Bestselling author of *Sword in the Storm*

DAVID GEMMELL

MIDNIGHT FALCON
A Novel of The Rigante

Look for Book Three of The Rigante by

DAVID GEMMELL

RAVENHEART

Coming in July 2001

Ballantine / Del Rey /
Fawcett / Ivy

Praise for
David Gemmell

"I am truly amazed at David Gemmell's ability to focus his writer's eye. His images are crisp and complete, a history lesson woven within the detailed tapestry of the highest adventure. Gemmell's characters are no less complete, real men and women with qualities good and bad, placed in trying times and rising to heroism or falling victim to their own weaknesses."

—R. A. SALVATORE
Author of *Mortalis*

"Gemmell's great reading; the action never lets up; he's several rungs above the good—right into the fabulous!"

—ANNE MCCAFFREY

"Everything a fan of heroic fantasy could desire: dramatic heroes, an exotic sorceress, deep evil [and] mood-drenched settings. . . . But the book also has something more, a quality which raises Gemmell's achievement to a much higher level: an empathetic and convincing grasp on the complexities and conflicts of real human beings. As a result, *Hero in the Shadows* has true power and poignancy."

—STEPHEN R. DONALDSON
(on *Hero in the Shadows*)

"A rousing tale . . . Think of Robert E. Howard meeting David Eddings. If you like headlong adventure, this one's for you."

—HARRY TURTLEDOVE
(on *Legend*)

By David Gemmell
Published by Ballantine Books:

LION OF MACEDON
DARK PRINCE
KNIGHTS OF DARK RENOWN
MORNINGSTAR

The Rigante
   THE SWORD IN THE STORM
   MIDNIGHT FALCON
   RAVENHEART*

The Drenai Saga
   LEGEND
   THE KING BEYOND THE GATE
   QUEST FOR LOST HEROES
   WAYLANDER
   IN THE REALM OF THE WOLF
   THE FIRST CHRONICLES OF
      DRUSS THE LEGEND
   THE LEGEND OF DEATHWALKER

The Stones of Power Cycle
   GHOST KING
   LAST SWORD OF POWER
   WOLF IN SHADOW
   THE LAST GUARDIAN
   BLOODSTONE

*forthcoming

Midnight Falcon

David Gemmell

A Del Rey® Book
THE BALLANTINE PUBLISHING GROUP • NEW YORK

A Del Rey® Book
Published by The Ballantine Publishing Group
Copyright © 1999 by David A. Gemmell
Excerpt from *Ravenheart* copyright © 2001 by David A. Gemmell

This book contains an excerpt from the forthcoming book *Ravenheart* by David Gemmell. This excerpt has been set for this edition only and may not reflect the final content of the forthcoming edition.

www.randomhouse.com/delrey/

Library of Congress Catalog Card Number: 00-111891

ISBN 0-345-43236-3

Manufactured in the United States of America

First American Edition: May 2001

10 9 8 7 6 5 4 3 2 1

During my school days I observed many teachers. Some were good, some were bad, and some were inept beyond belief. But only one was great. *Midnight Falcon* is dedicated with enormous affection to Tony Fenelon, a teacher of the old school, tough, uncompromising, and devoted to the children in his care. His belief in us gave us belief in ourselves. Those of us who were heading in the wrong direction owe him more than we can ever repay.

ACKNOWLEDGMENTS

Grateful thanks to the many test readers who helped steer me through the tough times, especially Jan Dunlop, Alan Fisher, Stella Graham, and Steve Hutt. Thanks also to my copy editor, Nancy Webber, and to the many readers whose letters and e-mails are a constant source of inspiration.

◇ 1 ◇

$\mathbf{P}$ARAX THE HUNTER had always despised vanity in others, but he knew now just how stealthily it could creep up on a man. The thought was as cold and bitter as the wind blowing over the snowcapped peaks of the Druagh mountains. From his saddlebag Parax drew a woolen cap, which he pulled over his thinning white hair. His old eyes gazed up at the majesty of Caer Druagh, the oldest mountain, but he could no longer make out the sharp, jagged ridges or the distant stands of pine. All he could see now was the misty whiteness of the peaks against the harsh, grainy blue of the sky.

His weary pony stumbled, and the old man grabbed at the pommel of his saddle. He patted the pony's neck and gently drew rein. The beast was eighteen years old. She had always been strong and steadfast, a mount to be trusted. Not anymore. Like Parax she was finding this one hunt too many.

The old man sighed. At thirty he had been at the peak of his powers, one of the foremost trackers in all the lands of the Keltoi. It did not make him boastful, for he knew he had been gifted with keen eyes and an intuitive mind. His own father, himself a great hunter and tracker, had taught him well. At five the young Parax could identify over thirty different animals by track alone: the leaping otter, the ambling badger, the cunning fox, and many more. His talent had been almost mystical. Men said he could read a man's life in the blade of grass crushed beneath a boot heel. That was nonsense, of course, but Parax had smiled upon hearing it, not recognizing the birth of vanity in that smile. What was true, however, was his ability to read a man from the trail he left; where he made his camp and placed his fire showed how well or little he understood the wilderness, how often he rested his mount,

1

how swiftly he moved, how patient he was in the hunt. All these things spoke of a man's character, and once Parax understood his prey's character, he would find him no matter how cleverly he hid his trail.

By the time he was thirty-five Parax's fame had spread to the lands of the Perdii, whose king, Alea, recruited him to the royal household. Even then he did not allow undue pride to color his personality. At fifty, in the service of Connavar the King, he allowed himself what he considered to be a quiet satisfaction in his achievements. Although his eyes were marginally less keen, his reading of trails still seemed almost magical to those who watched him. Even at sixty he could still follow a trail as well as any man, for by then he had a lifetime of acquired skills to give him an edge over younger men. Or so he believed, and in that belief vanity grew like a hidden weed unnoticed in his heart. Now past seventy, he had known for some years he was no longer preeminent, no longer even competent. The knowledge hurt the old man, but not as badly as the conceit that made him deny its truth to the man he loved most: the king.

Parax had served Connavar for over twenty years, from the day the young warrior had rescued him from the slave lines of Stone and brought him back to the towering mountains of Druagh. He had ridden beside him when the youngster became laird, and then war chief, and finally the first high king in hundreds of years. He had been beside him on that bloody day at Cogden Field when the invincible army of Stone had been crushed by the might of Connavar's Iron Wolves. He shivered again. Connavar the King had trusted Parax, and now age and increasing infirmity had made the old man betray that trust.

"Find the boy Bane," the king had said, "before the hunters kill him—or he kills them."

Parax had looked into the king's odd-colored eyes, one green and one tawny gold, and he had longed to admit the truth, to say simply, "My skills are gone, my friend. I cannot help you."

But he could not. The words clung within his throat on talons of false pride. He was one of the king's trusted advisers. He was Parax, the greatest hunter in the known world, a living legend. The moment he voiced the truth he would become merely a useless old man to be discarded and forgotten. Instead he had bowed awkwardly and ridden from Old Oaks, his mind in torment, panic lying heavily upon him. His fading eyes could no longer read the trails, and he had been forced to follow the hunting pack for days, hoping they would lead him to the young outlaw.

Then had come the final ignominy. He had lost the hunting pack. Twenty riders!

Parax had wept then, tears of bitterness. Once he could have tracked a sparrow in flight; now he could not find the spoor of twenty horses. He had been following about a mile behind them but had dozed in the saddle. His paint pony, tired and thirsty, had scented water and pulled away from the trail, wandering to the east. Parax had awoken with a start as the pony climbed a steep, wooded hillside. The old man had almost fallen from the saddle. Heavy clouds had obscured the sun, and Parax had had no idea where he was. The pony had led him to a bubbling stream, where Parax had dismounted.

His back ached, and his mouth was dry. Kneeling, he cupped water into his hands and drank.

"Outlived my usefulness," he said aloud. The pony whinnied and stamped its foot. "You know how old I am?" he asked his mount. "Seventy-two. I once trailed a robber for three weeks. Caught him on the high slopes, up in the rocks. The king paid me twenty silver coins and named me the prince of trackers." Removing his old woolen cap, he splashed water to his face and beard. He was hungry. There were muslin-wrapped slices of smoked bacon in his pack, along with black bread and a small round of cheese. He wanted to unpack them and prepare a fire, but then the late-afternoon sun broke through the clouds, and he dozed, his head resting on a round rock.

He dreamed of better days before his eyes failed, days of laughter and joy after the young king had driven the Stone soldiers from the northland. Laughter and joy, except for the king himself. The Demon King, they called him, because of his ferocity and because men recalled the terrible revenge he had taken for his wife's murder. Connavar, then a mere Rigante laird, had single-handedly wiped out the murderer's village, burning it to the ground and killing men, women, and children. From that day on Parax had never heard him laugh, had never seen joy in his eyes.

In his dream Parax saw the king, standing in the moonlight on the battlements of Old Oaks. Only now there were ghosts floating around them both, a young woman with long dark hair and a pale face and a giant of a man with a braided yellow beard. They were reaching out to the king. His scarred features paled as he saw them. Parax knew them both. The girl was his dead wife, Tae, and the man was his stepfather, Ruathain.

"You broke your promise, my husband," said the ghost of Tae.

Connavar bowed his head. "Oh, Tae," he said, "I am so ashamed."

"Will you still take me riding?"

Connavar gave out a groan and fell to his knees. Parax stood silently by, knowing the cause of the king's grief. He had promised to ride with Tae to a distant lake but on his way home had met with a woman he once had loved. Arian had held to him, and he had bedded her. Hours later, upon his return to Old Oaks, he discovered that Tae had ridden out with Ruathain and had been killed during a surprise attack by men who had a blood feud with his stepfather. Connavar remained on his knees, head bowed. The giant figure of Ruathain loomed over him. "Family is everything, Conn. I thought I taught you that."

"You did, Big Man. I never forgot it. I have looked after Wing and Bran, and Mam."

"And Bane?"

Connavar's face grew angry. "I regret that. But I could not bear to see Arian again. My lust for her killed Tae—and destroyed my life!"

"You made a mistake, Conn. All men do. But Bane was blameless, and he has grown to manhood without a father. He watched his mother, grief-stricken and broken, fade away and die lonely. He deserved better from you, Conn. You should have acknowledged him. It is not as if there was any doubt.

He looks like you, even down to the eyes of green and gold. And because you shunned him, all men shunned him."

The dream was terribly real, and Parax wanted to reach out and comfort the king, who seemed stricken by grief and ashamed. Then the vision faded, replaced by a stand of trees, branches gently swaying in the wind. Then—for the merest heartbeat—the old hunter saw a veiled woman standing close by. She was leaning on a staff. A huge black crow flew down from the trees and perched on her shoulder. Parax was instantly terrified. For this, he knew, was the dreaded Morrigu, the Seidh goddess of mischief and death.

He awoke with a start and cried out. He could feel his heart beating wildly in his chest. He gazed around at the tree line, but there was no veiled woman, no black crow. The smell of sizzling bacon came to him, and he thought he must still be dreaming. Turning his head, he saw a man squatting by a fire, holding a long-handled pan over the flames. The man glanced across at him and grinned.

"You were having a bad dream, old man," he said amiably. It was getting dark, and the wind was chilly. Parax moved closer to the fire and wrapped his green cloak tightly around his thin shoulders. He stared hard at the young man. He was beardless, his long blond hair tied back at the nape of his neck, a thin braid in the style of the Sea Wolves hanging from his right temple. Dressed in a hunting shirt of pale green, with a sleeveless brown leather jerkin, buckskin trews, and knee-length riding boots, he wore no sword but was turning the bacon with a hunting knife of bright iron.

"You are the Wolfshead Bane," said Parax.

"And you are Parax, the king's hunter."

"I am—and proud of it."

Bane laughed. "Men say you are the greatest tracker of all."

"So they say," agreed the old man.

"Not anymore, Parax," the youngster said, with a rueful smile. "I have been watching you. You've crossed my trail three times in the last two days. The third time I left a clear print for you to see, and you rode straight past it."

Parax leaned in closer. Now he could see the odd-colored eyes, one green and one tawny gold. Just like his father, thought the old man. Just like the king. He seemed older than his seventeen years, harder, more knowing than he should be. "Are you planning to kill me?" he asked.

"You want me to?"

"There would be a kind of poetry in it," said Parax. "The first time I met your father, he was around your age. He had come to kill me. I had tracked him for days with a group of Perdii warriors. Oh, but he was clever and killed seven of the hunters. And he did everything to throw me from the trail. Great skill he had for a young man. I tracked him over rock and through water. He almost fooled me one time. His tracks disappeared below the branch of an oak. He had hauled himself up, then run along the branch and leapt to a nearby tree. But I was not old and useless then. I found him."

"So why didn't he kill you?"

Parax shrugged. "Didn't know then, don't know now. We shared a meal, and he rode off to join the army of Stone. When next I saw him, he was the man who had killed the Perdii king, and I was roped and tied and ready for deportation to the slave mines. He recognized me and saved me. Now here I am with his son. So, are you going to kill me?"

"I have nothing against you, old man," said Bane. "I'd just as soon let you live."

"Then you'd better share that bacon," said Parax. "Otherwise I might starve to death."

"Of course. The food is yours, after all." Bane speared a strip of bacon on his hunting knife, then passed the pan across to the hunter. They ate in silence. The bacon was full of flavor but a little too salty, and Parax moved back to the stream for a drink.

"How did you evade the hunters?" he asked as he returned to the fire.

"It wasn't difficult. They didn't really want to find me. Can't say I blame them. Most are married men who wouldn't want to leave behind young widows."

"You are a cocky whoreson," snapped Parax.

"Indeed I am. But I am also very good with sword or knife. I have fought my battles, Parax. Twice against Sea Raiders and three times against Norvii outlaws." He tapped the thick gold clasp around his left wrist. "Uncle Braefar himself awarded me this for courage. It should have been awarded by the king, but that would have been too embarrassing."

Parax heard the rising anger in the young man's voice and changed the subject. "So why did you allow me to find you?"

Bane laughed. "You didn't find me, Parax. I found you. I felt sorry for you. It must be hard to lose one's skills."

"Aye, it is hard, though I doubt you'll live long enough to know how hard it is. So why are we having this meeting?"

The young man did not answer at first. He carried the pan to the stream, washed it, dried it with grass, then returned it to the old man's pack. Then he stretched out by the fire. "I was intrigued. I know why Uncle Braefar's men were after me but not why the king's hunter should have been sent or, indeed, why you did not ride with the other hunters."

"The king does not want to see you dead," said Parax.

Bane gave a scornful laugh. "Is that so? My father does not want to see me dead. How touching. In all my life he has not spoken to me except when I won the Beltine Race and he awarded the prize. 'Well done.' In my seventeen years they are the only two words I have heard my father speak. And now I am to believe he is concerned for my welfare?"

"I cannot speak for his concerns. He asked me to find you. Gave me a bag of gold to give you."

"A bag of gold? What a sweet man!" Bane spit into the fire.

"He is a good man," Parax said softly.

"Be careful, old man," warned Bane. "I am not known to be overly forgiving. I have killed two men in the past five days. A third will not trouble my conscience."

"My understanding is that they spoke slightingly of your dead mother, then waylaid you after you had beaten them with your fists. A trial would most certainly have seen you acquitted."

"And this bag of gold is to aid my trial?"

"No," admitted Parax. "It is to help you once you have left Rigante lands. The men you killed were kin to the general Fiallach. He has sworn a blood oath to fight you. The king does not want either of you hurt."

Bane laughed, the sound merry and full of humor. "He doesn't want Uncle Fiallach killed, you mean?"

"If that is what he had meant, then that is what he would have said," snapped Parax.

"I like loyalty," said Bane. "I don't have much experience of it, but I like it nonetheless. So I will let you live, and I will take the bag of gold." His voice hardened, and an edge of cold fury showed through. "But maybe I will not leave. Maybe I will stay and challenge Fiallach. And cut his throat in front of the king."

Parax was silent for a moment. "I have rarely seen such depths of anger in a man," he said. "It saddens me, Bane. Fiallach is headstrong. He is also a great fighter, but more than that, he is married to your mother's sister. You think your mother's spirit would rejoice in seeing the father of her nephews cut down by her son?"

"No, she wouldn't," he admitted, his anger fading. Parax saw the sorrow in his eyes. In that moment, with the ferocity disappearing, he looked much younger. "I will let him live," he said. "Did you know my mother?"

"No. I knew of her."

"And what does that mean?" Bane asked icily.

"It means I know the history, boy. She was Connavar's first love, but she married another man when she thought Conn was dying. That marriage did not succeed."

"No need to be coy, you old bastard! The marriage did not succeed because Connavar forced himself upon her and sired me. Then he left her in disgrace. Never spoke to her thereafter. Her life was ruined, and she died a sad and broken woman. Let us understand the full history."

"That is not even close to being the full story, but it is not for me to debate it. I will ask this, though: Did your mother ever say he forced himself upon her?"

"She didn't have to."

Parax sighed. "It seems to me men always believe what they want to believe. No point arguing over it. It is time for me to be going." He walked to his pony, opened his saddle-bag, and pulled forth the pouch of gold, which he tossed to the young man.

Bane laughed. "Now you can ride back to the king and tell him his old hunter is still the best there ever was. He found the Wolfshead when no one else could."

"I shall tell him the truth, and I shall hunt no more."

"Well," said Bane quietly, "if you're going to tell him the truth, tell him that I have always hated him and that one day I shall cut his vile heart out for what he did to my mother."

"You would have to be very, very good to defeat Fiallach," said Parax. "But to kill Connavar you would have to be the best there ever was. And you are not that, boy. Not by a damn sight."

"Perhaps I will be when next we meet," Bane said softly.

Parax climbed wearily into the saddle. "I don't think so," he said. "I may be old, Bane, and my physical skills faded and gone. But my mind is still sharp, and it hunts the truth as well as it ever did. Why did you not wait for the trial and walk free? And once you decided to run, why did you remain in these hills playing catch-as-catch-can with the hunters?"

"Because I am a free man and I live as I please."

"No, it is because you want it to end," said Parax. "Grief-stricken at the loss of your mother and hurting from a life of rejection and denial, you are waiting for death. Longing for it, perhaps. So I hope you are right, boy. I hope you will ride from here and spend time developing your skills. For like Connavar, you have it in you to be a great man. And, like him, I don't want to see you dead."

With that Parax heeled the pony forward and rode from the clearing.

Most people felt that the years had been kind to Vorna the Midwife. She was in her fifties, and her long hair was still predominantly black, though streaked with silver, her skin smooth. She looked like a woman ten years younger as she sat on the porch of her house, watching the last of the sunshine bathing the settlement of Three Streams.

Such is the power of Wicca, she thought. The earth magic ran in her blood, slowing down the aging process. Once she had been widely known as Vorna the Witch, respected and feared by the populace. Now, with them believing her powers to be gone, she had found popularity and treasured it. It was pleasant that people waved and smiled when they saw her. It was good when they invited her into their homes.

Yes, she thought, the years have been kind to Vorna.

She shivered suddenly, though it was not cold. From there she could see Nanncumal's forge and hear the steady thumping of his hammer and to the right was the house once occupied by Connavar's parents, Ruathain and Meria. Vorna sighed as the old memories flowed. She glanced at the towering peaks of Caer Druagh, the fading sunlight turning the snow to pale gold. So little has changed in the mountains, she thought, and yet so much in our own lives.

Looking back over the meadow to Ruathain's old house, Vorna pictured him strolling across the grass, her son on his massive shoulders. Ruathain had always seemed so full of life and strength. Vorna closed her eyes. Living with regret was futile, she knew, a waste of time and emotion. But as one got older, it became harder to avoid it. Best to endure it and let it pass.

Sitting in the sunshine, Vorna saw again her own husband, the little Stone merchant Banouin, setting off on his last ride, the young Connavar beside him. Banouin had turned and waved, then had blown her a kiss. The memory still brought a knot to her stomach and a lump to her throat. He had not lived to see his son born.

Now the young Banouin also had ridden away. He, too, had turned and waved from the hilltop. And Vorna was alone once more, just as she had been all those years ago, before Connavar had fought the bear. Before she had danced with Banouin on Feast Night. Before she had lost her witch's powers. Before she had secretly regained them.

Vorna stood and walked to the first stream, stopping to enjoy the beauty of the pale purple foxglove growing along the banks. Her thoughts were mellow, almost to the point of melancholy, and it seemed to her that the ghosts of the past were standing close: the mighty Ruathain, the earth maiden Eriatha, the crippled Riamfada, and the tormented Arian.

"I hope you are now at rest, child," whispered Vorna. Thinking of Arian brought thoughts of her son, Bane. Such a terrible name to give a child. It meant "curse" in the old tongue. Arian, in her selfishness and her grief, had wanted all the Rigante to know of her suffering.

Yet despite the burden of his name the boy had developed well except for his word blindness. The king had decreed that all Rigante children should learn to read and write. For some reason that Vorna could not understand, Bane, despite his intelligence and the quickness of his wit, could not grasp the skill. The druid Brother Solstice, who taught the children of Three Streams, sent Bane to her home to study with Banouin, who had mastered the lessons with ease. But even with the tireless help of Banouin the young Bane struggled.

Bane had other skills, however, and some of them brought great delight to Vorna. She smiled as she remembered the badger cub.

Looking around to make sure she was alone, she knelt and drew a circle in the air, then whispered three words of power—ancient words in a language no longer spoken by men. A silver circle glowed into life among the foxglove. Vorna gently blew a breath into it. The air within the circle rippled like a heat haze, and an image formed there. Vorna gazed once more at the nine-year-old boy and the blind badger cub. Kneeling among the flowers, Vorna watched the silent scene unfold, her mind drifting back to that early summer night eight years before.

The sun had been down for around an hour when she had heard the rap at the door. Climbing from her bed, Vorna had wrapped a shawl around her shoulders and walked out into the night. Bane had been standing in the moonlight, a very young badger nestling against his leg. As she opened the door, she had seen the badger's shoulders bunch, its black and silver head swaying from side to side.

"What are you doing with that beast?" asked Vorna, keeping her voice low.

"I was in the woods," said the child. "I saw it. It moved past me, then bumped into a tree. Then it stumbled over a rabbit hole. There's something wrong with its eyes, Vorna."

"How did you get it back here?"

"It took a long time," said the boy. "Watch!" He moved away from the cub, then knelt and made clicking noises with his tongue and teeth. The cub swayed from side to side, then moved toward the sound. As it reached Bane, the boy stroked its brow. "It was like this. I got him to follow me, but he kept wandering away. It took hours to get him here. Can you heal him?"

"There is no herb for blindness, Bane," she said.

"But can you heal him?"

"What makes you think that I can?" she asked warily.

"I can keep secrets," he countered. "And you can trust me."

She looked into the child's odd eyes and smiled. "I think that I can," she said. Then she knelt by the badger and gently placed her hands on its head, allowing her spirit to flow into the beast's bloodstream and on through its body. The badger cub fell into a deep sleep. It was badly malnourished and infested with fleas and worms, but the worst of the problems lay in the brain. A cancerous growth was pressing against its skull, causing the blindness. Opening her eyes, she turned to the boy. "There is a shoulder of cold ham in the larder. Put it in a bowl and fetch it here. And try not to wake Banouin."

Bane ran off and returned with the meat. Placing one hand on the ham and the other on the badger's head, she closed her eyes once more. Now she flowed within the cancer, feeling the pulse of its life, its need to grow. With infinite care she honed her concentration and began to draw the rogue cells into her own body, sucking them through her bloodstream, breaking them down, reconstituting them, transmuting them from flesh to energy. The cold ham began to writhe under her hand, maggots crawling over her fingers. Sweat beaded her brow and ran in rivulets down her cheeks. Still she held the focus. At last, satisfied that she had removed all trace of the cancer from the cub, she sat back and opened her eyes. Bane was staring in horror at the putrid, writhing mass that the ham had become.

"Those maggots were in the badger?" he asked.

"In a way. Take it and bury it. Then we will wake the little beast and feed it."

"I will tell no one, Vorna. Your secret is safe with me. I promise you that."

"How long have you known?"

"I saw you light a fire last year with a flick of your fingers. I was outside the window. I have told no one."

"Why did you keep the secret?"

"Because it was your secret," he said. "And I thought you would not want people to share it."

"You were right. Now bury that meat."

Vorna smiled at the scene in the circle, then flicked her fingers. The circle vanished, and she rose to her feet. As she did so, she saw a rider angling a dappled gray down from the eastern woods. "Reckless boy," she whispered. But she felt her spirits lift a little as the young fugitive crossed the bridge and cantered across the meadow. He drew up in front of the house and leapt down, a wide smile on his face, sunlight glinting on his golden hair.

"I hope you have food ready," he said. "I was tempted to stop and eat the horse."

"Foolish child!" she admonished him. "Of all the places to come. Do you want the hunters to find you?"

"Ah, you worry too much. Anyway, they are miles away and will not be back until well after dark." He grinned at her, then led the gray gelding into the barn. Vorna sighed, shook her head, and walked into the house. Cutting a large slice of meat pie, she scooped it onto a plate and laid it on the dining table. Bane stepped into the room, pushed closed the door, and sat down. Vorna poured him a mug of water, then sat by the hearth, waiting until he had finished his meal.

It was cool in the room, and Vorna whispered a word of power. Flames sprang up in the fireplace, licking around the dry wood.

"I never tire of seeing you do that," said Bane, rising from the table and seating himself in the old horsehide chair opposite Vorna.

She smiled as she looked at him. He had his father's eyes and his mother's beauty. "What are your plans?" she asked him.

Bane shrugged. "I have none. But I do have a bag of gold. A present from my loving father. Ah, but his kindness touches the heart."

"He was always kind to me," she said, "but let us not argue the point. I am far too fond of you to wish to see you angry."

"I couldn't be angry with you, Vorna," he said. "Next to my mother you have been my greatest friend. I see Banouin has already left. You think he'll come back?"

"That will depend on whether he finds what he's looking for," she said, her voice heavy with sadness. She looked into Bane's strange eyes. "It also will depend on whether he survives to find it."

"You think he is in danger? Have you had a vision?"

"I have many visions, but none concerning my son. Or you. I think my love for you both blocks my power. What I do know is that he is riding south, through a war-torn land full of violence and destruction. And he is not a warrior, Bane. You know that."

"Aye, I do. He is not . . . strong," he finished lamely.

"You are a good friend to him," she said with a smile. "You always were."

He blushed. "I know I always got him into trouble, and you were constantly scolding me."

She shook her head. "You never were very comfortable with compliments. Even as a child."

Bane chuckled. "Never received enough to become accustomed to them." He walked to the window and pushed open the shutters. Then he scanned the hills. The sound of hammering was still coming from Nanncumal's forge. "Poor Grandfather," he said softly. "First his wife, then his daughter. He has suffered much."

"You have forgiven him?" asked Vorna.

"Aye, I have. It was hard for him to have a disgraced daughter back in his house. In some ways I think he blamed me. But he was never harsh to me. He was even kindly in his own way. When I saw him weep at my mother's death, all the anger just flowed away from me." Turning back toward her, he gave a rueful smile. "Difficult to hate a man who loved someone you loved."

"That is a good lesson to learn," she said.

"I'm not awfully good at learning lessons," he admitted. "I can write my name and the word for 'horse.' " Returning to the fire, he sat back, resting his blond head on the back of the chair. "I have always liked this room," he said. "It is so calm here. I feel at peace."

"I know what you mean," Vorna told him. "It is a good house. Many happy memories are stored in these walls."

He sat up. "I spent three nights in your old cave. Threw the hunters off the scent. How long did you live there?"

"Twenty-five years."

"I was going out of my mind by the fourth morning. How could you dwell in such a desolate place?"

"I was a different person then. Younger, more bitter."

"That's where you saved Connavar's life," he said. "I thought of that often as I hid there."

"Had I not done so, you never would have been born," she pointed out. "And I would not have wed Banouin's father. Hence no Banouin. And what would the world have been without you two?"

"Duller," he said. His smile faded. "Tell me about Connavar and the bear."

"What is it you wish to know? Everyone knows the story."

"Aye, they do. But is it all true, Vorna? Did he really stand against the beast to save his crippled friend? Or was there another reason?"

"No other reason. He tried to carry Riamfada away from danger, but the bear was coming fast. So he put his friend down and turned to face it, armed with just a dagger. He was two years younger than you are now." Vorna sighed. "Do not look so disappointed, Bane. Would you want your father to be a coward?"

"Probably. I don't know, Vorna. Everywhere I go, men talk of his legend: his battle against the Sea Wolves, the ride of the Iron Wolves to smash the Stone Panthers at Cogden Field, the siege of Barrow Hill. The great Connavar! The hero! How could such a hero desert my mother? How could he let his son grow without even a gesture of parental affection?"

Vorna took a deep breath. "Perhaps you should ask him."

"Maybe I will one day."

She saw a touch of sadness cross his face. You are so young, she thought. Little more than a boy. But then another fear touched her. "What are you planning to do?" she asked him.

"Do? Why, I shall run the hunters ragged until they catch me." He gave a bright smile, but she held to his gaze.

"Speak to me with truth," she said softly. "What are you planning?"

"I have no plans, Vorna." He sighed. "Do you think my mother really liked me?"

"What do you mean? Of course she liked you. She loved you. Why would you ask a thing like that?"

"Sometimes she would look at me strangely, then she'd cry

and tell me to get out of her sight. Once she even told me I
was the cause of all her suffering."

"Aye, she could be thoughtless sometimes," said Vorna.
"You were not the cause, Bane. Neither was Connavar. We
are all victims of our own natures. Arian was not perfect. But
she loved you. I know this to be true, and you know I would
not lie to you."

"I know, Vorna. I saw the old hunter Parax yesterday. The
king sent him to find me."

"If anyone could find you, it is Parax," she said.

"Yes, indeed," he said. "He's a canny old man. Very wise.
Predicted my future. Anyway, I should be going. I want to
thank you for everything you've done for me."

The fear in Vorna grew. Reaching out with her talent, she
touched his mind. Grief, anguish, and emptiness filled her,
and with them a desire for death. "Wait!" she said as he
walked to the door. "If you have no plans, there is something
I would like you to do for me."

"I'd do anything for you, Vorna. You know that."

"Find Banouin. Travel with him and keep him safe. It
would mean a great deal to me," she added as he paused in the
doorway, "to know that you were together."

Bane glanced out of the open door. "Ah, here they come,"
he said. "Riding like the wind! Time for me to go." Then he
grinned, and Vorna relaxed, for it was the old Bane she saw
now, bright and full of life. "Don't worry about Banouin," he
said. "I'll find him and ride with him."

"I hoped that you would," she said. "But it does my heart
good to hear you say it. Now go quickly."

He gave a wide smile, stepped back into the room, and
hoisted her high, planting a kiss on both of her cheeks. "You
take care," he told her. "There are not many in this world I
love."

Bane put her down. Vorna reached up and stroked his face.
"Ride now!"

He ran from the house. Vorna stood in the doorway and
watched as he thundered the gray across the meadow, leapt
the three-rail fence, and galloped toward the southern hills.

The twenty hunters swung their mounts and gave chase.

"You will not catch him," Vorna said softly.

* * *

Not for the first time Banouin reined in his chestnut gelding and looked back toward the north. Through a gap in the tall pines he could still just see the distant peaks. He glanced to the south and the beckoning lowlands and knew that as soon as he crested the last rise, Caer Druagh would become but a memory. Sadness touched the young man, and this he found surprising.

Banouin had never enjoyed life among the Rigante. As a child he had loathed the boisterous play, the emphasis on physical strength, the feuding and fighting. The Rigante, he had discovered to his cost, were a hotheaded, volatile people, quick to anger, yet his spirit was heavy as he thought of his departure.

The day was bright and clear, the sun warm. Banouin pushed his hand through his dark shoulder-length hair. I must cut it before crossing the water, he thought. Citizens of Stone wear their hair short, close-cropped. They also shave daily, as beards and mustaches are for barbarians. His thoughts drifted away from the wild Druagh mountains, and he pictured the legendary city of Stone: the city of his father.

People had always spoken highly of the first Banouin, the little foreigner who had come to live among the people and who had married the former witch Vorna. A fine man, they said, kind and brave. He had been murdered by the Perdii king nineteen years before.

With one last glance at Caer Druagh, Banouin heeled the gelding forward and started down the slope.

"What was my father like?" he had once asked his mother.

"He was not tall, but he was handsome and dark-haired, like you."

"Did he have blue eyes like ours?"

"No, they were dark."

"Did people bully him when he was a boy?"

"We never spoke of his childhood, my son. They did not bully him as a man, however."

Banouin rode on. He had crossed the river the previous day and was, as far as he could judge, a day's ride from the southern Rigante settlement of Gilrath. His horse, a gift from the king, was still fresh and strong, though it was a little too spirited for Banouin's taste. Each morning it would stare at him balefully and, when saddled, would buck several times, jarring Banouin's bones. The young rider felt the horse did not like him, and was allowing him to ride only under sufferance.

"He's a good mount," Connavar had told him. "He will not let you down." Banouin always felt uncomfortable in the presence of the king. He was a man of immense physical power, a known warrior and leader, but it was the eyes that disturbed Banouin. They were just like Bane's, one green and the other gold. And when he looked at a man, it seemed as if he could read that man's heart.

"Thank you, sir. And thank you for all your kindness to my mother and me."

"Whisht, boy, I have done little enough. Are you sure you want to undertake this journey?"

"I am sure, sir. I want to see the land of my father."

"A man should always know where he comes from," said Connavar, "and find pride in it. Your father was a great man. He taught me much of value. I treasure his memory."

Banouin had been envious of that. He would love to have memories of his father that he could treasure. Instead, when he thought back to his early childhood, he could recall only the Big Man, Ruathain, who had carried him on his shoulders and taken him out to see the cattle herds.

Even now, so many years after Ruathain's death, Banouin still felt a deep sadness when he thought of him. With his wide smile, his long yellow hair, and the colossal breadth of his shoulders, he had seemed to the child to be immortal and invulnerable. When he had died after the Pannone battle, Banouin's small world had been rocked to its foundations.

Within the year the child had discovered other causes for sorrow. The Stone army had landed far to the south, and tales of battles and slaughter had begun to flow north. The other Rigante children had turned on Banouin, sneering at his bloodline, mocking him, taunting him. Then the beatings had begun, and the child had lived in almost permanent fear.

For years he suffered, especially at the hands of Forvar. The redheaded boy seemed to take enormous delight in causing him pain. Once he had tied Banouin to a tree and prepared a fire around his feet. He did not light it but constantly pretended to. The nine-year-old Banouin had wet himself in fear.

Childhood had few happy memories for Banouin. What joy there was—apart from his friendship with Bane—had come from his daydreams. He would travel to Stone and become a citizen. They had schools there and universities. A man could study and learn and live peacefully without fear of violence and threats. A merchant had told him once that there was a great library in Stone containing more than twelve thousand scrolls and many artifacts of wonder. From that moment Banouin had wanted nothing more than to journey there and sit in peaceful contemplation. He had badgered Brother Solstice the druid to teach him to read and write in Turgon, the language of Stone, and had spent many useful months at Old Oaks talking to Stone merchants, building a mental picture of the city of his dreams. He knew the names of each of the five hills and the positions of the parks and monuments. The Great Library had been built in the Park of Phesus, beside an artificial lake. It was approached along an avenue of flowering trees. In spring their blossoms were pink and white; in autumn the leaves turned to red and gold. Marble benches were set around the lake, and students would sit there in the sunshine and discuss philosophy with their tutors.

Banouin shivered with pleasure at the thought. No more running through the woods in fear. No more to hear the screaming and shouting of wild Rigante youngsters and listen to their bragging about their exploits in future battles. He doubted that the citizens of Stone ever boasted about who could fart the loudest or piss the farthest.

For several hours Banouin rode on. Then he began to look for a place to camp. Angling away from the open land, he steered his mount into a grove of trees, seeking a sheltered spot beside a stream. The gelding sniffed the air, and its head came up. Releasing the reins, Banouin allowed the animal to find its own way to water. Easing through the dense undergrowth, he saw a long oval pond decorated with white water lilies and surrounded by willows whose branches trailed in the clear water. Several white swans were gliding gracefully on the surface. It was an idyllic spot. Banouin dismounted and unsaddled the gelding, holding it back from the water while he brushed it down.

An hour later, with the chestnut hobbled and cropping grass, Banouin sat by the waterside watching golden fish just below the surface. He relaxed, savoring the moment. Then his talent touched him, an icy needle of fear pricking at his mind. His mother had always said that one day he would discover how to fully use the skills he had inherited from her, but he never had. He experienced no visions, had no healing touch, and could not read the minds of men. But when danger was close, Banouin would always know. That—so far—was the limit of his power.

And danger was close.

Banouin's mouth was dry as he rose slowly from the water's edge and turned. Three men were emerging from the trees: tough, grim-faced men. They wore no cloaks. Their clothes were ragged, and their breeches poorly crafted from buckskin. All wore swords and knives. Banouin struggled to contain his fear.

"Good day to you," he said.

The first of the three approached him. His left eye socket was empty, and Banouin saw that three fingers were missing from his left hand. In that moment he experienced his first vision. He saw the man running into battle, swinging an iron sword. He was wearing the green and blue checkered cloak of the Rigante. An arrow struck the bridge of his nose, cutting through his eye. He stumbled but then ran on at the enemy.

"Who are you?" asked the man, his voice deep and unfriendly.

"I am a Rigante, like you," said Banouin. "I am from Three Streams."

"I am not Rigante," said the man. "I am a cast-out, a Wolfshead."

"You fought bravely at Cogden Field. Why would they throw you out?"

The man looked surprised. "You know me? No, you are too young to remember Cogden."

"I'll take the tunic," said the second man, a hulking figure with a thick, matted black beard. Banouin glanced at him.

The man's face was flat and expressionless, his small eyes deep-set and cold.

"Why should you get the tunic?" asked the third man, who was smaller, with a thin, wispy blond mustache. "It'll be far too small for you."

"I'll sell it," said Black Beard. "You can have the breeches and boots."

"Why are you doing this?" asked Banouin, fighting to keep his voice calm.

The one-eyed man stepped in close. "Because we are robbers, idiot. Now, remove your clothing and perhaps we'll let you live."

Banouin looked into the man's single eye and saw no pity there. His legs started to tremble, and he felt just as he had when Forvar had tied him to the tree. His heart beat wildly, and he hoped his bladder would not betray him. "You will not let me live," he said. "You intend to kill me, but you do not wish my blood on the clothes or cuts through the cloth. What kind of men are you?"

"Scum of the worst kind," said a voice. Startled, the men spun to see a golden-haired warrior leading a dappled gray horse through the trees. Dropping the reins, he drew a long-sword from a scabbard attached to the saddle and strolled forward.

"Don't fight them, Bane," pleaded Banouin. "Just let them go."

"You don't change, do you?" the warrior said amiably. "Always softhearted. We can't just let them go. What about the next traveler who passes this way? We'll be dooming him. These creatures are vermin. They should be treated as such."

"Vermin!" hissed the one-eyed man. "Who do you—?"

Bane raised a hand. "If you don't mind," he said, "I was talking to my friend. So if you value the last moments of your miserable life, be silent. Take a lingering look at the swans, or the trees, or whatever." He turned back to Banouin. "Why do you want them to live? They were about to kill you."

Banouin pointed to the one-eyed man. "He was a hero at Cogden Field. He was proud and brave. In terrible pain, he fought and gave no ground. His eye was torn out by an arrow, his hand mutilated. Yet he stood firm with all the other heroes.

I do not know what has made him what he is, but he could be a good man again. If you kill him, he will never have the chance."

Bane swung his gaze to the other two men. "And what of these? You think they might choose one day to be gentle druids or healers?"

"I do not know anything about them. But I ask you to let them go. No harm has been done."

"Why are we listening to this?" Black Beard asked One-Eye. "He's just one man!"

"Indeed he is, you ugly whoreson," said Bane, "and he'd be grateful if you'd just draw your sword and put an end to this debate."

"Leave your sword where it is!" shouted Banouin. "Please, Bane, just let them go."

Bane sighed. Moving to One-Eye, he placed his hand on the man's shoulder. "He has been like this since he was a child," he said. "It is beyond understanding. I blame the mixed blood and the fact that his mother is a witch. You know, when other children tormented him, he never sought revenge. Has no understanding of hate at all. I've never known anyone like him." He sighed again. "And he brings out the worst in me. So, against my better judgment, I'll let you live." Suddenly he brightened. "Unless, of course, you'd prefer to fight."

One-Eye shrugged off Bane's hand and walked to where Banouin stood. "I am not afraid of death," he said. "You believe me?"

"I do," said Banouin.

"I am glad we didn't kill you," said One-Eye. "It was good to be reminded of what I once was. You really believe I can become that man again?"

"If you choose to," said Banouin.

"Probably too late for me," the man said sadly. Gesturing to the others, he walked away. The slim blond man followed instantly, but Black Beard stood for a moment, staring malevolently at Bane.

"Any time, goat face," said Bane.

"Karn!" yelled One-Eye. "Let's go!"

Reluctantly Karn followed the others.

Bane sat down on a fallen tree and looked at his friend. "That was a mistake," he said.

"What are you doing here?" asked Banouin.

"Looking after you, apparently. Do you have any food?"

It took Banouin an age to light a small fire, but finally tiny flames licked at the tinder. Bane had wandered off, and Banouin unpacked his saddlebag, removing an old copper pot, a wooden plate, a bag of dried oats, and a chunk of dry-cured salt beef. The sun was dipping below the horizon when Bane returned. He squatted down next to Banouin.

"Time to go," he said.

"Go? I've only just got the fire going."

"Life just isn't fair," said Bane. "But if you'd like to be alive in the morning, I suggest you saddle your horse."

"One-Eye won't come back," said Banouin. "I looked into his mind, and I know there is still some good in him."

"Maybe he won't, but the big ugly one will. And he won't come alone."

Bane moved to his horse and mounted. Banouin repacked his saddlebag, tacked up the chestnut, and went back to the fire. "Leave it," said Bane. "In fact, add a little more wood. It'll draw them, throw them off the scent."

Banouin did so and then climbed into the saddle, and the two men rode out of the woods and down the slope to the old road.

The horses plodded on as the sun fell. It was colder now, the wind sharp. Banouin lifted his cloak from behind the saddle, untied the thongs, and swung it around his shoulders. The sudden flaring of cloth alarmed the chestnut, which reared suddenly, dumping the young man from the saddle. He landed heavily. The gelding ran off to the south. Bane heeled his mount and raced after it. Banouin sat up. He felt sick and dizzy. Bane rode back, leading the runaway.

The stars were bright now, a crescent moon shining in the sky. "Are you hurt?" asked Bane.

"No. But you were wrong about me not knowing how to hate. I'm beginning to loathe that horse."

Wearily Banouin stepped back into the saddle. Bane led them away from the road and down into a tree-lined hollow, where they made camp.

Bane lit a small fire, its light shielded by boulders. Then he moved away into the trees. When he returned, he sat down beside Banouin. "You can't see the fire from the road," he said. "We ought to be relatively safe here."

Once again Banouin unpacked the utensils and the food. There was a stream close by, and Banouin filled the pot, added oats and salt, and set it over the fire.

"Thank you for saving my life," he said at last.

"That's what friends are for," Bane replied brightly. They ate in silence, and Bane lay down, his head on his saddle, using his cloak as a blanket.

Banouin was not tired and sat quietly by the fire, feeding it with dry sticks and watching the flames leap and dance. The incident with the robbers had left him both disappointed and dejected. It had shown how far he was from being a Rigante warrior. Not once had he even considered drawing the hunting knife at his belt. He had been paralyzed with fear and within moments of begging for his life.

He glanced down at the sleeping Bane. His arrival had surprised them, but it had been his confidence that had cowed them. It seemed to Banouin that his friend had radiated power and purpose. You ought to be a leader of men, he thought, not a Wolfshead, living outside the law.

And yet, Banouin knew, Bane's whole life had been moving inexorably toward this point. Beneath the easy banter, behind the reckless smile, there was a bottomless well of bitterness and anger that drove him on, rebelling against authority, creating enemies who could so easily have been friends.

Was it merely the lack of a father, Banouin wondered, or would his friend have been just the same regardless? Who could tell?

Banouin's thoughts swung to Forvar, the boy who had tormented him for most of his life. He had not hated him. Forvar's father and two uncles had been killed in the Battle of Cogden Field, killed by soldiers of Stone. Banouin understood how the boy had come to despise Stone and everything connected with it. Forvar did not truly hate Banouin, but Banouin represented a focal point for his hatred. By hound-ing and torturing Banouin he was releasing his own pent-up pain and sense of loss.

Understanding, however, did not help. It did not ease the suffering. Banouin had tried talking to Forvar, but his mind had been closed, his hatred overwhelming.

Two years earlier it had come to a head. Banouin had been walking in the hills near the Wishing Tree woods, when Forvar and a group of his friends had come walking back from the Riguan Falls, where they had been swimming. Seeing Banouin, they had chased him, yelling and whooping. Banouin had fled back toward Three Streams, but he was not a fast runner and they had overtaken him. They had beaten and kicked him. Then, as he lay semiconscious on the ground, Forvar had drawn a knife. Banouin remembered the moment and the sense of sick dread that had swept over him. He had looked into Forvar's tortured eyes and known, without any semblance of doubt, that the big youth was about to plunge the blade into his heart.

As the knife came up, a shadow fell across Banouin. Something dark flashed across his vision, and there was a sickening thud followed by a loud crack. Banouin blinked. Bane was standing there, a long, heavy lump of wood in his hands. Forvar was on the ground, his neck twisted at a bizarre angle. With trembling limbs Banouin pushed himself to his knees. Forvar was dead, his friends standing by, shocked and frozen.

"You killed him!" whispered Huin, Forvar's younger brother.

Bane tossed the blood-smeared club to the ground and swung to Banouin, hauling him to his feet. "How badly are you hurt?" he asked.

Banouin did not reply. He could not tear his eyes from the corpse.

There had been a full inquest, with a jury of nine, held under the direction of Laird Braefar. There it was decided that the death had been caused by misadventure. Forvar had died as a result of his unwarranted attack on Banouin. Bane had not intended to kill him but merely to stop him from killing another boy.

The fire died away, and Banouin settled down to sleep.

He awoke with the dawn and nudged Bane, who merely

grunted and turned over. Banouin shook his shoulder. Bane yawned and sat up. "You sleep too deeply," said Banouin.

"Aye, it has always been a problem to me. But I was having the most wonderful dream. There were these two sisters—"

"Please!" Banouin interrupted with mock severity. "No sexual fantasies before breakfast."

Bane chuckled and walked to the stream, where he stripped off his pale green shirt and doused his head and chest with water. After they had breakfasted on dried fruit and meat, they saddled their mounts and began to ride up out of the hollow. Bane was whistling a merry tune and seemed in good spirits. He steered his horse away from the trail.

Banouin called out to him. "That looks like a more difficult climb," he said.

"I think it might be quicker," said Bane.

"Well, you can go that way," Banouin told him, and continued on the easier route. At the edge of the trees he drew rein and gazed down, horror-struck. A man's body lay there, the throat cut, blood pooling on the earth. It was the black-bearded Karn. His eyes were open, staring sightlessly up at the morning sky.

Bane rode alongside his friend. "He and two others came back in the night," he said quietly.

"Two others?"

"Aye. They ran off. You were right, though. One-Eye was not among them."

"So you killed Black Beard, then came back to sleep?" stormed Banouin.

"I was tired. Don't you sleep when you're tired? What would you have had me do? Wake you when they were coming? For what purpose? I love you, my friend, but you are not a fighter. And there was no point in waking you after they'd gone."

Banouin dragged his eyes from the corpse and heeled the chestnut up the slope and out onto the road.

Bane followed him. "You want to hear my dream now?"

"No, I do not," snapped Banouin. "There is a man dead back there. Killed by you. And it means nothing to you, does it?"

"What should it mean? They came to kill us. Would you prefer it if we were dead?"

Banouin drew rein and took a deep breath, trying to ease the anger from his system. He looked at his friend and saw the genuine confusion in his eyes. "Of course I am glad we are alive," he said. "It is not the fact that you killed him, Bane, but that it did not touch you. Perhaps he had a wife and children. Perhaps he once had the chance to be a good man. Perhaps he might have had that chance again. Now he never will. Carrion birds and foxes will feast on his flesh, and worms will devour the rest."

Bane laughed. "He was just a turd floating on the stream of life. The land is better off without him."

"In his case that may be true," agreed Banouin. "But what I fear is that you kill too swiftly. You like to kill. But how long before a good man falls beneath your blade, a kind man, a loving man?"

Bane shrugged. "The only men who will die by my blade are those who choose to attack me. That is their choice, not mine. I knew that black-bearded whoreson would come back, so I rested a little, then went out to meet them."

"You enjoyed it, though, didn't you?" accused Banouin. "As you cut his throat, you felt a surge of exultation."

"Aye, I did!" snapped Bane. "And what of it? He was my enemy, and I vanquished him. That is what true men do. We fight and know pride—and we leave the women to sit in the corners and wail over the dead."

"True men?" Banouin said slowly. "Of course. True men do not wish to live quiet lives, in harmony with their neighbors. They don't waste time poring over useless scrolls and trying to assimilate the wisdom of the ancients. They don't long for a world without wars and bloodshed and death. No. True men joy in the slitting of throats in the dark."

Bane shook his head. "I won't argue with you, Banouin. If words were arrows, you'd be the deadliest man alive. But this is not a debate. They came to kill us. One of them died for it. And no, it doesn't touch me any more than it did when I aimed that blow at Forvar's neck."

All color drained from Banouin's face. "You mean you meant to kill him?"

"Aye, I meant to kill him. And I have not suffered a moment of regret since."

"That is where you and I are different," Banouin said sadly. "I have not known a day when I have not thought of it with regret."

"This is a pointless conversation," said Bane. "And you have made me forget my dream."

◇ **2** ◇

ON THE FIFTH day they entered the lands of the southern Rigante, a wide, rolling plain that seemed to stretch before them into eternity. Looking back, Banouin could see no sign of Caer Druagh. The mountains of his home were more than two hundred miles distant. For the next ten days he and Bane rode ever south, spending their nights in villages and settlements. They were always made welcome, for all the tribespeople were eager for news of Connavar, the Demon King. Did he have plans to ride south and smash the armies of Stone and the treacherous Cenii? Was he wed, and did he have an heir? Banouin had little to tell them, but Bane was a great storyteller and a fine singer, and he would sit with the tribesmen in the evenings, drinking ale, swapping tall stories, and finally leading them in a series of rousing songs. Not once did he mention that he was Connavar's son, nor did he speak disrespectfully of the king while with strangers. This surprised Banouin, and he asked his companion about it one morning as they rode away from a settlement.

"I have reason to hate him," said Bane, his expression unusually serious. "But he did save these people when Valanus led the Panthers north. It was Connavar and the Iron Wolves who crushed the advance and drove the enemy back into the lands of the Cenii. I cannot take that away from him. My hatred is mine alone."

On the eighteenth day they reached the River Wir and journeyed by flat-bottomed boat for two hundred miles. The days were pleasant on the water, watching the countryside glide by. At the start Banouin was nervous about the four-man crew, who seemed to him to be cutthroats. Bane laughed his fears away. He and the crew got on famously. Each night they would moor the craft near settlements, allowing the two com-panions to lead their mounts ashore to feed.

One evening, the day they crossed the border into Norvii lands, Bane got into an argument with a huge tribesman, and they moved outside to settle it with fists. The fight was fast, furious, and ugly, but at the close, with both men bloodied and bruised, Bane suddenly began to laugh.

"What is so funny?" asked his opponent.

"Well," said Bane, "you are the ugliest whoreson I've ever seen. But the more I beat upon your face, the better-looking it gets."

The men crowding around burst into laughter. At last even the fighter grinned. "You're a cocky little game bird," he said.

"I am, indeed. Can I buy you a drink?"

"Why not?" replied the man.

Banouin could not duplicate Bane's easy familiarity with the people they met and would often find himself sitting alone in a corner, observing. He envied, with just a touch of bitterness, Bane's ability to make friends. Banouin thought about the river crew. Hard men who would think nothing of killing a passenger and heaving his body over the side had warmed to Bane as if he were a blood relative. It was mysti-fying. Yet Bane was not always full of camaraderie. Often he would fall silent for long periods, his expression dark and brooding. Sometimes, when in such a mood, he would avoid settlements and the two travelers would go ashore and camp out in woods or hollows. He would talk then of his sadness for the life his mother had led and how she had been shunned by the folk of Three Streams.

"Not all of them," Banouin pointed out as they sat in the moonlight beside a small fire. "She used to visit my mother. And the Big Man was good to you both."

"I don't remember him," said Bane. "I was too young when he died. But my mother spoke of him often. She said she was sitting, cradling me, in Grandfather's forge three nights after her husband cast her out. Ruathain came to her there. He asked her if her husband had given me a soul-name. She said that he had not. The Big Man told her that he had been out walking on the night of my birth and had seen a falcon flying through the night sky. This was a rare thing, he

said, and he felt that it was an omen. Whenever she told me
this story, my mother's eyes would fill with tears. She said he
put his arm around her and asked if she would accept Midnight Falcon as my soul-name." Bane sighed. "It was the first
act of tenderness she had experienced since my birth. It was
said that Ruathain's wife was furious with him and demanded
that he see no more of my mother. He refused and often visited her to see how we were faring. I wish I could remember
him. He was a great man by all accounts."

"Aye, he was," said Banouin. "My mother warned him not
to go to that last battle. Told him he would die if he did. But he
went anyway, to protect Connavar. Mother knew he would.
Said it broke her heart."

"She was in love with him?"

"I never asked her. Maybe she was. It's not something you
think about with old people, is it?"

Bane laughed then, his good humor restored. "My grand-
parents used to make their bed creak most nights."

"Oh, that's disgusting," said Banouin. "Thank you for
putting that image in my mind before I sleep."

On the day they left the boat to continue their journey over-
land Banouin saw genuine regret in the eyes of the crew. They
wished Bane good luck on his travels and made him promise
to seek them out when he returned so that they could hear of
his adventures. Not one of them bade farewell to Banouin.

The journey south was slower as they entered the great
forest of Filair. Settlements were farther apart, and the riders
had to veer many miles east or west to purchase supplies and
food. At each stop they inquired about the location of the next
village before moving on. Banouin purchased a pack pony in
order to carry more supplies, and Bane traded in his old
bronze sword to acquire a leaf-shaped iron blade and a short
hunting bow with a quiver of twenty arrows.

It was pouring rain when the riders reached the forest's
end. The plain of Cogden stretched out before them, flat and
empty except for the four huge mounds erected above those
fallen in the battle. Banouin shivered when he saw the barrows. Twenty-eight thousand had died there on that terrible
day. He had hoped to arrive at the battlefield much earlier in
the day so that they might ride through it in daylight. But

Bane's horse had thrown a shoe, and they had been forced to detour to a settlement where a blacksmith had forged and fitted a new one.

Now, with dusk fast approaching, they would have to camp in that desolate place. It did not seem to worry Bane. As night fell, the rain eased away. Somehow Bane managed to light a fire, which hissed and sputtered against the damp wood. Spreading his cloak on the wet ground, Bane was soon asleep. Banouin sat alone, feeding branches to the flames.

Fear touched him, and he glanced around. Nothing was to be seen except the four barrows and the bright moon. The fear grew, unfocused and all-consuming. His mouth was dry, his heart beating wildly.

Then he felt their presence . . .

At first all he could see was the night mist rolling across the field; then it changed, flowing and rising until Banouin could see gray forms, the figures of men, cold and silent. For a moment he thought the scene was born of his fear, unreal, invented. Then the figures took clearer shape, becoming ten ranks of fighting men moving slowly across Cogden Field. Clad in helms of ghostly iron with embossed ear guards, they carried long rectangular shields and short stabbing swords.

This was the long-dead army of Stone. Banouin stared at them. Their forms were translucent and shimmered in the moonlight. When they reached the barrows, instead of climbing them, they passed right through. There was no sound. The advancing line broke into a run. Banouin glanced to his right. There, pale and spectral, was another line, this time of brightly armored horsemen. Silently they charged at the enemy, swords as pale as moonlight slashing into them. Banouin saw a man stagger back, his arm hacked from his body. Then a spear ripped through his guts, and he fell, the spear snapping in two. Horses fell, pitching their riders, who were stabbed mercilessly as they struggled to rise. All the terrible sights of war unfolded in eerie silence before his eyes.

A black crow glided down to the grass close by and stood, its baleful glare fixed on Banouin. Then a voice sounded from behind, startling him. "These are scenes men sing of, and brag of, and lust after." Banouin spun around. An old woman stood there, her shoulders hunched beneath a threadbare shawl, her hands clasping a long, crooked staff. Her hair was thin and wispy white, like mist clinging to her skull. She was impossibly ancient. Banouin's heart began to beat wildly. He knew of this woman, this creature of the Seidh. This was the Morrigu, whose promises tasted of nectar and burned like poison. The young man said nothing, but his dark eyes flicked toward the sleeping Bane. "He cannot hear me, and he will not wake," said the Morrigu. "Will you bid me welcome to your hearth?"

"You . . . are not welcome here," he forced himself to say.

"How that cuts me," she said with a sneer. "You, whom I delivered safe when nature had decreed your death."

"I don't know what you are talking about," he told her.

"Vorna did not speak of me, then? How disappointing. On the night you were born her life was in danger. The babe—the you that was to be—was breeched, and there were no mid-wives, no druids on hand to save her—or you. So I came. And you were delivered by these old hands."

"I don't believe you."

"Yes, you do, Banouin. It is part of the gift. You always sense when people are lying."

"Even if you did save me, I don't doubt you had your own reasons," he said, his voice firmer.

"Indeed I did." She paused. "Well, if I am not welcome here, will you at least walk with me awhile?"

"Why would I wish to?"

"Perhaps to prove to yourself that you are not the coward you believe yourself to be. Perhaps to repay your debt to me. Perhaps out of curiosity." She stepped closer, and he could see that the skin beneath her right eye had peeled back, exposing the bone beneath. Banouin recoiled. "Or perhaps because of your love for your sleeping friend." Once more Banouin looked down at Bane. Something moved on his friend's chest, and Banouin saw it was a coiled snake. It slithered up, then laid its flat head on Bane's neck.

"Don't kill him," pleaded Banouin.

"I have no wish to kill anyone," said the Morrigu. "All I wish for is a walk across this field of the slain."

"I will come with you," he said. "Make the snake disappear."

"What snake?" she asked.

Banouin glanced down. Bane was sleeping peacefully. The serpent had gone.

The Morrigu trudged past Banouin, leaning heavily on her staff. The young man followed, and they walked out onto the battlefield. The struggle was titanic, with neither side giving ground. The army of Stone fought with discipline and courage, while the tribesmen battled with passion and desperate bravery. Time and again Banouin saw acts of individual heroism that went unnoticed by the participants: a slim Rigante, standing astride a fallen comrade, trying to protect him; a soldier of Stone, his sword broken, charging into the mass of tribesmen, slamming his shield at them, and trying to wrest a fresh blade from the hands of the enemy.

"Why do they still fight?" he asked the Morrigu.

"They do not know they are dead," she answered.

"How can they not know?"

"The arrogance of man," she replied.

They walked on. Banouin saw a tall, handsome Stone officer with close-cropped hair waving his short sword above his head. Like a windblown echo he heard a thin, piping call to arms. "One more charge, lads! One more charge and we'll have the day!"

"Who is that?" he asked.

"That is Valanus, the most famous of all Stone generals."

"Famous?" queried Banouin. "It is my understanding that to speak his name aloud in Stone is a criminal offense. He was the first Stone general to lose a major battle against barbarians."

"That is still fame," she said. "Every man knows of him and his deeds. It is what he wanted. Indeed, it is what he asked for."

The ghostly fighting continued until not one of the combatants was still standing. Banouin and the Morrigu reached the top of the nearest barrow, and the young man looked down upon the field of the fallen. A cool breeze blew across the shimmering silvered grass, and slowly the dead began to rise again, whole and mended. Then they trudged back to their battle lines and formed up once more.

And the battle began again.

"Why does someone not tell them they are dead?" said

Banouin. "Then they could pass over the dark water and be free of this life."

The Morrigu laughed. The sound made him shiver. "Come, then," she said. "You can tell Valanus."

Banouin followed her back into the battle. As she reached the Stone general, she tapped at his form with her staff. He turned and looked not at her but directly at Banouin. "Who are you, spirit?" he asked.

"I am not a spirit, sir, but a man. You are the spirit. This battle was fought many years ago, and you died here. It is time to move on."

"Died?" Valanus said, with a wide smile. "Do I look dead to you? Get thee gone, demon. This is my day. And when it is over, I shall be lord of this land." Turning away, he raised his sword. "One more charge, lads! One more and we will have the day!"

"Well, you told him," said the Morrigu. "But it is in the nature of men never to listen. In death as well as in life."

"Why are you here?" he whispered.

"For reasons of my own. What is it you wish for?"

Banouin laughed. "Do you think me stupid enough to tell you? Like poor Valanus, whose name is now accursed?"

"Would your request be as his, child? Would you want fame and glory? Would you want riches?"

Banouin turned his back on the ceaseless, silent warfare raging around him and walked back to the campsite. Bane was still sleeping, and the fire was burning low.

The Morrigu moved alongside him. "Can you feel Caer Druagh calling you?" she asked.

"I find I miss the mountains," he admitted. "I had not thought I would."

"Do you know why the Seidh exist?"

"No."

"One day you will. And on that day you will return to Caer Druagh."

"What is it that you want from me?" he asked her. "I am not a warrior. I have no lust for battle and glory. My intention is to reside in Stone and study."

"Then do so, Banouin. Look through all the ancient texts. Look for the truth hidden within dusty pages and yellowing scrolls. You will not find what you are looking for. The answer, when it comes, will come from your heart." She sank down to the ground and rubbed her hand across her face. Skin peeled back and fell away, exposing more bone. Banouin turned his face away.

"Aye, not a pretty sight, am I?"

"I don't know why an immortal should choose such a grotesque countenance," he said.

"Perhaps I didn't choose it, child." Wearily she pushed herself to her feet. "Perhaps what you see is the very essence of the Morrigu." Her voice trailed away. "You have much to learn. And the first lesson is approaching. Understand this: You cannot conquer fear by running away from it."

The crow flapped its wings and soared toward the sky. Momentarily distracted, Banouin swung back to where the Morrigu had been.

She had vanished.

The dawn sun cleared the eastern mountains.

The battlefield was deserted now. With a deep sigh Banouin sat down by the dying fire.

Bane awoke and yawned. He looked up at Banouin through bleary eyes. "Have you been sitting there all night?"

"Aye."

Bane grinned. "Thought the ghosties would come for you, did you?"

"And they did," said Banouin.

By noon the riders had passed far beyond Cogden Field and were climbing low wooded hills overlooking the eastern coast. In the far distance they could see merchant ships hugging the shoreline, heading north.

"I have been thinking of Forvar and his death," Banouin said as they rode.

"Oh, no, not that again."

Banouin ignored the protest. "I often wonder if he might have changed as he grew older. He was very young, and the death of his father blinded him with hate."

"You think too much," Bane told him. "You always have. He was a brute, and he died because he was a brute. End of story, my friend. What he might have been is irrelevant. He's dead and gone."

"Perhaps he isn't gone," said Banouin. He told Bane of the ghostly battle and the arrival of the Morrigu.

His friend listened in silence. "Are you sure you didn't dream this?" he asked as Banouin concluded his tale.

"I am sure."

"And Valanus thought you were the ghost?"

"Yes."

"So why did the Old Woman appear to you? What did she want?"

"I don't know, Bane. But the whole scene was so irredeemably sad. To spend eternity endlessly reliving scenes of carnage and death. Valanus still believes he can win the battle."

"Well, there is nothing you can do about it, so let's concentrate on more important matters. I am hungry, and I need a woman." With that Bane swung his horse and rode off toward the highest hill to scan the countryside for signs of a settlement or village. Banouin watched him go and wondered if his friend truly had no feelings for the tormented spirits of Cogden Field.

An hour later Bane rejoined him.

"There is a large, stockaded town around five miles to the southwest. Maybe two hundred dwellings with two long halls." Banouin nodded but did not reply. Bane leaned across and thumped his friend on the shoulder. "You are a strange one," he said. "When will you learn?"

"There is much for me to learn," agreed Banouin, "but what exactly do you think I need to learn the most?"

"To live! To understand what it means." Bane halted his horse. "Look around you, at the hills and the trees. See the way the sunlight dapples the oaks. Feel the breeze on your face. This is life, Banouin. Last night, and the ghost army, is but a memory now. Tomorrow is yet to be born. Life is now! This very moment. But you never live in the now. You are always thinking back over some past tragedy or looking ahead to some distant dream. Is Forvar still haunting the hillside? Will the ghosts of Cogden ever find peace? Will the city of

Stone fulfill all my dreams? Why is the sun hot? Why is water wet? It is no way to spend one's life."

Banouin shook his head and felt his anger rise. "Better that than to ride around the countryside looking for earth maidens to rut with, to get drunk and fight with strangers, to be a wind-blown leaf skittering across the countryside."

"You think so?" Bane asked, with a smile. His expression grew suddenly more serious. "We are all leaves, my friend. Against the mountains and the sea we are as fleeting as heart-beats. Nothing we build lasts. To the north of Old Oaks there is a buried city. I have been there. A farmer unearthed the re-mains of a great wall. There are blocks of stone weighing fifty, sixty tons, all laid one atop the other. Farther on, in a sheltered valley, they found the head of a colossal statue. The nose alone was longer than a broadsword. What great man must this have been? A king, perhaps. No one knows his name or the name of his city. Perhaps he still walks the hills. Perhaps he and Forvar have become great friends." Bane sighed. "Ah, Banouin, you are a sweet and gentle soul. But in an hour or two, while you are sitting somewhere pondering all the unfairness of life, I shall be naked with a soft and yielding woman."

With that Bane heeled his horse forward.

Banouin rode after him. "Tell me about the statue they found," he said.

Bane sighed. "You didn't really hear a word I said, did you?"

"Of course. But tell me about the buried city."

"Connavar ordered the wall excavated, but it was too large and too long. They think it extends for miles. According to Brother Solstice, the men still working at the site are seeking treasure now. The Demon King needs gold to purchase weapons for his armies, and he hopes burial mounds will supply it."

"I wonder how they raised blocks of such size. And why," said Banouin.

"That does it!" Bane said suddenly. "You're off in the past again, so I'll see you in the near future."

He galloped off toward the southwest and the stock-aded town.

* * *

As with many Keltoi settlements, the town of Sighing Water bore no sense of overall design or planning. The original Norvii settlement of some twenty homes had been built close to a stream that flowed from the hills, cascading over a series of white rocks and down to a pear-shaped lake. Positioned as it was less than twelve miles from the eastern coast and close to a river leading to a wide estuary, it soon became a place of commerce. Timber was plentiful, the surrounding land was rich and verdant, and soon the town began to grow. With the lowlands ideal for corn and the higher ground for cattle, sheep, and goats, Sighing Water thrived. More and more houses were built. When iron ore and coal deposits were found less than two miles away, the settlement swelled even further.

Now some three thousand people dwelled within the stockaded town, with more than four thousand more in the surrounding countryside. There were warehouses, shops, stalls, forges, clothing makers, leather workers, jewelers, and merchants of every kind. There were mills, tanneries, wagon makers, horse breeders, and a host of allied trades, including a fleet of horse-drawn barges to ferry goods to the coast.

At seventeen Bane had never seen such a sprawling town. He had thought Old Oaks large, but there were twice as many people here, and as he rode in through the open gates, he felt uncomfortable, as if the sheer weight of multitudes were closing in on him. Pushing such thoughts aside, he located a hostler and left his gray in the man's care, asking that the beast be rubbed down and grain-fed.

The hostler, a middle-aged, round-shouldered man, asked if he planned to sell the gelding. Bane told him no.

"You could get a fine sum, boy. He's powerful and keen of eye. Is he fast?"

"He likes to run," said Bane. "Tell me, where is the best earth maiden?"

"The best what?" queried the man.

The response surprised the youngster. "Earth maiden," he said more slowly, wondering if his Rigante accent had confused the man.

"I do not know the term, boy."

"Young women who offer . . . company to a man."

"Ah, whores, you mean? Aye, there are plenty of those. But it is the weeks end, and the coal and iron workers are here in force. You'll be lucky to find a whore who hasn't already got her legs locked around a man's hips. You'll have no luck in the taverns, I'll tell you that for free. You could try the northern quarter. The expensive ones are up there."

"Expensive?"

"Ten silver pieces for an hour's pleasure, so they say. And a single night costs a gold."

"I'll try the taverns. I need a bed for the night, anyway."

"Avoid the Green Ghost," warned the man. "It's a place of trouble and violence. The Swallow is a good tavern, and they give a man a fine breakfast."

Bane thanked him and asked directions. As he was doing so, Banouin came riding up.

A short time later the two men were strolling through a packed marketplace and heading up a wending hill path toward a group of buildings set around an open square. The first of the buildings, the Green Ghost tavern, was large, around a hundred feet long, with two stories under a thatched roof. Several men were sitting in the fading sunshine outside, nursing pottery jugs of ale. They looked up as the newcomers approached.

"Just what we needed now the women have run out," said one, a sour-faced individual, his face seamed with dark coal scars. "Two pretty boys fresh from the farm."

Bane paused and laughed. "Look, Banouin," he said brightly. "There's a sight you don't see very often: a man who can fart through his mouth." He crouched down in front of the miner and dipped his finger into the man's ale. Then he licked it. "Good ale," he said. The man's eyes opened wide. Bane laughed at him, then rose smoothly and moved inside the tavern. There were some thirty long bench tables, most of them filled by burly men spooning stew or drinking ale.

"I don't like this place," whispered Banouin.

"This is the Green Ghost. It was highly recommended," said Bane. "You are too judgmental." He wandered to the rear of the dining room, where a fat, balding man was wiping the bar with a dirty cloth.

"You have a room for the night?" asked Bane.

"We always have rooms," said the fat man.

"What about women?"

The man shook his head. "All taken. You'll have to make do with Dame Wrist and her five little daughters. The room will cost you a half silver. In advance."

"Friendly place, isn't it?" Bane observed to Banouin. "Aren't you glad you came?"

Banouin sighed.

"You want the room or not?" said the fat man.

At that moment there was the sound of breaking crockery. Bane turned to see a young woman standing over three broken jugs, her thin woolen skirt stained with ale. The fat man stormed around the bar and rushed over to the girl. "You stupid clumsy cow!" he shouted.

"One of the men grabbed me," she told him.

His meaty hand slapped across her face, knocking her sideways. She fell against a table.

Bane was momentarily stunned. He could scarcely believe what he had seen. All color drained from his face, and he moved swiftly across the room. The fat man reached for the girl again, but Bane took hold of his arm, spun him, and delivered a right uppercut to his belly, followed by a left cross that sent him crashing to the sawdust-covered floor.

"Never in my life have I seen a man strike a woman," he said. "Find yourself a weapon. Then I'll open you from throat to groin." The fat man, his eyes frightened, crawled back from the angry tribesman.

"I don't want a weapon. I don't want to fight you."

"You don't want to fight? I have challenged you, man."

"I don't care! I'm not going to fight you."

The fat man rolled to his knees, crawled a few paces, pushed himself to his feet, and ran back to the bar. Once there, he fled through a doorway, slamming shut the door behind him. Bane shook his head in disbelief.

"How could he refuse to fight?" he said.

"He's just a coward. No shortage of cowards in the world," said a gray-bearded man sitting at a table close by. Bane looked at him. As with most of the men, his skin was deeply coal-stained.

The girl was on her knees, gathering the sharp shards of the broken jugs. Bane knelt down and put his hand on her shoulder. She looked into his face and gave a weary smile. Her skin was pockmarked, and a vivid red weal showed on the left side of her face.

"I am sorry that he hurt you," said Bane.

"He's done worse," she said. "And he will again."

"Better watch out, boy!" called the gray-bearded miner.

Bane glanced up. The rear door had opened. Two thickset men, both carrying cudgels, were advancing across the room.

The fat man was back in the doorway. He was smiling now. "You want to fight someone?" he shouted. "Well, now's your chance."

The two men rushed forward. Bane rose, took one step to the right, then lashed out with his foot. His boot hammered into the first man's knee just as his weight descended on it. The leg snapped backward. With a terrible scream the man fell. The second man lashed out, the cudgel catching Bane high on the shoulder. He swayed, then delivered a left hook to the man's bearded chin. The man stumbled. Bane kicked him in the face.

The fat man was standing framed in the doorway. Bane ran forward, vaulted the bar, grabbed him by his tunic, and threw him back against the wall.

"I'm sorry! I'm sorry!" wailed the man. Suddenly the sound was cut off. The fat man's jaw dropped, and he sagged down the wall, falling to his knees. Bane tore his dagger from the man's chest. The dying man's eyes flickered. "Don't hurt me!" he whispered. Blood frothed to his lips, and he toppled sideways to the floor. Bane wiped his dagger blade on the man's tunic, then rose, sheathing the weapon. All around him men were sitting in stunned silence. No one moved except the serving girl, who raised her hand to her mouth as if to stifle a cry.

Bane strode from the Green Ghost. Banouin ran after him. "We had better leave this settlement," he said. "They might decide to hang you."

"I did nothing wrong," argued Bane.

"You knifed an unarmed man," Banouin pointed out.

"He wasn't a man. He struck a woman, and he wouldn't fight. He had no honor. He was a vile thing, no better than vermin."

"I warned you, Bane. You kill too quickly," Banouin said sadly.

"And you nag worse than a wife," snapped Bane. "But you are right. Let's be gone from this place. Killing him has quite spoiled my day."

"Not as badly as it spoiled his," said Banouin.

They rode several miles from Sighing Water and camped in a cave overlooking the sea. Banouin lit a fire, but Bane wandered out and sat on the cliff top, watching the moon shining above the dark water. Banouin left him there for a while and tended the fire. Bane was in one of his dark, gloomy moods and would not appreciate company for a while.

There was little food left, and Banouin ate a stick of smoke-dried meat they had purchased several days before. He leaned back and stared at the cave wall, watching the fire shadows dance on the gray stone.

Bane did kill too swiftly. The fat man had been a bully and a coward, but that was no reason for him to die choking on his own blood. Worse, he knew that Bane had gone to the place seeking trouble. He knew the look that came into his friend's strange eyes, a kind of glint, a shining that always precipitated violence. Yet Bane had always been kind to him, seeming to understand his hatred of violence and his longing for a life of quiet study. The younger man had protected him and had been willing to be ostracized by his fellow tribesmen rather than give up their friendship.

It was all so baffling. When Bane was happy, he could charm the hardest heart and make friends with anyone. People genuinely liked him. Banouin thought back to the cutthroat river crew and their fondness for his companion. It was chilling to think that if any one of them had said the wrong word, Bane could just as easily have killed him. Would he have been different if Connavar had accepted him?

Adding dry sticks to the fire, he remembered asking his mother some weeks earlier why a great man like the king had turned his back on his son.

"That is a complex question," Vorna had said. "But it presupposes that greatness in one area must mean greatness in all. This is not even close to the truth. Connavar is a good man, and I love him dearly, but he is harsh and unforgiving. There is also within him—as there is within Bane—a burning need for violence that is barely held in check." She had looked into his eyes, then risen from her chair and moved to the window, which she had pulled shut despite the stifling summer heat that filled the house. "I want no one to overhear what I am to tell you, Banouin, and I do not want you to repeat it. Ever. Do I have your promise?"

"Of course, Mother."

She sat down in her chair and took a deep breath. "Many years ago Connavar wed a young Rigante woman named Tae. He loved her deeply. He had risked his life to save her from the Sea Wolves, and he had brought her to Three Streams. Then he became laird, and they moved to Old Oaks. One day Connavar went to the Wishing Tree woods to commune with the Seidh. There he was warned never to break a promise, no matter how small.

"One day, soon after, he had told Tae that he would be back at Old Oaks at around noon in order to accompany her on a ride to a pretty lake they had heard of. But as he was riding home, he saw a woman standing outside a hut built in the hills."

"And that was Arian," put in Banouin.

"I am telling this story."

"But I know it already," he argued. "He made love to Arian, and Bane was born."

"Listen!" hissed Vorna. "Arian was his childhood sweetheart, but she was . . ." Vorna hesitated. "This must never be repeated!"

"I have already promised that. Go on."

"She knew many men, even as a young girl. She would travel through the hills to the trade road, and she would rut with men for coin. There was a need in her that she thought no one knew of. No one save an earth maiden named Eriatha, who helped her abort several babes. But I knew. She was betrothed to Connavar, but when he fought the bear and everyone believed he would die of his wounds, Arian took up with Casta and married him on Feast Night. But as we know, Connavar did not die. He survived and grew strong. He never forgave Arian and avoided her always.

"On that dread day, when he saw her alone at the hut, all his old feelings came back. She wept and begged forgiveness. She clung to him." Vorna sighed. "Men are not strong, Banouin. The loins will inevitably betray the heart. Her husband was gone for the day, and Connavar bedded her.

"Back at Old Oaks his wife was waiting for the trip to the lake he had promised. When he failed to return, she asked Ruathain to take her to the lake. This he did. But on the way back a group of assassins were waiting to kill Ruathain. They shot an arrow, which missed him and killed Tae. Connavar had forgotten the warning of the Seidh. He had broken his promise, and his young wife lay dead upon the grass.

"When he heard what had happened, he lost his mind for a while. The men had come from a Pannone fishing village, sent by the Fisher Laird. Connavar went to that village alone, killed the laird and his sons, and destroyed the village by fire. Every house. He slaughtered many, including women and children. Does this behavior sound familiar to you?"

"Aye. Bane."

"Yes, Bane. He is his father's son. But when Connavar regained his senses, he felt a terrible burden of guilt. It is a burden he carries to this day. He could never look upon Arian again. He never spoke publicly of her or her child. Their very existence was a constantly painful reminder of his betrayal and the terrible deeds he committed."

"I always thought," said Banouin, "that Arian was a good woman."

"Stupid boy!" stormed Vorna. "Did I say she was not good? I said she had a need for men—a weakness, if you like. That does not make her evil. She was a good mother to Bane, and there was great kindness in her. It is my belief that she never stopped loving Connavar. Her burden of guilt was every bit as powerful as his own." Vorna sighed. "Their guilt was the same. And yet Connavar—as you said—is a great man, so he was forgiven. Arian was marked in men's minds as the whore who caused the death of Tae. It is unjust. Even members of her own family turned their backs on her. Govannan, mainly. But her sister, Gwydia, never invited her to Seven Willows."

"Why hasn't someone told Bane this?" he asked.

"For what purpose? He loved his mother, and he thinks her almost holy. He was the one person in her life who gave her complete love. It was for her to tell him, if she chose to. And she did not."

"It was all so tragic," said Banouin. "And it doesn't end, does it? Arian is dead, but Bane lives on, with all the bitterness."

"That bitterness would not be ended merely by understanding of the truth," said Vorna. "Trust me on this, my son."

"But none of this was Bane's fault," insisted Banouin. "His mother betrayed her husband, just as Connavar betrayed his wife. Bane is merely the innocent who has suffered."

"They have all suffered." She looked at her son fondly and reached out to stroke his face. "Men say that there is freedom in truth. Sometimes it is true. Mostly it is not. Truth can be a dagger to the heart. When your father died and you were born, I was torn between anguish and joy. It almost broke me. And on one day, as I looked at you within your crib, I felt as if I had been cursed by love, not blessed by it. In that one moment I wished that you had never been conceived, that I had never met your father, that I had never known love at all. That is a truth, Banouin. Tell me, how does it sit with you?"

"I can understand it," he said. "I feel no anger or hurt."

"Suppose I had told you this when you were five years younger, hated and despised by all the other boys?"

"I would have been devastated," he admitted. "I would have been too young to understand."

"Yes," she said, "the child would invest that truth with a perception of its own: 'My mother did not love me.' 'I was not wanted.' In many ways that is what the young Bane did. Connavar did not acknowledge him; therefore, Connavar hated him and hated his mother. Connavar was an evil creature. An enemy. This is the way Bane dealt with his perception of the truth. And it haunts him still."

"Then there is nothing we can do?"

"I would not say that. There is great strength in him, great loyalty and love. With good friends close by he may yet find his way. That is what we can do. Remain his friends."

"I will always be that," Banouin promised.

The dancing shadows on the cave wall were making Banouin sleepy. He glanced out at the skyline and saw his friend still sitting on the cliff top. Wearily he pushed himself to his feet and trudged out to join him. "It is a fine night," he said, hunkering down beside the blond warrior, his feet dangling over the cliff edge.

"Aye, it is," agreed Bane. "Some people find the night threatening, but I love the dark. It seems timeless and calm. When I was a child, maybe five or six, my mother would take me to the Riguan Falls on warm nights. We would swim there in the moonlight. I remember that I longed to be a fish, swimming forever. I loved those nights. When we climbed out, she would light a fire, and then we would sit and eat a supper she had brought with her. After that I always felt sleepy, and she would wrap me in a blanket and hold me close so that I slept with my head in her lap. They were the most peaceful of nights, and I never dreamed at all."

"It is strange," said Banouin, "how good memories can make you feel sad. I feel the same way about the Big Man. When I was young, I would constantly run out into the yard to see if he was coming to visit us. And when he did, I would whoop with joy and scamper off to meet him. Now, when I recall his face and his bright blue eyes, I feel a lump in my throat. So much would have been different had he not died in that battle."

"Perhaps. Perhaps not," said Bane. "I used to play that game in my head. What if . . . ? It is a stupid game. What's done is done. It cannot be undone. If I could have this day back again, I would avoid the Green Ghost. Or, if not that, then I would merely have thrashed the fat man. But I cannot have it back. Just as I cannot return to the Riguan Falls and sit with my mother, a blanket around me, the taste of a sweet cake on my tongue."

"Life does seem unfair sometimes," said Banouin.

Bane laughed. "Aye, but there are good times. Your mother and I rescued a badger cub once. It was blind, and she healed it. Then we took it back to the woods and watched it amble away to a new life. That was a grand night. I like to think that cub went on to become a fine beast, with a mate and cubs of his own. Maybe he did. Or maybe he was killed by hunters. Fortunately, I'll never know." Bane picked up a stone and hurled it high over the cliff, watching it drop to the water below. "I hope the sea is as calm as this when we cross," he said.

"You are coming across the water with me?"

"Of course. I promised your mother I'd see you safe all the way to Stone."

"I'll be safe," said Banouin, feeling suddenly uncomfortable. "I don't think you'll like Stone."

"If I don't, I shall bid you farewell," said Bane. "Anyway, I'm tired. I think I'll get some sleep." Rising smoothly, he wandered back to the cave.

Banouin sat alone for a while, lost in thought. He loved Bane, but the thought of arriving in Stone with him was a daunting and depressing one, like taking a wild bear to a wedding dance. The thought shamed him, but he could not push it away.

Bane lay in the cave, trying to deal with the now-familiar waves of sorrow and seeking a way through the desolation he felt. Parax had been right. He had planned to lead the hunters a merry chase and then go down fighting, putting an end to this bitter existence. Bane had not consciously realized it, and only when Parax had spoken the words had the truth of them registered. It was not that he particularly wanted to die. He loved life, the feel of the warm sun on his face, the sound of a waterfall, the call of a hunting falcon. Nor was it merely the death of Arian or the continuing hurt of his rejection by Connavar.

Rather, it was a combination of these and many other pressures, not least the sense of isolation after the early years of being shunned by his fellows and then, as he grew older, being offered only menial tasks because he could not master the relatively simple skills of reading and writing. It was almost as if the king had decreed this onerous duty on the peoples of the Rigante, Pannone, and Norvii merely to add to the already unbearable pressures of Bane's life.

He lay back in the cave and felt his anger rising. Vorna had probably saved his life by asking him to look after her son. And now that son, Bane's only friend, was ashamed of him. He had seen the look in his eye when he had talked of accompanying him to Stone, the sudden shock and dismay. He did not let Banouin know that he had seen it, and it hurt the more because he had to hide his pain.

But then, he had always hidden the pain. When have you ever let people see the real man? he wondered. When have you ever let fall the mask? Cheerful Bane, bright Bane, Bane the storyteller, the singer of bawdy songs. In settlements other than Three Streams Bane was popular with all he met, but the man they laughed and joked with was not the man behind the mask.

Even with his mother Bane hid his feelings. She had anguish enough, he thought, and so he joked and laughed with her. No one else could bring a smile to her face. No one else really tried.

Now she was gone. Even Vorna's skills had not been enough to save her. This had confused Bane, for Vorna had taken the cancer from the blind badger and restored its sight, and Bane had railed at her.

"Magic alone was not enough," Vorna had said. "Arian no longer had the will to go on."

Bane understood it now. He had felt it for himself up in the hills as the hunters searched for him.

He felt it now in this cold cave.

Thoughts of Arian filled his mind. When, he wondered, had she finally lost the will to live? Often she would walk the high hills, staring toward the north. Bane always believed she was waiting for Connavar, hoping he would one day ride by and would stop and talk to her. He never did.

Two years earlier, at age fifteen, Bane had decided to meet with the king, meet with him in a way that would force Connavar to speak with him. And when they spoke Bane would ask him why he shunned them. The plan was simple enough. All Bane had to do was win the Beltine Race, five miles over rough country. The problem was that there were at least seven other youngsters faster than he among the Rigante of Three Streams alone.

Bane trained every day for months, building his stamina, pounding along mud-covered trails, running up high hills, pushing himself to the point of collapse. In the early weeks he would sometimes stagger to a halt and vomit beside the trail.

Then he would run on, lungs afire, muscles burning. Gradually he became stronger, driven on always by the thought of meeting his father, seeing at last pride in his eyes.

The race had been hard fought. One boy from the northern Pannone had stayed with him for four of the five miles, but Bane had powered away from him in the last mile, finishing fast and sprinting toward the feast fires at the foot of Old Oaks. The last two hundred paces had been run between lines of cheering tribesmen, and at the finish he saw the king, standing alongside his brothers Braefar and Bendegit Bran.

Connavar was a big man, wide in the shoulders. He was wearing his famous patchwork cloak, bearing the colors of the five tribes, and at his side was the legendary Seidh sword that men said could cut through stone and iron.

Heart pounding, lungs close to bursting, Bane had slowed at the finish, then stood, hands on hips, staring into the eyes of the king. It was like looking into his own eyes, and their gazes met and locked. There was no expression on Connavar's scarred features, and he did not smile. He stepped forward and said: "Well done." Then he turned away before the breathless Bane could answer and strode back through the crowd.

For a moment there was silence in the crowd, then Bendegit Bran stepped forward and put his arm around Bane's shoulder. "The champion is from Three Streams," he shouted. He patted Bane on the shoulder. "That was a fine run." The crowd cheered again, and Bran led Bane away as the other runners started to pound down toward the line.

"Are you all right?" asked Bran.

Bane looked into his uncle's handsome face and nodded. "Just tired," he said, looking beyond him at the distant figure of Connavar, walking up the hill path toward Old Oaks. "Is the king not staying for the feast?"

Bran looked embarrassed. "He is a solitary man. He rarely stays among crowds for long."

"Last year I heard he sat the winner of the race beside him at table," said Bane.

"Then you shall sit beside me this year," said Bran.

"I think I'll go home," Bane replied.

"That's a two-day ride, Bane. Stay. Enjoy the feast."

Bane walked away, saddled the borrowed pony, and set off into the darkness.

Eighteen months later, when he fought his first skirmish against the Sea Raiders, killing two and wounding a third, he was awarded the gold clasp he still wore on his wrist. It was a tradition that these were given out by the king. Bane had received his from Braefar. It was no surprise by then.

It was around that time that Arian began to fade. She ate like a sparrow, and the weight dropped from her. Even Bane could no longer make her smile.

Bane pulled his blanket around himself and rolled to his side, resting his head on his saddle. He heard Banouin's soft footfalls as he entered the cave but kept his eyes closed.

I will see you safely to Stone, he thought, and when the walls of the city are in sight, I will say farewell.

The wagon trundled on through the driving rain, the two weary horses moving slowly, heads down against the wind. The driver sat huddled below the canvas canopy, his right hand holding the reins, his left arm around the shoulders of the teenage girl beside him.

Despite the canopy the rain had soaked them both, and the girl shivered. "How long, Father?" she asked.

"According to the map, we're about a mile from the bridge," the old man told her. "After that maybe five miles. We should be there before dusk."

He smiled as he said it. The sky was so dark now, it already felt like night. Appius lifted his whip and cracked it over the heads of the team. They surged into the traces, and the wagon picked up speed. His daughter snuggled in close. He patted her back and, reaching over, tugged her hood forward to try to protect her from the rain. The hood was already drenched. She looked up at him and smiled. His heart leapt. So like her mother, he thought. So beautiful.

Appius looked back at what the map indicated was a road. The thought made him shake his head in frustration. Road? It was a wide, muddy track, pitted and irregular, and his wagon was trundling along in the deep grooves made by other lumbering vehicles. Only an idiot or a barbarian could call this a road. Back in Stone there were roads! Roads of well-laid stone over gravel and sand.

He sighed. Back in Stone there were also the Crimson Priests, the blood trials, the burnings. The wind died down, and the rain began to ease. No longer did it lash into their faces but now pattered against the canopy above their heads. To the west the sun broke through the clouds. Appius pushed back his hood, exposing his close-cropped white hair.

Lia looked up at him and smiled. "Everything looks so wonderful when the sun shines," she said.

"What would look wonderful right now is a bathhouse with steam rising from perfumed water," he said. "And then a massage and a long sleep."

"Barus said the town was quite civilized. There should be a bathhouse."

"Just so long as there's no temple," he said, his good humor fading.

"The priests have not crossed the water," she said. "But they will." Lia leaned back and stretched, removing her hooded cloak and shaking the water from it. He glanced at her and felt immediately renewed and revived. Her dark hair was cut short, after the latest fashion in Stone, and it emphasized the extraordinary beauty of her features, her large, dark eyes, and the radiance of her smile. He wondered if he was merely seeing her with a father's eye but then recalled the effect she had on his young officers. Most were struck dumb in her presence. Maybe here, he thought, at this ass end of the empire, she will put aside the stupidities her mother instilled in her. Then, after a reasonable period, they could return to Stone and take up their positions in respectable society. Lia could marry a man she loved and know true happiness, and he could sit in the sunshine and watch his grandchildren grow.

I should live so long, he thought miserably. His back ached, and he could feel his knee joints swelling with the wet and the cold. Fifty years a soldier, marching in all kinds of weather, sleeping on cold ground. It is a marvel I can walk at all, he thought.

But never in his worst nightmares did he expect to end his days across the water, in the very land that had seen the destruction of a Stone army. He shivered at the memory. Of all the participants in that reckless exercise, Appius alone had emerged with credit, organizing his Panther into a fighting retreat to the safety of the previous night's fortified camp. Even then he had lost half his men.

The man Connavar had been a devil in human form. He had organized his troops brilliantly, and Valanus, expecting the usual Keltoi tactics of a massed charge, had fallen into a trap. Cut off from supplies, unable to build a camp, the weary, hungry army had been attacked first by heavy cavalry and then by mounted archers. Cogden Field. The name made his skin crawl. Twelve thousand soldiers of Stone had died there.

Back in Stone the shock had been colossal. Appius had been arrested and returned for trial, but he and three other officers had been acquitted of negligence, the full brunt of the city's fury falling upon the dead Valanus, who had, it was said, led his fifteen thousand men against an enemy a million strong. It was such arrant nonsense that Appius could hardly credit it, yet the people believed it. Their pride would not let them even consider the idea that a Stone army could be defeated by a mere thirty thousand Rigante. No one wanted to hear the truth except Jasaray, and then only in secret.

He remembered the day the general—not yet the emperor—had summoned him to his home, forcing Appius to relive every moment of the battle, sketching out fighting lines, recalling tactics. First the Rigante had killed all the Cenii scouts used by Valanus, and the army had been forced to march blind. Then a detachment had cut behind them, savaging the supply column, killing the drivers, and burning the wagons. At the last they had surrounded Valanus on Cogden Field, a combined force of Rigante, Norvii, and Pannone tribesmen, all under the command of Connavar.

"I trained him," said Jasaray, and Appius thought he detected a note of pride in the general's voice.

"You trained him too damned well," Appius said. "We'll have to take an army back, and swiftly."

Jasaray shook his head. "All in good time. The defeat has frightened the populace. They no longer trust the council to make strong decisions. Neither do I. It is my belief that a single figure should rule Stone: a single mind controlling the destiny of our city."

"Your mind, General?" Appius asked.

"If they call upon me, it would be unpatriotic to refuse. Where do you stand, my old friend?"

"As I always have, Scholar. By your side."

"I expected no less," admitted Jasaray.

The wagon lurched as a wheel hit a sunken stone. Appius backed up the horses and moved around the obstacle. He could see the bridge up ahead now. It was a wooden structure no more than fifty feet across.

Aye, he had supported Jasaray, watched him become emperor. But when his own family was in trouble . . . ? "Put not your faith in emperors," he whispered.

"Did you say something, Father?"

"No, I was just thinking out loud."

"Will Barus get into trouble for loaning us his house?" Lia asked suddenly.

"No, there will be no trouble. We are not runaways, Lia. They did not serve the papers. We have committed no crime."

"But we knew they were coming when we fled."

"We did not flee," he snapped. "We sought the emperor's permission to remove ourselves from Stone. He granted it. That was the sum of his help. So we did not flee."

"You are bitter. It does not become you. Anyway, we left in the dead of night while friends of ours were being taken to prison. It felt like flight."

"No friends of mine were arrested, Lia. I have never subscribed to their foolish ways. I never will."

"I do not think they were foolish," she said. "And I do not believe the Source would think them so."

"Aye, a god of real power, this Source. All who believe in him are put to death, and he raises not a finger. But let us not argue it again. I had all this with Pirae."

Both fell silent at the mention of her name. Appius had not been present when the Crimson Priests arrested her. He was serving on the eastern border, helping to put down a bloody revolt. He arrived in Stone the night after her trial and missed her execution. Pirae had refused to recant and had faced down her accusers, calling them "small men with small dreams."

It seemed strange to him that a woman who had spent her life in the pursuit of every illicit pleasure should have come to her end with courage and dignity. He glanced at Lia. She was not his daughter. She had been sired by one of Pirae's many lovers. He doubted if even Pirae had known which one. Yet he loved Lia more than he had ever loved anything. She was sunlight upon his soul, cool clear water in the desert of his life.

Pirae had betrayed him at every turn. Sullen and spoiled, she had spent much of his fortune on ludicrously expensive clothes, silks and satins, jewel-encrusted gowns, baubles of every kind. She had never shown the slightest interest in any worthy cause. And then, at the age of forty, she had stood against the might of the priests and defied them, knowing they would kill her.

"And all for a tree!" he said aloud.

"Why does the thought of the tree upset you so much?" asked Lia.

"What?"

"You mentioned the tree again."

"I didn't realize I said it aloud."

"The tree is merely a representation of the power of the Source, spirit that flows upward, outward, inward, and downward, mirroring the seasons. It has nothing to do with tree worship. That is a silly lie put about by the priests."

"And why can you not understand?" he countered. "The priests represent power in Stone. To go against them is willful and dangerous. It has left us here, in this forsaken cesspit of a land."

"I was happy to stay," she reminded him.

"To stay and die," he pointed out.

"Some things are worth dying for."

"Aye, but not trees," he said.

The team halted before the bridge. Appius stood and stared at the raging river as it gushed past the supports. The structure looked insubstantial and neglected. With a silent curse he sat down and cracked the whip. The horses moved out onto the wooden boards. Below, in the black churning water, the swollen body of a dead bull was swept along by the flood. It rammed against one of the supports, which buckled and fell away. The wagon lurched. Appius rose in his seat, cracking his whip once more. The frightened horses lunged into the traces.

Then the bridge collapsed.

Appius was thrown clear, his head striking a post. Then he was pitched unconscious into the water.

Banouin had been miserable for most of the day, and not just because of the hissing winds and the driving rain. He had not slept well, his dreams full of anxiety and humiliation. Happily, he could not remember most of the dreams, but one had clung to his conscious mind. He was standing naked in the center of Stone, and crowds of people were laughing at him. Deep down he knew the reason for the dream, and it made him feel like a traitor and an ingrate.

It was quite simply the thought of Bane's accompanying him to Stone that had brought about this mood of depression and the anxiety dreams that accompanied it. Banouin's plan had been to purchase suitable clothing, cut his hair, and enroll in the university, in short, to become a citizen of Stone, to blend into the life of that wondrous place. No more jeers and taunts, no more feelings of inadequacy. He had planned to become a scholar, living a quiet life of contemplation and study. Now he was riding toward the city of his dreams in the company of a man of ferocious violence, the epitome of the best and worst of Rigante manhood.

Yet this man had protected him for much of his young life and had endured the hatred of his peers for doing so. The thoughts that plagued Banouin left him feeling melancholy and unworthy.

The rain eased away for a while during midmorning, and Bane tossed back his hood and rode in closer to his friend. "You are not such a lively companion today," he said.

Banouin forced a smile. "It's the rain."

"Come, now," said Bane, slapping him on the shoulder. "I've known you too long. When you wear that long face, there is something troubling you. Are you still concerned about the fat man?"

"No. I was thinking about my life among the Rigante," said Banouin, which was at least partly true.

"What about it?"

"It was not happy," Banouin said lamely. "It is hard to be hated for something you can do nothing about. I am not responsible for the blood that flows in my veins. Why could they not just accept me as Vorna's son?"

Bane shrugged. "Aye, life was difficult for you, right enough."

"I never did anything to harm any of them," continued Banouin, anger creeping into his voice. "And they hated me. You, on the other hand, constantly got into fights and rows, and they liked you. Or they would have, had you let them. There's no sense to it."

Bane turned toward him and looked as if he were about to speak. Then he changed his mind and rode on a little ahead, the gray picking his way carefully through the mud. It was an abrupt end to the conversation, and Banouin thought back over his last statement to see if he had unwittingly said anything offensive. Puzzled, he urged the chestnut forward. As he came alongside his friend, he glanced at Bane's face. There was no anger there but no good humor, either. "What? What did I say?" asked Banouin.

"For a man who wants to be a scholar," said Bane, "you see things too simply."

"Would you care to elaborate?"

"For what purpose?" asked Bane. "You are leaving the Rigante. The past is gone."

"I would still like to know."

Bane glanced at the roiling clouds above. The rain would soon start again. A clap of thunder sounded in the distance, making the horses react nervously. Bane stroked the long neck of the gray and whispered soothing words to it. Then he looked at Banouin. "There's an example for you," he said. "The horses were spooked. What did you do?"

"What do you mean?"

Bane hauled on the reins and angled in close. Banouin's chestnut was still skittish, and he calmed it. "You complain about this horse all the time," said Bane. "It bucks. It doesn't like you. Yet when it is frightened you don't pet it or speak to it. To you it is just a beast of burden to carry you to the sea. You sit upon it, but you do not ride it. You have made no attempt to communicate with the horse, to become its friend."

"What have horses to do with what we were talking about?"

Bane shook his head. "You really don't see, do you? You have complained all your life about people disliking you. Yet when have you done anything for anyone else? Last year when Nian's barn caught fire and everyone rushed there to try to save it, where were you? You stayed home. As we walked back through Three Streams, covered in soot and ash, you came walking by, clean and bright. You might just as well have been carrying a sign that said 'I care nothing for any of you or your troubles.' One day you will realize that you are what you are because you choose to be that way. It has little to do with your blood."

"That is not fair! A man with half an eye could see that Nian's barn was beyond saving. It was a waste of effort."

"That waste of effort brought people closer together. It showed that people cared for one another and were willing to take risks for one another. When his barn was destroyed, Nian could at least sit back and know he had true friends who would stand beside him. And two days later those same people got together again to raise a new barn. Was that a waste of effort? And you were missing on that day, too."

The clouds opened, and rain lashed down over them. Bane pulled his hood into place and drew his leather cloak around his shoulders. Banouin was furious, but any words he could have summoned would have been whipped away by the storm. Bane's comments ate away at him as they rode. All his life he had been taunted and beaten by the Rigante. Why, then, should he care about their barns or their lives?

Toward dusk, with the rain easing and the sky brightening to the west, the two companions were riding along the bank of a swollen river. Up ahead a broken-backed wagon was caught up against the bank. A horse was thrashing in the water, desperately trying to keep its head above the flood. Bane kicked the gray into a run and rode alongside, leaping from the saddle and clambering over the ruined wagon. Unbuckling his sword belt, he threw it to the bank, then leapt into the river alongside the weakening horse. With his dagger Bane sawed at the traces, then ducked under the water.

Banouin watched from the bank. Three times Bane surfaced and dived again. At last the horse moved clear of the wagon, but it was too exhausted to climb the slope. Bane swam alongside it.

Then he shouted up at Banouin. "Don't just sit there, you bastard! There's a rope in the back of the wagon." Shocked by the outburst, Banouin stepped down from the saddle and climbed to the wagon. There were several chests there and two coiled ropes. Taking them both, he looped them over his shoulders, then climbed down the side of the wagon. He slipped and almost fell but grabbed at the half-submerged wheel. The wagon tilted. For a moment Banouin thought it would roll over him and, almost panic-stricken, lunged at the bank and scrabbled up through the mud. Taking up one of the rope coils, he made a loop. His hands were shaking as he approached the slippery mud slope above the water, and twice he failed to drop the loop over the flailing horse's head. But the third throw was a success. The loop drew tight, and Banouin tried to haul the horse from the water. His feet slipped, and the weary beast slid back and fell to its side. A flailing hoof cracked against Bane's skull, and he cried out. Banouin saw him fall back into the torrent. He was swept along for a hundred yards, then grasped a low branch and hauled himself clear. When he returned, Banouin saw a wide, blood-smeared gash on his forehead. Pushing past Banouin, Bane ran to the gray, and vaulted to the saddle. Easing the gray forward, he took the rope from Banouin and looped it around the horn of his saddle. Carefully Bane and the gray drew the exhausted horse from the water. It scrambled up the bank and stood shivering in the fading light. Bane dismounted and moved alongside it, stroking its neck and flanks. "You fought well, brave heart," he said, keeping his voice low. Suddenly the wagon broke clear of the bank, turned over, and floated away, carrying with it the body of a second horse, which had been submerged.

Blood was dripping from Bane's brow. He wiped it away. "I'm sorry," said Banouin. "I should have thought of tying the rope to a saddle."

Bane said nothing for a moment, then shrugged. "We rescued the horse, so it all ended well." Banouin examined his wound. It was not deep and required no stitches, but it was bleeding profusely, and a lump was forming above Bane's left eye.

The wind died down, and a faint sound came to Banouin. He swung around. "Did you hear that?" he asked.

"Yes. It sounded like a cry."

It came again more clearly. "Help us!"

Ahead of them the riverbank rose steeply, the waterline below strewn with boulders. Banouin ran ahead, climbing the slope. He gazed down at the rushing water and saw a young woman clinging to a jutting rock some thirty feet from the shoreline. White water was crashing against the rocks, and at any moment she was likely to be swept away. Then he saw that she was also holding on to another figure, a white-haired man who was feebly trying to haul himself farther onto the rock.

Bane joined him and gazed first at the trapped pair, then down at the shoreline. "Can't get the horses down there," he said. Then he swore softly.

"What can we do?" asked Banouin.

Bane ran back to where Banouin had left the ropes, looped a coil over his shoulder, and carefully made his way down to the water's edge. Banouin climbed down the slope to where Bane was standing. The blond warrior was tying one end of the rope to his waist.

"You can't go into that torrent," said Banouin.

"What do you suggest, my friend?" said Bane, his eyes angry. "Perhaps we should sit and watch them die rather than take part in a waste of effort."

"That's not what I meant," Banouin said sadly. "I meant that you can't go in. Your head is bleeding, and you are exhausted from getting the horse clear. And even if you did reach them, I would not have the strength to pull you all in. I'll go."

Bane offered no argument. He removed the rope from his waist and tied it around Banouin. "You'll have to enter the water farther upstream," he said. "Otherwise the current will sweep you straight past them. Strike out at an angle. When you get close, swing around so that your legs can take the impact of the rocks. Otherwise you'll smash your ribs." He looked into Banouin's eyes. "Are you sure you want to do this?"

"Of course I don't want to," snapped Banouin. "Now let's get on with it."

The two men ran back along the bank for around a hundred paces; then, with Bane letting out the rope, Banouin dived into the water and began to swim, using a fast overhand crawl. The current was far more vicious than he had realized, and his arms tired fast as he swam. Bane was racing back along the shoreline, holding on to the end of the rope, but he was still some way behind as Banouin saw the rocks rushing toward him. Desperately he swung his body, but he did not have time to extend his legs fully and was dashed against the stone. Agonizing pain seared through his shoulder and right wrist as he struck the rock. He would have been swept clear if the woman had not grabbed him. She hauled him back, and he managed to get a handhold on the rock.

"Your friend will not be able to pull us all clear," she shouted. "You help my father. I will make it to the shore along the rope."

Banouin was in too much pain to argue. The girl took hold of the rope and began to pull herself along it. Banouin reached out with his right arm and tried to hold on to the white-haired man, but his fingers were numb. The old man gave a weak smile and hooked his fingers into Banouin's sleeve. As his weight came down on the arm, Banouin cried out. The man let go instantly and almost went under. Swinging, Banouin hooked his legs around the man's body, drawing him close. He surfaced.

"Put your arm around my neck," Banouin told him. The old man did so. Banouin transferred his gaze to the shore. The girl made it to the bank, then joined Bane at the rope. Bane raised his hand, gesturing to Banouin to let go.

Grabbing the old man with his left hand, he pushed himself clear of the relative safety of the rocks. Water surged over them both, and the rope tightened. For a while Banouin thought he was going to die as his lungs came close to bursting. Then he bobbed to the surface and felt the pull of the rope. His feet touched bottom. The old man was unconscious now, but still Banouin clung to him.

Leaving the girl to hold the rope, Bane waded in and hauled them both to the bank. Banouin collapsed and lay back, breathing heavily. He heard the old man groan, then Bane was alongside him.

"My arm is broken," said Banouin. Bane tenderly examined the swollen wrist.

"Aye, I think it is. We'll bind it tight and get you to a healer."

The girl came and knelt beside him. Her hair was short and dark, her violet eyes large beneath strong brows. Just looking at her beauty made the pain recede. "You are very brave," she said, her voice low, almost husky.

He could think of nothing intelligent to say and tried to smile instead. Then he began to tremble violently. "What is wrong?" asked the girl.

"It is just shock," he heard Bane say. "Get a fire going, and I'll tend to him."

Bane half carried him to the tree line and laid him down beneath a spreading pine. It was quite dry there. A little way to the left the old man was lying on his back, his breath coming in ragged gasps. The girl was trying to start a fire, rasping Bane's knife against a flint rock and sending sparks into a small pile of shredded dry leaves. Banouin was still shivering and was now feeling nauseous. His arm was throbbing, his fingers swelling. Bane brought him a blanket, which he draped over his shoulders.

Banouin lay down and closed his eyes. "You did well," he heard his friend say.

Then he fell asleep.

◇ 3 ◇

T HE FORMER GENERAL Appius sat on the balcony, enjoying the sunshine and the distant view of the sea. From the walled garden below the scent of jasmine drifted up to him. If he closed his eyes, he could almost believe he was back in his own home, overlooking the harbour of Cressia and the white cliffs of Dara Island. Appius sighed, his good humor evaporating.

This poorly constructed house, with its creaking timbers and drafts, was not his home. Accia was a frontier settlement, and the attempts by the outcasts to make the Stone settlement even a rough copy of the home city were almost pathetic. The houses were timber-built and merely dressed with stone and plaster. The roads—except for the open area outside the council building—were not paved, and there were no playhouses, theaters, or arenas. The one bathhouse was still uncompleted—the funds having been delayed—and the racetrack boasted no seating.

The residents were the flotsam and jetsam of Stone society: corrupt politicians, exiled merchants, and criminals escaping justice. Even the three hundred soldiers stationed there were rejects, governed by officers who had committed a breach of discipline or were otherwise out of favor.

In the twenty-four hours Appius had been in the house of Barus he had already been visited by two disgraced citizens: the merchant Macrios—accused of bribery and fraudulent dealings—and Banyon, the former senator, whose nepotistic behavior had been the talk of Stone. He had greeted them courteously, accepted their welcomes graciously, then bade them good day.

It hurt the pride of the old soldier that he was now one of

them, a man living in disgrace in a frontier town far from civilization. He wondered if they looked at him the same way he viewed them. Did they wonder what grubby crime he had committed to be banished there? Appius shuddered inwardly. All his life he had fought to be a man of honor and dignity. He had never accepted a brass coin in bribes from merchants anxious to supply his Panther regiments. Not once in his adult life had he acted in petty jealousy, greed, or envy. Yet here he was, living among criminals and runaways in a shoddy replica of a Stone city. The plaster of the balcony balustrade was already cracking, and flakes had fallen to the terra-cotta tiles of the floor. He gazed out over the settlement. From there some of the houses seemed almost habitable, but he knew that if he approached them, he would see the same poor workmanship.

Spinning on his heel, the old soldier strode back into the main room. The furniture, three couches and four deep chairs, had all been shipped from Stone, and its quality only made worse the contrast with the badly plastered walls and clumsily wrought ceiling. But then, what carpenter or stonemason worth his salt would want to live here? he thought.

There was a tap at the door, and the stoop-shouldered surgeon Ralis entered.

"How is he?" asked Appius, gesturing the man to a chair. Ralis sat and ran his thin hand over his balding head.

"The fever has broken. He will be fine. I have instructed one of the servants to sit with him. I would guess he swallowed river water and it contained some effluent that has upset his system. I managed to get him to swallow an herbal tincture. That should settle his stomach. And I have set his arm. It was a clean break. His heartbeat is strong, and I would think he should be back on his feet in a day or two."

Appius offered his guest a goblet of wine, and they sat in companionable silence. Appius had known the elderly surgeon for years. Ralis had accompanied him on three campaigns. His skills were solid though without flair, and he had performed his duties well. Appius glanced at the man, remembering the scandal. Ralis had exiled himself to this desolate place after an affair with a young senator, whose wife had subsequently committed suicide. Her relatives had killed the senator and sent assassins to dispatch Ralis, but the surgeon had been warned and had fled the city during the night. The scandal surrounding the affair had been talked of for years in Stone.

"The young man looks familiar," said Ralis.

Appius nodded. "He is the half-breed son of Banouin, the Ghost General."

"Well, well," said Ralis, "Banouin, eh? Didn't he become a troubadour or something?"

"A wandering merchant. He was killed in the Perdii campaign almost twenty years ago."

"Men say he was as good a general as Jasaray."

"No one is as good as Jasaray, but he was skilled," said Appius. "He was a charismatic leader, worshiped by his men. But more than that, he had an intuitive feel for battles."

"Didn't he marry some slave or suchlike?"

"A northern witch woman."

"Baffling," said Ralis. "He could have been rich and powerful in Stone. Instead he took to the highlands and married a savage. I wonder why."

"We'll never know. Do you miss the city?" Appius asked suddenly.

Ralis gave a rueful smile. "Who would not? But we are doing our best here. This time next year the roads should be paved, and Macrios is raising funds to complete the bathhouse by the spring. Small beginnings, I know, but progress at least. Is Barus coming back this year?"

Appius shook his head. "He has been given a command in the east. Lia and I will look after his house for a while until we decide whether to settle here or go home."

Their eyes met, and Ralis had the good grace to look away. No citizen came here through choice. Either their funds had vanished or they had made powerful enemies back home. "How are things in Stone?" asked the surgeon.

"Lively," answered Appius, and did not expand on it.

"Well, they are not so lively here, General. We have no Crimson Priests, and people feel they can speak freely and live their lives according to the wishes of their hearts."

"Sounds pleasant," observed Appius. "Though perhaps ill

advised." He rose, signaling to his guest that the conversation was over.

Ralis bowed. "It was good seeing you again, General. If there is any worsening of your guest's condition, please feel free to call upon my services."

Appius shook the man's hand, walked him to the door, then returned to the balcony. In the garden below Lia was walking with Bane. She seemed happy and carefree. It mattered nothing to her that they were thousands of miles from home. The sound of her laughter hung on Appius like a lead weight.

There were no Crimson Priests in Accia.

Not yet.

It was just past midnight when the scream ripped through the silence of the night. Bane was the first to react. Coming awake, he rolled from the bed and raced naked into the next room, where Banouin was sitting up in bed, pointing toward the far wall. He screamed again. Bane ran to him, grabbing his friend by the shoulders.

"The walls are alive!" shouted Banouin. His face was drenched in sweat and gleamed in the pale moonlight. "And there is a demon hunting you, Bane. Ah! I see him. Talon and claw. He is coming for you."

"If he is, I'll kill him," said Bane. "Don't fret. Lie back. Sleep."

"Watch out for him, Bane. Watch the tail. It flicks just before the demon leaps!"

"I'll watch the tail. Now, do as you're told. Lie back."

Banouin sagged against him, then let out a long sigh. He allowed Bane to lay him down. His eyes flickered. "It was not a dream," he said, his voice calm. "It was a vision, Bane. You were walking through . . . through corridors, but the walls were alive and writhing. You were carrying a short sword, and there was a man with you, an older man. And a demon was stalking you." He shuddered. "A terrible beast of incredible speed and strength."

"All in all," Bane said softly, "I would have preferred your first vision to have been of a beautiful young woman—maybe two beautiful young women—nursing me back to health after killing the beast. But no matter. Rest now."

Banouin's blue eyes closed, and his breathing deepened. Bane rose and walked out into the torchlit corridor beyond. Appius was standing there, dressed in a pale gray night robe. Beyond him was Lia.

"He had a vision," said Bane.

"Yes, yes, we'll talk about it in the morning," Appius said sharply, moving to stand between the naked Bane and his daughter.

"Are you all right, Appius?" asked Bane. "As I said, it was only a vision. And it didn't concern you at all."

"Lia! Go to your room," Appius snapped, without turning to look back at her. Bane moved to the right.

"Sleep well," he said.

Lia laughed aloud, shook her head, and moved from sight.

"You are naked," Appius said sternly.

"So are you beneath that robe," observed Bane.

"Exactly! Beneath the robe. In civilized societies it is considered . . . offensive to parade naked."

"What is a parade?" asked Bane.

"To appear naked in public."

"And why would that be?"

"Why? Because . . . it just is. I don't know why these customs appear. But it is especially offensive for a man to appear naked before a young virgin."

Bane grinned. "Are you mocking me, Appius?"

The older man sighed. "No, I am not mocking you. If you appeared naked on the streets of Stone, you would be arrested and flogged. And if you appeared so before a young woman of good family, you would be either hanged or thrown into the arena to fight for your life. Now go to your room; take the robe that is hanging on your door and put it on. I feel the need of a goblet of wine. Then you can tell me about this . . . vision."

Moments later, garbed in a fine robe of white ankle-length cotton, Bane entered the main room. Appius handed him a silver goblet, and the two men sat on the balcony, overlooking the town of Accia and the star-dappled sea beyond.

"Why are you going to Stone?" asked the old general.

Bane shrugged. "I promised Vorna I would see Banouin

safe. He is not a fighter, but he draws trouble like flies to cow shit."

"That's another thing you might want to consider," said Appius. "Your language. You speak Turgon well and seem to have picked up some . . . interesting phrases. In polite company you should avoid using words associated with bodily functions or the nature of human intimacy. A citizen of Stone, for example, doesn't rise from the dinner table, as you did this evening, in order to 'piss.' He excuses himself and says he will rejoin the company presently. He doesn't open his leggings in order to scratch his privates."

"Privates?" queried Bane.

"Balls!" snapped Appius.

"Ah. When is he allowed to scratch them?"

"In private. Hence 'privates.' You see?"

Bane nodded sagely, then drank his wine. "You are a very strange people," he said. "You think nothing of enslaving tribes, butchering men, and bringing war and destruction to all the lands around you. Yet you find the sight of a penis offensive, and you don't talk about pissing. That is civilization, is it? War, murder, and butchery are respectable, but a man without clothes risks a flogging?"

Appius laughed. "I have not heard it argued quite so simplistically before, but yes, perhaps that is the essence of our civilization: personal privacy, national expansion. However, the rights and wrongs of it are meaningless. The fact is that these laws apply. You must walk and speak warily in Stone, Bane. It will be different for Banouin. He is the son of a prominent citizen and will be carrying papers I shall give him, signifying his position. He will be accepted. You, however, will be watched carefully for any sign of barbarous behavior."

"You think me barbarous?"

"I am an old soldier, boy. I have seen men like you. Warriors, a little in love with death. Life without risk is nothing to you. A waste. If you find a chasm, you must stand on the very tip and dare the void to drag you in. If you see a horse no man can ride, you must tame it. And if you see a man no one can beat, you must challenge him."

"You see a lot, General."

"More than you think. What is Connavar thinking of to send his son into Stone?"

"You know Connavar?" Bane asked warily.

"I fought alongside him in the Perdii wars and against him at Cogden Field. Aye, I know him well enough to see him in you—even without the strange eyes. Tell no one of your bloodline, Bane, or you will be dragged before Jasaray himself and used against your father."

"I shall bear that in mind," Bane said coolly. "The gods know how much I love Connavar."

Appius looked at him sharply but said no more on the matter.

Bane stood and stretched, then asked the general a direct question.

Appius laughed aloud. "The correct way to ask that is: 'And where can a man find a relaxing spot with pleasant female company?' And my answer is: I have not been here long enough to find out, young man. When I do, I shall let you know. Perhaps tomorrow you should take a walk down to the docks. I don't doubt some publicly minded citizen will approach you and guide you to what you seek."

"Baffling," said Bane. Then he left the room. As he did so, he heard Lia's door click shut. He looked in on Banouin, who was now sleeping deeply, then returned to his bed.

As he lay down, he found himself thinking of Lia. When first he had seen her at the river, he had thought her a pretty girl, nothing more. But earlier, when he had walked with her in the garden, he had found himself noticing the tilt of her head as she laughed, the slender perfection of her neck, the fullness of her lips. And when they had sat upon the bench, beneath the canvas canopy, he had caught the scent of her hair.

You've been without a woman too long, he told himself. And he fell asleep thinking of the dark-haired girl and picturing himself walking with her on the slopes of the Druagh mountains, with the morning sun clearing the peaks and the mist seeping from the Wishing Tree woods.

Oranus, the captain of the watch, was tired, his stomach full of cheap red wine, his head pounding. Midweek was usually quiet in Accia, and he had brought the flagon of wine to the small office fronting the cells. It would, he hoped, help give him a good night's sleep. Instead it had left his mood as sour as his belly.

He glared balefully at the small group of angry people crowding around his desk. They were all talking at once, their discordant voices matching the angry pounding behind his eyes. The woman he knew well, a whore who operated in the eastern dock area. The man beside her, sporting a broken nose and a swollen eye, was her pimp, Nestar. He was also the owner of a waterside tavern renowned for foul practices, including robbery, extortion, and the fleecing of customers. Two of his men stood close by. All bore signs of recent violent activity. The captain would have liked nothing better than to close Nestar's tavern, but the pimp had many friends in high places, including the merchant Macrios and the councillor Banyon. At forty-four, only eight months from retirement and a free parcel of land, Oranus had no desire to incur the wrath of powerful men.

Oranus rubbed his eyes and transferred his gaze to the thin man standing by the door. He did not recognize him. The man's face was dotted with spots of blood, and there were wooden splinters in the skin of his forehead. Just for a moment the sheer incongruity of the man's injuries lightened his headache. But only for a moment.

The morning had been quiet until the barbarian had been brought in. He glanced back at the chained tribesman, sitting glowering in the cell. He was young and powerfully built with long blond hair, a single braid hanging from the temple. He wore no tribal cloak, but Oranus felt sure he was not Cenii. There was something untamed about him that suggested he had not endured the yoke of Stone. Perhaps Norvii or Rigante, he thought. Oranus filled a cup with water and drained it. Then he turned his attention back to the angry group.

"Silence!" he bellowed as hammers of fire thudded at his temples. He pointed at the redheaded whore. "You, Roxy. You speak first. The rest of you keep your mouths shut."

"The bastard assaulted me, sir. Robbed me of my life's savings. Kicked in my door, he did, when I was with a friend. Hurled the friend through the window."

"That's me," said the man at the back with the splinters in

his forehead. "We were talking when the savage burst in. I tried to remonstrate, but he grabbed me and sent me flying into the shutters. I went straight through. Luckily, there was a canopy under the window, which broke my fall." He sighed. "Bet he didn't know about the canopy," he said. "Strong canvas, luckily. Well made. Didn't even tear."

"It is not even remotely possible that I could care about the canopy," said Oranus, leaning forward and pinching the bridge of his nose. "Did you know the tribesman?" he asked the whore.

"He enjoyed my company some time earlier," she said coyly.

"Which is when she stole my pouch of gold," the prisoner said, in passably good Turgon.

"What a liar he is," said the woman, her voice full of outrage. "Has it come to this, that a businesswoman can be maligned in the office of the law?" She smiled sweetly at Oranus. "I could help you with that headache, sir."

"That's just what I need," snapped Oranus. "A headache—and a dose of pox. You!" He pointed to the pimp Nestar, a thickset man with short, greasy black hair. His nose was swollen and bloody, his right eye almost closed. "How did you come into this?"

"I was downstairs, and I heard Roxy cry out. I took up my cudgel and ran up the stairs. When I stepped into the doorway, he came at me and butted me. I fell back down the stairs. That's when he robbed Roxy of our savings," he said, casting a murderous glance at the whore. "He came down the stairs, and I yelled out to my men to stop him. I say 'my men,' but they're not anymore, sir. A more useless pair would be hard to find. He swatted them like they were flies and walked out into the street. I mean, to look at them you'd think they were tough. Big hands, strapping shoulders. Fooled me, though. He treated them like the farm boys they are."

"That's not fair," said one of the men. "He took us by surprise."

"You're paid not to be surprised, donkey brain!"

Oranus slammed the flat of his hand onto the table, the noise making them jump. He lifted his hand, holding his index finger a hair's breadth from his thumb. "I am this close to locking you all in for the rest of the day and for tonight," he said. "Now, will you continue with your story and hopefully finish it before year's end?"

Nestar nodded. "I'm sorry, sir. Anyway, after swatting these imbeciles, he ran out into the street, where happily several soldiers of the watch were on hand. They grabbed him. I think you'll find he lashed out at them, too, sir. That's what comes of allowing these barbarians into a civilized township, if you don't mind me saying so."

"I do mind you saying so," said Oranus. He rose from his chair and swung to the prisoner, who was sitting on a cot bed within the cell. Oranus looked into the man's eyes and felt suddenly cold. Memories of the past almost overwhelmed him, and his hands began to tremble. Fighting for control, he took a deep breath. "What have you to say?" he asked the prisoner.

The man stood and stared through the wooden bars at the assembled group. "The woman says I stole her money. Then I ran from the building and was grabbed by your soldiers. Is this correct?"

"That would seem to be their evidence," said Oranus. "Your point is . . . ?"

"Ask her how much was in the pouch."

"You heard him," said Oranus. "How much was there?"

"Oh, around twenty-five gold coins," she said. "Maybe thirty. I don't recall exactly."

"There are thirty-two gold coins, three half silvers, and five copper," the prisoner said coolly. "And doesn't it seem remarkable that I had time to count them all while running down the stairs and into the street?"

"Aye, remarkable," said Oranus, turning a cold stare to the whore. "So you stole his pouch. That's a flogging offense, Roxy. Fifty lashes."

"You going to take his word over that of a taxpaying businesswoman?" she shouted, her eyes fearful.

"Not his word, whore! His arithmetic."

"I knew nothing about any theft," said Nestar, holding up his hands. "As you know, I run a lawful establishment."

"I know what you run," said Oranus, his gaze holding to the frightened eyes of the redheaded woman.

"I can't take another flogging," she whimpered, backing away toward the door. "It'll kill me."

"Perhaps you should have thought of that before robbing him," said Oranus.

"I don't want to see her flogged," said the prisoner. "Do I have a say in this?"

Oranus felt a wave of relief and a lessening of his headache. If the barbarian wished to bring no charges, the whole matter could be forgotten and his office would be quiet again, peaceful. There would be no papers to fill in, no further inquiries to make. He could remove his breastplate, step into the cell, lie down on the cot bed, and close his eyes. Keeping his expression stern, he looked at the whore, then back at the prisoner. "It is your pouch," he said at last. "The crime was against you, not against town property. If you are happy to see the matter forgotten, then there is little I can do." He tried to sound regretful and gave the whore a withering look.

"What about me?" asked the man with the splinters in his brow. "He threw me through the window!"

Oranus gave a bleak smile. "You are quite right," he said. "There should be a public trial. You can appear and explain how you were in a whore's room when one of her other customers broke in and assaulted you. Let's see," he said, opening a ledger on his desk. "Court will be in session tomorrow at noon."

"I don't want to go to court," mumbled the man.

"And what about you, Nestar?" asked Oranus. "Do you want to go to court?"

The pimp shook his head.

"Right," said Oranus. "Everyone out! And if I see you brought before me again, Roxy, I'll have you hanged."

The woman fled from the room, as did the other men. Oranus unlocked the cell door and removed the chains from around the prisoner's wrists. "Where are you from?" he asked the man.

"North."

"Rigante?"

"Aye."

"You are a long way from home."

"I like to travel." The young man scooped up his pouch and tied it to his belt.

"Why didn't you wish to see her flogged?" asked Oranus. "She deserved it, you know."

"She was a very good companion," the man said, with a wide smile. "And it was my own fault for falling asleep. Am I free to go?"

"That depends on where you are going. Do you have friends in Accia?"

"I am staying with the general Appius while my friend recovers from a fever."

"Ah, Appius! I heard he had arrived. The gods alone know what he did to be consigned to this flea-infested cesspit." Oranus took a deep breath. "You'd better be leaving," he said. "It'll be dark soon, and tribesmen are not allowed out after curfew. And watch out on the way back. The pimp Nestar may lie in wait for you. That's a lot of gold to be carrying."

The man grinned widely. "He won't be waiting for me." Then he was gone.

Oranus moved to the door and slid the bolt. Then he took off his breastplate and stretched out on the cell bed.

Tomorrow he would call on Appius and pay his respects. He closed his eyes, remembering the bloody retreat from Cogden Field. With the memory came the awful fear that had dogged Oranus ever since, that had burned away his ambition and corroded his courage. In his mind's eye he saw again the broken line and the slashing blades, heard the choking, bubbling screams of his comrades as their throats were slashed or their limbs hacked away. It was as if a host of devils in human form had materialized out of the mist, their bodies daubed with blue paint, their eyes gleaming with evil intent. Oranus shuddered. He had been lucky. He and around forty other panic-stricken men had managed to run to the safety of the rear guard organized by Appius. They had then fought their way back to the previous night's fortified camp. Throughout the long night the enemy had attacked, but Appius, with great skill, had marshaled the defenses. Then the enemy had withdrawn.

Even then the terror did not stop.

As they waited on the earth-built ramparts, they saw the enemy pushing the three captured catapults toward the walls. There was no fear at first, for there were no stones for them. But the tribesmen did not hurl stones. They loaded the firing basins with severed heads and rained them down on the camp. By morning the open ground within the walls was filled with them.

As dawn came, a rider on a gray horse approached the walls, reining in his mount just out of bowshot. Oranus and all the other defenders stared at the man. This was Connavar, the Demon King. They had seen him fight the day before, cutting and killing like a man possessed. He sat now on his gray, his patchwork cloak billowing in the dawn breeze. Appius strode to the battlements, stood silently for a moment, then glanced at Oranus.

"Follow me," he said. To the horror of the terrified Oranus, he clambered over the battlements and climbed down into the trench and up the other side. Oranus scrambled down after him, and the two men walked out onto open ground.

Appius walked slowly, arms clasped behind his back, as if he were out for a morning stroll. Oranus looked at him and saw no fear in the patrician features. They reached the horseman. Oranus looked up once. He was wearing a white-plumed, full-faced helm of gold-embossed iron. Only his baleful eyes showed through the curved slit. He seemed somehow inhuman. Oranus focused instead on the hilt of the sword in the scabbard at the king's side. He heard Appius speak.

"Your men fought well, Connavar."

Connavar ignored the compliment, and when he spoke, his voice, distorted by the helm, sounded metallic and cold. "You have two choices, Appius. You can stay here and we will destroy you, or you can march your men back to the lands of the Cenii. If you give me your word that you will not stop until you reach the sea, I will allow you to pass unhindered. And I will see that supplies are brought to you on your journey."

"Will you return to us the body of Valanus?"

"I doubt I could gather all the pieces or recognize them if I tried," said the king.

Oranus felt his legs begin to tremble, and he almost passed out with fear.

"Then it shall be as you say, Connavar. But I have badly wounded men in the fort. I will need some wagons for them."

"You will have them. Be ready to leave in an hour."

"I'll need a little more time to bury the heads you . . . returned to us."

"Two hours, then," agreed Connavar.

The king swung the gray and cantered back to the waiting Keltoi army.

Oranus turned to the general. "If we leave the fort, sir, they will surely massacre us."

"Perhaps, though I doubt it. Connavar is a cunning strategist but also a man of his word."

"But why should he allow us to leave?"

"Because although he has won the battle, his forces have taken huge casualties. Any full attack on us here would see him lose three men to our one. Yes, we would die, but it would achieve nothing. As it is, we will march away with our tails between our legs, and every surviving man will talk of the Demon King of the Rigante. We will carry his legend home, and it will spread like a plague. The next army to march here will march with fear in their hearts."

The long, slow march to the coast was a painful one. Many of the wounded died on the way and were buried by the roadside. All along the way Keltoi tribesmen gathered to watch the defeated men of Stone trudge wearily back to the sea.

For Oranus it was the end of a bright career. Throughout the years since that time he had rarely known a night to pass without terrible dreams in which severed heads called out to him and sharp swords were piercing his flesh.

Had it not been for the skill of Appius, he would have died on Cogden Field.

Oranus sighed. The best part of me did die there, he thought sadly.

Banouin lay in his bed, his splinted arm throbbing, his head aching. But those discomforts were as nothing to the terror haunting him. He had believed he had known the nature of fear, being chased and tormented, being beaten and threatened. He knew now that his years among the Rigante had merely touched the surface. The fears he had lived with had been caused by external forces such as Forvar and his friends. Nothing he had ever experienced could have prepared him for what he had now discovered.

Banouin had always felt safe within his own mind, but now it was as if a gateway had opened inside his skull that at any moment he could fall through and spin away into a bottomless pit of dread from which there would be no return. He could feel it pulling him even now, as if he were standing on the edge of an abyss and losing all sense of balance. He shivered and sat up, drawing the blanket around his shoulders. I should never have ventured into the water, he told himself. That was my undoing.

Vorna had always assured him that his talent would one day flower, that he would develop skills beyond those of normal men. Banouin had eagerly looked forward to the day. But the skills had not manifested themselves, and he had spoken to Brother Solstice about the problem. The druid had been walking the high hills and had stopped at the house for a cool drink. Banouin had approached him at the well, where Brother Solstice had splashed water onto his black and white beard and run his large hands through his silver-streaked hair. A huge man, broad of shoulder and thick of waist, Brother Solstice had looked more like the fighter he once had been than the druid he had chosen to become.

Banouin had asked him about developing his talent. Brother Solstice had sat down on a bench seat beneath a spreading oak and gestured Banouin to sit beside him.

"Why is it that you want these powers?" he asked.

"Why does anyone want power, Brother?" he countered.

"You think they will make you special and earn you respect among your peers."

"Of course. And how wonderful it must be to see the future or read a man's thoughts."

"Why would it be wonderful?" asked the druid.

"I would know if a man intended me harm."

"I see. So you perceive these powers to be merely of use to you?"

"Oh, no, Brother. I would use them for good purposes."

"And people would be grateful to you and shower you with praise. You would become, perhaps, a great and valued man."

"Yes. Is that wrong?"

Brother Solstice shrugged. "I try to avoid examining issues on the basis of right or wrong. It seems to me they always come down to perspectives. What is right for one man becomes wrong for another. The talent you seek is a gift from the Source. And such gifts fall like seeds. In the right soil they prosper and grow. If they fall upon rock, they wither and die. Are you rock or soil, Banouin?"

"How can I tell?"

The druid smiled. "Look to your actions and how you live your life." Then he climbed to his feet, patted Banouin on the shoulder, and walked away.

Now, a year later, Banouin knew the answer. He had been rock. He recalled Bane's words just before they rescued Lia and her father from the river. "You really don't see, do you? You have complained all your life about people disliking you. Yet when have you done anything for anyone else? Last year when Nian's barn caught fire and everyone rushed there to try to save it, where were you? You stayed home. As we walked back through Three Streams, covered in soot and ash, you came walking by, clean and bright. You might just as well have been carrying a sign that said 'I care nothing for any of you, or your troubles.' One day you will realize that you are what you are because you choose to be that way. It has little to do with your blood."

And that was the truth of it. When he had ventured into the torrent to save Lia and Appius, he had risked his life to save others. It was that selfless act that had opened the gateway in his mind. Now he wished with all his heart that he had stayed on the riverbank, for the gift was not wonderful at all. All he could see when his frightened inner eyes peered beyond the gateway was violence and death.

And then he saw the face, flat and expressionless, the pale eyes that knew no pity. The man was tall and wide-shouldered, wearing armor of black and silver, and he carried a shining sword that dripped with blood. No one could stand against him, for he was the greatest killer, fast and deadly. Banouin could see crowds cheering him, thousands of people chanting his name. Then the man, with two others in similar armor, was on a ship, standing at the prow, staring out over the gray waves. He is coming here, thought Banouin. He is coming here to kill us all. Despair washed over him, and he began to weep.

Bane had almost reached the house of Barus when he heard movement behind him. He spun and saw the two toughs previously hired by the pimp Nestar. Both of them were armed with knives.

The first ran at him and aimed a clumsy thrust at Bane's belly. Bane blocked it with his left arm, then hammered his right elbow into the man's face, spilling him to the ground. He fell directly in the path of his comrade, who tripped over him and stumbled. Bane kicked his legs away, and he, too, fell. Bane sat on a low wall and shook his head.

"By Taranis, you are the clumsiest robbers I've ever seen. Are you intent on being killed?"

"He broke by doze," said the first man, the words horribly mangled. He sat up and tried to stem the blood oozing from his nostrils.

"I told you to go wide," said the second man, rubbing a bruised knee. "Didn't I say that? Go wide to the right; leave me a clear thrust?"

"By doze!" moaned the first man.

"Where did you learn this trade?" asked Bane.

"It's not a trade," said the second man. "We've no money now. Nestar ordered us gone. We thought we'd try for your gold."

"Well, you tried," said Bane. Opening his pouch, he fished out two silver pieces and tossed one to each of the two men. Startled, the first man dropped the coin, then scrabbled for it. The second caught his cleanly. "Find yourselves an occupation," advised Bane. "What are you trained for?"

"We worked a farm for our da," said the second man. "It was a small farm. When the Stone army came, he was told to leave. He refused, so he was hanged. We signed on as sailors after that, but Durk spent three months being seasick, so we came ashore and worked for Nestar. It was all right till you came along."

"Never look at the dark side," Bane said brightly. "Think on this: Someone would have come along some time, and he might not have been as easygoing as me. He might well have plunged a blade in your bellies."

"Thad's drue," said the first man, his nose swelling badly.

"Find work on a farm. A man should always do what he's best at. And trust me, lads, thievery is not a choice for you."

With that Bane stood and wandered along the lane. The side gate was locked, so he scaled it, dropping lightly to the garden beyond. Lia was sitting on a curved stone bench. Looking up, she saw him and smiled. His breath caught in his throat, and his pulse quickened. That surprised him.

"Why didn't you call out?" she asked. "I would have opened the gate."

He shrugged. "It was easy to climb. How is Banouin?"

"The fever is gone, but he has a haunted look in his eyes. When I was sitting with him, he put up his hand and pushed me away. Then he shuddered and began to weep. He says he must be gone tomorrow. My father has given him letters of reference and has booked charter on a merchant vessel sailing to Goriasa. It leaves at dusk tomorrow."

"Not much time to get acquainted," said Bane, sitting beside her. Her lips were moist and glistening in the moonlight.

"You are staring," she said.

"I apologize. I am a mountain lad and unused to such beauty."

She laughed gaily. "That compliment rolled a little too smoothly from your tongue. I think you are a rogue, sir."

"A rogue would surely demand a kiss," he said.

"And are you a rogue?"

"I am, indeed." He leaned in and lightly brushed his lips against hers. Then he drew back and took a deep breath. "You should have slapped me," he told her.

"And why would I do that?"

"For my impertinence."

"How do you know it was not what I desired? How do you know I have not been sitting here waiting for you to return?"

"Have you?"

"No," she told him with a smile, "but I might have been."

Bane laughed with genuine good humor. "I would have to be a rogue indeed to seduce the daughter of my host, so I shall content myself with the delights of your company."

"You'll have to make do with the delights of my company," Appius said gruffly, emerging from a side door.

"I'm sure that will be equally delightful," said Bane. Lia rose from the bench, blew him a kiss, then walked away. He watched her, noting the sway of her hips beneath the cotton gown. "She's very beautiful," he said as Appius settled down alongside him.

"Aye, she is. My treasure, Bane. Lia is sweet, courageous, and foolhardy. Like her mother." Appius fell silent for a moment. "She was burned in the arena with fifty other heretics. It was said that the smoke from the pyres made them unconscious before the flames ate into them. Even so, it was a savage death."

"What are heretics?" queried Bane.

Appius waved his hand. "Religion, boy. All nonsense. My wife became enamored of the tree cult, a group outlawed in Stone. They talk of achieving harmony with the earth and with all the peoples of the earth. They worship the Source of All Things, a being of such dazzling weakness that he cannot save a single one of his followers. I piss on him! Lia was to be arrested, like her mother, but I took her from Stone. Sadly, I didn't remove her before she publicly insulted Nalademus, the Stone elder, calling him a vain and stupid old man. I saw his eyes. Hatred burned there."

"And these elders can order deaths?" asked Bane.

"Aye, they can. They employ killers, though they give them fine armor and a noble name. The knights of Stone. Hard men and deadly. They make the arrests, drag people from their homes to stand trial before the elders."

"And the emperor permits these actions?"

"Why would he not? Most of those arrested are former supporters of the republic, and all have voiced their protests at the emperor's continued expansion of the empire through war. The tree cult believes that all war is evil."

"How foolish," said Bane. "Without war there would be no glory."

"Exactly! And what would I have been, eh? A cobbler? A blacksmith? But I have brought Lia here to see her safe, to wait until the Crimson Priests themselves fall. Then we can return to Stone."

"And who is it that these priests worship?" asked Bane.

"Stone itself. They claim the city is a god, eternal and holy. All other gods are false, the creations of weaker peoples." He looked Bane in the eye. "What do you worship, boy?"

"Nothing. My own strength, perhaps. And you?"

"I believe there is a greater power beyond that of man. I have to believe that or else we are all just parasites rushing hither and yon to no purpose. Anyway, that is enough of my philosophy. I have booked you passage tomorrow. Banouin has offered to carry letters for me. If you like, I will write some for you that will, at least, ensure that you have somewhere to stay in Stone."

"I will find somewhere to stay, General. Do not concern yourself. And I will not be staying long. I promised Banouin's mother I would see him safely to the city. Then I shall view it and return home. I miss the mountains already."

"I would like to have seen the Rigante mountains," said Appius. "They are said to be magnificent." His expression changed, and sadness touched him. "I rather fear that my successors will do just that when the Stone army finally marches north."

"You did not learn your lesson at Cogden Field?"

"Stone does not learn lessons," Appius said, with a sigh. "We are a people afflicted with colossal arrogance. Jasaray had other matters on his mind after Cogden, and Connavar was clever enough to return the Panther standards to him. Jasaray sold this act to the people as a gesture of contrition and managed to place the blame for the entire venture on the head of the dead Valanus. But Jasaray has not forgotten the Rigante, Bane. Of that you can be sure. At the moment he is fighting a war in the east, but when it is concluded, he will march against Connavar."

"The result will be the same," Bane said coldly.

"I can see why you would think that, but I am an old soldier and I disagree with you. Valanus advanced too far, too fast with only five Panthers—fifteen thousand men. By the time of the battle the supply lines had been sundered, and the troops had eaten nothing for five days. Even so, they killed sixteen thousand tribesmen. Jasaray will not come with twelve thousand. More like forty. And he will lead them."

"He's an old man." Bane sneered.

Appius smiled and shook his head. "Ah, the wonderful arrogance of youth! Yes, he is an old man, boy, but he is an old man who has never lost. A general does not need the lightning reflexes of the young to see an opening in an enemy's line or to read the ebb and flow of a battle. What he needs is skill, experience, and iron nerve. Jasaray has all those qualities. His supply lines will not be sundered. He will move slowly, with infinite care. You enjoy your Rigante mountains while they are still Rigante mountains."

◇ 4 ◇

A FEROCIOUS STORM broke over Accia during the night, the thunder deafening, rain and fierce winds lashing the town. Tiles were ripped from rooftops, and to the north a barn collapsed, killing two horses. The morning sky was dull and overcast, lightning flashing ominously in the east. Bane was nervous about the sea crossing later that day but kept his fears to himself. Banouin said very little. He was withdrawn, and his eyes retained a haunted look. Several times Bane tried to engage him in conversation, but Banouin's answers were monosyllabic and he spent much of the day in his room, sitting on the balcony and watching the road to the sea.

"I don't know what is the matter with him," Bane told Lia as they sat under an awning in the garden, watching the rain in the late afternoon. "I have never seen him like this. It's as if he's not really here at all."

"I tried to speak to him," said Lia, "but he will not look me in the eye. I wonder if I have said something to offend him."

"Perhaps it is the result of his fever and the pain of his broken arm," offered Bane. "He's always been terrified by the thought of physical pain. And with his mother a healer, there was never any lingering sickness."

"You like him, but he saddens you," said Lia.

"Aye, well, I'm an embarrassment to him. He wants to leave Rigante ways behind him. We're barbarians, you see. No place for someone like me in Stone."

"Oh, Bane, you are not the barbarians. We are. I heard what you said to Father the other night about nakedness. You were right. While we preach sexual morality, we rape the world, enslave its men and women, and slaughter its children. We are worse than barbaric, Bane. We are so far beyond evil that it has no meaning anymore." She smiled sadly. "Banouin wants to be a part of that? Let him. For me, I would rather journey into the mountains and live among those my people call savages."

Bane lifted Lia's hand to his lips and kissed it.

"Why did you do that?" she asked, blushing.

He shrugged. "It felt right." He looked into her dark eyes. "I shall miss you."

"You can always come back," she said softly. "I will be here."

Bane leaned toward her, and she did not move away. Their lips met, and the kiss lingered. He felt his heart beat faster. In his short life he had bedded a score of earth maidens, yet this one kiss filled him with an awareness of life he had never before experienced. He drew back, aware that something magnificent was occurring yet frightened of its intensity. He rose from the seat and kissed her hand once more. "I will come back," he said, his voice husky. "I promise you that. And I will take you to the Rigante mountains."

"I will be ready," she told him.

At that moment Banouin came out into the garden. The rain had eased, and the sky was clearing. "Time to go," he said. "The ship sails in an hour."

Bane was torn. He was tempted to tell Banouin to sail without him, but he had made a promise to Vorna. One of the two house servants, an elderly man, came into sight beyond the gate, leading their horses. Banouin walked quickly along the path without a farewell to Lia. His rudeness annoyed Bane, but the feeling was momentary, for Lia threw her arms around his neck and kissed him again. The kiss was passionate and long, and when she pulled away, she gave an impish smile. "That's for you to remember me by," she said.

"Oh, I will remember," he told her.

Appius stepped into view as they parted. Bane looked him in the eye and saw the disappointment there but also the resignation. He offered his hand, and Appius took it. "Come back safely," said the old general. Bane walked along the path, reached his horse, and vaulted to the saddle. Then he waved and rode after Banouin.

"You didn't even say good-bye," he said as he drew alongside his friend. Banouin ignored him, and they rode through the town, then out onto the open stretch before the port.

Three riders were traveling in the opposite direction. Bane watched them approach. They wore black cloaks and helms of black-stained iron embossed with silver. Banouin pulled his horse from the road to let them pass. Bane remained where he was. As the lead rider came alongside, he glanced at Bane and their eyes met. Bane felt a thrill of fear as the pale gaze touched him. The man was tall and wide-shouldered, his bare arms powerfully muscled. He smiled as he rode by, and Bane felt his anger rise. In that moment each man had recognized the warrior in the other, and the smile had been one of contempt.

Then he was past. Bane swung in the saddle and watched them ride on. "Now, that was an evil whoreson," he said.

"We have to go!" said Banouin. Bane looked at him. Banouin's face was white with fear, and he was trembling.

"What is wrong with you?" said Bane. "I have never known you to behave like this. You are beginning to unsettle me."

"We have to get away!" said Banouin, urging his horse into a run.

Bane swore and heeled the gray after him. He caught him swiftly and leaned over, grabbing Banouin's reins.

The horses slowed. "I'm sick of this behavior," said Bane. "Now talk to me. What is wrong with you?"

"We have to get to the ship. Once we are on the ship, I'll tell you everything. The ship!"

"A pox on the ship. You tell me now."

"Please, Bane, trust me. I have had a vision. A terrible vision."

"You told me that. A demon stalking me."

"No, not that. Come with me, please . . . Your life depends on it!"

"My life? I have no enemies here."

Banouin's eyes flickered to the distant riders. "They are knights of Stone," he said. "Former gladiators. Killers. You could not stand against them. Believe me."

"Why would I want to?" Bane smiled. "I think you are a victim of bad dreams, my friend, not visions. They rode past.

If they were looking for me, they would have . . ." He fell silent. "They were not looking for me, were they?"

"We have to leave," said Banouin.

"You miserable whoreson," hissed Bane. "They've come for Appius, haven't they?"

"Trust me! You can't save them!"

"Them? Oh, sweet heaven!" Swinging the gray, Bane raced back toward the town. He could not see the riders now and urged the gray into a gallop. A woman moved out onto the road, dragging a handcart full of linen to be washed. Bane leapt his gray over it. Terror was upon him as he rode, and he prayed to Taranis that he would not be too late. In his mind he heard again Appius talking about the knights of Stone and how Lia had insulted their chieftain. And he remembered the kiss and all that it promised for their future together.

He was close to panic as he reached the lane outside the garden gate. Bane leapt from the saddle. Three horses were tethered there, the riders nowhere to be seen.

The gate was open, and drawing his sword, Bane ran into the garden. The old servant who had brought the horses was lying on the path, his throat slashed open, blood pooling on the stone. Bane ran into the house. One of the warriors he had seen earlier was in the hallway, wiping his blood-drenched blade across the gown of the second servant, an old woman. He glanced up as Bane entered and swung to face him. He was fast, but Bane was already moving, his sword slicing across the man's throat and cleaving his neck. Even before he fell Bane ran past him and on to the stairs.

The body of the general Appius was lying sprawled on its back at the foot of the stairs, a terrible open wound in the chest. Bane took the steps two at a time, emerging into the up- stairs corridor. Just as he reached it, a second black-garbed warrior came into view. Bane ducked under a slashing sweep, then kicked out, catching the warrior on the knee. As the man fell, Bane rammed his sword toward his throat. The blow was mistimed and went in through the man's mouth, spearing up into the brain. Dragging the short sword clear, Bane raced along the corridor to Lia's room, throwing open the door and rushing inside.

The leader was there, holding Lia by the throat, a short

sword in his hand, the blade pressed against Lia's chest. He was taller than he had looked while riding, several inches over six feet, and the black and silver helm he wore accentuated the cold, pale eyes. Bane felt a moment of dread as he looked into those eyes, and his warrior's heart sensed that he was in the presence of a true killer. Lia was no longer struggling. She was looking directly at Bane, and there was hope in that gaze.

"Let her go," ordered Bane, "or I'll kill you as I killed your men."

The man grinned, then rammed his blade into Lia's body, wrenched it clear, and tossed her aside. Time froze in that moment. Lia's body fell slowly, her wide-open eyes staring up at Bane. She struck the floor, and Bane saw her eyes close, blood staining her bright blue gown.

He looked up from the body into the cold eyes of her killer. "You were saying?" said the man.

Bane gave a terrible cry and hurled himself forward. Their blades met. Bane hacked and slashed, thrust and cut. Every attempt was blocked with ease. Suddenly the man spun on his heel, turning full circle and crashing his elbow into Bane's face. The young tribesman fell back, blood streaming from a cut to his cheekbone.

"You could have had promise, boy," said the man. "You are fast and strong."

Bane attacked again, seeking an opening. The man dropped his guard for a heartbeat. Bane lunged. It was a trick! His opponent swayed aside, then slammed his blade into Bane's body. The sword struck Bane's hip then ripped up through his flesh. He lashed out, and the warrior leapt back, Bane's sword opening a shallow cut in his upper arm.

"Well, this has been enjoyable," said the warrior, "but sadly, it is time for you to die."

Bane leapt for him, but the man spun away. Bane's charge carried him past his opponent. Terrible pain exploded in Bane's back as the man's iron sword plunged home. Bane dropped to his knees onto the balcony. A shadow fell across him, and he threw himself to his right. The warrior's sword clanged against stone. Bane surged to his feet and once more lashed out. This time his blade nicked the skin of his opponent's cheek.

"You could have been good," said the man.

Bane's vision was blurring. The man's sword lanced toward him. Bane tried to throw up his arm to block it, but the sharp metal rammed home in his chest.

A distant bell began to toll as Bane fell from the balcony. It seemed to him then that he was falling forever. His body struck the rain-drenched grass, but he felt no pain. With a groan he rolled to his belly, seeking his sword. It had plunged into the earth some feet away. He reached for it, but then the pain hit him, searing from the wound in his back. His face touched the damp earth. With a tremendous effort of will he dragged his torn body across the grass. His hand curled around the hilt of the sword.

Then he passed out.

It was almost dusk when Oranus led the ten-man honor guard to the house of Appius. He had made sure that the soldiers had shined their armor and their belt buckles and greaves. Light oil glistened on their leather tunics and kilts, and their red cloaks were new, fresh from the stores. Each of their helms boasted a crimson horsehair plume, neatly brushed. These and the cloaks would be returned as soon as this visit was over, but Oranus was determined that his men would find approval in the eyes of the general.

The front gates were locked. Set into the wall beside them was a bronze bell with a hanging rope. Oranus rang it. There was no response. Irritated now, he led his men around the garden wall to the rear gate. It was open. As the captain of the watch stepped through, he saw the first body. Drawing his short sword, he ran along the path.

By the house he saw the blond Rigante warrior Bane lying facedown on the grass. Blood was drenching his dark clothes and pooling beneath him. Oranus knelt beside the man and turned him. Bane's eyes flickered open. His face was gray, and Oranus saw another terrible wound in his upper chest. Bane tried to speak, but blood bubbled from his mouth and he passed out.

A tall figure moved from the house. Oranus glanced up and

felt the onset of fear. The man wore the black and silver armor of the Stone knights. Oranus knew him at once. He had seen Voltan fight in the Great Arena in the days before he had been recruited to the service of Nalademus. The man was a deadly killer.

"Does he still live?" asked Voltan.

"Barely," answered Oranus.

"Then step aside and I shall finish him."

Anger washed over the fear, and Oranus rose and turned toward his waiting men. He pointed at one of them: "Fetch the surgeon Ralis. And do it quickly," he said.

"I gave you an order," Voltan said softly.

"I am the captain of the watch, Voltan. You do not order me. Show me your papers of warrant," replied Oranus.

Voltan gave a wry smile, then reached inside a hidden pocket in his black cloak. From it he produced a section of folded parchment. This he handed to Oranus. The captain read it slowly, his heart sinking. Carrying the authorized seal of the Crimson Temple, it named Appius and Lia as enemies of the state, to be dispatched wherever found. Oranus pretended to study the document as he gathered his thoughts. He could feel the tension in the men around him. No one wanted to find himself at odds with a Stone knight.

"I take it that sentence has already been passed on General Appius and his daughter?" he said, passing the parchment back to Voltan.

"It has. Now stand aside while I finish this wretch."

"I do not see his name on your warrant, Lord Voltan, or the name of that poor wretch of a servant upon the path."

"The savage killed two of my knights and tried to prevent the execution of our duty."

"Ah, then you will wish him to be charged with that offense, and you will no doubt take the time to remain here in Accia while a court is convened. There will, of course, be a second hearing before the Cenii king since one of his subjects has been accused of a crime. This, as I'm sure you know, is part of our treaty with the Cenii. It will take no more than a month, perhaps two, Lord Voltan. You are welcome to share my home during that time."

Voltan gave an easy smile. "I like a man with nerve, Captain. They make better opponents." He glanced down at the blood-drenched body. "He had nerve." His cold blue eyes locked to Oranus. "Perhaps we shall meet again," he said. Then he sheathed his sword and strolled past the honor guard. He paused at the last man, then chuckled. "This man has specks of rust on his sword," he said. "Be thankful I spared Appius from seeing it. He was notoriously strict about such matters." Voltan placed his hand on the unfortunate soldier's shoulder. "You'd probably have received ten lashes," he said. Then he walked from the garden, mounted his horse, and rode away.

"Check the house," Oranus ordered his men, "and find something to stanch these wounds." Removing his cloak, he rolled it and placed it under Bane's head. Then he cut away the wounded man's blood-drenched shirt. He had been stabbed three times: once above the hip, once in the chest, and once in the lower back. The chest wound was by far the most serious, and from the bubbling of the blood Oranus knew his lung had been pierced. One of the soldiers returned with some cloth. Oranus made a compress and pressed it down against the chest wound.

"He'll not live, sir," said the soldier.

Oranus said nothing. The light faded, and he ordered lanterns lit. The bald and stooping surgeon Ralis arrived, examined the wounds, then turned to Oranus. "There's little I can do," he said. "His lung is pierced, and the wound to his lower back has probably sliced through any number of vital organs."

"Do what you can," said the captain.

"Let's get him inside."

A crow flew over them, cawing and screeching. Oranus shivered. "How do they know when death is close?" he whispered.

"They can see the spirits pass over," said a voice. Oranus looked around and saw an old woman, her face veiled, a heavy fishnet shawl over her bony shoulders.

"What do you want here, woman?" he asked her.

"I have some skill with wounds, soldier. Best you leave him in my care."

"Our own surgeon is here, but my thanks to you for your offer."

Her laughter was cold, and Oranus shivered suddenly. "Your surgeon wishes to be gone to his home, for he knows the boy has perhaps an hour to live. Is that not so, Ralis?"

"It is so," admitted Ralis.

"Then carry him to a bedroom and I shall tend him until he dies."

"You are a witch woman of the Cenii?" asked Oranus.

"I am a person with some . . . shall we say . . . talent in these matters, Oranus."

"Then it shall be as you say."

Soldiers carried Bane to a bedroom on the first floor and laid him down on a bed. Then they left him and the old woman. Oranus stood in the doorway. "I shall return tomorrow for the body, lady," he said. "We must be careful to prevent disease spreading."

Her veiled face turned toward him. "You did well to protect him from the Cold Killer. It was an act of courage. Perhaps it will bring you peace now."

"Peace would be pleasant," he said.

"Is that what you wish for?"

Oranus sighed. "I would wish for him to live," he said.

Closing the door behind himself, he walked down the stairs and out into the night. The bodies were being carried out to two waiting wagons. Appius and his daughter were laid side by side in the first, the two elderly Cenii servants and the dead knights in the other. The surgeon Ralis climbed into the first wagon and sat beside Appius and Lia. Oranus ordered the honor guard to walk beside the first wagon and follow it to the death house.

After the bodies were carried inside, Ralis stayed with them. "He was my general," said the surgeon, "and a great man. I shall prepare the bodies for burial."

"Do not place your name on the grieving list," warned Oranus. "They were murdered on the orders of Nalademus."

"I know."

Then Oranus returned to his home. He felt a sense of sorrow at the murder of Appius. The old man had served Stone well, and Oranus could not imagine what crime he had committed to be so summarily butchered. Toward midnight, weary and spent, Oranus took to his bed and prepared himself for yet another night of nightmare and terror. But he slept without dreams for the first time in years and awoke to see a blue sky and bright sunlight shining into the room. He rose and walked to the window, staring out over the green hills and the distant forest.

"A new day," he said aloud and, even as he said it, felt the awesome fears of the past lose their power and drift away like woodsmoke in a breeze. He felt free and alive, and the future that had yesterday seemed bleak and shadow-haunted now shone brightly in this new sunlight. How can this be? he wondered. Then he remembered the old woman and the words she had spoken to him. "Perhaps it will bring you peace now." Amid the drama and horror of the events in the house of Appius he had not fully registered what she had said. How had she known of his fears and his endless torment?

Perhaps she is a seer, he thought.

Banouin waited until the death wagons had been drawn away, then walked slowly into the house. He avoided looking at the bloodstained rugs, and climbed the stairs to the upper bedroom. As he opened the door, he heard the voice of the Morrigu.

"You were not worthy of your talent," she said.

Banouin did not reply but gazed down on the deathly pale face of his friend. "He is dead, isn't he?"

"No, he is not dead," said the Morrigu, "though his soul has fled this damaged shell. He should be dead, however. His lung was pierced through, and his liver."

Banouin moved to the bedside. Bane was lying naked on the bed. There were stitches to the wounds in his chest and hip, and a little blood was seeping through them.

"Why did you save him?"

"A soldier of Stone wished it, and it is my destiny to grant wishes. I might ask you a similar question: Why did you not save him? He is your friend."

"What could I do? I am no fighter."

"No," said the Morrigu. "You are not, not in any sense of the word. Why did you come back? Now you have missed your ship and your journey to the towering greatness of Stone."

Banouin felt the contempt in the words. "I don't know why I came back." He sat down by the bedside and took hold of Bane's hand. "Why do you say I could have saved him?"

"Why did you not warn Appius of the impending attack? He could have fled the house with his daughter. They would still have been alive. Then Bane would not have attempted his valiant rescue."

"It was a vision. It was the truth. I could not have changed it."

"The words of a man with the heart of a weasel," she hissed. "Best you go from here, Banouin. Run away to Stone. Hide yourself from all confrontation and danger. Live out your miserable life lost in the words and the works of better men."

Banouin backed away toward the door. "You are just like all the rest," he said, tears in his eyes. "You value the killers like Bane, the bringers of death. You cannot tolerate those who find violence appalling and seek a better way."

The Morrigu turned toward him. Banouin tried to run but found himself frozen in place. "It is the nature of weak men," she said softly, "to see their weaknesses as strengths and other men's strengths as weakness or stupidity. Bane risked his life a few days ago to save a horse trapped in a swollen river. A horse, Banouin! And why? Because he has a heart. He has feelings for others. He does not live his life whining about unfairness. He lives his life. On your travels you envied his popularity, the way men and women warmed to him in a way they could never warm to you. You felt they were some-how foolish and were taken in by his easy smile. Not so. They sensed that Bane was a man who cared, a man to be relied on. You, they knew, cared only for yourself and could not be re-lied upon.

"I am a spirit, born of spirit and fed by spirit. This land is also fed by spirit. No tree can grow, no flower bloom without it. And where does it come from, this life-giving energy? It comes from men like Connavar and Ruathain, from women like Vorna and Eriatha and Meria. People who know love and warmth, people who will risk their lives for all they believe in." The Morrigu stepped in close to the terrified Banouin and lifted her dark veil. Her face was dead, the skin gray and peeling back from white bone. "Look upon the Morrigu, child. Gaze upon her beauty. You feel sick, do you not? Can you smell the corruption? Aye, I guess that you can.

"Once, a long time ago, man understood the nature of spirit. His deeds caused it to flower, and he lived in harmony with the creatures of earth and spirit. Then came more and more men like the Cold Killer and his masters, Banouin. Selfish, greedy, small men who drank of the spirit but did not replenish it. And the creatures of spirit began to pass away, drifting across the multitudes of universes in search of more pleasant habitations. With immeasurable lack of speed this earth began to die. Oh, it will take many thousands of years, but it will die when the last whisper of spirit passes.

"The men of Stone are the latest parasites. They hack down the forests, gouge the earth for precious metals, and kill and conquer, breeding hatred and malice that will last for a hundred lifetimes. They believe in nothing save themselves. That is why you are drawn to them. They are like you, Banouin, utterly selfish. Yes, Bane is violent, and some of his deeds do him no credit. But when he risked himself to save the horse, he added to the spirit of the world. He fed the earth. And when he came into this house to save the innocent, he fed it again—this time with his blood. You did not remember my warning, did you, Banouin? No man conquers fear by running away from it. Now go away from here. Enter the rats' nest that is Stone. Become a part of the death of the world."

She turned away from him and returned to the bedside.

Banouin stumbled from the room and ran out into the night.

The man had no idea where he was, except that the sky was gray and gloomy and there were no trees, no flowers, no grass. All around him the hillside was covered with gray dust and tall, jutting boulders the color of smoke. He felt pain and glanced down at his chest. A flame was burning on his skin, turning the flesh black around it. He slapped at it with his hand, but the flame burned on.

Something moved to his right. He swung around, sword in

hand, and saw a huge serpent slither into view. It was color-less, and as it moved, it left white slime on the gray dust. The man backed away from the creature. Suddenly it reared up, its head flashing toward him. For a moment only he was shocked into immobility. The head of the serpent was human, though its fangs were as long as knives.

At the last possible moment the man snapped into action, his sword cleaving the thick neck of the snake. The creature disappeared in an instant. More and more strange creatures appeared from behind the rocks, and the man felt his skin crawl as he heard their moans. He stood, sword in hand, and watched as the creatures edged toward him. Some slithered on their bellies, and others crawled, their talons pulling them for-ward. Still more crept on all fours, bright yellow eyes staring at him with open malevolence. A scaled beast darted forward, then leapt. He stepped in to meet it, sending his sword slashing through its chest. It, too, disappeared in an instant.

He backed away, farther up the slope. There were scores of the creatures now, and more were coming. Each one of them was demonic in appearance, yet all carried aspects of hu-manity, some in the eyes and others in the features or limbs. The flames were still burning on his chest, but he felt no weakness. Only pain. The ground below his feet was corpse-gray and thick with dust, which eddied up like smoke around his ankles. He had no recollection of coming to this place, no memory of a life before it. All he knew was that here, on this dark mountainside beneath a gray sky with no stars or moon, he was in deadly peril.

The beasts edged closer. He moved back. Soon, he knew, they would come at him in a rush, and there was no way he could kill them all. Their hatred enveloped him like an in-visible mist, cold and unrelenting. The man moved ever up the mountainside until his back touched a wall of dark, dagger-sharp shining glass. There was nowhere left to retreat. Within the mist of pulsing hatred he felt their unholy joy. They gath-ered themselves, moving around him in a semicircle, ever closer.

Then they swept forward.

In that moment a bright light burst upon the scene, and as the man hacked and cut with his blade, he felt a presence beside him, guarding his back. From the edge of his vision he saw a sword of bright light slashing through the gloom. Once more the beasts fell back. The man's savior strode after them, then plunged his sword into the gray earth, cutting a long curving line into the dust. Bright fire leapt up along the line, rearing high in the air, a golden half circle of flame through which the beasts could not pass. Then the shining warrior turned back toward him. He saw that the warrior was completely human, a big man, wide-shouldered and yellow-haired, with friendly blue eyes.

"You should not be here, young Falcon," he said. "This is no place for the living." Gently he laid his hand on the flames scorching the man's chest. The fires died down instantly, the pain vanishing and the skin instantly healed.

Weariness swept over the young man, and he sank to the ground, laying aside his sword and sitting with his back to the rearing cliff of black glass. "I don't know how I came to be here," he said. "Where is this place? Why do you call me Falcon?"

"I call you Falcon because this is your soul-name," said the other man, sitting beside him. "As for this evil land, it is the Vale of the Lost, a place of the damned. Your enemies were once men. Now they wander here, cursed and forlorn."

"Why did they attack me?"

"You drew them to you, boy. You are alive. Your spirit burns them, reminding them of all they have lost. They must destroy you to end their pain."

He looked into the face of the big man. "And what of you? Why are you in this place?"

The yellow-haired warrior smiled. "You drew me here, Bane. It was I who gave you your soul-name, and when your soul was in peril, I sensed it. Do you know who you are?"

"You called me Falcon and now Bane. The names are familiar, but I cannot get a grasp of where I have heard them before."

"That happens here sometimes," said the man. "Sit quietly for a while. Let your mind relax. Think of a mountain with green flanks, a cloak of woods, and peaks of white snow like an old man's hair. Can you picture it?"

"Aye, I can."

"Give it a name."

"Caer Druagh," said Bane. It was as if sunlight suddenly had pierced the darkest corners of his memory. "I am Bane of the Rigante," he said. "I was with Banouin, and we were traveling. Then . . . then . . ." He gave a groan. The big man placed his hand on Bane's shoulder.

"Aye, then you tried to save them."

"I could not defeat him."

"But you tried, boy. You almost gave your life for it. I'm proud of you."

"Proud of failure?" Bane gave a harsh laugh.

"Aye, proud," the man said again. "A heroic action should never be judged on the basis of its success or failure but on the heart, passion, and courage that inspired it."

"You are the Big Man," said Bane.

"I am Ruathain."

"I know of you," Bane told him. "You treated my mother with kindness." He smiled suddenly. "I always wanted to know you, Big Man."

Ruathain clapped him on the shoulder. "I would like nothing better than to sit and talk with you, Grandson, but the sword flame will not last much longer, and you must make a choice. You can stay and I will lead your soul to the haven, or you can try to return to the world of the living."

"Then I am not dead?"

"Not yet."

"How do I return?"

Ruathain gestured up at the glass cliff. "You must climb it, Bane, to the very top. It will be mercilessly hard. Agonizing. The sharp glass will cut away at you, tearing your flesh. Most men would fail. But you will not fail. Your courage and your fighting spirit will carry you on through all the agony. Do you believe me?"

"I believe you, Big Man."

"Then go now, my boy," said Ruathain, drawing Bane to his feet. The spirit warrior embraced Bane, hugging him close and patting his back. Then he released him. Bane felt a wave of warm emotion threatening to engulf him. No one except his mother had ever embraced him. He looked into Ruathain's eyes.

"I am glad that we met," he said.

"And I. Now climb back to the sunlight and the life beyond."

Leaving his sword on the ground, Bane reached up for a handhold, then began to climb. At first it was easy, but then his foot slipped and sharp glass cut through his boot, slicing the skin of his foot. The pain almost made him lose his grip. Gritting his teeth, he pulled himself up. At first he suffered only small cuts and scratches, and each one stung like salt on a wound. After a while his shirt and breeches were in tatters, his boots sliced away. Deep cuts had been gouged into his chest and belly, and he was smearing a trail of blood on the cliff face. He glanced down. Ruathain was no longer there, and the sword flame had disappeared. A huge throng of creatures had gathered at the foot of the cliff, but none attempted to climb after him.

The pain was intense now, clouding his thoughts, filling his mind. He looked up but could not see the top. He struggled on. The flesh of his arms had been stripped away, and he could see sinews and muscles and the whiteness of bone. Each hand- or foothold now brought increasing agony, and his mind screamed at him to let go, to fall away from the torturous climb. He closed his eyes and felt his spirit failing.

"Courage, Grandson," came the voice of Ruathain.

Bane climbed on.

There was no flesh now on his fingers, only white bone and ligament. Strips of skin were hanging from his arms, belly, and thighs, and his body burned as if on fire. Once more he stopped, all strength seeping from him. If he climbed much farther, he would be torn to shreds. There would be nothing left of him.

Again the voice of Ruathain whispered into his ear. "The man who brought death to the house of Appius still lives, Bane. His name is Voltan. Men say he is the greatest swordsman in all the world. I saw him laugh as he stabbed you!"

Anger flooded through Bane, washing over the pain. He fought his way ever higher, dragging himself inch by agonizing inch.

At last he pulled his mutilated body over the lip of the cliff. He felt a cool breeze on his face and looked around. He was standing on a flat section of glass no more than twenty feet square.

"Proud of you, boy," came the voice of Ruathain.

And Bane awoke.

Oranus waited for the death wagon to arrive and then climbed up alongside the driver. Two stretcher bearers were sitting on an empty wooden coffin in the back. The sun was bright in a clear sky as the driver flicked his reins across the back of the two ponies and the wagon moved on through the streets.

"It is a beautiful day," said Oranus. The Cenii driver looked at him quizzically, then nodded agreement. As the wagon trundled on, Oranus saw the old Cenii witch woman moving from a doorway. He called out to her, but she did not hear him and walked into the shadows of an alleyway. A crow cawed loudly, then launched itself from a rooftop and flew away to the north.

"What is her name?" Oranus asked the driver.

"Whose name?" replied the man.

"The old woman we just saw."

"I saw no woman, sir."

The wagon lurched as it left the only paved area of road in Accia and headed up the rutted slope to the house of Barus. Leaving the wagon and the driver at the side gate, Oranus led the stretcher bearers through the house, stepping over the pools of dried blood on the floor and climbing the stairs. The captain paused at the bedroom door, preparing himself for the sight of the dead Rigante. Then he pushed open the door and stepped inside. He stopped suddenly, and a stretcher bearer walked into him, mumbling an apology.

Bane was sitting up in bed, his face pale but his eyes open. Oranus glanced at the stitched wounds and the bruises around them. It was not possible the man could be alive. He stood for a moment, uncertain, then drew in a deep breath and ordered the stretcher bearers to wait downstairs. Then he walked to the bedside, drew up a chair, and sat down.

"You should be dead," he said. "Your lung was pierced."

"Your surgeon did well, then," said Bane, his voice weak. There was dried blood on his chin and neck.

"It wasn't my surgeon. An old Cenii witch woman tended you."

"Then she was very skilled. What happened to the man I was fighting? Did you catch him? He killed Appius and . . . his daughter."

Oranus saw the pain in the man's eyes.

"I saw him," said Oranus. "He was a knight of Stone. He carried orders to execute the general and his family. There was nothing I could do. He left last night on a ship for Goriasa."

Bane closed his eyes and said nothing for a moment. "I'll find him," he said.

"Best you don't, young man. Look what happened the first time." Oranus removed his helm. On a nearby table was a pitcher of water and three goblets. He filled one. "Drink this," he said. "You've lost a lot of blood."

Bane opened his eyes and reached out for the goblet. He winced as the stitches pulled. Then he drank deeply. The effort seemed to exhaust him, and he sank back to the pillow.

"You need to regain your strength," said Oranus. "I'll hire a nurse to tend you and have some food delivered."

"Why would you do this?"

"In honor of the general," Oranus replied instantly, "and because you fought so hard to save him."

"Who is Voltan?" Banc asked.

Oranus sighed. "He is a former gladiator. He killed forty men in the arena and won a hundred other duels which did not result in death. Who told you his name?"

"I dreamed it," whispered Bane. He fell silent, and Oranus saw that he was sleeping.

Oranus quietly left the bedside, walked downstairs, paid the stretcher bearers, and ordered one of them to go to the field hospital and have the surgeon Ralis and a nurse sent to the house. The second man he handed a silver piece and told him to run to the market and buy bread, cheese, milk, and fruit. Then he walked out into the garden and stood beneath the awning, staring at the mass of blood on the ground. Bane had been stabbed three times by a master swordsman. One terrible strike had pierced his lung. Of that there was no doubt. The wound in his back should have speared a kidney. Yet Bane was alive, his wounds healing.

Oranus had heard of the skills of the Keltoi witch women but had dismissed some of the wilder stories as fantasies. Now he knew different.

Returning to the house, he walked through to the kitchen. Milk was curdling in a jug, but in the larder there were several eggs. He was about to light the cookfire when he heard people moving around in the hallway. There were four women, all carrying mops and buckets. Oranus remembered ordering that the house be cleaned and wandered out to them. They were all Cenii women, and they stood staring silently at the blood on the walls, floor, and rugs.

They curtsied as he entered. "There is more blood on the upstairs landing," he said, "and in the far bedroom."

The women stood together, gazing nervously around. "What is wrong?" asked Oranus. "It is only blood. It will not harm you."

"Is the Old Woman still here, sir?" one of them asked.

"No, she has gone."

"Is she coming back?"

"I don't know. Who is she?"

The women remained silent, exchanging glances. The oldest of them, a woman of around fifty, stepped forward. "The soldiers said a crow was with her. It sat on the wall when she walked into the garden. Is this true, sir?"

"Aye, there was a crow. Death always brings them." The women began speaking in Keltoi, a tongue Oranus had never been able to master fully. "What is the matter with you?" snapped the officer. "She was a Cenii witch woman, and she saved the young man. Nothing more than that."

"Yes, sir," said the older woman. "We'll work now."

Oranus left them to it and returned to the garden, where he sat awaiting Ralis and the nurse. After a little while he heard a wagon draw up. A young army doctor and a slender, dark-haired young woman entered the gate.

Oranus stood. "Where is Ralis?" he asked.

"He had urgent matters to attend to," said the young man, saluting. "He has remained at his home today. Where is the dying man?"

"He's not dying," said Oranus. "A witch woman healed him."

The young man laughed scornfully. "Then his wounds could not have been as severe as was thought."

"I saw him," said Oranus, an edge of anger in his voice. "He was choking on his blood." He pointed to the blood-soaked paving. "That is where he lay."

"Yes, sir," replied the doctor, but Oranus could see that the man retained his scepticism.

"He is upstairs. Examine his wounds." Turning to the nurse, he told her to prepare some food for the injured man.

"You wish me to stay with him, sir?" she asked stiffly. Her pretty face held a look of cold disdain.

"Yes, I do."

"He is a tribesman, is he not?"

"He is."

"I am a citizen of Stone and should not be required to tend savages. I will stay with him today, but I expect a Cenii woman to be recruited from tomorrow on."

Oranus knew the young woman. She had been expelled from Stone for illegal prostitution and extortion. Since arriving in Accia, however, she had been a model citizen, attending temple and working voluntarily in the field hospital. "It will be as you say," he told her. "I am grateful for your assistance. He is a brave young man who fought to save two citizens of Stone."

"Two traitors," she pointed out.

"Yes, but he didn't know that. There are some eggs in the kitchen and some bread. I would be grateful if you could prepare a breakfast for me also."

"Of course, Captain," she said, and walked away.

The young doctor returned some minutes later. "As you say, Captain, he is not dying, though he has lost a great deal of blood." The man chuckled suddenly. "I heard the cleaning women talking. They believe a Seidh goddess healed him. The Morrigu, they called her. That's obviously the answer, then." He laughed again. "I must be getting back."

"Thank you for your time, Doctor."

"See that he drinks plenty of water and eats red meat. He should start regaining his strength in a week or so."

"I shall."

The young man returned to the waiting wagon, and Oranus walked back into the house and through to the kitchen. The nurse, Axa, had scrambled some eggs. She put them onto two wooden plates, handed one to Oranus, and took the other upstairs. Oranus sat quietly in the kitchen eating his breakfast. The eggs were good, and he cut two slices of bread, smearing them thickly with butter.

He felt different today. He had half expected the good feeling he had experienced upon waking to drift away like a dream once the day began, but it was quite the reverse. I feel strong again, he thought. Casting his mind back to the horrors of Cogden Field, he found he could view the memories without terror.

Axa returned with an empty plate and sat at the table opposite him. "I am sorry, Captain," she said. "I feel I was a little harsh earlier. I will do my duty and remain with Bane until he is well." He glanced at her and saw that her face was flushed.

"That is good of you," he said.

The cleaning women had completed their task as he returned to the bedroom. Bane was asleep again, but he woke as Oranus entered.

"I feel weak as a newborn foal," said the Rigante.

"Your strength will grow day by day," said Oranus.

Bane smiled. "I thank you for your kindness. Do you know what happened to my friend?"

"Friend?"

"I was staying here with Banouin. He's another Rigante. We were traveling to Stone together."

"No, I have not seen him. I will make inquiries."

"Tell me, what is a gladiator?"

"A man who fights to entertain the crowds at stadiums. Some are former soldiers; some are criminals. They train daily to hone their skills. They can become very wealthy—if they survive. Most don't."

"And it was this training that made Voltan so deadly?"

"I think he was probably deadly before it. But yes, the training would have sharpened his skills."

"How does one become a gladiator?" asked Bane.

*   *   *

A cold wind blew across the arena floor, causing snow to flurry over the sand. Persis Albitane heaved his ample frame from his seat high in the owner's enclosure and watched the meager crowd snaking toward the exits. Fewer than four hundred people had paid the entrance fee, which meant that with only two event days to come, Circus Orises would make a loss for the second year in a row.

Persis was not in a good mood. Debts were mounting, and his own shrinking capital would barely be able to meet them. As the last of the crowd left, the fat man strolled up the main aisle to the small office, unlocked the door, took one look at the huge pile of debt papers on the desk, pulled shut the door, and walked along the corridor to a second, larger room that boasted four couches, six deep hide-filled chairs, and an oak cabinet. A badly painted fresco adorned the walls, showing scenes of racing horses, wrestling bouts, and gladiatorial duels. Persis hated the fresco. The artist must have been drunk, he thought. The horses looked like pigs on stilts. He sighed. The fire had not been lit, and a west-facing window was banging in the wind, allowing snow to drift across the sill. Persis moved to the window. Down in the harbor of Goriasa he saw three fishing boats heading out into the iron gray of the sea. Better them than me, he thought. In the far distance he could see the white cliffs of the land across the water. Two of his uncles had died there, officers serving Valanus. Another uncle had survived, but he had never been the same man again. His eyes had a haunted, frightened look.

Persis tried to shut the window, but the catch was broken and the wind prized it open once more. Several old wooden gambling tickets were strewn on the floor. Stooping, Persis plucked one and used it to wedge the window shut. Then he went to a poorly made cabinet by the far wall. Inside were four small jugs. One by one he shook them. The first three were empty, but the fourth contained a little uisge, which he poured into a copper cup. The hospitality room was cold, but the uisge warmed him briefly. He sank down into a chair, stretched out his legs, and tried to relax.

"Happy birthday," he told himself, raising the cup. He swore softly, then chuckled. Persis had always believed that by twenty-five he would be fat, rich, and happily settled in a villa on a Turgon hillside, perhaps overlooking a bay. And he might have been except for this money-sucking enterprise. At eighteen, with the ten gold coins his father had given him, he had invested in a shipment of silk from the east. That had doubled his money, and he had bought five shares in a merchant vessel. By the age of twenty he owned three ships outright and had purchased two warehouses and a dressmaking operation in Stone. Two years later he had amassed enough coin to buy a small vineyard in Turgony.

Moneylending increased his fortune further, that is, until he had met old Gradine, owner of the Circus Orises in Goriasa. He had lent the man money, and when he had failed to pay, Persis had taken a half interest in the stadium and the circus. When Gradine died of a stroke a year later, Persis became sole owner. He chuckled to himself. Sole owner of a run-down circus with a mountain of debts and only two assets: the little slave Norwin and the aging gladiator Rage.

I should have closed it down, he thought.

Instead, in his arrogance, he had traveled from Stone to the Keltoi port city of Goriasa, believing he could make Circus Orises into the gold mine Gradine had always prayed it would be: a venture to rival the mighty Circus Palantes.

He had known the enterprise was doomed virtually from the beginning but had carried on, injecting capital, acquiring new acts, paying for repairs to the creaking timber-built stadium. One by one he sold his other profitable interests to finance the project. First to go was the vineyard, then the warehouses, then the ships.

"You are an idiot," he told himself. Fat and rich by twenty-five! He smiled suddenly and patted his stomach. "Halfway there," he said.

A bitterly cold draft was seeping under the door. Rising, Persis emptied the last of the uisge into his cup and walked out into the open.

A team of Gath workers was moving through the stadium, clearing away the litter left by the Stone spectators. A small boy was working close by. Persis saw that he was wearing only a thin cotton tunic and that his arms and face were blue with cold. "Boy!" he called. "Come here!"

The lad walked shyly toward him. "Where is your coat?" asked Persis. "It is too cold to be dressed like this."

"No coat," said the boy, his teeth chattering.

"Go below and find my man Norwin. Tell him Persis says to give you a coat. Understand?"

"Yes, lord."

Persis watched the boy move away, then returned to his office, where at least a fire was blazing. Sitting at the desk, he gazed balefully at the debt papers. There was enough coin left to pay most of the debts, and two reasonably good event days would see to the rest. But the next season was another matter. Persis spent some time going through the papers, organizing them into neat piles. They seemed less threatening stacked in that way.

The door opened, and his slave Norwin entered. Just over five feet tall, his gray hair thinning, Norwin shivered with the cold despite the heavy sheepskin coat he wore.

"Please let this be good news," said Persis.

The little man grinned. "The horse-riding acrobats have quit," he said. "Circus Palantes has offered them a two-season contract."

"One day you must explain to me your definition of good news," said Persis.

"Kalder has a pulled hamstring and will not be ready to fight for six weeks. By the way, the surgeon says you have not paid his bill, and unless he receives his money in full by tomorrow, he will not be available any longer."

"I've known plagues that were better company than you," grumbled Persis.

"Oh, and it's good to know we are now in the happy position of being able to give away coats. By tomorrow every beggar and his brother will be at the door. Perhaps we should set up a stall."

"Tell me," said Persis, "did you ever act like a slave? Yes, sir, no, sir, whatever you desire, sir . . . that sort of thing?"

"No. I have one year left," said Norwin, "and then I shall be free of this indenture, my debts paid. And you will have to offer me a salary. That is, if the circus is still operating by then. Did you know Rage is approaching fifty? How long do you think he will still pull crowds for exhibition fights?"

"Oh, you are a joy today."

Norwin sighed. "I am sorry, my friend," he said. "We took less than ninety silvers today, and without the horse acrobats we'll take less in the future. Have you thought about the Palantes offer?"

"No," said Persis.

"Perhaps you should. Crowds love to see blood."

"I know. It is one of the reasons I despise people—myself included. But the Palantes offer would ruin us. We have fifteen gladiators, all of them veterans. Palantes has more than fifty, all of them young and ambitious. Can you imagine what would happen to our old men if we were to pit them against the highly trained young killers of Palantes?"

"The majority of our men would die," Norwin said coldly. "Against that we could draw maybe three thousand people, clear all debts, and leave this stadium with enough coin to invest in a truly profitable business."

"Are you truly that callous, Norwin? Would you sacrifice our people for money?"

The little slave peeled off his sheepskin coat and stood by the fire. "They are gladiators because they choose to be. Fighting is what they live for, what they know. As matters stand we will not be able to pay any of them winter wages, which means that for the next three months they will be begging for work at the docks or the timber yards."

Persis stared down at the debt papers and sighed. "I do not want my people killed," he said.

"They are not your people, Persis. They are performers who work for you."

"I know that. I also know Rage says he will never take part in another death bout. I don't blame him. He had ten years of it."

Norwin added several chunks of wood to the fire. "Rage is getting old, and he wants a pension. This could be his chance. He has money saved. He would bet it all on himself. If he won, he could retire."

"If he won," said Persis.

"If he didn't, he wouldn't have to worry about a pension," observed Norwin.

"You are a hard man, but rightly or wrongly, I care about the people of Orises and their lives."

"As I said before, they are the lives they chose to lead," pointed out the little man.

"That was true in the past. But they joined Circus Orises because we do not engage in death bouts."

Norwin stepped to the table and lifted the first pile of debt papers. "In Baggia last month," he said, "Circus Palantes drew eighteen thousand and charged double the entrance fee. Everyone wanted to see the fight between Jaxin and Brakus."

"I know that."

"Well, at least think about it," advised Norwin. "Put it to the gladiators. Let them make the choice."

"I'll talk to Rage," said Persis.

Persis Albitane eased his large bulk into the seat and gazed around the vast wooden building. He had never liked visiting Garshon's establishment. It was a haunt, he believed, of robbers and cutthroats. Few Stone citizens gathered there. At the far end of the building a horse auction was being held in a circle of sand surrounded by tiered wooden seats. Close by several whores were trying to interest newcomers. Their perfume hung in the air, mixing with the smell of horses, damp straw, and sweat.

The odor was far weaker in the eating section, where several open windows allowed the sea breeze to filter through, and Persis found that the aroma of cooking meat more than compensated for the occasional noxious scent from the main hall. There were more than fifty bench tables in the eating section, and most were full, a testament to the quality of fare served there. A serving wench approached him, but Persis told her he was waiting for a guest, then sat with his gaze fixed on the double doors.

When Rage arrived, he was immediately surrounded by well-wishers who clapped him on the back as he moved through the throng. Rare to see a man of Stone popular among the Gath, thought Persis. He smiled. Rage, despite his grim features, was a charismatic figure still, with the trademark red silk scarf tied over his shaved dome and his muscular upper frame clothed in a tight-fitting shirt of black satin beneath a heavy cloak of black wool. He still looked every inch the warrior who had fought eighty duels, thirty-three of them death bouts. Persis had seen the last. It had been exactly twelve years earlier, and his father, as a birthday treat, had taken him to the Giant Stadium, where, after the horse races and the tableau, the great gladiator Rage was to fight the unbeaten warrior Jorax. Both men represented the finest circuses of the day: Palantes and Occian. Huge amounts of coin were placed in bets, and the crowd was utterly silent as the two men stepped out into the arena. Persis shivered with pleasure at the memory. Rage had been garbed in the armor of Palantes, bright bronze, his helm embossed with a black eagle. Jorax's helm was iron polished like silver. Since this was a death bout, neither man wore a breastplate. At the center of the arena slaves had dug out a pit thirty feet long and twenty wide, which was filled with hot coals. Ten feet above it was a narrow platform on which the men would fight.

They climbed the steps to the platform, then drew their short swords and saluted the lord of the games. Persis could not remember who it was that day, but it might have been Jasaray. The swords were lowered, and trumpets blared out. Both men advanced along the platform, and the fight began. The crowd erupted, cheering on their chosen favorites. Persis was not able to hear the clashing of the weapons, but he saw the bright swords licking out, lunging, parrying, slashing, cutting.

It went on for some minutes, then Jorax slipped and fell to the coals. He rolled across them, the skin of his arms, back, and legs blistering badly. Then he scrambled clear. Rage leapt from the platform, clearing the coals. He charged at the stricken man. Jorax defended brilliantly for a little while, then Rage's gladius slipped under his guard, cutting through his right bicep. Jorax dropped his sword, tried to retrieve it with his left hand, but was then punched in the jaw. He fell heavily. Rage's sword touched the base of his opponent's throat, and Jorax lay very still.

The crowd began to bay for the finish, including Persis. "Death, death, death!" they cried.

Rage had stood for a moment, then plunged his sword into the sand and strode across the arena.

The crowd erupted in fury, hurling seat cushions at the departing gladiator. He had made a mockery of the fight! The stadium authorities had withheld his purse—six thousand in gold—and all bets were canceled while an inquiry was launched. The inquiry found that Rage had besmirched the integrity of gladiatorial combat, and he was fined ten thousand in gold. He paid the fine and announced his retirement from Circus Palantes and the arena.

A year later Jorax was proclaimed Gladiator One, a title he held for three years before being cut to pieces and killed by Voltan. Rage was offered fabulous sums to return to the arena and fight the new champion but declined them all.

But Rage had returned to the arena several years later to fight in what were termed exhibitions of swordplay and martial skills and for a number of years pulled in good crowds for Circus Orises. Even now several hundred would turn up just to glimpse Rage in full battle armor.

Persis waved as Rage approached. The tall warrior removed his cloak and eased himself into the seat opposite. Persis looked into his night-dark eyes. "How are you feeling after your bout? No pulled muscles, I hope."

"No. No problems." Rage's voice was deep and almost musical.

The serving wench returned, bringing a platter of bread and a slab of salted butter. Persis ordered the game platter: wood pigeon, duck, and goose prepared with a raspberry sauce. Rage asked for a rare steak accompanied by uncooked vegetables.

"What was it you wanted to discuss?" Rage asked, as the girl moved away.

"We have had an offer from Circus Palantes."

"No death bouts," said Rage.

Persis fell silent for a moment. "Circus Orises is almost bankrupt," he said. "I do not like the idea of death bouts myself, but I thought I would at least put it to you. You have a one-fifth stake in the circus, and if we do not find a way to draw the crowds, that stake will be worthless. How is your farm prospering?"

"It has been a bad year," said Rage.

"One big crowd, say, five thousand or more, and we would

clear all debts and make a strong profit. Then I could buy out your stake for a reasonable sum."

"Some of the others might be interested," said Rage.

Persis looked away. "They could not draw the crowds as well as you." Steeling himself, he looked again into the dark eyes. "I understand your moral objections to killing, but—"

"You do not understand me at all," Rage said, without a hint of anger. "And I do not need your understanding. What has Palantes offered?"

"Five thousand in gold as an agreement fee, but they receive two-thirds of all receipts from the crowd."

"And the named gladiators?"

"They say they will use only new fighters, no Names—and none of the bouts to figure in the championship."

Rage considered the information. "They seek to blood new talent," he said at last. "They don't want to risk putting poor performers into a major arena. So they will bring them out here to the ass end of the empire to practice on aging fighters no one cares about." Rage shook his head. "Nothing changes. I will put it to the others."

"They have asked for you, Rage. You are an integral part of the offer," said Persis. "They will not bring their fighters unless you agree to take part."

Rage's eyes narrowed, the only hint of the anger he felt. When he spoke, his voice was still even. "Of course. They will pitch their best new talent against me, and then they can proclaim him as the man who killed Rage. So much for old loyalties. Does Absicus still own Palantes?"

"Yes."

"He is the man who told me he would value me always. He said I had helped make Palantes rich, and he was pleased I had survived to retirement. He wished me well, though he offered me no financial support when the games authority stripped me of all savings. Now, for the sake of a few extra coins, he wants to send a young man to kill me."

"You are still the best," said Persis.

"Do not speak like an idiot!" said Rage. "I am two years from fifty. I was the best; now I am merely good. In another five years I will be an embarrassment. No man can hold back time, Persis. It eats away at you like a cancer."

The sound of a scuffle broke out some distance away. Persis swung to see the cause of the commotion. A young blond tribesman was being attacked by three men. The first of the attackers was felled by a savage right hook; the second grabbed the tribesman but was thrown by a rolling hip lock. The third smashed a straight left to the tribesman's face, sending him staggering backward. As the attacker moved in to finish him, the tribesman leapt forward, taking two more hard blows but grabbing his attacker's tunic and hauling him into a sickening head butt. The third man's knees buckled. At that moment Persis saw the second of the attackers rise from the floor behind the tribesman, a shining dagger in his hand. The circus owner was about to cry out a warning when he saw Rage rise to his feet, a wooden platter in his hand. His arm swept forward. The platter sliced through the air and slammed into the temple of the knifeman, who dropped like a stone.

The blond tribesman knelt by the first of the men and retrieved a pouch. Then he rose and walked across to Rage.

"Good throw," he said. "Never thought to see a bread plate used as a weapon."

"Now you have," said Rage, turning his back on him and returning to his seat. Persis was watching the young man and saw his face grow pale with anger.

"I am Persis Albitane," he said, rising and offering his hand. The tribesman hesitated for a moment, then turned toward him, accepting the handshake. Persis saw that his eyes were different colors, one green and the other tawny gold. "You fought well."

"He fought like an idiot," said Rage. "Now can we conclude our conversation?"

"I am beginning to dislike you," said the tribesman, turning his attention to Rage.

"Be still, my terrified heart," said Rage.

"Perhaps you would like to step outside, you old bastard, and I'll show you what terror is," said the young man.

Persis moved around the table to step between them. "Now, now," he said. "Let us not forget that my friend saved your life. A brawl between the two of you would be unseemly."

"Aye, but judging from what I've seen, it would be short," said Rage.

One of the downed men climbed to his feet and rushed at the tribesman, who turned and delivered a bone-crunching left that sent his attacker skidding back across the sawdust-strewn floor. He did not rise.

"That, at least, showed a little skill," said Rage. "Nicely timed, the weight coming from the feet, with good follow-through."

"So glad you approved," muttered the tribesman.

"It's not about approval or disapproval, boy. It's about survival. You just faced three men. You took them out well at first, but the man you threw over your hip was not stunned. You momentarily forgot about him. In a fistfight that could be considered careless. But he had a dagger, and that carries it far beyond carelessness, straight into the realm of stupidity. Now, that is an end to the lessons for today."

The tribesman grinned suddenly. "It was a good lesson, and I thank you for it." He swung to Persis. "My name is Bane," he said. "I came here looking for you. I have a letter from your uncle, Oranus. He said you would help me become a gladiator."

◇ 5 ◇

A LIGHT SNOW was falling as Bane walked up the hill. He paused at the crest to gaze down on the L-shaped white farmhouse below. The young Rigante was nervous and on edge. Persis Albitane had told him to report to Rage just after dawn and had said that the old gladiator would assess whether Bane could join Circus Orises. It had not occurred to Bane that he would have to prove himself. He was a fighter and had killed men in combat. Surely, he had thought, that was all that was needed. But no. After their meeting Persis had walked with him through the city center and back to Stadium Orises, explaining that Rage would make the final decision.

"The man does not like me," Bane said, as they sat in the fat man's small office.

"Rage does not like anyone," Persis put in brightly. "Do not let that concern you."

"I need to learn the skills of a gladiator," said Bane. "It is important to me."

"Rage will test you fairly, young man. I can assure you of that. Go to his farm early tomorrow, soon after dawn. He will assess your strength, your speed, your endurance, and your fighting skills. If he is satisfied that you have the talent, then we will make an agreement."

Now, in the early chill of a winter morning, Bane trudged down the slope toward the farmhouse. He did not feel confident. As he approached the building, he saw the gladiator emerge from a doorway. Rage was wearing a sleeveless black shirt, a loose pair of black woolen leggings, and thin leather moccasins. The bitter weather did not seem to affect him at all. Just looking at him made Bane feel colder.

Rage offered no greeting. His face was expressionless as

115

he approached the younger man. Gesturing Bane to follow him, he strolled to the back of the farmhouse and onto a stretch of snow-covered open land on which had been erected a number of curious wooden frames. "Do you understand the nature of discipline?" he asked suddenly.

"Discipline? I believe so. In war, some will be officers and some will be fighting men. It is important for the fighting men to carry out the orders of the officers."

"I meant self-discipline," said Rage.

"Giving orders to oneself? I'm not sure what you—" At that moment Rage struck him, open-handed, in the face. Bane was knocked sideways. For an instant he was paralyzed with shock, then fury swept through his system. He hurled himself at Rage, who sidestepped, tripping him to the ground. Bane rolled and came up fast, his hand reaching for the knife in his belt. Rage stepped in, grabbed his arm, and threw him again. Bane hit hard but rose once more to see Rage sitting calmly on a wooden bench.

"Heart and head," Rage said softly. "It is a difficult balance to find. Without heart and passion a warrior cannot function at his best, but without the head he will not survive. You know why they first called me Rage?"

Bane took a deep breath, fighting to control himself. In that moment he wanted nothing more than to kill this arrogant whoreson. "No," he said, his hand still hovering over the knife hilt.

"Because I never get angry. It was a joke, you see. I hold it all in here," he said, tapping his broad chest. "I stay smooth on the outside, allowing my body to accomplish what it is trained to do."

"Good for you," said Bane, still trembling with suppressed emotion.

"Calm down, boy. That's why I asked about self-discipline," said Rage. "Without it you'll fail. I am forty-eight years old, and I just downed you twice. The first time because you were taken unawares, the second time because you reacted with heart but no brain. I know you've got nerve. I saw that in Garshon's hall. I saw also that you have speed and good coordination." Rage rose to his feet, removed a red silk cloth from the pocket of his black shirt, and tied it over his shaved head.

"I thank you for your compliments," Bane said coldly. "But I'd like to see you best me now that I'm prepared."

"Takes you some time to learn, boy, doesn't it?" said Rage. "Whenever you're ready."

Bane advanced cautiously, then threw himself at the man. Rage grabbed his outstretched arm, twisted on his heel, and threw Bane over his hip. Keeping hold of the arm, he flipped Bane to his belly, then touched the young man's throat with his index finger. "If that was a knife, you'd be pumping blood right about now."

Bane sat up. "You've convinced me. How do I acquire this . . . self-discipline?" he asked.

"That is just one of many skills," said Rage. "Have you breakfasted yet?"

"No. Persis told me to be here just after dawn."

"Good. Can you run?"

"Of course I can run."

"How far?"

"As far as I need to."

"Then let's begin," said Rage, setting off slowly toward the eastern hills. Bane removed his cloak, left it hanging over one of the wooden frames, and set off after the older man. Coming alongside, he said: "Where are we going?"

"Over the hills," responded Rage.

"Why are we running so slowly?"

"We're warming the muscles. We'll stop at the first crest and stretch, then the real work can begin."

Bane settled in alongside him. On the hilltop Rage slowed to a walk, then moved through a series of stretching exercises. Bane watched him. His legs were lean, and there was not an ounce of fat on his powerful frame. Then the two men ran on, moving easily for several miles. From the high ground Bane could see the port city of Goriasa. According to Brother Solstice, it had once been one of the most ugly settlements on the mainland, a mass of clumsily constructed wooden buildings set close together and separated by winding, claustrophobic alleyways. The conquest by the armies of Stone sixteen years previously had seen much of the city burned, and now there were stone-built temples, houses, and places of business, all linked by a series of streets branching off a wide avenue through the center of the city. Some three thousand citizens of Stone now lived there among twenty-five thousand Gath.

Rage and Bane ran along the crest of the eastern hills, then cut down into a wooded valley. Rage increased his pace, and Bane matched him, still breathing easily. His legs were a little tired now, his calves burning. After the Cenii witch woman had healed him, he had recovered fast but then had come down with a fever. It had stripped him of flesh and sapped his strength, and he had been forced to spend three months recuperating in the city of Accia. He had thought his stamina to be fully restored, but now he realized just how weak he had become.

Rage cut to the left, climbing a slippery slope. Bane fell and rolled back, then scrambled up after the older man. Once more on the flat, Rage picked up the pace again. Bane was now breathing heavily and struggling to keep up. Rage noticed his distress and grinned at him. Anger touched Bane, sending new power to his tired limbs.

They ran on, covering another three miles before climbing over a low drystone wall and loping back toward the distant white-walled farmhouse. Once there Rage stretched again, while Bane slumped down onto a bench, sucking air into his lungs.

"Strip off your shirt," said Rage.

"Why?"

Rage stood silently for a moment. "Let us understand something, boy," he said. "Persis asked me to assess you. As a favor. I told him I would if you proved yourself willing. But in my company you are my student. When I tell you to do something, you will do it. Instantly. In that way you will learn self-discipline. Now I think you are intelligent, so understand what I am now going to say: Disobey me one more time and I will send you away, and you will have to travel to another city to fulfill your dream. Am I clear on this?"

Bane looked into the man's dark eyes. "Aye, you are clear," he said.

"Then strip off your shirt and stand."

Bane did so. Rage looked at him closely, turning him around and examining his muscle development. "The biceps and shoulders need work," he said. "But you are built for speed and strength. You came from good stock." He paused and peered closely at the scar on Bane's chest. "Short sword. Should have pierced the lung and killed you. How did you survive?"

"I don't know," said Bane. "Luck?"

"The wound in your back is also from a gladius. Were these wounds from the same fight?"

"Yes."

"More than one assailant?"

"No. Just the one."

"He stabbed you first in the back?"

"No," said Bane. "Here." He tapped at the scar on his hip.

"Ah, I see. You rushed him. He sidestepped and stabbed you in the back as you went past. Then you tried to turn and fight him, and he finished you with a lunge to the chest. Skilled man. Very skilled."

"Aye, he was that," muttered Bane.

"A gladiator?"

"I have been advised to be wary when speaking of . . . my wounds," said Bane.

"Good advice," said Rage. "All right, put your shirt on and let's get to work."

He took Bane to one of the wooden frames. A round pole had been extended between two supports ten feet above the ground. Rage extended his arms, leapt lightly, and hung on the pole. Then he drew himself up until his chin touched the wood. He repeated the move twenty times, then dropped to the ground. "Now you," he said.

Bane found the exercise easy for the first ten raises. The next five were difficult, the last five excruciating.

For the next hour Rage put him through a series of agonizing routines. Bane completed them all until, exhausted, he sank to the cold ground.

"Time for breakfast," said Rage.

"I don't think I could eat," said Bane.

Rage shrugged. "Suit yourself," he said, and wandered into the farmhouse. Bane joined him and sat quietly while Rage prepared a pan of oats and milk, which he placed on a black iron stove.

"Why are you still fighting in the arena?" Bane asked, as the warrior stood over the pan, stirring the contents.

"Why would I not?"

"Persis said you earned fabulous sums as a fighter."

"Indeed I did. I managed to save almost ten thousand in gold. But it was stripped from me when I quit. All I had left was this farm."

"Why did they take your money?"

"I brought the noble name of gladiatorial combat into disrepute. Now you tell me why you want to become an arena warrior. Glory, riches, revenge?" He glanced back at the blond-headed young man.

"Aye. One of those."

"I thought so," said Rage. "You want to find the man who almost killed you and prove to yourself that you are the better man."

"No," snapped Bane. "I want to kill the whoreson for what he took from me."

"Interesting," said Rage. "But your friend's advice still remains good. Let us talk no more of it at this time."

The door opened, and a young girl entered the kitchen. Bane judged her to be around thirteen years old, very slim, with long, white-blond hair. She was wearing a brown cotton nightdress, and she yawned as she moved to the table. "Good morning, Grandfather," she said sleepily.

"You slept late, princess," said Rage. "Did you have nice dreams?"

"I never remember dreams," she said. "You know that." Then she noticed Bane and turned toward him. Her eyes were cornflower blue and very large. Bane smiled at her. She did not respond.

"Who are you?" she asked him.

"I am Bane of the Rigante."

"I am Cara," she told him, sitting opposite him at the table. "You look exhausted."

"Indeed I am." Bane found her directness both engaging and off-putting.

Rage served the thick porridge into three wooden dishes, which he placed on the table. "There is honey, sugar, or salt, whichever is your preference," he told Bane.

Bane shook his head and drew a plate toward himself.

"It will be very hot," said Cara. "Best to leave it for a while or add some milk. Otherwise you'll burn your tongue."

Bane chuckled and shook his head.

"Why do you laugh?" she asked him. "Did I say something amusing?"

"I was just thinking how like your grandfather you are, princess," he said.

"I am not a princess," she said sternly. "That is just what Grandfather calls me. But you may call me princess if it pleases you."

"Then I shall," said Bane. "Is your mother still sleeping?"

"My mother is dead," said Cara, pouring cold milk onto her oats.

"I am sorry."

"Why?" asked Cara. "Did you know her?"

"No. I meant I am sorry for you. My mother died earlier this year. I miss her."

"I don't miss my mother," said Cara. "She died when I was a baby. I don't remember her."

"Did your father die, too?"

"No. He went away. He might be dead now. We don't know, do we, Grandfather?"

"We have not heard from him," said Rage.

"So, is it just the two of you that live here?" asked Bane.

"We have four herdsmen who have rooms at the far end," said Rage, "and two servants who live down the hill."

After breakfast Rage sent Cara back to her room to wash and dress. Then, after cleaning the porridge pan and dishes, he took Bane outside once more.

"I will train you," he said. "You will stay here. I will have a room prepared. Every morning this week we will run and work. Next week we will begin on your sword skills. Now you will excuse me. I need to see to my dairy herd."

With that he wandered back into the house. Bane gathered up his cloak, swung it around his shoulders, and set off back to Goriasa.

Having paid for his room at the tavern, Bane saddled the gray and rode back to the farmhouse just before noon. A fat, middle-aged Gath woman took him to a Spartanly furnished room facing west. There was a narrow bed, a chest for his clothing, and two wooden chairs. The walls were white and unadorned except for an empty shelf to the right of the door. The room was spacious, some twenty feet long and fifteen wide, and there was a large window with red-painted wooden shutters that opened outward. A fire was blazing in the hearth.

"If there's anything you need, you have only to ask," said the woman. "My name is Girta, and I cook and clean here three times a week."

"Thank you, Girta," said Bane.

"You are Rigante, aren't you?" said Girta.

"Yes, I am."

"I have a cousin who dwells among the Rigante now. He left years ago with Osta and other fighting men to serve Connavar. I have often thought of crossing the water to join him. Don't suppose I will now, though. I have no wish to see more wars and death."

Bane did not respond, and Girta moved to the doorway. "The others will be here within the hour. I'll serve the meal then," she said.

"Others?"

"The other gladiators," she told him. Then she pulled shut the door behind her, and Bane heard her walking away down the corridor. Taking off his cloak, he draped it over the back of a chair and then pushed open the window. From there he could see a line of wooded hills and the distant stone road that led to Goriasa. The sky was clear above the hills, but in the distance dark storm clouds were bunching over the sea.

Tired from his efforts that morning, he pulled off his boots and lay down on the bed. He thought of Banouin and wondered again why his friend had deserted him. Oranus had told him that Banouin had boarded a ship the morning after the killings. It made no sense to the young Rigante. They had been friends. Did I misjudge him so badly? he wondered.

Then he slept lightly and dreamed of Caer Druagh and of Lia. He was holding her hand on the mountain slope and pointing down at the settlement of Three Streams. Then she began to float away from him. He ran after her, but she was swept along like a leaf in the wind, ever higher, until she vanished among the clouds.

A sharp rapping on the door roused him from sleep. "Come in," he called.

Cara pushed open the door. She was dressed in a knee-length tunic of bright blue. "The day is not for sleeping," she chided him.

He grinned at her. "Ah, but I am old and tired," he said.

"You are not old. Grandfather is old, and he doesn't sleep in the daytime. Anyway, Polon and Telors are here. Would you like to meet them?"

Bane pulled on his boots. "They are gladiators?"

"Yes. Grandfather has called a meeting."

Bane followed the girl downstairs, through the kitchen, and into a long room containing a dozen chairs and six couches. Two men were lounging there, one tall and wide-shouldered with a neatly trimmed black beard flecked with silver and the second smaller, sandy-haired with close-set gray eyes. Cara ran to the black-bearded man, who grinned widely and lifted her into a hug, kissing her cheek. Bane paused in the doorway.

"Telors," said Cara, "this is Bane. Grandfather is teaching him to be a fighter."

Black-bearded Telors lowered the child to the floor and stepped forward, hand outstretched. Bane shook hands. "Good to meet you," said Telors.

"You'll make no money with Orises," said the sandy-haired man, not offering his hand.

Telors shook his head. "Polon is not in a good mood today," he said. "He spent last night gambling and now is without a copper coin to his name."

Polon swore at him.

"That is not nice," said Cara. "Those were bad words."

"Aye, but he's a bad man—and a worse gambler," Telors said, with a grin. "Now, why don't you run along and fetch us some hot drinks, princess."

Once the girl had left, Telors' expression hardened. "You shouldn't use language like that in front of her," he said sternly.

"Like I should give a shit?" answered Polon, moving to the window.

Telors turned to Bane. "Are you Gath?"

"No. Rigante."

"That will draw the crowds. Especially in Stone. Demon fighters, the Rigante. Or so we're told." He gave an easy smile as he said it, and Bane found himself liking the man.

"Here they come," said Polon.

Bane glanced out of the window and saw five riders approach the farmhouse. A servant took charge of their horses, and the men came inside. All were in their middle to late thirties, lean, grim-faced men. No one introduced Bane, and he wandered to a seat against the wall, where he sat and observed the group. The clothes they were wearing were of good quality but not new, and their boots were worn. Three more riders arrived within minutes, then four more. Girta and Cara brought cups of hot tisane, leaving them on the table at the center of the room. Telors took one, but the others ignored the drinks. Finally, with fourteen men gathered, Rage entered the room. He was dressed now in simple farm clothes, a sleeveless leather jerkin over a thick woolen shirt and leather leggings. Even so, he created a magnetic center to the room. Bane watched him. The man radiated power and purpose, and all conversation ceased as he moved to the hearth and stood with his back to the fire.

"You have all heard of the offer from Palantes," he said. "Persis Albitane needs to send them an answer. So let us discuss it. Who wants to begin?"

"How much coin?" asked Polon.

"Five thousand in gold guaranteed to the circus, plus a third of the gate. I would think at least four thousand people would attend. Persis has agreed to give one-tenth of the receipts to the eight who agree to take part. That should mean around two hundred in gold for the fighters."

"For the survivors of the eight, you mean?" said a swarthy, thin-faced man at the back of the room.

"Aye, Goren, the survivors," agreed Rage. "Money earned by those who die will be paid to their kin or to any named by the fighters before the bouts."

"That's fair," said Telors. "I have an ex-wife and two daughters. If I were to . . . fail . . . I would expect my tenth to be given to them."

"She left you, man," snorted Polon. "She's not worth a bent copper coin."

Telors ignored him.

"Are they sending Names?" asked another man.

"No Names," Rage told him. "All are young gladiators, yet to be blooded in the arena. But we are talking about Palantes, and they do not sign cowards. All will have been soldiers, and all will have proved themselves in exhibition displays."

"How do you feel about this, Rage?" asked a stocky man with close-cropped blond hair and a flattened nose.

"I am against it, Toris. But if seven are willing, I will be the eighth. One fact needs to be made clear: Circus Orises has made another loss this season, and there will be no money to pay winter wages. Now, some of you obtained employment at the docks last year, others with the timber men in the high country. This year, with the crop failures, there are some six thousand extra workers seeking employment in the city. Work will not be so easy to find. If the Palantes offer is accepted, every man will be on half wages until the new spring season."

"I want no part of it," said the thin-faced Goren. "I quit the major arenas ten years ago. I knew then that I was no longer as fast or as strong. I would not have lasted another season. Now I'm ten years older and certainly no faster. I have no wish to die on the sand."

"I understand that view," said Rage, "and I share it. It is eminent good sense. We are none of us here young men."

"He looks young to me," said Polon, pointing to Bane.

"He's not ready," said Rage, "and has no vote in this. You should all, I believe, consider the words of Goren. We are past our best, and Palantes would not have made this offer without first sending scouts to watch us. It is my belief that should we go ahead with this venture, few will survive to claim the gold. Now let us have a show of hands. How many believe this death bout should be refused?" He raised his own hand, the move echoed by Goren. All the others sat very still. Bane thought they looked uneasy. Rage lowered his arm. "Those for?" he asked. The thirteen others raised their hands.

"Very well. Now the question is, Who will compete?"

No one moved. Rage shook his head and smiled. The gesture shamed the fighters.

"I'll fight," said Polon. "The gods know I need the money."

"And I," said Telors.

Five others raised their hands, including the flat-nosed Toris. "I don't relish begging for winter work again," he said.

There was a brief moment of silence, then Telors looked at Rage. "Why are you fighting, my brother?" he asked. "The farm may not shower you with gold, but it does keep you fed."

Rage shrugged. "Palantes have a new man they are seeking to promote. They think killing me will enhance his reputation."

"Is it pride, then?" asked Goren. "Or do you think you are immortal?"

"I expect to find out," Rage told him.

The conversations went on for a little while, but then Rage dismissed the men and they filed out. Telors was the last to leave. He approached Rage, and they shook hands. "Not a good day, Brother," Telors said sadly.

"Poverty makes fools of us all," replied Rage.

When they had gone, Rage sat down in a wide chair and drank some cold tisane. Then he glanced at Bane. "That's the reality, boy," he said. "Menial labor on the docks or an agonizing death in the arena."

"Then why do it?" asked Bane.

"It is all they know."

"I meant you."

Rage took a deep breath. "Without me there would be no contest. I am still a Name. The man who kills me will become one." He leaned back in the chair. "Palantes is the largest and richest of the circuses. For seventeen of the last twenty years they have owned Gladiator One, the greatest of fighters. I was with Palantes, as was Voltan and now Brakus. But in order to stay at the top Palantes must acquire new fighters, fit, strong young men. Brakus is close to thirty now, and it is said he was cut badly in his last fight. So they need to blood young fighters, prepare them for the noise and the crowds, the tension and the fear. What better way than to bring them to border cities and towns, pitting them against old and tired men who have forgotten how to fight for their lives?"

"You sound bitter."

"Aye, I am a little bitter." He rubbed his hand across his face and pulled clear the red silk scarf. He looked older without it, thought Bane. "So," said Rage, "how did you enjoy your first morning?"

"It was tough. I have been . . . ill for some time. I am weaker than I thought."

Rage nodded. "I have been doing some thinking about you, Bane. Word reached us here three months ago that two knights of Stone were killed during the execution of the general Appius across the water. A third knight completed the execution and in doing so slew the young tribesman who had killed his comrades. This was in Accia. You came from Accia. Would I be right in thinking that the tribesman did not die?"

"You would be right," admitted Bane.

"He fought to save a Stone general, or so it is said. Why would he do that?"

"Perhaps he liked him. Perhaps he liked the man's daughter."

Rage fell silent for a moment. "Did he save the daughter?"

"No. He arrived to see the killer plunge his blade into her heart."

"Did he know the name of the killer?"

"Not at the time."

"But he knows now?"

"Aye, he knows."

"I suppose it would be reasonable to assume that the tribesman will seek out Voltan and challenge him?"

Bane looked directly into Rage's deep brown eyes. "What do you think?"

"I think Voltan is the best I have ever seen. He is uncanny. Almost mystical. He has a talent, like a stoat with a rabbit, for making his opponents feel mortal. He casts a spell over them. They become clumsy or reckless."

"Why did he quit the arena?"

Rage shrugged. "He ran out of good opponents. Then Nalademus, the Stone elder, offered to make him the lord of the Stone knights. Voltan accepted. He got a title, estates in Turgony, and the opportunity to kill without consequences."

"He will find there are consequences," said Bane. "I—"

"Say nothing more, boy!" snapped Rage. "I have no wish

to know of your feelings on this matter. If this tribesman we are talking about does hunt Voltan, I hope he has the sense to train first and to learn from his betters. But that is all I have to say on the matter."

"Why are we being so careful?" asked Bane.

"These are difficult times. There are spies everywhere. Some spy for Jasaray, others for Nalademus. I have no interest in politics or religion, and so I am safe. I will not be drawn into conspiracies, nor will I lie. So the less I know, the better for all concerned."

For five days Rage pushed Bane through an increasingly grueling routine. Leather straps with lead weights sewn into the lining were placed on his wrists and ankles for the six-mile run that began each morning's work. Bane was almost constantly exhausted. On the morning of the sixth day, after the obligatory run, which was made without added weights and at an almost leisurely pace, Rage led Bane back into the house.

"No more work today," he said.

Bane hid his relief. "Why not?" he asked.

"The body needs a little time to recover from heavy exercise. Today is a rest day. Work five, rest one."

"Do all gladiators use these methods?"

"No," said Rage. "Most rely on what they perceive as their natural strength and skill. Telors runs most days, but the others . . ." Rage opened his hands. "They do not see the need to punish themselves."

"But you do."

"Aye, I do. Always have." Outside the sky darkened, and heavy snow began to fall. The farmhouse was empty. Cara was attending lessons at the home of a teacher and the house servants had not yet arrived.

"You'll have to think of armor," said Rage. "Persis will offer to have some made for you, but he uses a cheap armorer with no pride. Do you have coin?"

"Aye."

"Then tell Persis you wish to find your own man. I would recommend Octorus. He is one of the best. You will need a good breastplate, greaves, a kilt of bronze reinforced with leather strips, wrist guards, and a well-fitting helm."

"No mail shirt?"

"Mail shirts are outlawed in the arena, as are neck torques. Even the breastplate is not worn in death bouts. They are meant to be bloody. That is how the crowd obtains its pleasure. Nothing pleases them more than seeing a brave man stagger back, his lifeblood pumping from a severed jugular."

"Were you always so contemptuous of your calling?" Bane asked him.

"Always," Rage told him. "And it was not a calling. I went into the arena because it was the only way I could make money. I never learned to love it."

The snow began to ease around noon, and Bane saddled the gray and followed the directions Rage gave him to the forge of Octorus. It was two miles north of Goriasa in a small settlement of some twenty stone-built houses constructed close to a garrison fort. Children were playing in the snow as Bane rode up, hurling snowballs at one another. One sailed close to the gray, which reacted skittishly and almost slipped on the ice.

"Sorry," yelled a boy with ginger hair. Bane grinned at him and rode the gray into a paddock beside the forge. A young man came out and took charge of the horse, asking Bane if he was staying the night. Bane told him no, then walked into the forge.

It was almost unbearably hot inside, with two charcoal fires burning and several men beating hammers upon red metal. Bane called out for Octorus, and one of the metalworkers cocked his thumb toward a door at the back of the forge. Bane moved through the forge, sweat beading his brow, and pushed open the door.

Beyond the forge was a gallery containing armor, helms, and weapons of all kinds, from longswords to axes, lances to pikes. At the far end sat an elderly man carefully burnishing a handsome helm with gold-edged ear guards.

Bane approached him. The old man looked up. He was still powerfully built, with a bull neck and massive forearms. His eyes were the color of slate, his hair still dark, his skin wrinkled and dry. "What do you want?" he asked.

"I need some armor made."

"Then go back to Goriasa. There are craftsmen there more suited to your pocket."

"I was told you were the best."

"I am the best," said Octorus. "But the best costs more, and I have no time to waste with poverty-stricken tribesmen."

Bane laughed. "Rage told me that you were a cantankerous old bastard but that I should make allowances in deference to your skill."

Octorus put aside the helm, laying it gently on a cloth. "If Rage sent you, then you cannot be as poor as you look," he said. He glanced at Bane's short sword and gave a derisive snort. "You don't have much judgment, though, judging by the pig sticker you carry."

"It has served me well so far," said Bane.

"Aye, fighting other savages who wear no body armor. Three whacks on one of my breastplates and that . . . thing would be either blunted or broken. So what are you looking for?"

Bane told him. Octorus listened in silence. Then he walked to the western wall, beckoning Bane to follow him. For the next few minutes he pointed out various breastplates and helms, highlighting the strengths and weaknesses of each. "This one will withstand a thrust from a charging lancer," he said, "but it is too heavy for arena work. It would slow you down. This one is light enough for a rider but would not withstand a prolonged assault by a fighter who knew what he was doing. Well, let's try a few and see how they feel."

After an hour Bane had settled on a burnished iron helm, an iron breastplate embossed with the shapes of pectoral and solar plexus muscles, a pair of bronze greaves, and an iron sword with a steel edge.

"That will be twenty-five in gold," said Octorus.

"I didn't think I was buying the forge as well," muttered Bane, opening his pouch and emptying the contents into the palm of his hand.

"Still time to change your mind," said Octorus.

Bane smiled. "I like your work. It is worth the money," he said, counting out the coins.

"Persis will give you eight back," said the old man. "That's what he normally pays, I understand. I'll have the armor sent to you. Now we'll have a drink to celebrate the transaction."

Octorus took him back through the gallery and into the house beyond, and the two men sat before a warm fire, nursing goblets of uisge.

"So," said Octorus, "are you fighting in this crazy death bout?"

"No. Rage says I am not ready."

Octorus shook his head. "No one is ever really ready," he said. "I fought twelve such bouts myself. Dry mouth, full bladder. When the gates open and you step out onto the sand, you never feel ready."

"You survived," Bane pointed out.

"Aye, I survived. Barely. Bastard pierced my lung just before I opened his throat. I was good but not great. After that I wasn't even good. Didn't have the wind anymore. Lung never really healed properly." He drained his uisge and refilled the goblet. "Now, Rage was great. Utterly deadly. Never seen a man more focused. Crowds didn't like him at first. He was too fast. Walk out, take the salute, wait for the trumpets, then move in." Octorus snapped his fingers. "Then, just like that, his man was dead and Rage was marching back to the exit gate. No entertainment value, you see. Then, of course, people began to bet on just how fast Rage would win. A drummer would sound a slow beat after the trumpet blast, and when the poor bastard facing Rage died, a man would call out the number of beats. Don't suppose there'll be a drummer this time." Octorus shook his head. "Rage is a fool to go back. You can't hold back the years. They march on, stealing a little from you with every passing season. Has it been announced who is to face him?"

"No," said Bane.

"It'll be Vorkas."

"Vorkas?"

"Circus Palantes took him on this season. He's a five-year veteran of the eastern wars. His first death bout was in the spring. He fought a good man—a Name. Killed him fast. Since then he's had around six, maybe seven, death bouts. But he needs a really big kill to become a crowd puller."

"Why do you think it will be him?"

"He ordered a new gladius from me. Said not to deliver it—he'd pick it up himself. I don't think Vorkas will be coming all the way from Stone just to spectate."

"Does Rage know this?"

"He may be old, but his mind is sharp enough. He'll have guessed."

It was snowing heavily when Bane rode the gray from the settlement, and it was growing bitterly cold. Wrapping his cloak around himself, he eased his mount out onto the road. His face and hands were blue as he reached the last rise above the farmhouse. Glancing down, he saw a black speck moving on the distant hillside. It was Rage running the training route. Bane angled the gray down the hill, dismounted, and led him into the stable. Unsaddling him, he rubbed him down, then walked him to a stall, forked hay into the feeding trough, and moved back to the house.

Cara was sitting on the windowsill of the main room, watching the snow-covered hillside for signs of Rage. She glanced up as Bane entered. "You should be fighting, not my grandpa," she said, her blue eyes angry.

"He would not let me, Cara. And anyway, without him there would be no fights at all."

"I know," she said. "Circus Palantes wants him dead so they can earn more money. I hate them!"

"He's very strong and tough," said Bane, removing his cloak and hanging it on a peg by the door. "Perhaps you shouldn't worry so much." The words sounded lame, but he could think of nothing else to say.

"Grandpa is an old man. He's enormously old. They shouldn't do this to him." Her face crumpled, and she began to cry. Bane grew increasingly uncomfortable.

"He is a man, and he makes his own decisions," said Bane.

"He is a great man," she replied, wiping her eyes and returning her gaze to the hills. "And he's coming back now. I'll make him a tisane. He always has a tisane after training." Jumping from the sill, she ran from the room.

Bane walked to the window and watched as Rage ran into the yard, then slowed and began to stretch. Stripping off his shirt and leggings, he lay down and rolled in the snow, then stood and stretched out his arms. He saw Bane, nodded a greeting, pulled on his leggings, and entered the house. Cara brought him a hot tisane, which he sipped in a wide chair by the fire. Cara sat on the arm of the chair, her hand on Rage's shoulder.

"I thought you said this was a rest day," observed Bane.

"It is for you, boy. But I've been resting all week nursing you along. I needed a good run to clear my head. Did you see Octorus?"

"Yes. He took almost all my coin."

"You won't regret it. His armor is the finest." To Cara he said: "Would you fetch me something to eat, princess?" She smiled happily and left the room. Rage drained his tisane and rose.

"He said you would be fighting someone named Vorkas."

"That's no surprise," said Rage. "Word has it Palantes is grooming him for next year's championship." Removing his red silk head scarf, he walked to the window, pushing it open. Scooping some snow from the outer sill, he rubbed it over his bald head.

"Is there anything I can do to help you?" asked Bane.

"Help me? In what way?"

"Well, you said I was slowing you down. Perhaps I should train alone."

Rage was silent for a moment, then he smiled. "Do not concern yourself, boy. It is not your problem. And I was only half-serious. You are coming along well. I saw you talking to Cara as I ran back. She looked upset."

"Very upset—and frightened."

"I'll talk to her." Rage walked back to his chair and slumped down. He looked dreadfully tired, thought Bane. The young Rigante looked closely at the aging warrior, seeing the many scars that crisscrossed his arms and upper body.

"I'd be fascinated," said Bane, "to hear what you're going to say to her. You know you shouldn't be fighting this bout. It is madness."

"It is all madness, Bane," Rage said sadly. "It always was. But I cannot change the way the world works. The farm is almost bankrupt, and my stake in Orises is worthless. All I have of worth is my name. The coin I make will ensure a comfortable life for Cara, at least until she is wed. I have named Goren as her guardian, and he will take good care of her."

"You talk as if you expect to die."

"I will or I won't, but either way Cara will be protected."

◇ 6 ◇

Persis Albitane always felt uncomfortable in the presence of Crimson Priests. Not that he had anything to fear, he thought hastily, but they had a knack of making a man feel that he did. He glanced at the man and was unnerved to find the priest staring at him. As with all priests, he had a shaven head and a forked beard dyed blood red. He was wearing an ankle-length tunic of pale gold, unadorned except for a long pendant of gray stone in a setting of cold iron.

"Are you sure you wouldn't like to sit down?" asked Persis. "They may be some time yet."

"I am comfortable, Persis Albitane," replied the priest. Persis shuddered inwardly at the use of his name.

"So," he said, forcing a smile. "Is this your first visit to Goriasa?"

"No. I came in the spring for the arrest of two traitors."

"Yes, of course. I remember now. And how are things in Stone?"

"Things?"

Persis could feel sweat trickling down his back. "It is a long time—almost two years—since I was last in the great city. I was wondering . . ." What was I wondering? he thought, his mind close to panic. How many innocent people have you dragged from their beds to be burned at the stake? What new levels of horror and cruelty have you managed to achieve?

"You were wondering?" prompted the priest.

"One so misses the city," said Persis, recovering his composure. "The theaters and dining houses, the parties and gatherings. Time moves on, and one wonders if everything is as it was in the golden rooms of memory. I always like to hear

135

news from Stone. It lessens the sadness at being so far from home."

"The city remains beautiful," said the priest, "but the cancer of heresy is everywhere and must be hunted down and cut out."

"Indeed so," agreed Persis.

"How many of the tree cult thrive in Goriasa?" asked the priest.

"I don't know of any," lied Persis.

"They are here. I can smell their vileness."

The door opened, and the little slave Norwin entered. Seeing the priest, he bowed low. Then he turned to Persis. "The Palantes representatives are downstairs," he said.

Relief swept over the fat circus owner. "Bring them up," he told him.

Norwin bowed again to the priest and backed out of the small room. All contracts over one thousand in gold now had to be witnessed by a priest, who then pocketed two percent of the money.

"I understand Rage is to fight again," said the priest.

"Yes, indeed. Are you partial to the games?"

"Bravery is what makes our civilization great," said the priest. "It is good for our citizens to see martial courage."

The door opened once more, and Norwin led two men inside. Both were middle-aged and wearing expensive clothing, their cloaks edged with ermine. Seeing the priest, they bowed. Persis was delighted to see that they were as tense as he in the man's presence. Who wouldn't be? he thought. In ten years they had grown from a scholastic order compiling a history of Stone to become the most feared organization in the land.

The first of the two men, powerfully built, his long dark hair drawn back into a ponytail, produced two papyrus scrolls, which he handed to Persis. The man bowed. "Lord Absicus sends you his greetings. I am Jain, first slave to Palantes. This is my colleague, Tanyan."

Even their slaves are better dressed than I, thought Persis, noting the quality of Jain's long blue woolen tunic edged with gold, the chest embroidered with an eagle's head in black silk.

Persis offered them seats, then perused the scrolls. They

were standard contracts, outlining the amounts payable and the conditions of the day. He read slowly through each of the clauses. Towards the end he hesitated, then looked up at Jain. "It says here that Circus Orises shall pay the cost of travel and hospitality for the Palantes team. This was not mentioned in our earlier negotiations."

"That must have been an oversight," Jain said smoothly.

"The clause will be removed," said Persis.

"I think not," said Jain. "You are receiving a fine sum for your part in this . . . little tourney. Lord Absicus made it very clear to me that there was to be no change to the contract."

"Ah, well," said Persis, "then what can I say?" He looked into Jain's dark eyes and saw the glint of triumph and the barely masked contempt. Glancing up at the priest, Persis gave a rueful smile. "I am so sorry for wasting your time, sir." Pushing himself to his feet, he gathered up his cloak and walked toward the door.

"Where are you going?" asked Jain.

"To the bathhouse," said Persis. "I shall have a long soak and then a massage. Please convey my respects to Lord Absicus."

"You haven't signed the contract!"

Persis paused in the doorway. "There is no contract," he said. Then he left.

"Wait!" wailed Jain, rising from his chair so fast that he knocked it backward. He scurried after Persis, catching him in the outer corridor. "Come, come," he said, "we are reasonable men. Let us negotiate."

"There is nothing to negotiate," said Persis. "Either we walk back in, remove the clause, and sign or I leave."

Jain leaned in close, and Persis could smell the perfume on his oiled hair. "Let us be frank, sir. You are in debt and close to insolvency. This contract is a lifesaver for you. You do not really want to see it fail."

"Good-bye," said Persis, pushing open the outer door and stepping into the sunshine.

"I agree!" shouted Jain. "The clause will be removed! Now let us conclude our business."

Persis stood for a moment, then walked back inside.

Later, when all the visitors had departed, Norwin returned

to the office. "If you were as good at running a circus as you are at negotiating, we wouldn't have found ourselves in this position in the first place," he said.

"That's teetering on the edge of being a compliment," said Persis.

"Damn, it wasn't meant to be," said Norwin. "Perhaps I phrased it badly."

Persis grinned at him. "Tomorrow you will see that all our debts are paid, the longest to have interest added. We will need goodwill for next season."

"We'll need more than goodwill," said Norwin. "With Rage dead there won't be a Circus Orises. What is wrong with you, Persis? You are a bright, intelligent man. You were a phenomenally successful merchant. Why can you not see that Orises is a doomed venture?"

"I can see it," said Persis. "But I can't help it. I love the circus, watching the crowd applaud, seeing the delight on their faces as the horses ride and the athletes compete. I get a greater thrill from this than any I ever experienced making profits. And I dream of seeing this stadium full of people—all cheering."

Norwin pinched the bridge of his long, thin nose. "Yes, yes," he said, "nice dream. But let us take a long, cool look at the reality. Goriasa is a conquered Keltoi city, inhabited largely by Gath tribesmen who have little interest in the circus. Our people number less than three thousand. There are simply not enough Stone citizens to fill the stadium. And as for watching the horses run, need I remind you that Palantes stole our horse-riding acrobats?"

Persis sat lost in thought. "That's it!" he said suddenly.

"Horse acrobats?"

"No. Filling the stadium. We must put on shows for the Gath. Find something they would want to see."

"Sheep shagging springs to mind," offered Norwin.

"Be serious, my friend," chided Persis. "The Keltoi are not the barbarians we pretend them to be. Their metalworking is exquisite, their culture older than ours."

"I accept that," said Norwin. "However, think on this: They are a warrior race, but even when death bouts were common here, the Gath did not come in any great numbers."

"I know. They did not want to pay to watch men of Stone fighting one another. But would they pay to see one of their own fighting a man of Stone to the death?"

Norwin said nothing for a moment. "Now, that is something to consider," he whispered.

Magistrate Hulius Marani was bored. Not that anyone in the court would notice, for his sharp, hooded eyes appeared to miss nothing, his heavy face holding a serious expression as he listened—apparently intently—to every shred of evidence. His gaze only occasionally flickered toward the ornate hourglass and its trickling sand.

He sat and pretended to concentrate on the case before him, in which a young Gath farmer was arguing that his lands had been tricked from him by a Stone citizen. The case was well presented, but since the citizen had already paid a large bribe to Hulius, the issue was not in doubt. The Gath was an idiot. Hulius had invited him to his home and given him every opportunity to offer a larger bribe, but the man, like the rest of his barbarous tribe, had no understanding of the manner in which civilized people conducted disputes. He had ranted on about justice and foul business practices, just as he was doing now.

Hulius waited for the man to finish his argument—which was only good manners—then found against him. The man shouted abuse, and Hulius ordered the court guardians to take him away, sentencing him to twenty lashes for his impertinence.

After the brief excitement boredom settled on him once more like a shroud.

As Goriasa's first magistrate, the recipient of one-fifth of all fines paid, Hulius Marani would have been wealthy even without the numerous bribes. He had ordered a shipment of fine marble from Turgony so that a suitable house could be constructed for him to the south of the port. He had a loyal wife and a beautiful Gath mistress and was treated with respect and courtesy wherever he traveled. That was a far cry from his days as a shipping clerk in Stone, where he had worked all day in a cramped office, earning one-quarter of a silver piece a day. Hulius had labored for two years before discovering his route to high office and a measure of fame.

On difficult sea voyages some bales of cloth became damaged by salt water and thus were rendered unsalable. They were then dumped unceremoniously alongside the warehouses. One day Hulius cut into such a bale, green silk from the east, and found that only the outer layers had been seriously damaged. At the center of the bale he found that four of the twenty-five rolled lengths of silk were in perfect condition. Those he sold, creating his first profit. As the months passed, he amassed ten times his salary from such items and in doing so made valuable contacts in the local industries. One day a ship's captain saw him, late in the evening, examining a damaged bale. The man called him aside and suggested a business partnership. All merchants accepted a small percentage of loss during sea travel. For the right sum the captain would put aside good bales and between them he and Hulius could label them damaged goods.

It had worked beautifully.

Within the year Hulius had put down a deposit on a piece of land and commissioned a house. His wife, Darnia, had been delighted at his growing wealth. Not so his employers, who descended one day with ten soldiers from the watch just as Hulius was overseeing the loading of a wagon with ten undamaged bales.

The captain also was taken. He was hanged four days later. But then, he had no friends in high places. Hulius, by contrast, had used some of his profits to fund the political career of his wife's cousin, a man who had now risen to a high rank in Jasaray's government. Thus, an agreed sum was paid to the employer, and Hulius was offered the post of first magistrate in Goriasa. And now he was close to becoming rich despite a large part of the money made being sent back to Darnia's powerful relative.

Yet despite his wealth and the ease of his lifestyle, Hulius was bored with Goriasa and the interminable petty cases brought before him: broken contracts, matrimonial disputes, and arguments over land rights and borders. He longed for the dining rooms and pleasure establishments of Stone's central district, the magnificently skilled whores, the musicians, and the beautifully prepared food with recipes from a dozen different cultures.

Hulius glanced down at the list before him. One more hearing and then he could visit his mistress.

Three men filed into the new courthouse, bowed before the dais on which Hulius sat in his white robe of justice, then took up their positions to the right of the two engraved wooden lecterns. Hulius recognized the gladiator Rage and the circus owner Persis Albitane. Between them stood a Gath tribesman, a lean yet powerful young man with golden hair and odd colored eyes. The door at the back of the room opened, and a Crimson Priest strode in. He did not bow before the dais but walked immediately to stand to the left of the lecterns. Hulius noted the surprise on the face of Persis Albitane and felt a small knot of tension begin in the pit of his stomach.

The magistrate stared down at the document before him, then spoke. "The registration of the tribesman Bane to be allowed to take part in martial displays for Circus Orises," he read aloud. "Who sponsors this man?"

"I do," said Persis.

"And who stands beside him to pledge his good faith."

"I do," Rage said solemnly.

Hulius looked at Bane. "And do you, Bane, pledge to uphold the highest traditions of courage and—"

"I object to these proceedings," said the Crimson Priest.

Sweat began to trickle from Hulius' temple. "On what grounds, Brother?"

"The law. It is forbidden for Gath tribesmen to carry swords for any reason save those employed as scouts in the service of the army of Stone."

"Yes, indeed," said Hulius, thankful that the matter could be dealt with simply. He had no wish at all to offend a priest. "In that case—"

"Bane is not a Gath," said Persis Albitane. "He is of the Rigante tribe and was recommended to me by Watch Captain Oranus of Accia. As a Rigante he is not subject to the laws governing the Gath."

Hulius felt sick and glanced nervously at the Crimson Priest. "Even so," said the priest, "the man is a barbarian, and it should be considered below the dignity of any honest citizen to employ him in the capacity of gladiator."

"It may be argued," said Persis, "that such employment in itself is 'below dignity,' but it is certainly not illegal. Therefore, I respectfully request that the objection be ruled inadmissible. There is no law to prevent a foreigner being gainfully employed by a citizen of Stone. Indeed, there are many gladiators, past and present, from foreign lands."

Hulius would have loved to rule against Persis Albitane, but all his rulings were written down and sent on to Stone, and this was not a matter of a magistrate's judgment—which could be bought at a price—but of the law of Stone. Hulius sat silently, his mind whirling, seeking some way to accommodate the priest. But there were no subtleties to the issue, no gray areas to exploit. The case was simple.

Hulius looked into the fat face of Persis Albitane. Perhaps there was still a way out. "I would think that a loyal citizen of Stone would accede to the wishes of the venerable order of Crimson Priests," he said smoothly. "You are quite right when you say that the Rigante are not under the jurisdiction of Stone, but equally they are Keltoi, and the spirit of the law is what—I believe—concerns the brother." Surely Persis would understand what he was saying. No one wanted to come under the scrutiny of the temple. Hulius looked at the man and saw he was sweating. Then Persis spoke.

"With respect, Magistrate, there is no such creature as the spirit of the law," he said. "The laws of Stone are drafted by intelligent, farseeing men, among them the senior priests of the Crimson Temple. If you believe the law to be carelessly drafted, then you should write to the council forthwith. However, as has already been established, my request today does not break the law, and I once more submit the name of Bane."

In that moment Hulius understood the true joys of boredom. To be bored was to be free of danger, far from perilous activities. "I agree," he said miserably. "We will continue with the pledge."

The Crimson Priest said nothing more but stalked from the room.

Hulius Marani listened to the pledge, signed the necessary document, added the wax seal of justice, and rose from his chair.

The day had soured considerably, and he had no desire now to visit his mistress.

Stadium Orises had never looked better, thought Persis as he strolled out across the fresh sand to the center of the arena. For two weeks, much to Norwin's disgust at the expense, carpenters and workmen had been laboring to repair the more run-down sections of the tiered seating areas. The stadium had been hastily constructed eleven years earlier, mostly of timber supported on stone columns. The original owner, Gradine—a man of limitless ambition and little capital—had not been able to afford the normal embellishments: statues, fresco-decorated areas for the nobility, dining halls, and public urinals. Stadium Orises was at best functional. The arena floor was two hundred feet in diameter, surrounded by an eight-foot wall beyond which were twenty rows of tiered bench seats. Many of them were warped and cracked. Shading his eyes, Persis watched the carpenters at work on the last section. The new benches gleamed with linseed oil.

Norwin trudged across the sand to join his master. "Well, once more you have managed to battle your way to poverty," he said. "I have completed the accounts. With most debts paid, half wages for the gladiators throughout the winter, and—assuming we get around three thousand people for the games, with a further thousand in revenue—we will be coinless by the first day of spring."

"Spring is a long way off," Persis said happily. "Look at the stadium, Norwin. It is beginning to look very fine."

"Like a seventy-year-old whore with dyed hair and fresh face paint," said Norwin. "Anyway, the carriage is here. I told the driver to wait. Are you ready?"

Persis glanced at the sky, which was clear and blue. The day was cold but not overly so. "We should get a good crowd at the field," he said.

"Of course we'll get a good crowd," said Norwin. "It is a free day, and you have spent a fortune on fire breathers, acrobats, jugglers, and food. Of course people will come. But they would have come anyway. Palantes has brought an elephant."

"An elephant? Ah, what it must be to have unlimited funds.

Can you imagine how many people we could draw if we had an elephant?"

Norwin shook his head. Then he smiled. "You are a good, sweet man, Persis, and I love you like a brother. But you lack foresight. How many times does one need to see an elephant before one is bored? If we had such a beast, the crowd would come once. After that we would be left with enormous feeding costs. Then there would be trainers and handlers and special housing for it. Then, with debt collectors stalking us like rabid wolves, I would urge you to sell the creature. You would say no because you had grown to like it."

"True," Persis agreed affably. "But an elephant!"

"Let's go to the carriage," said Norwin, "before I find a club and beat you to death with it."

Persis laughed, and the two men walked across the sand to the western gladiators' gate, on through the darkness of the sword room and the surgeon's ward, up the stairs, and out once more into the sunshine.

The carriage was a converted wagon drawn by two sway-backed horses. Persis climbed the steps to the rear and sat down. "I should have brought my cushion," he said as Norwin moved in alongside him. "And didn't I ask you to hire the gilded bronze chariot from the garrison?"

"Aye, you did. But Palantes was there before me, which I thank the Source for, since the cost was obscene."

"You should not mention the Source so publicly," Persis rebuked him.

Norwin nodded. "It was a slip of the tongue. But it hurts me to be so secretive. I sometimes feel that I am betraying the Source by not speaking out, by hiding my faith."

"They are burning heretics in Stone," whispered Persis. "Or casting them into the arena to be torn to death by wild animals. Yours is a perilous religion, my friend. Your faith could kill you."

"That's true. It frightens me sometimes. But last night I went again to listen to the Veiled Lady, and she filled us all with the power of spirit. And she healed a man, Persis. Laid her hands on him, and all his sores vanished. You should come and hear her."

"I can think of nothing I would rather do less," said Persis. "One day soon the priests will come in force to Goriasa. I do not wish to become kindling for their fires. Have you seen Rage today?" he asked, changing the subject.

"No, but he'll be there."

"It is to be Vorkas. I had rather hoped the rumors were untrue."

"Rage made the decision, not you, Persis. He is his own man."

"I fear he is angry with me over Bane."

"Rage doesn't get angry. And anyway, the news that a Keltoi is fighting a gladiator is already the talk of the city. It should draw in a good crowd."

Out on the open road the wind was more chilling, and Norwin pulled a woolen cap from the pocket of his heavy coat. Tugging it over his balding head, he glanced at his master. "Bane has more chance of surviving than the man he replaced. And Bane himself was delighted to fight. He is a Keltoi. They live to rush around with swords and butcher one another."

As they reached the high road, the wagon moved more slowly, for the road was packed with people moving toward the field. From the highest point Persis could see the tents and food stalls below. Already there were more than a thousand people gathered there, most of them crowding the eastern section. "There it is!" said Persis, pointing. "There's the elephant!"

"I have seen elephants before," Norwin told him.

"It is really big."

"That's a novelty," said Norwin. "I thought maybe they'd bring one of those famous small elephants."

Kall Manorian had only ever taken part in two death bouts, the first against a young criminal sentenced to fight in the arena and the second against a fine young gladiator from Circus Poros. Kall still felt a shudder go through him as he recalled that second fight. The man had been more skilled, faster, and Kall had seen in his eyes a blazing cruelty and confidence that had chilled him to the bone.

The fact that Kall still lived was due to the carelessness of

an unnamed circus employee who did not adequately cover
with sand the blood from the previous fight. Kall's opponent
had slipped just as Kall attacked. He literally had fallen sideways onto Kall's blade, which had lanced up under his chin
strap, slicing his jugular. Kall had made an offering to the god
of Stone and walked away from the arena.

Often in the intervening years he had suffered nightmares
about the fight. Now, at thirty-seven, he had walked away
again. When Rage had first told them about the offer from
Palantes, Kall had volunteered. In part this was to test his
courage, but also—if he was being honest with himself—it
was because he had believed more of the others would step
forward and Rage would not choose him. But the others had
not volunteered in sufficient numbers, and Kall had gone
home that night in a state bordering on terror.

Three days later he had secretly visited Persis Albitane. He
had intended to lie about being called back to Stone after a
family bereavement. Instead he had found himself blurting
out all his fears. In his shame he had begun to weep. He had always held fat Persis in faint contempt, but on this day he had
found the man to be more than considerate. Persis had risen
from his seat behind the desk, walked around, and patted him
on the shoulder. "You are a good man, Kall," he had said, "and
a brave one. You proved your courage in the arena. Now calm
yourself. It is no disgrace to know one's limitations." Persis
had poured him a goblet of wine, then perched himself on the
edge of the desk. "I do have a plan. I believe the young man
Bane would like to fight. I shall ask him today. If he agrees, I
shall tell Rage that you are being replaced. I will not tell him
you requested it. No one need know of our conversation."

The relief had been total.

But now, sitting in the armor tent, Kall felt wretched. The
other gladiators were putting on their armor, ready to share
the warriors' cup, and several of them had approached him,
commiserating with him, telling him how they believed
Persis had treated him unfairly in striking him from the team.

Kall sat in the corner, nursing his shame. He saw Rage
buckle on his breastplate and strap his scabbard to his hip.
Rage glanced across at him, his face expressionless. Kall

looked away. Rage was an old man, and tomorrow he was going to die. But he had not walked away even when he had learned he was to face Vorkas. Kall shivered.

He had seen Vorkas a few moments before, walking with other gladiators from Palantes. The man looked like a lion among wolves. Palantes had said they were bringing no Names—no fighters listed for the next season's championship. Technically this might have been true, but there was still a month to go before registration was needed, and there was no question that Vorkas would be among those listed. Seven successful death bouts, each of them apparently won with ease. People were speaking of him as a new Voltan.

Kall stared down at his hands. "Walk with me," said Rage. Kall jerked, for he had not heard the big man approach. He rose and followed Rage out into the weak sunlight. Crowds were everywhere, and Rage led him to the rear of the tent. "You want to talk?" asked Rage, tying his red silk scarf around his head.

"What about?"

"About what is troubling you, Kall."

Kall closed his eyes. "I wish I was more like you," he said. "But I'm not. Never was, never could be." He drew in a deep breath. "But I do not like to deceive my friends. Everyone's been telling me how sorry they are that I have been so badly treated. I wasn't badly treated, Rage. I went to Persis and told him I was too frightened to fight. There! It is said!"

"Aye," whispered Rage. "It is said. You think yourself a coward?"

"I am a coward. Have I not proved it?"

"You listen to me, Kall, and be sure you understand what I am saying: You are not a coward. If I were beset by foes, I would be more than relieved to know you were by my side. And you would be by my side, Kall. For you are a man of honor, a man to be relied on. But this . . . this farce is not about honor. It is about money. Palantes wants its young lions to taste blood, to taste it without too much risk. They have spent huge sums promoting these warriors, and they expect to make—eventually—a hundred times their outlay as a result. Now stop punishing yourself. You hear me?"

Kall nodded. At that moment the young barbarian Bane

strolled around to the rear of the tent. "Persis is asking for you," he told Rage. The old gladiator swung on his heel and walked away.

Kall looked at the tribesman, noting his new armor. It looked expensive. Kall had never been able to afford such a breastplate and helm. "Do you know who you'll be fighting?" he asked.

Bane shrugged. "They told me a name. It means nothing to me."

"What name?"

"Someone called Falco."

"Three fights," said Kall. "Never been cut."

Bane seemed uninterested. Then he leaned in toward Kall. "Why are we meeting them today?" he asked. "And why are we dressed for battle?"

"Did Rage not tell you?"

"He said that we were to share the warriors' cup, that we were to drink with our opponents. Why should we drink with people we are going to kill?"

"It is a ritual," said Kall. "It shows the crowds that we honor each other and that there is no hatred in our hearts." He smiled. "It also helps sell tickets."

"Ah," said Bane. "That I understand."

Together the two men walked back to the tent. Out on the field a trumpet sounded, and the crowd fell silent. Two men climbed to the back of a wagon. The first man's voice boomed out, in Turgon, welcoming the citizens. The second spoke moments later in Keltoi, repeating the message. Then they introduced the first gladiator from Circus Palantes. The warrior, in magnificent armor, strode from the Palantes tent to stand before a long table upon which were set sixteen golden goblets filled to the brim with watered wine. Then Polon's name was called out.

The sandy-haired warrior, holding his helm under his arm, stepped up to the table, waving to the crowd.

One by one the names were called. Kall felt a second wave of relief that he was not among them. Falco was called. Kall glanced across the field and saw a tall man stride forward. He moved well. Then came the shout: "And his opponent, Bane of the Rigante." A mighty roar went up from the Keltoi section of the crowd. Bane waved to them, then walked across to the table.

Then Vorkas was summoned. Kall felt a ripple of fear as he saw the man. Vorkas was impressive, broad-shouldered and well over six feet tall.

Lastly came Rage. Once again the crowd cheered, but Rage did not acknowledge them. He moved to the table to stand opposite Vorkas. Then the warriors raised their goblets, offering a toast to their opponents.

Kall turned away and trudged back into the armor tent.

For Bane the ritual at the field was baffling almost beyond belief. Enemies were people who sought one's death. They were not men one drank a toast to or shook hands with. He looked at the man opposite him. Falco was lithe and lean, the bones of his face flat, his mouth a thin, tight line. The eyes were light blue, and no fear showed in them. He met Bane's gaze and seemed about to speak. Then the gladiators around him raised their goblets. "To valor!" they shouted. Applause rippled from the crowd. Bane tasted the wine. It was sour on the tongue.

Bane glanced to his right and saw the mightily muscled Vorkas lean forward. "By the Stone, you look old and tired," he told Rage. "I shall take no joy in killing you. It will be like killing my grandfather." Rage smiled and said nothing. He sipped his wine, then placed his goblet back on the table. "And I can see the fear in your eyes," continued Vorkas.

The toast over, the gladiators moved away from the table. Bane walked alongside Rage. "You should have broken his face," he said.

"Why?"

"He insulted you."

"He was trying to intimidate me. Tell me, what did you notice about your opponent?"

Bane thought about the question. "He had blue eyes," he said.

"He was left-handed," snapped Rage. "Now let's get out of this armor and go home. There is work to do."

"I thought we were supposed to walk among the crowds and let people see us."

"They have seen us," said Rage. "And we have no time for this foolishness."

An hour later, back at the farmhouse, Rage, carrying two wooden short swords, led Bane out into the training area. Tossing one weapon to Bane, he took up a fighting position, feet well apart.

They had practiced in this way for some days now, and Bane had learned many secrets. The first was—as Rage had explained some days before—that all gladiators had their own rhythms and mannerisms. The longer a fight went on, the more of them would be revealed to a man with a keen eye. "Some men," Rage had said, "will narrow their eyes just before they attack; others will drop a shoulder or lick their lips. These actions are unconscious, but if you read them, they will give you a heartbeat's advantage. All the best gladiators take a little time at the start of a bout to learn the opponent's moves."

"You didn't," said Bane. "Octorus told me they beat a drum when you fought and bet on how many beats it would be before your man died."

Rage shook his head. "I used to go to the other circuses and sit in the crowd. I watched future opponents, then I went home and wrote down what I had observed."

"Have you seen Vorkas before?" Bane had asked.

"No, but I know how he will fight."

"How?"

"He will seek to extend the bout, wearing me down—a nick here, a cut there. But he won't let it last too long. He won't want people to think he had to struggle against an old man, but he will milk the moment."

"You don't sound too concerned."

"I am concerned, but about you, boy. Have you not understood yet why, when we practice, not one of your lunges ever gets through?"

Bane smiled. "I thought it was because you were too fast and too skillful for me."

"It is your left hand that gives you away. The fingers flick open just before you lunge."

"I will work on that."

"Best to be aware of it but to let it happen naturally. Falco will begin to read it. Then, at some point in the bout, clench your left fist, hold it closed, then attack. That one moment of misdirection could win it for you."

Day after day they had worked, and Bane had improved rapidly.

Now Rage stood before him yet again, but this time he was holding the wooden sword in his left hand. "Attack me," said the older man. Bane had—or so he believed—begun to read Rage's moves. Moving in suddenly, he lunged at Rage's chest. Instead of parrying the blade, Rage swayed to his left, and his wooden sword smacked against Bane's right ear. Bane tumbled forward, righted himself, then swung back to face Rage.

"There is no point in adopting a fighting pose, Bane," Rage said softly. "You are dead. Left-handers are pure poison. They have a great advantage in that most of the people they fight are right-handed, so they get used to such combat, whereas their opponents are forced to rethink all their attacking moves."

"How do I fight him?" asked Bane, rubbing his ear.

"Generally you would attack a left-hander to his right, circling away from his sword arm. But I do not know this man's style. Attack me again."

For another hour the two men practiced. Several times Bane managed to get behind Rage's defense and once touched the wooden blade to Rage's throat.

"That was good," said Rage, "but do not get too cocky. I am not a left-hander. Let us take a break, and then we'll work on a little strategy I've used twice against lefters."

Inside the farmhouse Rage lit a fire, and the two men ate a light meal of toasted bread and cold beef washed down with water.

"Are you worried about tomorrow?" asked Bane.

"No. You?"

"No."

Rage smiled, which was a rare sight. "Then we are a pair of fools. Have you placed a wager?" Bane shook his head. "Then you should. You've been given good odds. Four to one."

"Odds?"

"Do the Rigante not gamble?"

"Aye, we gamble."

152 MIDNIGHT FALCON

"But not for coin?"

"No. Not in my settlement."

"I see," said Rage. "Well, here we gamble incessantly. The odds merely reflect your perceived chances of success. Four to one means that if you wager one gold coin on yourself and you win, you'll get four back plus your original stake. In other words, you'll start with one gold coin and end up with five."

"What are your odds?" asked Bane.

"Ten to one."

"Which means that you are considered to have a one in ten chance of surviving?"

"Yes. Vorkas is young and strong."

"He is also arrogant, and I didn't like him," said Bane.

"I was arrogant once, so I am a little more forgiving. Now let us get back to work."

They trained for another hour, then the snow began to fall once more. Bane was tired, but he was grateful to the older warrior for the time spent. As they were finishing their exercises, two riders came down the hill. Telors and Polon dismounted, led their horses into the stable, then strolled out to where Bane and Rage waited.

"You missed some great fun," said the black-bearded Telors. "The elephant broke loose from its chains and ran into the crowd. It was last seen heading over the hills, being chased by a dozen Palantes slaves."

"Anyone hurt?" asked Rage.

"No one dead," Polon put in, with a wide grin. "You should have seen the crowd scatter."

"You are in a good mood," Rage said to Polon.

"Aye, I am. The man I am to fight has frightened eyes, so I've spent the morning wondering how to spend my gold. Telors and I are going into Garshon's place tonight. Find a couple of whores. You want to come?"

"No," said Rage.

"It will relax you," said Telors.

"I am relaxed, my friends. And I'll feel more relaxed when I'm in my bed and sleeping like a babe."

They stood in silence for a moment, then Telors stepped

forward and held out his hand. "Well, once more we spit in his eye," he said softly.

"Once more," agreed Rage, gripping his hand. Polon also shook hands, then both men returned to their horses and rode from the farm. Rage watched them go.

"Spit in whose eye?" asked Bane.

"Death," said Rage.

Bane sat quietly in the windowless sword room below the stadium, two lanterns flickering on the wall. Through the doorway he could see the body of Polon. Blood no longer oozed from the gaping wounds in his chest and throat, but it still dripped from the table on which he lay, each drop making a small plopping sound as it struck the pool of dark liquid on the floor below. Polon's head had lolled to the left, and no one had closed his dead eyes.

His bout had lasted for some time, and the men then in the sword room—Bane, Rage, and Telors—had all begun to think Polon might be the first to prove victorious for Circus Orises. Four Orises men had been killed already, their bodies dragged from the arena, carried through the sword room, and laid out of sight.

Then the door known as the gladiators' gate had opened, and sunlight had poured into the darkness. Two men entered, carrying Polon's body, laying it on the table in the room beyond. Telors rose and put on his iron helm. His chest was bare, but a coarse linen bandage had been wrapped around his belly to prevent his guts from spilling to the sand. Rage rose alongside him. The old gladiator said nothing, and the two men shook hands. Then Telors walked out into the light. The two slaves followed him, pulling shut the door and plunging the room back into gloom.

Another figure entered the room from the rear. It was the surgeon Landis, a stout, balding man, round-shouldered and bull-necked. He sat quietly, his canvas tool bag beside him.

First came the sound of trumpets, then the roar of the crowd filled the room and the occasional clash of metal on metal filtered through to the waiting men. Bane found the situation bizarre. He had fought before. Indeed, he had killed before. But always there had been passion. Here, in the semi-darkness, there was an unnatural calm as he sat with the dead. He glanced at Rage, who was tying his red scarf into place. The big gladiator moved to the far side of the room and began to stretch.

Bane took a deep breath and closed his eyes. There was a huge roar from the crowd, then silence. He became aware that the blood had stopped dripping from the table on which they had laid the dead Polon. Bane rose, put on his burnished helm, and stood quietly. His heart was beating fast, and he felt suddenly breathless.

The door opened, and Telors walked in, removing his helm and hurling it at the far wall. It clanged like a bell as it rolled to the floor. Blood was flowing from several wounds in Telors' upper arms, and there was a cut just above his left knee. The surgeon rose as Telors entered and beckoned him through to the back room. Telors strode after him.

Bane drew his short sword. He walked toward the door. Rage's voice stopped him. "Stay focused. Put the crowd from your mind and concentrate on your opponent. Do not use the strategy too quickly."

Bane's mouth was dry. The door opened, and he walked into the sunlight. The noise of the crowd was thunderous. Eleven thousand people were crammed into the stands. Bane halted and scanned the crowd. He had never seen so many people in one place, and for a moment he was awed by the multitude. The Gath had come in their thousands to watch a Rigante fight a warrior from Stone. Bane drew in a deep breath. The sky above was clear and blue, and there was no breeze. Bane started to walk once more toward the elevated section containing Persis Albitane and his guests. The gladiators' gate at the eastern end of the arena opened, and Falco stepped out. Bane did not look at him but kept his eyes on the small group of men in the owner's enclosure.

Persis was sitting alongside a thin man in a purple robe, and ranged about them were their guests, the rulers of Goriasa. There were several men in full armor, and Bane took them to be the officers of the garrison. The magistrate Hulius was there, and several children were clustered by the front rail. Bane found their presence distasteful. Children should not watch while men fought and died.

Putting such thoughts from his mind, he approached the enclosure and waited for Falco to join him.

Then the two men raised their swords in salute to the guests, and Bane spoke the words Rage had taught him. "Those who are about to die salute you!" He turned to Falco and offered his hand. The man from Palantes shook it. Then they turned away, walked back to the center of the arena, and waited. Persis rose and signaled the trumpeters. Three notes pealed out.

The crowd erupted. Falco attacked. For a single heartbeat Bane did not react, then he parried wildly, spinning away from the ferocious onslaught. Their blades met again and again. As Rage had predicted, fighting a left-hander was more than difficult, and Bane felt clumsy and uncoordinated.

Screening out the baying of the crowd, he focused on his opponent. Falco moved well, always in balance. He was fast and confident, and Bane was hard-pressed to hold him at bay. A part of his mind was filled with gratitude for the training Rage had put him through, for without it he would have been dead in moments.

They fought furiously for some while. Neither drew blood in the opening exchanges as they sought to read each other's moves. Rage had told Bane over and over again that a duel was like a dance. It had its own rhythms. Falco dropped his right shoulder and lunged. Bane parried. Falco's right foot lashed out, hooking behind Bane's heel and tripping him. Bane hit the ground hard. Falco rushed in. Bane rolled, his opponent's gladius striking the sand. Bane scrambled to his feet. Blocking another thrust, Bane lashed out with his fist, striking Falco full in the face and hurling him back. Bane charged—and almost died. Falco, recovering quickly, stabbed out. Bane swayed to his right, slashing his own sword swiftly downward. The blade clanged against Falco's bronze wrist guard. Falco threw a punch into Bane's belly, and the two men backed away from each other and began to circle.

Bane leapt in, sending a vicious cut toward Falco's throat. Falco swayed away, his gladius licking out and cutting the top of Bane's shoulder. Blood sprayed from the wound, and once more the crowd erupted.

"The beginning of the end," said Falco. "I have played with you long enough, savage."

The Stone gladiator now attacked with renewed frenzy, his swordwork dazzling. Bane stayed cool, blocking every attack, waiting for his moment. Falco's right shoulder dropped. Bane brought his hands together, transferring his gladius to his left. Falco lunged. Bane parried it with his wrist guard. In that fraction of a heartbeat Falco registered the move that would kill him. His eyes widened in terror. The gladius now in Bane's left hand plunged into Falco's unprotected belly and up through his heart. Falco sagged against his killer. Bane pushed him away, dragging his gladius clear.

Even as Falco hit the sand, slaves came running to remove the body and clear away the blood.

Bane raised his bloody sword in the air and drank in the roars from the mainly Gath crowd. They were delirious with joy. Bane stood for some moments, elation surging through him. Then he cleaned his sword on the sand. The wound on his shoulder was shallow, and Bane had no desire to return to the gloom of the sword room. He strode across the arena, the sound of applause in his ears, and climbed to the stands. Men surrounded him, clapping him on the back. Then he turned to see Rage walking across the sand.

All elation drained away from him. He had known the man only a short while but had come to regard him highly. Now he felt a sense of sick dread. He had not thanked him or said good-bye or even wished him good luck.

Rage moved across the arena, his sword sheathed, his helm tucked under his arm, his red scarf bright as blood in the sunlight. From the other side of the arena came Vorkas. Bane stood, hands gripping the front rail, and watched as the two men came together before Persis and his guests. They saluted and drew back.

Rage donned his helm and took up his position. Vorkas faced him. The trumpets sounded.

A heartbeat later Vorkas lay dead on the sand.

Rage sheathed his sword and walked back to the sword room. The crowd was silent. They stared at the fallen Vorkas, saw the blood pumping from his throat. Bane stood in shock. Even he had not seen the deathblow. He replayed the move in his mind. Vorkas had lunged high, and Rage had parried. Then the shock of realization struck Bane. Rage had killed Vorkas before the parry. As Vorkas' sword had lanced forward, Rage had stepped in and slashed through his opponent's throat, the blade continuing its sweep to block the lunge. It had been a desperately dangerous maneuver.

Some of the Stone citizens in the crowd began to shout their displeasure at the lack of spectacle. Others merely sat, trying to make sense of what they had seen. Bane vaulted down to the arena and ran across the sand. Inside the sword room Rage was removing his wrist guards.

"You were magnificent," said Bane.

Rage said nothing. Unbuckling his sword belt, he dropped it alongside his wrist guards and greaves. Then he loosened his leather kilt and threw it to a nearby seat. "Are you all right?" asked Bane.

Rage turned to him, his face tight with suppressed emotion. "Five of my friends are dead, boy."

"But you are not," Bane said softly.

"No, I am not."

"You had that move planned from the beginning, didn't you? You said to yourself that Vorkas would want to extend the fight. He would not open with a lethal attack. So you risked everything on that one strategy."

"Risk is what we are paid for, Bane. Did you use the switch from right to left?"

"Aye, I did. He saw it too late."

"Get that cut on your shoulder seen to. Don't let Landis clean it. The blood flow will have done that."

Telors came into the room, his wounds stitched. The black-bearded warrior gave a weary smile. "Good to see you alive, my friend," he told Rage, and the two men gripped hands once more.

"Did you wager on yourself?" asked Rage.

"No," Telors told him. "I thought my man looked too good." He sighed. "And he was—but he didn't have the heart. If I'd had his talent, I would have been Gladiator One." Telors slumped down to a nearby bench seat and glanced through the doorway at the dead Polon. "He knew he was going to die. I could see it in his eyes last night," he said.

The surgeon Landis entered, saw the shallow wound on Bane's shoulder, and called him through to the back room. He did not speak but sat Bane down and took up a crescent-shaped needle and thread. Swiftly and expertly he stitched the cut. Then, as he snipped the last thread, he looked into Bane's eyes. "Well, lad, this is what you have chosen. Are you pleased with yourself?"

"I am alive," said Bane.

"And eight men are dead," said Landis. "Eight souls cast out of the world. More mothers to grieve, more children to know sorrow. Is this a life you want for yourself?"

"No, it is not," Bane told him. "But we do what we must."

"Not true! We do what we choose. And we face the consequences."

Bane thanked the man, returned to the sword room, and removed his armor. Then he put on his leggings and tunic and a thick fleece-lined jerkin. Rage and Telors were already dressed. "Let us leave this place," said Rage. "I need to get back to the farm."

Crowds were still leaving the stadium as the three gladiators made their way to the stabling area. They cheered as they saw Bane, who waved back at them.

Snow clouds were bunching as the three riders came in sight of the farmhouse. Cara was sitting in the doorway, a thick blue blanket around her shoulders. She threw it off and ran toward them as they rode down the hillside. Rage drew rein and dismounted as Cara flew into his arms. He hugged her close. "I am well, princess. I am well," he whispered.

"No more fights," she pleaded. "No more fights, Grandfather."

"No more fights," he agreed.

Bane took the mounts to the stable while Telors, Rage, and Cara went inside the farmhouse. Unsaddling the horses, Bane rubbed them down, forked hay into the feed boxes, then climbed to the loft and sat, staring out over the hills. He felt drained but not tired. Memories of the arena filled his mind: the rising roar of the crowd, the look in Falco's eyes as his blade plunged home, the soaring elation as his opponent died, and beyond it all the smiling face of Voltan.

"I will find you," whispered Bane. "And I will kill you."

Climbing down from the loft, he went back to the farm-house. Rage was sitting in a wide chair, Cara on his lap. The girl's arms were around his neck, her blue eyes still bright with remembered fear. Both Rage and Telors were sitting silently, and Bane felt like an intruder. He left them to their quiet companionship.

The fire in his room had been lit, and the room was bathed in a warm red glow. Removing his clothes, Bane slipped under the covers, laying his head back on the pillow. The stitches in his shoulder were tight, the wound itching.

Pushing the discomfort from his mind, he thought of Lia and all that might have been.

It was past midnight, and still Bane could not sleep. Pushing back the covers, he rose from the bed. The fire had burned low, and the room was cold. Moving to the fireplace, he blew gently on the coals, causing them to flicker to life, then added a few sticks. Tiny flames licked at them, and once they had caught hold, he added thicker chunks. The smell of woodsmoke was strong in the air, and he walked to the window, pushing open the shutters. The moon was high in a clear sky, and a chilly fresh breeze brushed across his face and chest. From the room next door came the sound of Telors snoring.

Bane stared gloomily out over the snow-covered hills. Nothing moved in the silence of the night. He shivered and pulled on a thick woolen shirt and leggings. Melancholy thoughts continued to assail him. His failure to save Lia was at the fore-front of his mind, but also there was his mother's death. They both seemed connected somehow, and Banc felt a sense of guilt like a weight around his neck. Had he been more clever and able to master the skills of reading and writing, perhaps he would have found a way to win Connavar's approval. And, had he done so, might the king not also have been reunited with Arian? It was despair that had killed her, but had Connavar come to her, she might even now be alive and happy. As for Lia, *if only I had taken her away,* he thought, back to Caer Druagh.

Or fought harder or attacked Voltan more swiftly, then the deadly sword would not have ended her life.

Feeling the need to walk and think, he tugged on his boots and draped his new fleece-lined cloak around his shoulders. Moving quietly downstairs and out into the snow, he was surprised to see fresh footprints leading away toward the hills. He could still hear Telors snoring upstairs and wondered why Rage should be walking out into the night.

The footsteps led him past the training area and on into the hills to a shallow cave where Rage was sitting before a small fire. The old gladiator looked up as Bane approached.

"Would you rather be alone?" asked Bane.

"I am alone whether you are here or not." Rage gestured for Bane to sit alongside him on the fallen log.

"You'd have been more comfortable in front of the fire in your own hearth," said Bane, sitting down and holding out his hands to the small blaze.

"It is a stone-built house. It keeps the world out. I felt the need to be part of the hills, to see the stars above me. You ever feel that way?"

"No."

Rage sighed, and Bane smelled the uisge on his breath. "You Keltoi are supposed to be close to nature, to walk the path of spirit. But you don't know what I'm talking about, do you?"

"Does it matter?"

"Probably not. Did you enjoy today?"

"Yes. I felt a surge of exultation as my enemy died. And the cheers of the crowd were like wine. I know it was not the same for you. Was it ever?"

Rage reached behind the log and produced a two-pint cask of uisge. Pulling the stopper, he drank deeply, then passed the cask to Bane. "I shouldn't have fought today," said Rage. "It was arrogant and wrong. I tried to tell myself I was doing it for the circus, for my comrades. Truth is, I was . . . irritated. I once fought for Palantes. They earned a mountain of gold from my duels. Now here they were wanting a few coppers more from the old farmer's death. I should have told them to . . . go away. That would have been manly. No amount of false pride is worth the pain I caused Cara."

"You hurt them, though," said Bane. "Killed their best prospect."

"Pah, it will mean nothing to them. They'll find another. My pride wasn't worth killing a man for. And it certainly wasn't worth the deaths of five comrades." He drank again, then glanced up at the sky. He almost fell from the log, but Bane caught him. "That's where we came from," he said, his voice slurring.

"Where? The sky?"

"Somewhere out there," said Rage, waving his hand high. "A wise woman—a seer—told me that. We are created from the dust of stars. A very wise woman, she was."

"She sounds like an idiot," said Bane. "I was created by a lustful man who forced himself upon my mother."

"The dust of stars," said Rage. He gazed blearily at Bane. "A long time ago—long, long time—a star exploded, and its dust was scattered across the heavens. This magical dust covered the earth, and from it all life was born. Fishes and . . . things. Trees. And when these living things die, the magical dust is freed again and makes new trees and . . . and . . ."

"Fishes?" offered Bane.

"Yes. Fishes." He sighed. "I felt sorry for Vorkas today. He should not have lost, and he knew it in the moment of his death. He expected me to be defensive, to try to read his movements. As my sword opened his throat, his eyes changed. He looked like a child then, lost and bewildered." Rage drank again, several deep, long swallows.

"I thought you didn't drink, old man."

"I don't. Can't abide the stuff. Have you ever seen a ghost?"

"I think so. I had a dream when I was wounded. In it my grandfather came to me."

"Every now and again I see her ghost," said Rage. "Her dress is covered in blood, and she is holding a knife in her hand. She was standing at the foot of my bed tonight. I saw her mouth move, but I couldn't hear any words. Then she faded away." He shivered. "Getting cold," he said.

Bane found some more wood close by and banked up the fire. "Did you know the ghost?" he asked.

"Aye, I knew her."

"Was it your wife?"

"Wife? I never had a wife, boy. I was a soldier for ten years, then a gladiator. No time for wives. Whores, yes. Plenty of those. Good girls, most of them."

"Then how do you have a granddaughter?"

Rage lifted the jug and shook it. "All gone," he said. "Full and now empty." He chuckled. "Like life."

"You drank all of that?" said Bane, worried now, for he had known of men who had died after consuming that much uisge.

"I think I'll sleep now," mumbled Rage. He leaned back and fell from the log. Bane tried to rouse him, but the older man was unconscious. Bane took hold of his arms and tried to heave him upright so that he could drape him over his shoulder and carry him home. But Rage was a big man and too heavy to lift as a dead weight. Bane laid him down.

The temperature was below zero, the little fire making no impact on the cold. If he could not get him back, Rage would die out there. Bane swore, then pulled Rage close to the fire and covered him with his own cloak. He would have to go back to the house and wake Telors. Even as he thought it, he knew Rage could die of cold before they returned. He cast around, gathering more fuel for the fire. It was growing colder, and Bane shivered and huddled close to the flames.

Suddenly the cold eased away, and Bane felt the warmth of a spring breeze on his back. A crow fluttered down to stalk around the unconscious Rage. Bane turned slowly.

An old woman, leaning on a staff, came walking from the edge of the trees.

"Greetings, Rigante," she said, her voice muffled by the heavy veil she wore. Sitting down on the log, she stretched out her hand to the fire. Flames leapt up, circling her fingers, then danced on the palm of her hand. Her fingers closed around the flames, and Bane saw her fist glowing like a lantern. He glanced back the way she had come. There were no footprints in the snow. Fear touched him then. All Rigante knew of the Seidh, the gods of the forest. But of them all the Morrigu was the most feared, and few among the Keltoi tribes ever spoke her name aloud. It was said to bring ill luck.

"You are the Old Woman of the Forest," he said. "You came to Banouin at Cogden Field and made the ghosts appear."

"I did not make them appear," she said. Her veiled head tilted down to look at Rage.

"He is a good man," said Bane. "And my friend. Do not seek to harm him."

"I have no wish to harm him, child." The crow hopped along the ground until it was alongside Rage's head. Bane drew his knife.

"If that foul bird pecks at him, I shall cut its damned head off," he said.

"How like your father you are," she told him. "Using anger to drown fear. You sit there, heart hammering, limbs trembling, yet still you are defiant. Your knife, however, is useless here."

"What do you want? I need no gifts from you to torment me and see me die."

"Such is the arrogance of man," she said. "When the Seidh were first formed, the world boiled and storms raged across the planet, storms of a ferocity you could not possibly imagine. Molten rock spewed from broken mountains, and the earth trembled and crashed against itself. The Seidh were there, Bane. We have seen the death of stars and the birth of man. We watched your slug-eating ancestors creep from their caves and slowly, oh, so slowly, begin to learn. And we helped you, inspired you. We lifted you from the mud and showed you the sky and the stars beyond. We fed your spirit. And so you grew. But your minds are small and filled with pettiness. You make everything small to match your own lack of understanding. Torment you? See you die? Child, I saw your great-grandfather die and his great-grandfather. And what torments could I offer that you do not already possess?"

"I know the stories of you," said Bane. "Your gifts are perilous."

She turned her face toward him. He blanched as he glimpsed the corruption under her veil. "When you run these hills with your friend, you occasionally crush an insect beneath your heel. How might the other insects view your purpose in life, Bane? Would they say, 'He was created to kill us'? Would they believe in you as some grim demon fashioned to bring destruction to their race? My purpose here is not to torment man. I care little for man. We inspired you to an understanding of the beauty of the world, but we could not change your nature. You are killers. Greed and lust and cruelty bedevil you, creating in every man a war that is seldom won by the spirit." She fell silent for a moment. "I am not your enemy, Bane, nor am I man's enemy."

Rage moaned in his sleep. "His dreams are tormented," said the Morrigu. Rage's fists were clenched, and he groaned again. Lightly she touched him with her staff, and he sighed and slept peacefully. "You sleep well, Vanni," she whispered. "Sleep without dreams." There was a moment of tenderness in her voice, and that surprised Bane.

"You know him?"

"I have known him longer than I have known you, Bane. I saw him first as a young soldier. Four of his fellows had dragged a Keltoi girl into the woods to rape and kill her. Vanni stopped them. Many such small acts of kindness I have seen from him. And then there was Palia."

"Palia?"

"The girl he raised as his daughter. The mother was a prostitute, what the soldiers of Stone call a unit whore. She followed the army on campaigns and attached herself to Vanni's unit. She became pregnant and decided to have the child. The unit paid for her to return to Stone. They joked about which one had fathered the child. It could have been any of the twenty who had paid for her services, including Vanni.

"Then the real fighting began. It was fierce and terrible. Vanni's unit was trapped in the mountains and all but wiped out. Vanni fought his way clear and carried the one other survivor to safety. That man died under the surgeon's knife. When Vanni returned to Stone, he sought out the whore and discovered that she had been killed in a side street by an evil man. The child she had borne was being raised by the wife of the man who owned the brothel where she plied her trade. Vanni bought the child and had her cared for by a good family. He paid for her clothes and food and lodging, then for her schooling."

"Why would he do that?" asked Bane. "He did not know who fathered her."

"Why did you save the horse in the river?" she countered.

"You were there?"

"I am everywhere, Bane. But I was talking about Vanni. He called the child Palia, and she grew to be a beautiful girl in both body and nature. Yet she was delicate of soul. She fell in love with a man who used her and cast her aside when she became pregnant. Her mind was unhinged by what she saw as his betrayal of her, and soon after the birth she took a knife, slashed her wrists, and died."

"The ghost Rage sees," whispered Bane.

"Aye, the ghost."

"So all he did was for nothing," said Bane.

"Stupid child!" hissed the Morrigu. "Such acts of kindness and love are never for nothing! They feed the world. Like a stone dropping into a pool, they send out waves in every direction. They inspire and, in doing so, enhance spirit."

"Did Rage kill the man who betrayed her?"

"No, he did not. The man was a soldier. His only crime was that he had seduced Palia. He had made her no promises, and he had already left the city with the army to go on campaign. Vanni had become Rage by then, Gladiator One. But the death of Palia all but destroyed him. He fought on for a while, but his heart was broken. Then came the day when he could fight no more. He walked away from the arena and brought his granddaughter to Goriasa."

"You say you are fond of him," said Bane, "and yet he is a killer. Is this not a contradiction?"

"You are all killers," replied the Morrigu. "But there is in Vanni a desire for spirit and a great measure of goodness, kindness, and compassion. He has what the Seidh term a great soul."

Bane glanced down at the sleeping Rage. The cold of winter swept over the snow, and Bane shivered.

"Ah, there you are," said Telors, emerging from the tree line. Bane flicked a glance to his right, but the Morrigu had gone. The black-bearded gladiator trudged across the snow and knelt by Rage. "I knew he'd do this," he said. "That's why I stayed the night."

Together they hauled Rage upright. Dipping down, Telors heaved the sleeping man over his shoulder, staggered, then began the long walk back. Halfway there, with Telors exhausted, Bane took over. Both men were more than weary as they reached the farmhouse. Bane laid Rage down on the rug by the fire in the main room. Telors took a cushion from a couch and placed it under Rage's head, then they covered him with a blanket and walked back into the kitchen. Telors lit a lantern and poured himself a goblet of water.

"He drank a great deal," said Bane. "I've heard of men dying after imbibing like that."

"I'll sit with him."

Bane cut a slice of bread from a loaf, smeared it with butter, and joined Telors at the table. "I thought he didn't drink strong spirit," said Bane.

"He doesn't usually. It started back in Stone after . . . a personal tragedy. Death bouts began to affect him, and after them he would get drunk and then wander off somewhere. I always found him and brought him home." Telors moved to a cupboard and took out a small jug of uisge, adding a measure to his cup of water. He offered the jug to Bane, who lifted it to his mouth and took several deep swallows.

"Did he talk much?" asked Telors.

"What about?"

"Oh, life . . . his past?" Bane saw the worried look on Telors's face.

"No. He said something about coming from the stars. That's all."

Telors looked relieved. "He'll be fine in the morning. Cara will cook him breakfast. She's a sweet girl. I wouldn't like to see her hurt."

Bane suddenly understood Telors's concern. Cara did not know of her mother's suicide or the truth of her background. Bane took another swallow of uisge. It was very strong, and he felt its effect almost immediately.

"Rage was magnificent in that bout yesterday," he said, changing the subject. "Fast, sure, and deadly."

"That's Rage," said Telors, his face relaxing into a smile.

"Would he have beaten Voltan?"

"I see you're learning your history. Well, the answer is that

I don't really know. Both were awesome in their prime. I guess if I had to put all my money on a fighter, I'd pick Voltan. But if someone was fighting for my life, I'd want it to be Rage. Does that answer your question?"

Bane swayed in his seat, the room beginning to swim. Telors laughed. "Better get off to bed, lad. I'm too tired to carry you up those stairs."

◇ **7** ◇

BANE FLOATED IN a sea of dreams, faces and images floating across his mind, merging and changing. He saw his mother Arian, then Vorna, then the elderly hunter Parax, then Falco the gladiator. An endless stream of people flowed past him. He tried to reach out to them, but his fingers passed through them, rippling the images as if they were water. He awoke in a cold sweat and threw back the covers. The room was cold, and ice had sealed the shutters.

He sat up and groaned as hot hammers began to beat inside his skull. Rising, he dressed swiftly and left the room. In the kitchen Cara was helping the fat Gath woman Girta clean the breakfast plates. "You slept late," said Cara. "I could toast you some of yesterday's bread."

"That would be welcome," said Bane.

The pounding in his head eased slightly, but a dull ache had begun behind his eyes. He sat down at the table and rubbed his temples. The veins below the skin were hard as copper wire. Girta dropped a muslin pouch of herbs into a cup and filled it with hot water. A sweet scent filled the room. She placed the cup in front of him.

"Wait awhile," she said, "then drink it. You'll feel better."

Bane forced a smile. "Do I look that bad?"

"You are very pale, and there are dark hollows under your eyes. Uisge hollows." She grinned at him. Bane rubbed his eyes. He thought he had taken only a few swallows of uisge, but he remembered the strength of it. It had been like swallowing fire.

A few minutes later Cara returned with a plate of hot buttered toast. Bane thanked her and sipped his tisane. Girta had

168

been right. His head began to clear almost immediately. "Where are Rage and Telors?" he asked.

"They had breakfast an hour ago, then went for a run," said Cara. "Telors said not to wake you because you had been drinking uisge." She gave him an accusing look. "Grandfather says gladiators should not drink strong spirits. It is like poison, he says."

"He's a very wise man," observed Bane.

"He's not going to fight again," said the girl. "Not ever."

"I'm glad to hear it."

She looked at Girta. "Yesterday was a terrible day, wasn't it, Girta? Sitting here not knowing if Grandfather . . . It was a terrible day."

"But today is not so terrible," said Bane.

"Today is my birthday," said Cara. "I am fourteen. Grandfather and I are going into the city. He is going to buy me a horse. Not a pony! A horse. And we are going to buy more cattle. Grandfather is rich now. That's why he doesn't need to fight again."

As Bane was finishing his breakfast, Rage and Telors ran into the open ground beyond the kitchen window. Bane glanced through the window. Telors waved at him and walked over to lean on the sill. "The young just can't handle strong drink," he said with a grin.

"It wasn't the drink," said Bane. "It was your snoring. I hardly slept a wink."

Telors flicked snow at him from the sill, then turned as a rider came into sight. The man wore an expensive cloak edged with ermine and fur-lined riding boots. His horse was a fine beast, well groomed and keen-eyed. Rage walked out to meet him.

Bane wandered to the window. "Who is he?" he asked Telors.

"Judging by the eagle embroidered on his tunic, I'd say he's from Palantes," Telors told him, then wandered off to join Rage.

Bane headed through to the main room and sat down by the fire. His headache was almost gone, but he felt drained of energy. The chair was deep and comfortable, and he stretched out his legs and closed his eyes.

"Someone here to see you," said Rage. Bane sat up. The

visitor, a tall man running to fat, dipped his head in a short bow. Bane picked up the scent of perfume.

"I am Jain, first slave to Circus Palantes," said the newcomer, his voice smooth and melodious. "It is a pleasure to meet you."

Bane stood and shook the proffered hand. The man's grip was soft, the fingers clammy. "I watched you fight yesterday. You were very impressive." Bane said nothing. "I have spoken to Persis Albitane about you and made him an offer for your contract. In short, Circus Palantes would like to sponsor you."

"Sponsor me?"

"They want you to fight for them," said Rage.

"Five hundred in gold upon your signature and a guaranteed two hundred each time you fight. Your lodgings and personal expenses will be paid by the circus, and we will supply you with armor and weapons."

Bane looked at Rage. "Is that a fair offer?"

"Yes, but no more than that."

"What do you advise?"

"Think on it," said Rage.

Bane looked at the man from Palantes. "I will give you my answer tomorrow," he said.

"You won't get a better offer," said Jain, holding his smile in place.

"Tomorrow," Bane repeated.

"Yes, yes, of course. Well, as I said, it was a pleasure, and congratulations on your duel." He turned to Rage. "My congratulations also to you, sir. We all thought Vorkas was destined to be Gladiator One. You showed us the error in that judgment."

"Good-bye," said Rage, opening the door for him.

The man left the farmhouse, climbed on his horse, and rode away.

"As I told you," said Rage, "Palantes does not grieve for long. There is always another fighter waiting to be sucked dry."

"I did not like the man," said Bane. "Yet his offer takes me closer to my . . . quest."

"Aye, it does that," said Rage. "They are a disciplined circus with good trainers and fine facilities: their own bathhouses, masseurs, surgeons. They even have a whorehouse purely for the gladiators and owners. They will rent you a house and pay for up to four servants and a personal trainer."

"You make it sound very tempting," said Bane. "Now tell me why I should refuse them."

"No reason I can think of, boy. You dream of revenge. This will help you to prepare for that day. Either that or you'll die on the sand."

"Circus Palantes wanted you dead," Bane reminded him.

"Aye, they did. But there was no malice in it, no passion whatsoever. Merely a cold desire to make money. Such people do not warrant hate, merely contempt. Were I young again, I would not fight for them. We are not, however, talking about me but about you. You have no reason to despise Palantes. They do what they do. That is their nature." Rage moved toward the doorway. "Now I need to bathe and get ready to take Cara into the city. You think about what I have said. Discuss it with Persis. I don't doubt he'll be here within the hour."

Two hours later, as Bane returned from a run over the hills, he saw two horses tethered outside the farmhouse. He slowed to a jog and stood for a while, stretching, allowing the cold winter wind to chill the sweat on his skin. Salt from the sweat was stinging the stitched wound in his shoulder, but his headache had cleared. The events of the night before kept returning to haunt him. Why had the Morrigu appeared to him? What was her purpose? But above it all he felt a great sadness for Rage. In the weeks he had known the aging gladiator Bane had come to regard him highly, had seen him—despite the occasional flashes of bitterness—as a contented man. Now he knew Rage carried an enormous sorrow.

He shivered as the cold cut into his cooling skin and stepped into the kitchen. Girta was there, preparing food for the evening meal.

She gave him a smile and nodded toward the main room. "You have two visitors," she said. "How popular you have become." Bane went upstairs, removed his clothes, and toweled himself down. Pulling on a fresh pair of leggings and a clean shirt, he tugged on his boots and returned to the ground floor.

Persis Albitane rose as he entered, his fat face beaming.

Striding forward, he shook hands with Bane. "You are looking well, my friend," said Persis. "Allow me to introduce you
to Horath, who is here representing Circus Occian. He was at
the stadium yesterday."

The man was in his early twenties, slim and dark-haired,
his brown eyes deep-set. His clothes were expensive: a shirt
of heavy gray silk that shone like silver and black leggings of
good wool edged with glistening leather. At his hip he wore a
jewel-encrusted dagger with a golden pommel. Bane accepted the man's handshake, which was firm and brief, then
moved to a chair by the fire. "Horath came to see me this
morning," said Persis. "He was inquiring about your contract
with Circus Orises."

"I am much in demand, it seems," said Bane.

"Indeed you are, Bane," said Horath, returning to his seat.
"The crowds in Stone would flock to see a Rigante warrior."

"What are you offering?"

Horath smiled, and there was genuine humor in it. "Whatever Jain offered plus one gold piece," he said.

"And I suppose Circus Occian will value me highly and
treat me like an honored son?"

This time Horath laughed aloud. "There will be those who
will tell you exactly that," he said. "The reality, as I am sure
you are aware, is that you will be a valuable commodity and
treated as such. When you win, you will be lauded and ad-
mired, and Circus Occian will become richer. When you lose,
your body will be cast into a pauper's pit and you will be forgotten within days. I will then be dispatched to find another
fighter to replace you."

"You make it sound very tempting," said Bane. "I especially liked the reference to the pauper's pit."

"I despise deceit," Horath told him. "I have little appetite
for pretty falsehoods and insincere flattery. I do it, of course.
In the higher circles of Stone it is a required practice. But not
when I can avoid it. I think you would be a valuable addition
to our circus, and you will certainly help fill the stadium."

"They will come to see the savage barbarian?" asked Bane.
"Indeed so."

"What is your view?" Bane asked Persis.

The fat man spread his hands. "There are only three major

circuses: Palantes, Occian, and Poros. Two of them want you. Both are highly respected, and both offer you a chance to become a good—and rich—gladiator. You must decide, Bane."

"What of Circus Orises? Do you want me to stay?"

Persis smiled. "I will have no more death bouts. It was good to see the stadium full, but I hated watching men die for the joy of others. No, I have other plans. You would be most welcome to stay, but I have to say that with the money I shall receive for your contract, I can expand the circus into other areas. In short, I am the wrong person to ask for advice, for I will profit greatly by your departure." He chuckled and turned to Horath. "Damn, but this honesty business is infectious."

Bane leaned back in his chair. In order to kill Voltan he needed to learn to fight as well as the Stone knight. There was no better way to do that than to join a major circus. Finally he looked at Horath. "If you hire Rage and Telors as my personal trainers, I will accept your offer. If they refuse, then I refuse."

"Your services do not come cheaply," said Horath, "but then, nothing good ever does. Very well. I shall speak to Rage. I have to say that Circus Occian would be delighted to have him." He rose from his chair and swung his cloak around his shoulders. He and Bane shook hands, and the three men walked out into the weak sunlight. Bane swung to Persis.

"So what will you do with all this money you are making?" he asked.

"I intend to buy an elephant," Persis said happily.

Rage was uncomfortable and shifted uneasily in his chair. Telors was sitting on a couch, his long legs stretched out before him.

"What do you think?" said Bane. "Would you be interested?"

"I'm interested," said Telors, glancing toward the old gladiator. "What about you, Vanni?"

"I don't know. I'd like to see Stone again, and it would be good to enroll Cara in a good school, prepare her for life in the city."

"But?" said Telors.

Rage gave a tight smile. "I want to do it for the right reasons, yet deep inside I see it as a way of making Palantes pay."

"Nothing wrong with revenge," said Telors.

"It darkens the spirit," said Rage, looking directly into Bane's eyes. "What will you do if I refuse this offer?"

"I will stay here and hope that you will continue to train me. I believe you to be the best, and I will learn more from you than from any other man."

"That is not so, Bane. Training can only carry you so far. The reality of combat will teach you much more. Let us understand something from the outset: You are a gifted fighter with good heart and natural speed. It could be that you have the potential to be great. I don't yet know whether that is true. What I do know is that you are a long way from being able to . . . fulfill your quest. If I do agree to train you, I want your promise that you will not seek that which you desire until I say that you are ready."

"I'm not sure I can promise that," said Bane.

"If you cannot, then we must part company."

"Would it be easier to talk if I wasn't here?" asked Telors. "You both seem to be skirting around something."

Rage looked at Bane and said nothing. Bane turned to Telors. "A man from Stone killed a woman I had come to love. I was there. I watched his sword cleave her ribs. It is my intention to hunt this man down and kill him."

"Understandable," said Telors. "So what is the problem?"

"The man was Voltan," said Rage.

"Oh. I see." Telors scratched his black beard and leaned back, staring up at the ceiling.

"I know he's good," said Bane.

Telors laughed. "He would have to lose half his talent to be merely good. Have you considered walking up behind him and plunging a knife into his back?"

"No. I want to face him."

"I have seen hundreds of fighters," said Telors. "Good, bad, mediocre. Some were even great. But I have only ever seen two men whose talents were godlike. One is Vanni, the other Voltan. Men like them are rare, young man. They are the stuff of legend. Some years ago Voltan was due to be fighting a young pretender. Someone managed to poison his wine. Voltan almost died. Two days later, having lost ten pounds in weight, his body weakened by fever, he stepped out into the arena and killed his man."

"I don't care how good he is," said Bane. "I will kill him when we meet."

Telors spread his hands and glanced at Rage. "What do you think?"

"I'll accept the offer—if you make the promise," Rage told Bane.

"How soon will you know if I can beat him?"

"A year. Perhaps two."

Bane sat silently for a moment. "Very well. I promise to wait a maximum of two years. After that I will make my own decision. Is that sufficient?"

"It will do," said Rage.

"I have missed Stone," said Telors. "There is a whorehouse off the Avenue Gabilan that is second to none. Paradise could not be more satisfying than a night spent there."

"Then it is agreed," said Rage. "We will go to Stone with you."

Banouin left the Great Library and wandered along the tree-lined white gravel path leading to the artificial lake. Once there, he settled himself on his favorite bench of curved stone, set beneath a tall weeping willow. The branches trailed all around him like a green veil, the tendrils caressing the grass. It was a place of quiet beauty, and Banouin experienced a dreamlike state there, a freedom from the cares and worries of this alien world. For years, as a child among the Rigante, he had pictured himself in this place of calm and tranquillity. In the depths of his despair he had thought of this park. When Forvar and the others had tormented him, he had dreamed of escaping from them all and coming here. And still, almost two years after his departure from the lands of the Rigante, the Park of Phesus remained a special place of harmony. He never tired of the park, even in winter, when the lake was frozen and snow covered the ground. He would wrap up warmly and come to this bench and sit and dream.

And yet . . . ? Truth to tell, there was something missing. Banouin was, he realized, mostly content but never happy. As with the Rigante, he had not made friends here. There were people he liked—old Sencra, his history tutor, and Menicas, the keeper of texts—but no young people. Banouin knew the names of many of his fellow students and would smile and exchange greetings with them, but none had invited him to their parties and gatherings or sought greater intimacy with him. Banouin had come to the realization that Bane was probably right about him. He was a loner, and people recognized this and avoided him. Yet this alone, he knew, was not the reason for his lack of happiness. He could sense that much. The real reason, however, was one that he did not wish to analyze.

The two years in the city had been kind to him. The letters of introduction from Appius had allowed him access to the university and, through the goodwill of the general Barus, let him apply for Stone citizenship, which had been granted. Then his tutor, Sencra, had offered him employment as a copier of texts. The payment was not great, but it enabled Banouin to hire a suite of rooms close to the university. Luckily, he did not have expensive tastes or desire to frequent the eating houses, theaters, and stadiums. Banouin was content merely to study, copy ancient texts, and wander the city, marveling at its architecture: the broad roads and avenues, the colossal structures, the magnificent statues and parks.

Often he sat alone in the antiquities section of the Great Library, and this solitude puzzled him. Here were stored the histories and philosophies of many ancient races, yet few Stone scholars bothered to study them. Banouin had found a map of the stars, the parchment so brittle that it almost cracked under his fingers. He copied it with great care and replaced it in its niche. There were other maps of far distant lands and parchments written in languages none could now speak. He pored over them, trying to make sense of the glyphs and strokes. What knowledge is contained here? he wondered. Sencra had chuckled when Banouin had brought one such parchment to him. "It is probably just a tale of magical heroes," he had said. "Of no importance."

"How can we know that, sir?"

"Quite simply, my boy. We know that Stone is the greatest city ever built and that our culture is the finest the world has seen. Therefore, we will find little of consequence in ancient writings. Our own philosophers are far in advance of any in the ancient world."

Banouin had not found that convincing, but he had not argued with Sencra. The old man was a good tutor, mostly easygoing and kind, but he reacted badly to criticism.

Banouin sat under the willow and found himself thinking of Caer Druagh. He glanced around to see if anyone was close by, then, satisfied he was alone, lay back and closed his eyes. His spirit drifted clear of his body, floating up through the willow. It was one of the reasons Banouin loved this spot. Here—and only here—he could release his spirit from the cage of flesh. When he had first developed this talent, it had filled him with fear, but he had learned swiftly that he had merely to wish himself back in his body and it would be so. Gradually during the first year he had ventured farther abroad, finally soaring back to Caer Druagh and hovering over the settlement of Three Streams. The sheer joy at seeing the cluster of wooden homes had surprised him.

This time he saw there was a new building, huge and conical, to the north of the settlement. Banouin floated inside. It was a meeting hall, and several hundred Rigante were there, enjoying a feast. Connavar's half brother, Braefar, was sitting at the head of the table, a slim yellow-haired man with quick darting eyes. He was laughing at some jest and drinking from a golden goblet.

Banouin drew back and flew on to his mother's house. Vorna was dozing before the fire, her head resting on a cushion. She looked tired, thought Banouin.

Vorna's dark eyes flared open, and she looked directly at him. She yawned, stretched and sat up. "Are you well, my son?" she asked him.

"I am," he told her. "But you look weary."

"I returned from Old Oaks last night. There is plague there. Forty dead. I think I have cleansed the settlement. Have you heard from Bane?"

"No. He is becoming famous now. Six kills and fifteen other victories in less than two years. He has become a Name."

"You should make your peace with him. He was a good friend to you."

"He is a killer of men, and we have nothing in common."

"You think not? You are both Rigante, born in the shadow of Caer Druagh."

"I am a citizen of Stone, Mother," he reminded her.

"Aye, you are. But that was through choice. You are Rigante by blood, and your soul-name was heard in the mountains and the Wishing Tree woods."

"We have had this conversation before," he said with a smile. "I did not accept it then, nor do I accept it now. I am content, Mother. I am who I am."

"You do not yet know who you are," she told him. "And contentment is not enough."

"It is good to see you well," he said.

He opened his eyes back in the Park of Phesus. As always after his astral journeys, he had returned refreshed and curiously uplifted. Rising from the bench, he pushed aside the willow branches and walked out to the edge of the artificial lake. Just below the surface he could see multicolored fish gliding through the water. He looked up and saw the distant towers and rooftops of Stone, glistening white in the afternoon sun.

Stone was the future. One day all over the world there would be cities like this, places of great beauty and culture. Wars would have a place only in history texts.

He heard the sound of running feet and swung to see a young man racing along the tree-lined path. He was being chased by several men on horseback. The first came alongside him, knocking him to the ground. Then the horsemen leapt from their saddles and beat the young man with cudgels. Banouin stood very still. He could see from their black cloaks and armor that they were knights of Stone. One of them glanced at Banouin.

The knights hauled the young man to his feet. His hands were tied, and he was forced to stumble along ahead of the riders. One of the knights peeled his horse from the group and rode back to Banouin.

Waves of violent thought radiated from the rider, washing over Banouin. His mind reeled, and his stomach turned. Summoning his talent, he released a ripple of calm and harmony, focusing it on the knight.

"You know that man?" asked the rider.

Banouin shook his head. "I have seen him in the library, sir, but I do not know his name." Banouin centered a field of harmony around the rider, feeling the harshness within the man subsiding.

"And what is your name?"

"Banouin, sir. I am a student and a copier of texts."

"Banouin, eh? Are you a loyal citizen, Banouin?"

"I am, sir. And proud to be so."

The knight swung his horse and cantered back after the others. The spiritual odor of violence still hung in the air, and Banouin shivered. He trudged back along the path to the library. The previous week two tutors and a dozen students had been arrested and hauled from the university. Nothing had been heard of them since. Banouin did not interest himself in politics or religion and had no wish to be drawn into any debate. It had frightened him when old Sencra had raised the subject in his study one evening.

"Have you come across the tree cult, young man?"

"No, sir. Nor do I wish to."

"Interesting ideas, though I find most of their arguments specious and their pacifism positively revolting."

"I do not wish to speak of them, sir."

Sencra chuckled. "You think the priests might come for you in the dead of night, eh? Well, so they might—were you to join the cult. But it is not yet a crime to speak of them. You are a Keltoi. You believe in spirits and such? The Seidh, you call them?"

"I do, sir."

"And are they benign or malevolent?"

"They can be both," said Banouin, more comfortable now that the conversation had seemingly veered away from the tree cult. "They exist separately from us. There are woods, magical places. Men do not go there."

"Creatures of spirit, are they?"

"Aye, sir. Yet they can appear in the flesh, so to speak. Connavar the King was helped by both the Thagda and the Old Woman of the Forest."

"The Thagda . . . ah, yes, the tree man. I remember reading

of him. He has a body of bark and lichen for a beard." Sencra chuckled. "And the Old Woman . . . the Morrigu, isn't it?"

Banouin shivered. "It is best not to speak her name, sir. It brings ill luck."

"It seems to me that there are similarities between the tree cult and the beliefs of the Keltoi. Both speak of spirit and matter and the necessity of harmony between the two. As far as I can understand the principle, it is that the body is an imperfect vessel for the spirit and that the spirit cannot function to its full potential while the body is driven by carnal desires or anger or hatred. What do you think?"

"I think, with respect, we should not be talking about this," said Banouin. "It is dangerous."

"You Keltoi are said to be insanely courageous and great fighters," said Sencra. "You disappoint me. Very well, let us discuss the works of Habidaes and the iron rule."

Banouin remembered the conversation as he walked toward the library. He was a citizen of Stone, not a Keltoi, and it stung him that even here his tribal shortcomings should be thrown in his face.

The library was huge and white, fifty massive pillars supporting two hundred rooms under a domed roof. Exquisite statues had been placed all around the building, and other equally magnificent carvings adorned the walls and the many niches set within the columns. Banouin climbed the forty-two steps to the main doors and entered the Hall of Nature. Here, set on plinths, were scores of stuffed animals and birds of every kind. A huge elephant, covered in fur, stood at the far end, trunk lifted, caught in midcry. The tusks were more than ten feet long. There were crocodiles, turtles, several bears— one albino white—and other creatures from distant lands: a striped horse, a huge spotted lion, and an animal with an immensely long neck. This last one was half rearing, its dead lips nibbling at an artificial tree set on the gallery of Level Two.

Banouin climbed the stairs to Level Three and the antiquities section. Upon entering, he was surprised to see four young men in the far corner, sitting huddled together. They looked up as he entered, scrutinized him, then returned to their whispers.

Taking a scroll from the shelf of the Keltoi, Banouin moved to a small table set against the wall. Then he carefully opened the scroll and began to read. The author of the piece had been dead for two hundred years, and much of what he said concerning the Keltoi people was wildly inaccurate. In one section he talked of human sacrifices and the eating of human flesh, claiming it to be a fetish among the tribes. Banouin had never heard of human sacrifice being practiced by any Keltoi. Irritated by the lack of scholarship in the scroll, Banouin returned it and drew another.

This one dealt with, among other matters, the spiritual beliefs among tribesmen and talked of tree worship. It also maintained with great seriousness that the Keltoi were a childlike race, incapable of serious intellectual thought, who believed thunderstorms to be the clashing shields of the gods. It pointed out, however, that if treated with firm discipline, the Keltoi made good slaves.

Banouin returned it to its place. At the back of the shelf he saw a faded scroll that had slipped from its niche. Carefully he lifted it clear. It was bound with an old ribbon, frayed at the edges. It contained in note form a description of a Keltoi ritual in which a druid blessed the land of a farmer whose crops had been blighted since he had built his farmhouse three years before. The druid maintained that a battle had been fought on this land a hundred years before, and the spirit had departed from it. In order to bring the spirit back, the druid arranged for a wedding feast to be held on the land. Hundreds of Keltoi were invited, and they danced and sang and made merry throughout the day and long into the night. The writer, a Stone merchant, had added a postscript to the scroll, saying that the following season the farmer enjoyed a successful crop.

The writing was crisp, authoritative, and beguiling. There was no comment concerning the scenes witnessed, merely detailed observations. Banouin wanted to read on, but he became aware of a growing tension within the large room. It was flowing from the group of young men talking in the corner. Fear was present, and an immense sadness. Banouin pretended to read. He wished he could float from his body and listen to their conversation, but such separation was impossible here. For his spirit to soar, Banouin had to be close to the willow.

He strained to hear what they were saying but could make out no words. At last they stood to leave. Banouin returned to his studying but glanced up as they passed. The last of them, a tall handsome young man with close-cropped black hair, paused at Banouin's table. "You are Banouin the Healer?" he asked.

Banouin's heart sank. He had helped his tutor, Sencra, removing a huge abscess from his back, and twice now had been recommended by the old man to his friends. Banouin had masked the use of his power by first applying sweet-smelling poultices filled with aromatic herbs such as mint and lavender. Having done this, he would then close his eyes and heal the wound. With Sencra it had been an abscess, and with both the other older men it had been inflammation of the joints caused by arthritis. Banouin wished he had never used the skill at all, for he did not want to stand out in Stone. He wanted peace and relative anonymity.

"I do have some skills with herbs," he said. "A small skill, however," he added.

"Maro, son of Barus," said the young man, offering his hand.

"Your father was kind to me when I arrived," Banouin answered. "Please convey to him my best regards."

Maro smiled. "He is away fighting again, but I'll try to remember for when he gets back."

Despite the smile, Banouin could tell Maro was worried about him. Tension and fear were still radiating from the young man and from his fellows waiting in the corridor outside.

"I have not seen you here before," said Banouin. "What are you studying?"

"History, obviously. Why else would we be here?"

"I meant what period of history," Banouin said smoothly.

"The early history of the city," answered Maro. "We all have examinations in the spring. You? What brings you here?"

"I am paid to copy the oldest and most fragile of the parchments and scrolls. Strange, really, since many of them lie unread for years. Some are even in languages no one now knows how to read. Yet still I copy them as faithfully as I can."

Maro relaxed. "Well, perhaps I will see you here again. Good day to you."

Banouin tried to return to his studies, but his heart was not in it.

Seeing the knights beat and arrest the student had brought his dilemma home. While he loved the architecture of the city and its libraries and museums, he could no longer blind himself to the terror being faced by many of the inhabitants. Cultists were rounded up daily and herded to the dungeons below the Crimson Temple. Many would be hanged, others burned. Only a week earlier forty men had been taken to the Circus Palantes stadium, where they had been tied to stakes and surrounded by oil-soaked brushwood. They had then been set alight. The crowd, apparently, had cheered as the screams sounded.

Banouin had not wanted to see the evil in Stone, but it was all around him.

You must stay clear of trouble, he told himself. Do not engage in any religious debate. One day the terror will be over. Until that day keep yourself safe.

Three days later old Sencra was arrested. Four black-cloaked knights entered the university, marched through to the lecture hall, and dragged Sencra from the podium. At first the old man was furious, shouting at them to release him. Then a knight cuffed him on the ear, sending him sprawling. Then Sencra's cries were piteous.

Banouin was one of a hundred students gathered to hear the tutor, and he could not believe what he was seeing. Sitting as he always did close to the door, Banouin found himself rising from his seat and moving to stand before the knights as they dragged the crying man toward the exit.

"Of what is he accused?" Banouin heard himself say, his voice echoing in the domed hall.

The first of the knights loomed over the young man. "Do you seek to hinder us?" he asked.

"Of what is he accused?" repeated Banouin. "Sencra is a good citizen and a fine teacher."

The knight looked into Banouin's eyes. "He has been named as a tree cultist. He will be taken to the temple for a hearing."

"It is a mistake," said Banouin. "Sencra has always spoken against such cults."

"It is true! It is true!" wailed Sencra. "It is a mistake!"

The knight stepped in close to Banouin. "You are trying my patience, young man, and I have no more time for debate."

Banouin was about to speak again when the man's fist lashed into his temple, sending him sprawling to the floor. He lay there, his head spinning. Hands helped him to his feet, and he was led away from the hall to a small side room, where someone sat him in a chair.

Maro brought a damp cloth and dabbed at his temple. Banouin was surprised to see blood on the cloth. "I must get to the temple," said Banouin. "This is not right."

"Sit still," said Maro. "Right has nothing to do with it."

"He is not a cultist," said Banouin.

"Of course he's not. But he has been named."

Another young man entered, bearing a cup of water, which he offered to Banouin. He sipped the liquid. His stomach felt queasy, and his head was pounding. "I . . . need to lie down," he whispered. Once more he was helped to his feet. He leaned against Maro, feeling the room spin.

They took him along the corridor and into a second, windowless room, laying him upon a cot bed. Banouin lost consciousness almost immediately. When he awoke, he saw that a lantern had been lit on the far wall. He lay very still. His stomach was still uneasy, but the pain in his head had eased. He touched his temple. There was a lump there, and a scab had formed upon it.

"How are you feeling?" asked Maro. Banouin rolled onto his side and saw the dark-haired young man sitting at the bedside.

"They took him away," said Banouin.

"Aye, they did."

Banouin closed his eyes. "Why?"

"Stone is in the grip of the terror. There's no point in asking why another innocent man is taken. There have never been more than a thousand cultists in Stone, yet four thousand people have been executed in just three years: hanged, burned, or beheaded. Some of the richer, more influential citizens have been allowed to take poison."

Banouin did not reply. He felt the mists drawing away from his vision. He had so wanted to believe in Stone and all it stood for that he had blinded himself to the truth. By not talking about the terror—not even thinking about it—he had created for himself the image of the perfect city, a place of learning and culture.

"I want to go to my home," he said, struggling to sit.

"Where do you live?"

"I have rooms near the White Plaza."

"I'll help you," said Maro, taking his arm. Banouin stood and swayed. Maro helped him out into the corridor and through the deserted university, out into the wide avenue beyond. It was almost dusk, and the fresh air revived Banouin. He began to walk unaided. Within minutes they reached the White Plaza, where the fading sun made rainbows dance around tall fountains and early-evening diners were sitting at tables outside the many eating houses. Servants were lighting colored lanterns and hanging them from ropes strung between the buildings. The sound of laughter echoed from one group.

Banouin sat down on the rim of a fountain pool. Maro joined him. "How does the emperor gain by these . . . these killings?" asked Banouin.

"In the beginning he profited because the first people arrested were supporters of the republic. In short, they were Jasaray's enemies. But now? I don't believe he gains at all. Quite the reverse, in fact. Naladernus becomes more powerful day by day."

"Then why doesn't Jasaray stop it?"

"He can't. Most of his Panthers are committed to the war in the east. There are now more knights in the city than loyal soldiers. Were he to move against Naladernus, he would lose. He will probably lose anyway. Jasaray is over sixty, with no wife and no sons. He will be toppled before the year is out."

"And Naladernus will be emperor?"

"That is my belief. But my father says Jasaray is a cunning old fox and shouldn't be dismissed lightly."

"Does your father know you are a cultist?" asked Banouin, keeping his voice low.

"I am not a cultist, though I have listened to their teachers. I think their philosophy of love and harmony is wonderful, but I have not the strength for it. And I have no wish to embrace my enemies and make them my friends. I will meet my enemies with a sharp sword and a strong arm. Though when I listen to the Veiled Lady, I could almost believe."

An empty pony trap came clattering by. Banouin shouted to the driver, asking if the trap was for hire. The man drew rein. "Where did you want to go?" he asked.

"The Crimson Temple."

"Climb in, young sir," the driver told him.

"Are you insane?" whispered Maro, grabbing Banouin's arm.

"I must speak up for Sencra," he said.

Maro shook his head. "My father said you Rigante were courageous to the point of madness. Now I see he was right."

"I am not courageous, Maro. All my life I have been a coward. But this I must do."

"You must be very fond of the old man."

"Not even that, though I like him well enough."

"Well, why, then?" asked Maro, confused.

"Because it is right to do so," said Banouin. "If they take him for the burning and I do not speak, it will be as if I lit the torch myself. You understand?"

"You can't save him, my friend."

"It is not about saving him. It is about saving me," said Banouin, climbing into the rear seat of the pony trap.

The driver cracked his whip, and the trap moved out along the avenue.

Banouin leaned back against the cushioned seat and watched as the city of Stone slid slowly by him. Crowds were moving along the avenue, seeking places to dine before attending the many theaters, and scores of pony traps and carriages flowed by, filled for the most part with expensively dressed nobles. Huge lanterns set on iron posts were being lit in the main thoroughfares; smaller lights were being hung from ropes and wires in the side streets.

Stone at night was like a gleaming jewel, but the beauty of it was lost on the young Rigante. He sat silently in the carriage, his heart heavy.

"Which of the temple entrances did you require?" asked the driver.

"I'm not sure. How many are there?"

"There's the main entrance off the Lion Road, but they'll be closing that soon. Then there's the administrative center, the museum, and the knights' barracks."

"I have a friend who was wrongly arrested today."

The driver tensed. Banouin could feel the rising fear in him. "You'll want the prison building," he said.

The trap moved on, cutting left through the Remembrance Garden and under the Arch of Triumph, moving farther into the center of the city. There were not so many people there, and fewer lanterns had been lit.

Banouin's headache was returning, and he felt a little sick. He considered seeking a vision. He had not used this talent since the dreadful day back in Accia when he had seen the knights of Stone coming for Appius and his daughter and had known what they would do. Sweat broke out on his brow, and his stomach tightened. Those without the power would never understand the panic that had swept over him. To sit with living people who were already dead, to watch them smile and laugh and know that tomorrow they would scream in agony, their lives torn from them. To be filled with power and yet be powerless. Banouin had been consumed by the desire to run, to leave, to put the vision behind him. He had wanted to save himself and his friend.

But Bane was a Rigante, and even the knowledge of certain death could not prevent him from trying to save Appius and Lia. How Banouin envied such courage.

"There is the entrance," said the driver, drawing the pony to a halt some way from the gates. Banouin paid him and stepped down. The driver swung the trap and moved away swiftly.

Banouin walked toward the building. Like all great structures in Stone it was dressed in white marble and decorated with statues. The huge bronze latticed gates were open, and two knights carrying iron-tipped spears stood guard outside them. Their cloaks were white, indicating that they were guardsmen, the elite who protected Naladcmus.

The young Rigante approached the first of the guards. "I am seeking someone in authority," he said.

"You wish to name traitors?" asked the man.

"No, sir. My tutor was arrested today, and I wish to speak on his behalf."

"If he was arrested, then he's a traitor," said the knight. "You wish to speak in defense of a traitor?"

"He is not a traitor, sir. He was falsely accused."

"Oh, is that right?" the knight said with a sneer. "Well, then. Wait here." He walked back inside the gates and clanged his spear point against a bronze bell hanging outside the guard-house. A middle-aged servant emerged from the building, spoke to the guard, then ran toward the main building. Banouin waited patiently. After some time two more knights appeared, grim-faced men with emotionless eyes.

The first guard approached Banouin. "These men will take you to where you can make your complaint," he said.

"Thank you, sir."

Banouin followed the two knights along a path of white gravel and through a tree garden to a side door leading to a narrow corridor. Their footsteps echoed inside the building. They climbed stairs, turning first left and then right, and soon Banouin felt lost within the maze of corridors and rooms. At last they halted before double doors, which the soldiers opened. Beyond the doors was a large room with high, arched windows. The walls were unadorned, but a beautiful mosaic pattern had been laid upon the floor, a series of interconnected lines of shimmering gold on a field of white. In the center of the room was a semicircular table behind which sat a priest. His head was shaved, his beard dyed blood red. He glanced up as the knights entered, then sat back in his chair, idly fingering the pale gray pendant that hung from his neck.

"You are here to defend a traitor, I understand?" he said, his voice sibilant.

Banouin stood very still and opened the pathway to his talent. He could feel the emotions of the knights on either side of him. Both were enjoying this scene and waiting for the moment when they would drag him screaming to the cells. Reaching out, he touched the mind of the Crimson Priest and recoiled. His thoughts were of torture and vileness. Banouin was about to speak when he felt the presence of a fourth, unseen man. He focused the talent. The man was observing the proceedings from behind a velvet curtain. Banouin sensed a cold, calculating mind and a powerful, magnetic personality. The observer was also in pain and struggling to deal with it.

"Well, do you have a tongue?" asked the priest at the table.

"I do, sir, but I have to say that I am confused. My understanding was that following arrest, a suspected man would then face a hearing to decide his guilt or innocence. Yet you, not knowing which arrested man I have come to speak for, have already decided his guilt. How is this so?"

The priest's pale face reddened. "You dare to question me? Give me your name!"

"I am Banouin the Healer, student to Sencra, who teaches history at the university."

"I do not like your attitude, Banouin. It lacks respect. To disrespect a priest of Stone is to disrespect Stone itself. That alone is treachery. As to your foul master . . . His hearing was held two hours ago. He was found guilty and will face the consequences."

The velvet curtain flickered at the far end of the room, and a huge man carrying a golden staff and wearing a voluminous red robe moved into sight. The Crimson Priest stood and bowed. Both of the guards dipped their heads. Banouin also bowed but then looked up into the man's swollen face. It was impossibly large, and white hair framed it like a lion's mane. The man moved with great difficulty, pain etched on his features. The Crimson Priest moved away from the chair, and the figure in the red robe eased his enormous weight down upon it.

"You call yourself a healer," said the newcomer, his voice rumbling like distant thunder. "What do you heal?"

"I can ease all pains, lord," Banouin told him, "and cure many ailments."

"All pains?"

"Yes, lord."

"How old are you?"

"Twenty-one, lord."

"Twenty-one," repeated the man. "Where did you learn these wondrous skills? At the university?"

"No, lord. I was born among the Rigante tribe. My mother is a healer, and she taught me the mysteries of herbal lore and also the gift of diagnosis."

The huge man winced as he leaned forward, resting his massive forearms on the table. "And how would you diagnose my condition, Banouin the Healer?"

"You are suffering from anasarca, lord. Your body is swollen with water—a sign that either your heart, liver, or kidneys are not functioning as they should. Do you sleep upright now?"

"Yes. I choke if I lie down."

"Then your heart is weak, lord."

"Can your . . . herbs make it stronger?"

"I can heal you within ten days," said Banouin.

"Ten days? So confident?"

"Yes, lord."

"What if I were to tell you that should you fail, I will have your eyes pierced by hot irons, your tongue ripped from your mouth, and your limbs sawn away? Would you still be so confident?"

The words were spoken with chilling relish, and Banouin gazed into the man's cold eyes. "You have an illness, lord. I can cure it," he said softly. "I do not lie. As, indeed, I do not lie when I say that my tutor, Sencra, is no cultist. Whoever named him as such is the liar. He has spoken to me often about what he regards as the stupidity of the cultists and of his admiration for the work you are doing, lord," Banouin said, lying smoothly.

"Are you saying that you will heal me only if I release your friend?"

The words hung in the air, and Banouin knew his answer had to be the right one. "No, lord, I will heal you because I can. What I am saying is that Sencra is innocent."

"I will look into the matter. What herbs will you need?"

"A small amount of figwort seed and leaves from a number of flowering plants, including marigold. Also some nettles. And some oil, perfumed with lavender. I shall return with these items tomorrow, and the healing can begin."

Nalademus pushed himself to his feet. "My guards will go with you, and you will return with them within the hour. The healing will begin tonight," he said.

Just under two hours later Banouin was ushered into the lavish private apartments of Nalademus the Stone elder. Velvet curtains hung over the windows, and ornaments of gold and silver adorned the many shelves and tables. The couches were all covered with richly embroidered silk, and even the lanterns glinted with gold.

Nalademus was sitting propped up on a couch, cushions all around him. In the lantern light his face had a waxy sheen. He had removed his crimson robe, and the bare flesh of his shoulders seemed impossibly stretched and swollen.

Banouin placed his medicine pack on a table.

"Did you obtain all you needed?" asked Nalademus.

"Yes, lord, though the apothecary was terrified to see knights of Stone at his door."

"Terror has its uses," said the sick man. The two guards positioned themselves by the door and stood silently. "You mentioned figwort earlier," said Nalademus. "I take it you mean to use the seed."

"Yes, lord. It will help your heart."

"I understand the seed is a deadly poison."

"Indeed it is," agreed Banouin. "A little too much and the patient dies. I will not use too much."

Nalademus's head sagged back on the cushion. "What I told you about hot irons was no idle threat. You understand this?"

"I understand. Now, what you must understand is that I need you to relax. Your body is under great stress, and that is not helping your heart. What have your own surgeons prescribed?"

"I have been bled constantly, and I have swallowed several gallons of noxious potions. Now you will prepare me another."

Banouin mixed some ground seeds with powdered chamomile and elder flower, then added it to a goblet of water. This he passed to Nalademus. The Stone elder drained it in a single swallow. "Lean your head back on the cushion," said

Banouin, "and close your eyes." Nalademus did so. Banouin took hold of his right arm. The flesh was clammy and hot. Closing his eyes, Banouin gathered his talent, then let it flow within the stricken body. The heart, as he had feared, was not strong, and the kidneys were on the point of collapse. He waited for the digitalis to begin its work. This would have an immediate twofold action, as Vorna had explained to him years before. The heart contractions would be strengthened, and the beat slowed. This meant increased power to the muscle and a longer period of relaxation between beats. With Nalademus there would also be a third advantage. Pressure from a stronger heart would force more blood into his fading kidneys, aiding the diuretic effect. This alone, however, would not save Nalademus. In normal circumstances, even with the aid of digitalis he would be dead within weeks.

Still holding on to the man's arm, Banouin strengthened the kidneys and directed energy into the liver, which was also in the first stages of terminal disease.

"I feel it working," whispered Nalademus. "There is not so much pain. You have done well."

"I need you to lie upon the floor, lord," said Banouin.

"I will not be able to breathe."

"Yes, you will. Your heart is stronger now. But I have to help move the water that is flooding your muscle tissue." That was a lie. It was important, however, for Nalademus to believe that the healing was the result of physical medicine and natural practices. Banouin had no wish for his power to be recognized.

He helped Nalademus stretch out on a thick rug and placed a cushion under his head. Then he began a series of smooth massaging strokes on the man's chest, shoulders, and arms. Lastly he placed his hands on the Stone elder's temples and gently pressed his fingers to the skin. Nalademus closed his eyes, and his breathing deepened.

Banouin rose to his feet and stretched his aching back. Then he called the guards to assist him in helping Nalademus to his feet and through to the bedroom. Nalademus lay down. "It feels so good to stretch out on a bed," he said. "I have been sleeping in chairs for weeks."

"Do not overstretch yourself tomorrow, lord. You are stronger, but your kidneys will need time to heal."

"I feel better than I have in months, Banouin. But I will heed what you say."

"I also think, lord, that I should stay close for the next few days. There may be a relapse."

Nalademus smiled. "I have rooms prepared for you." With a grunt he sat up and walked through a narrow doorway. Banouin waited, and after a while the Stone elder returned. "By the Stone," he said. "I've not pissed like that in five years."

Banouin forced a smile. "You will find that the action is repeated a great deal over the next few days, lord. There is a great amount of liquid to be expelled."

Nalademus sat down on the bed. "This has been a fortunate day for me, young man. It has also proved fortunate for your tutor, Sencra. I did reexamine the evidence, and he will be released forthwith."

"Thank you, lord. That is most kind of you."

"My kindness is legendary," Nalademus said coldly. "Now my guards will show you to your rooms."

Lanterns had been lit in the suite of rooms assigned to him, and Banouin stood in the doorway and marveled at the opulence of the interior. A magnificent fresco had been painted around the main room: a vineyard scene with leaves and grapes. The vines seemed to be growing out of the walls, and the grapes looked good enough to pluck from the plaster. The furniture was elegantly crafted, and the rugs below his feet were woven silk.

Banouin stepped inside, and the guards pulled shut the door. There was no fireplace in the main room, but warm air was circulating up through two metal grilles in the floor and the temperature was comfortable despite the open doors leading to the balcony.

He strolled outside and found himself overlooking the knights' barracks and the bronze gates through which he had walked with some trepidation earlier. Alone at last, Banouin allowed himself to relax. His hands began to tremble. There was a curved seat on the balcony, and he sank gratefully into it. Doubts assailed him. He was pleased that Sencra had been freed and felt a small pride in his achievement. Against that, however, was the knowledge that he was in the process of saving a monster. It had been hard to touch the swollen flesh of Nalademus. Evil emanated from the man like a seeping, invisible mist, corrupting as it touched. Banouin shivered and walked back into the warmth of the room.

The tables and shelves contained many small ornaments, mostly porcelain figures and objects of colored glass. Banouin stared at them for a moment. These, he realized, were personal items gathered by a man—or woman—who took pleasure in the delicate beauty of the pieces. He moved to a closet at the far wall and opened it. The shelves and hooks within were bare, but unnoticed in a corner, a single sandal lay against the wall. Moving around the suite, he opened all the drawers and found not a solitary item in any of them. Whoever had dwelled here had left in a great hurry, not even bothering to pack the beautiful porcelain. Perhaps they will return for it, he thought.

Someone tapped at the outer door. Banouin walked through the apartment. A young man was waiting outside, bearing a silver tray on which was a selection of cooked meats and vegetables and a jug of water. The servant bowed his head and entered the suite, laying the tray on a lacquered table.

"Who dwelled here before me?" asked Banouin. The servant bowed again, and Banouin saw fear in his eyes. Then the young man hurried away. "Thank you," Banouin called after him.

Moments later there was another knock at the door. This time it was two older servants. One was carrying folded clothes, the other a copper bucket filled with hot water. Banouin saw that the clothes were his own. The first servant laid the clothing in the empty closet, then withdrew. The second moved through the suite to a room Banouin had not noticed, behind a paneled door. He followed the servant and watched him pour the hot water into a tub shaped like a giant shell. Other servants entered the room, each carrying buckets. Within minutes the shell tub was three-quarters full. The first servant returned, carrying fresh towels and a small phial of perfume, which he added to the water. Then they all withdrew. Not one spoke a word.

Banouin removed his tunic and sandals and climbed into the tub. The water rose around him, the sweet perfume filling his nostrils. The feeling was exquisite. Splashing water to his face and hair, he lay back, remaining in the bath until the water cooled. As he climbed out, his foot touched something in the base of the tub. Reaching down, his finger hooked into a ring of metal. He tugged it. Immediately the water began to bubble down the exposed hole. In panic he struggled to replace the plug, frightened that he was flooding the apartments below. He could hear water splashing from outside the tub room window. Moving to it, he glanced out. An exit pipe protruded from the wall, the water gushing to the ground below. Banouin smiled, returned to the tub and pulled the plug once more, then ran back to the window, leaned out, and watched the water flow away. For some reason this small activity lifted his spirits, and he returned to the main room and ate the food that had been left for him. Weariness was heavy upon him, and he went into the bedroom. The bed was of gilded wood, but curiously, the mattress was slightly overlarge, jutting over the wooden frame. He lay down upon it, and immediately his anxiety returned. Sitting up swiftly, he realized that something had touched his talent. He lay back once more and honed his concentration.

In an instant he saw a vision of two soldiers looming above the bed and the swollen, angry face of Nalademus beyond them. The soldiers had knives in their hands and were reaching for him. In terror he sat bolt upright.

The vision vanished from his mind.

Clambering from the bed, he grabbed the edge of the mattress and pushed it back. In the lantern light he saw a patch of wet on the planks of the bed frame below it. When he touched it with his finger, it felt sticky. Banouin lifted his hand and saw that it was blood. Running to the washroom, he cleaned his hand, then hurled the bloodstained towel to the floor. His heart was hammering, his mind awash with fear.

The man who had lived in this room had been murdered that day, killed in his bed while Nalademus watched. Then servants had removed the blood-drenched mattress, replacing it with another that did not quite fit. The murdered man had not been killed swiftly, for the blood had continued to flow, seeping through the mattress to the frame beneath. What had been his perceived crime? Banouin wondered.

Back in the main room Banouin drank some water and gazed once more at the little porcelain figures. When at last exhaustion overcame him, he walked back to the bed and pulled the mattress back in place.

Then slept fitfully on the couch.

A bad dream awoke him in the middle of the night, and he sat up shivering with fear. The memory of the dream drifted out of his consciousness like water falling through his fingers. All he could remember were sharp knives pricking at his skin.

Rising to his feet, Banouin wandered out to the balcony. Stars were bright in a clear sky, and he felt the tension easing from him. He wished he could close his eyes and let his spirit soar free, but that was impossible here, surrounded by stone. A cold wind blew, and Banouin walked back to the couch and threw the blanket around his shoulders. Back inside the room he felt suddenly claustrophobic, as if the walls were closing in on his spirit. Returning to the balcony, he sat down under the starlight and gazed out over the city of Stone.

From there he could see the towers of the university building and the awesome, moonlit majesty of the Palace of the Republic, where the emperor now dwelled. Stone is truly magnificent at night, he thought, and found himself filled with both sadness and shame. This was the city of his dreams, and because of that he had blinded himself to the truth. Yes, Stone was beautiful, but it was the beauty of the tomb, its glorious exterior merely hiding corruption and decay within.

The buildings had been designed and constructed by men of awesome talent, using only the finest materials. Those materials had been purchased by conquest, by the butchering of neighboring races and civilizations. The foundation of Stone was blood. Every column, every statue, every block of every road was drenched in it.

Anger flared in Banouin, fueled by self-loathing. Why did I not see it? he asked himself. The truth was as nakedly bright as the moon above. He had seen it but had pushed it away to a dark and hopefully forgotten corner of his mind, concentrating instead on the more positive aspects of city life: the university and the Great Museum, the libraries and the architecture. In this way his selfish dream had stayed alive. But coming here, to the temple, this place of concentrated evil, had lit a torch, and by its light all the ugliness of Stone had been laid bare.

He wished he could run from there all the way to the Park of Phesus to sit beneath the willow and free his spirit to soar in the sweetness and purity of the night.

"Come sit with me, Banouin," came a voice.

Banouin surged to his feet and spun around. The doorway to his room had disappeared. Where the frame had been was now a bower of honeysuckle, thick and heavily scented. The room had disappeared also, and he saw the Morrigu, heavily veiled and sitting on a tree trunk just beyond the honeysuckle. A fire was glowing in a circle of stones before her, and Banouin could smell the musky odors of the forest: wet earth and rotting leaves.

The Morrigu beckoned to him, and he moved to the fire, squatting down beside it and pushing his hands into the soft earth. The scent and sounds of the forest soaked into him, filling his spirit. Drawing his hands from the earth, he held them to his face and drew in a deep breath.

"Look at you, citizen of Stone," said the Morrigu, "grubbing your hands into the soil like an animal. Do you miss the dirt, Banouin?"

"You may mock me, lady, and perhaps I deserve it. But I never smelled a sweeter scent in all my life."

"And do you know why?"

"Yes, I do," he told her. "There is life in this earth, vibrant life. There are seeds waiting to grow and insects are burrowing through the soil. It is rich and fertile and crying out for growth. It is beautiful," he said.

"Ah, then perhaps you can take a handful back to the city with you. You can carry it to the university and say to them: 'Look, the Rigante boy has brought you some mud.' And they will garland you with flowers and perhaps declare a day of celebration in your honor."

"You are in a foul mood today," he said.

"I delivered you, Banouin. Your little eyes were closed against the brightness of the lantern's glare. They have remained closed ever since. Now they begin to open. You want me to applaud? You hold that earth in your hands, and you talk of its fertility. All that is true. But why is it feeding you now? Why does it lift you? Answer me that!"

"I . . . I don't know."

"Stupid child. It is not your flesh that it feeds. It is your spirit. And from your spirit comes your power. I have watched you in Stone, running to old willow and freeing your spirit to fly back to Caer Druagh. Oh, how happy you were. Did you never question why the old willow brought you freedom or why you could not use your talents to the full anywhere else in Stone? No, of course you did not. You were so full of your selfish dreams. The old willow stands on the last sacred spot in these five hills. All the others are covered now. Entombed. And the spirit of the land withers and dies."

"I know it now," said Banouin. "I understand that Stone is a city of evil. And I am sorry it has taken me so long to realize it."

"Trust me, child, you still do not realize the significance. This world—all worlds—survive only because of the harmony between spirit and matter. The dirt in your hands is charged with spirit, fresh and full and wondrously magical. Without the spirit it would be lifeless. No seeds would grow, no insects thrive. Once—when I was young—this world was ablaze with spirit. Throw a seed into the air, and wherever it landed it would sprout and grow tall. The Seidh prospered here, along with scores of thousands of spirit creatures. Men called us gods and worshiped us. And we helped man. We raised him from the earth and taught him to look at the stars. Did we do this because we loved man? No. It was because we saw in man a creature capable of feeding the spirit of the world. Each act of selflessness, of love, of courage and compassion added to the world's energy." She gave a harsh laugh and threw another dry stick to the fire. "Of course every act of greed and vileness drained the spirit. It will surprise you not at all to learn that evil men devour the spirit many times faster than good men can enhance it. Like a statue, I suppose. A good craftsman can create a masterpiece in four or five years. A fool with a hammer can destroy it in a few heartbeats.

"We labored long to find a balance. We struggled to teach man the error of his ways. Quite simply we failed. And one by one the spirit creatures left this world in search of other, more pleasant homes. The more foolish of us stayed behind, still trying to teach errant, arrogant man. And as the spirit withered, so, too, did we. You asked me once why I chose to look this way. I did not choose it, Banouin. You chose it. You and your race."

"I am sorry," he said, the words sounding lame and entirely inadequate.

"Don't tell me how sorry you are, Banouin. Show me!"

The world spun. Banouin opened his eyes. He was still sitting on the balcony. There was no ivy clinging to the door frame, no fire dying in the circle of stones.

But upon his hands there was the smell of sweet earth.

For three days Nalademus continued to improve, but on the fourth day he suffered a pounding headache. Banouin heard him hurling crockery across the room and shouting obscenities at a servant. He hurried along the corridor.

"I'll pluck out your eyes, you clumsy oaf!" screamed Nalademus as the servant cowered by the door, his head in his hands.

Banouin felt the rage from Nalademus like a blow that almost made him step back. Instead he fastened to the emotion, gentling it and radiating it back to its bearer, softened and changed. The Stone elder stood towering over the servant, and his fists unclenched. He shook his massive head. "Get out," he told the frightened man. "Go on, away with you." The servant scrambled clear and sped along the corridor. Nalademus turned to Banouin. "My head is splitting."

"Sit down, lord. I shall soothe it for you." The big man sank into a deep chair, and Banouin moved behind him. Nalademus tensed instantly. "I will do you no harm, lord," Banouin said softly, placing his fingers on the elder's temples. Closing his eyes, Banouin drew out the pain, easing the rigid muscles of the neck and shoulders.

"That is good," whispered Nalademus. "The pain is almost gone."

"I fear it is my fault, lord. Some of the herbs I use do have secondary effects. Headaches are not uncommon, and they can be extremely severe. I shall lessen the amounts."

Banouin moved away from the elder, but Nalademus bade

him sit in a chair opposite. "You have great skills, young man. How may I show my gratitude to you?"

"You already have, lord, by freeing Sencra. By your leave, I will remain here for two more days until your recovery is complete, then return to my studies and my work at the university."

"You will reside here, Banouin," said Nalademus. "You will receive a handsome salary, and a carriage will take you to the university on any days you choose."

"Thank you, lord," said Banouin, his heart sinking.

"Now tell me about Bendegit Bran."

Banouin's jaw dropped. "Why, lord?" he stammered.

"He arrived in the city ten days ago as a guest of our emperor. He and a brutish general named Fiallach traveled under escort from Goriasa. They are staying in a villa overlooking the bay. I will probably have to meet them myself and would be grateful if you could tell me something of them."

Banouin gathered his thoughts. "Bran is the half brother of our king, Connavar, lord. He is also a general of the horse archers and governs the northern lands of the Pannone. He is a good man and was always very kind to me and my mother."

"Is he a married man?"

"Yes. He had two children when I left Caer Druagh."

"What of his ambitions? Does he seek to rule himself?"

"I don't believe so, lord. He is devoted to Connavar. Might I ask why the emperor invited them here?"

"That is for the emperor to know, Banouin. Not mere servants like you and me." Banouin sensed the anger underlying the words. "And what of Fiallach?"

"He is a mighty warrior, probably the strongest man in all Rigante lands. He must be over fifty now, but he is awesome to behold, six feet, six inches tall, with enormous shoulders. He is ferocious in battle, utterly fearless and without mercy. He is one of three generals who lead divisions of the Iron Wolves, Connavar's heavy cavalry."

"You like him?" asked Nalademus.

"He is a hard man to like, lord. But I do not dislike him."

"And you would class him as loyal to Connavar?"

"Utterly. They were enemies once, when Connavar was a

young man. Both loved the same girl, and she chose Connavar. But they have been friends now for twenty years."

"And what of Braefar?"

"Is he here, too, lord?"

"No, but I have heard him spoken of."

"He is the laird of Three Streams and another half brother
to Connavar. He is a very clever man."

"Do I hear a 'but' in your voice?"

"I believe he feels he should have had greater duties than he
has. He complains publicly about his talents being underused."

"And are they underused?" Nalademus asked softly.

"I don't believe they are," said Banouin. "Whenever Connavar has offered him more responsibility, something has always gone wrong. Braefar always blamed others for their
shortcomings, accepting no responsibility for the errors and
mistakes."

"Interesting," said Nalademus. "I thank you for your time.
Now I must get to work. I shall have a carriage ready for you
to attend the university. Please convey my good wishes to
Sencra."

"I shall, lord," said Banouin, rising. "And I shall return by
dusk to prepare more medicine."

Banouin bowed and left the Stone elder.

An hour later he was strolling through the main hallway of
the university building and out into the Park of Phesus. A light
rain was falling, but Banouin ignored it and ran along the
white path to the willow. Pushing aside the trailing branches,
he sat down on the curved stone bench and relaxed his mind.
His spirit soared free, floating high above the city. Swiftly he
sped over the waters of the bay, hovering over the fine villas
with waterside views. One by one he flew through them,
seeking out his countrymen.

And then he saw them, walking together in a terraced garden. Bran seemed worried, his handsome features grim as he
listened to his companion. Fiallach looked older, and there
was silver in his braided yellow hair and drooping mustache.
It felt good to be close to them, and Banouin realized in that
moment just how much he missed the mountains of home. He
wanted to eavesdrop on their conversation but decided that
would be rude and flew back to his body.

He opened his eyes and saw the dark-haired Maro leaning over him. "I thought you had fainted," said Maro. "Are you all right?"

"I am fine."

"We thought the worst when you failed to return. Then Sencra came back and told us you had spoken up for him with Nalademus himself. That was a fine deed, Banouin."

"He was innocent. I just explained it, that's all."

"Heroes should always be modest," said Maro. "Or so my father always tells me. Come, let's go to the library. You can tell me of your adventures."

◇ **8** ◇

BENDEGIT BRAN STOOD before the emperor and bowed low. Beside him the huge General Fiallach followed his lead. Straightening, Bran waved his hand, and Fiallach stepped forward, bearing an ornately carved wooden box. "I bring you greetings from my king," said Bran, "and a gift."

Jasaray, seated on a gilded throne, summoned the tribesman forward. Bran noted that the three guards in silver armor standing close to the emperor were tense and ready to spring forward at the first sign of treachery. Hardly surprising, thought Bran. Fiallach was a massive man with fierce blue eyes and a long-standing and well-chronicled hatred of Stone. Jasaray himself seemed perfectly at ease. Fiallach lifted the lid of the box. Inside, nestling on velvet, was an exquisite dagger with a blade of silver steel and a hilt of gold encrusted with pale blue gems. The pommel held a huge black opal that had been superbly carved into the shape of a panther's head. Jasaray reached out and lifted the dagger clear. It seemed to Bran that the weapon looked incongruous in the old man's hand, and he understood in that moment why he was once known as Scholar to his men. Jasaray could not have looked less like a warrior emperor. He was skinny and slightly round-shouldered, his hair thinning, his face long and ascetic. He could have been a philosopher or a teacher rather than the most gifted general Stone had produced.

"It is a charming piece," said Jasaray to Bran, ignoring Fiallach. "Please convey my gratitude to your brother, Connavar."

Bran looked into the emperor's eyes and felt the thrill of fear, for in that gaze he saw the keen intelligence of the man.

203

"My king says to tell you that he remembers with great affection the time he spent with you on the Perdii campaign, and he will be delighted to hear that you are in good health."

"Indeed I am, Lord Bran. Which is more, I understand, than can be said for your brother. How are his wounds?"

"I had not realized the news had traveled this far, Majesty. Connavar is well, his wounds minor. The assassins, however, did not fare so well. He slew three himself. The fourth was taken and put to the questioning."

"Do you mean tortured?" asked Jasaray, still examining the dagger.

"No, Majesty. We have a druid with great skill. He spoke to the man and elicited the truth from him."

"Ah, the truth. And what was the truth?"

"He and the others were hired by a merchant to kill the king."

"Tricky creatures, merchants," said Jasaray, replacing the dagger in its box. "They yearn only for money. I take it the king had refused him some request."

"We have yet to ascertain that, Majesty. The merchant fled across the water and took refuge in Stone."

"Well, you must supply the name and I will see he is hunted down and brought to trial." Jasaray rose from his throne. "My men will show you and your aide to your quarters, where you may bathe if it pleases you. This afternoon you will both be my guests at the Palantes Stadium. Later we can talk of political matters."

"Thank you, Majesty," said Bran, offering another bow. He waited until Jasaray had left the throne room. One of the king's guards took the dagger box, then he and Fiallach followed another silver-garbed soldier to a suite of rooms. Once inside, Bran sat down in a deep chair, while Fiallach cast off his cloak and stretched out on a couch.

"He's a cold man," said Fiallach, speaking in Keltoi.

"Aye, but canny. He showed no reaction when we spoke of the merchant. Perhaps he knew nothing of it."

Fiallach said nothing. Brother Solstice had warned them both about hidden chambers behind the walls where spies might lurk, noting down their conversation.

Beyond the main room was a garden, and Bran gestured Fiallach to follow him out. Once outside, they wandered along a curving, neatly paved path, stopping here and there to look at the many flowers. Bran glanced around, sure that from there they could not be overheard. "You kept your temper well, my friend," he said.

"Perhaps I'm getting older and wiser," said Fiallach, but there was anger in his eyes.

"They all know of you and your skills. They probably also know of your legendary temper. It is vital you do not react to any . . . discourtesy."

"I know that, Bran. By Taranis, you have been belaboring the point for the entire journey!"

Bran smiled. "You are right. My apologies. I wonder if Nalademus will be at our meeting."

"I don't much care who is there," said Fiallach. "I still don't know why Conn accepted this invitation. And there is more than a chance we'll be held hostage."

Bran nodded, and the two men continued their walk around the garden. They came to a small man-made pond over which a wooden bridge had been raised. Bran leaned on the rail and looked down into the still water, gazing at his reflection. Like Fiallach he had not relished this trip and was missing Gwen and their three boys terribly. He thought of them constantly, wondering whether little Orrin had mastered his fear of riding and if his eldest son, Ruathain, had regained his strength after the fever. The boy had been so weak. Brother Solstice had tended him well, but Bran knew that secondary illnesses could prove fatal.

"We cannot refuse the invitation," Connavar had told him. "It would be seen as both weak and hostile. Obviously Jasaray needs something from us. Find out what it is and report it back to me."

"What about Wing?" Bran had asked, referring to their brother Braefar by his soul-name, Wing over Water. "He is skilled with words and might enjoy a trip to Stone. He has no wife, no sons. And he constantly talks of being bored."

"You are more suited to this task, Bran. Take Fiallach with you."

This had surprised Bran. Fiallach was known for his

seething hatred of all things Stone. "Would that not cause offense, Brother? After Cogden, Fiallach cut the heads from thirty Stone officers and had them set on spears at the border. According to Brother Solstice, only two Rigante names are well known to the people of Stone: yours and Fiallach's."

"Precisely why he should go," Connavar had said. "Although you are wrong about two names. There is a third. Many of the merchants who seek our favors are talking about a Rigante warrior who fights in the arenas of Stone."

Bran had heard the stories but had never spoken about them with Connavar. "You want me to meet with him?" he had asked.

"No. He has made his life, barren though it is."

"I liked him," Bran had said.

Connavar's eyes had narrowed briefly, and he had scanned Bran's face for signs of criticism. Then he had sighed and for a brief moment lost the haunted look Bran had come to know so well in the years since the death of Tae.

"I might have liked him, too," he had said at last. "He is one of many regrets I carry. If I could turn back the years and live my life again, I would live it differently. I would have taken Tae to the lake. There would have been no war with the Pannone."

"You know, Conn, this is something I have never understood. You are my brother, and I love you. But how long will you allow yourself to carry this burden? Take a wife, sire sons. You owe it to yourself—and to the people. You must have an heir, Conn."

Connavar had smiled. "You are my heir, Bran. And your sons will follow you." Connavar had walked to the window and stared out over the countryside. Light clouds were casting dappled shadows over the flanks of the mountains.

"You could invite Bane back home," said Bran.

Connavar had swung around, his face once more set, his expression hard. "We will talk of it no more."

"As you wish, my king," Bran had said.

Connavar had been instantly contrite. "I am sorry, Brother. I had thought the hurt would lessen as the years passed. But it sits like a canker on the soul."

"Ah, dammit! I am sorry, too, Conn. I'll not mention it again. So what is it you think Jasaray wants from us?"

"It is hard to say. He has many troubles. The war in the east has meant that most of his regular troops are far from Stone. Brother Solstice tells me that there are now more Stone knights in the city than loyal soldiers. Jasaray apparently believes Nalademus is loyal to him, and perhaps he is. But the political situation there is precarious. The arrival of Rigante ambassadors will cause a stir and perhaps deflect criticism of the eastern campaign. In short, Brother, I do not know."

Bran had now been in Stone for ten days, he and Fiallach quartered at a villa to the south of the city, awaiting the call from Jasaray. Now it had come, and still there had been no talks.

A servant came running down the path. "The bathhouse is ready, sirs," he said. "And your clothes have been moved from the villa. I have taken the liberty of having them washed for you. They are currently drying."

"That is kind of you," said Bran.

The private bathhouse was some forty feet long, with a sunken bath large enough to take perhaps twenty people. Bran and Fiallach removed their clothes and climbed in, sitting back and relaxing in the perfumed water. Fiallach sighed and ducked his head below the surface. He came up sputtering, water dripping from his braids and his long yellow and silver mustache.

Bran chuckled. "You are being corrupted by such decadence," he said.

"It eases the pain in my back," said Fiallach. "I am not as young as once I was. I do not heal so swiftly."

They lazed contentedly for some time, and then two servants arrived, holding hot towels. The Rigante warriors climbed from the bath and dried themselves, then walked through to the massage room, where two young men waited.

Bran lay on his stomach and felt the warm oil poured onto his back. He relaxed instantly, and the masseur expertly stroked and probed the muscles of his neck and shoulders, easing the tension. He glanced across at Fiallach, who was lying facedown with his eyes closed. When the massage was finished, the oil gently scraped from their bodies with rounded ivory blades, they rose and dressed and returned to their rooms. Food had been laid there, cold cooked meats and sweet pastries alongside two jugs, one of wine and one of water. They ate, then sat back to await the call from Jasaray.

"One could almost come to like this place," said Fiallach.

The door opened, and two silver-armored warriors entered. "Your chariot is here," said the first, his voice echoing the contempt in his eyes.

Fiallach rose and strode across to tower over him. He looked at the man closely.

"Isn't that remarkable," he said to Bran. "Do you remember the first Stone head I rammed on the lance? It was just like his, though I think this man's neck is thicker. Probably take two cuts to sever it." The soldier blanched and licked his lips. Fiallach smiled at him. "Do not concern yourself, little man. Today I am in a good mood."

Horath bowed deeply as the emperor and his entourage entered the Royal Enclosure and took up their seats overlooking the golden sand of the arena. The sun was shining, and the stadium was almost full: twelve thousand citizens of Stone waiting to see that day's death bouts.

Horath led the emperor to his high-backed, velvet-covered chair. With Jasaray were two tribesmen, one handsome and beardless with golden hair and the other an enormous figure with a long drooping mustache. The giant looked fearsome, and his bare arms showed many scars. He would have made a fine gladiator, thought Horath.

Six silver-garbed warriors filed in and stood in a line behind the emperor. Jasaray sat down, leaning his back against a plump cushion. He glanced up at Horath. "You are looking well, young man," he said.

"Thank you, Majesty. You honor Circus Occian with your presence."

"May I introduce my guests? This is Bendegit Bran, a lord of the Rigante tribe, and his aide, Fiallach."

"A pleasure to meet you, sirs," said Horath, offering a slight bow. "Have you come to see your comrade in battle?"

He saw the surprise in their faces. "Bane is fighting today," he said swiftly. "He is Gladiator Seven now, a magnificent fighter and a great asset to our circus. Today he meets Dex from Circus Palantes. Dex is Gladiator Four, and it should be a classic encounter. If you wish to gamble, I would be delighted to have your bets placed with the circus bank."

Bendegit Bran shook his head and exchanged glances with Fiallach.

"Well, enjoy your day, sirs." With a deep bow to Jasaray, Horath withdrew to his own seat. Every few minutes he cast nervous glances back toward the door. He had invited Nalademus and Lord Voltan to the enclosure but had received no reply. Even so, chairs had been prepared for them. This had caused him some concern, for Nalademus was a large man and needed a big chair. That would have been fine except that the emperor insisted on a straight-backed seat for himself, with a single cushion. Horath could not seat Nalademus in a chair more grand than that of the emperor and had instead placed a wide couch to the rear of the enclosure. Unfortunately, this meant that Nalademus, should he arrive, would be sitting behind Jasaray and his guests. Horath comforted himself with the rumor that the Stone elder had been in ill health for some time and was therefore unlikely to attend.

A blare of trumpets sounded, and six horsemen rode into the arena. The crowd cheered as the men galloped their white mounts around the perimeter. Then, in unison, the riders lifted their feet and smoothly rose to stand on the backs of the horses. The mounts came into a line. The riders began to leap from one horse to another, landing lightly, timing each jump to perfection. Then they sat back in their saddles and rode from the arena. The crowd applauded their skills. Horath glanced at the two Rigante warriors. They sat expressionless, arms folded across their chests. At that moment the rear door opened, and Horath mouthed a silent curse.

The Stone elder Nalademus moved into sight, leaning on a long golden staff. Horath leapt to his feet. "Welcome, lord," he said. "You honor us with your attendance."

Nalademus nodded, then glanced at the couch. Jasaray rose. "Good to see you, my friend," he said warmly. "Please, come sit beside me. Horath, have another chair brought in."

Horath hurried out, signaled two servants, and gave them instructions. Moments later they carried in a beautifully carved and gilded chair that was taller and deeper than that used by the emperor. "You should sit here, Majesty," said Nalademus as the chair was placed beside the emperor's.

"Nonsense, my friend. You have been ill, and your well-being is far more important to me than small matters of ego. Sit yourself and be comfortable."

Nalademus bowed and lowered his massive frame into the gilded chair.

Horath breathed a sigh of relief and returned to his place. Nalademus was introduced to the other guests, and then the party returned its interest to the events in the stadium. A precision cavalry display was followed by a lion hunt. Two beasts were set loose in the stadium, and two horsemen armed with hunting bows galloped out. The first lion was killed swiftly, but the second, wounded and enraged, charged at a rider. The horse reared, throwing the man to the sand. Instantly the lion was upon him, and the beast's talons ripped open his back. The satisfied roar from the crowd startled the lion, which swung its great head just as the second rider bore down, sending an arrow into its heart.

The audience applauded wildly as slaves ran out to carry the mutilated rider from the stadium. The bodies of the lions were dragged clear, and slaves with buckets of sand and long rakes covered the blood.

"The riders are men of great courage," said Horath to Bendegit Bran.

"The lions were starved," said Bran, "their strength almost gone."

Horath smiled and turned away, casting his eyes over the crowd, which was more than two thousand more numerous than at the last event three weeks before. Circus Occian was close to becoming the most profitable circus in Stone. Ah, thought Horath, how that must taste like poison to the owners of Palantes. Part of the success was due to the tribesman Bane, who had become immensely popular with the crowds, but the greater part was due to the influence of Rage, who now trained all the gladiators, driving them hard, building their strength and speed. It was rare now for an Occian man to lose a death bout.

The trumpets sounded for the intermission, and the party rose and moved back to the long room, where food and drink had been laid out on a twenty-foot table. Nalademus engaged Bendegit Bran in conversation, while Jasaray stood talking with Fiallach. Horath hovered close by, close to the silent guards lined up across the doorway.

"I understand you have children," Nalademus said to Bran.

"Three now," said Bran. "All boys. The youngest is but four months."

"The children are our future," said the Stone elder. "They should be cherished."

"Indeed," agreed Bran, visibly relaxing. "It is a joy watching them grow and learn. Do you have children?"

"Sadly, no. The priesthood demands total abstinence from all desires of the flesh. It is a source of regret to me, which is perhaps why I take such joy from the happiness of family men such as yourself."

Horath wandered away. The honey dripping from Nalademus was almost nauseating. Another figure moved into the room, the guards stepping aside for him. He was tall and wide-shouldered, wearing armor of black and silver. Horath hurried over.

"Lord Voltan, many, many thanks for taking the time to attend. Circus Occian is honored by your presence."

"Fetch me some wine," said the tall warrior.

"Indeed so," said Horath, holding to his smile. As he filled a goblet, Horath became aware of a change in the atmosphere within the room. He glanced back to where the former gladiator stood. The guards looked nervous and ill at ease, and even the emperor was watching him closely. Jasaray strolled over to where Voltan waited. For a moment it seemed the Stone knight was not going to bow, but then he dipped his head. Jasaray summoned the captain of his guards. The man stepped forward.

"Lord Voltan," said Jasaray, "is a loyal and good friend, and I can see from the dust on his cloak that he has ridden hard to be with us today, which is why I excuse him for coming into my presence armed with a sword. In his haste to pay his respects he probably forgot he was wearing it. What, then, pray, is your excuse for allowing him to enter?"

"I am sorry, Majesty," said the man. "It will not happen again."

"Indeed not. You are dismissed from my service. Report to your commander and await my pleasure."

"Yes, Majesty," said the man, bowing deeply. He backed away.

"Before you go," said Jasaray, "be so good as to remove the weapon of which we were speaking."

With a speed that made Horath blink, Voltan's sword flashed into his hand, and for a moment the air was charged with danger. Then Voltan reversed the blade, handing it to the disgraced captain, who swiftly left the room. Horath stepped in, handing the goblet to Voltan, who received it without a word of thanks. Naladcmus introduced him to the guests, and Horath saw his gaze lock to that of the mighty Fiallach. "Ah, yes," said Voltan, "you fought at Cogden Field. I have heard of you. Are you not the general who beheaded captured Stone officers and raised their heads on poles at the Cenii border?"

"The very same," said Fiallach.

"A sound strategy," said Jasaray. "Terror is a potent weapon in war. The placing of the heads on the border sent a clear and concise message to the enemy while at the same time instilling fear in them. Now let us take a little refreshment before the main events."

Bane grunted as Telors probed the injured rib. Blood was still oozing from the four-inch-long gash on Bane's left side.

"The rib's broken," said Telors. "You were lucky, Bane."

"Oh, yes, I feel really lucky," said Bane, wincing as Telors wiped away the blood.

"Damn careless," snapped Rage. "I spent many hours watching Dex, and I told you how fast he is on the counter-attack. Did you read the notes I left with you last night?"

"Yes, I read them," lied Bane. "And I didn't fail. Dex is dead, isn't he?"

"Yes, he's dead," agreed Rage, "but a better man would have cleaved your ribs or disemboweled you. A man like Brakus, perhaps."

Suddenly Bane grinned. "You are never satisfied, are you? After my last duel you were telling me how if I fought like that when I met Dex, he would cut my head off. And before that there was the deadly Kespus. Now both are dead."

"Perfection is what we strive for, boy," said Rage.

"No one achieves perfection," said Telors. "You know that, Vanni."

Rage sighed. "If it could be achieved, it wouldn't be worth striving for. The object is to get as close as you can." He looked at Bane. "You fought well for most of the bout. Good footwork, fine concentration. But right at the start he lured you in with a feint. Only your speed saved you, and even with that he snapped a rib. An extra ounce of pressure and that rib might have pierced a lung."

Telors opened a small leather medicine bag, removing a crescent needle and some dark thread. For some moments he tried to thread the needle. Finally Bane took it from him, threaded it, then handed it back. "My eyes aren't what they were," grumbled Telors.

"That's because you're getting old," Rage told him.

"I'm ten years younger than you," Telors responded.

Rage smiled at him. "That's true." The big man sat down alongside Bane. "Don't mind me, boy. You frightened me out there. For just a moment I thought he had you."

"I thought so, too," admitted Bane. "And you are right. I was careless. But the shock of seeing Bendegit Bran and Fial-lach with the emperor rocked my concentration." He swore as Telors tightened the first stitch.

"Be brave, little soldier," Telors said with a grin.

Rage patted Bane's shoulder. "Well, you are Gladiator Four now, and you are almost at your best. You've done well, Bane."

"Well enough?"

"To take Voltan? I don't think so. Ask me in three months. If you beat Brakus, we'll talk again."

"I promised you two years. I kept that promise."

"Just three more months," said Rage. "Give me that and then make your decision."

Telors finished the stitches and snapped the thread. Bane lowered his arm. "What is troubling you, Rage? Be honest with me."

"There's a time for honesty, boy, and this isn't it. Now wash the sweat and sand from yourself. We've been invited to meet the emperor and his guests."

"I don't know that I want to," said Bane.

"There isn't a choice, my friend."

Bane rose and walked through to the rear of the sword room and the bathhouse beyond. Telors put away his needle and glanced at Rage. "What is it, Vanni?"

"The boy is good. Very good; fast, strong, courageous. But he isn't ready for Voltan."

"Why don't you just tell him?"

"No point, my friend. He will fight him anyway at some time. I don't want to destroy his confidence."

"You might be wrong, Vanni."

"Let's hope so."

"Am I invited to meet the emperor?"

Rage laughed. "Why would he want to talk to an ugly bastard like you?"

Telors chuckled and began cleaning Bane's sword and helm before packing them away with his wrist guards and greaves. Minutes later Bane returned. His blond hair was combed back and tied in a ponytail, and he was wearing a pale blue tunic, gray leggings, and riding boots of the softest leather. At his waist was a silver-edged belt from which hung a hunting knife with a hilt of engraved horn.

"You'll have to leave the knife behind," said Rage. "No one enters the emperor's presence armed."

Bane lifted the knife from its sheath and handed it to Telors. Then the two men left the room, climbing the stairs to the second level and emerging out into the stand. The last of the crowd was moving down the aisles as Bane and Rage made their way ever higher toward the Royal Enclosure. Several people recognized Bane and called out to him. He responded with a wave and a smile.

A guard in silver armor met them at the enclosure door, searched them for weapons, then ushered them inside. A second guard led them along a corridor, through a food hall, and into a large private room. Expensive rugs adorned the mosaic floor, and a dozen beautifully crafted couches were set around the walls. The emperor was reclining on a couch below a high arched stained-glass window. Bendegit Bran and Fiallach were sitting on either side of him. On a couch opposite sat an enormous figure in crimson robes, his huge head framed by a mane of white hair. And behind him stood Voltan.

Bane tensed, his hand moving unconsciously to his empty knife sheath. Rage gripped his arm. "Bow to the emperor!" he whispered. Bane's hands were trembling, but he fought for control, took two steps forward, and offered a deep bow to Jasaray.

"I thought you might like to meet your countrymen while they visit Stone," said Jasaray.

"That was . . . most thoughtful, Majesty," said Bane.

"Good to see you, lad," said Bran, rising and offering his hand. Bane shook it. Fiallach remained where he was and folded his arms across his enormous chest.

Jasaray rose from his couch. "Let me introduce you to my friend Nalademus." Taking Bane by the arm, he walked him across the room. Bane bowed to the Stone elder.

"An entertaining duel, young man," said Nalademus. "You are certainly not dull to watch."

"And this is Lord Voltan," said Jasaray. "He leads the Stone knights."

"We have met," said Bane, his voice cold.

"Have we?" asked Voltan. "I do not recall."

"We only spoke briefly," said Bane, his voice trembling with suppressed emotion. "You had your sword buried in a young girl's heart at the time."

Voltan looked closely at him. "Well, well," he said. "The tribesman from Accia. Did I not say you had potential?" He smiled broadly. "And here you are as the new Gladiator Four. I always was a good judge of fighting men. Good to see you again."

"You have no idea how much I have been looking forward to meeting you," said Bane.

"Gratifying to be so highly thought of," said Voltan.

Bane tensed, but just as he was about to attack, Rage's hand clamped to his shoulder. "There is a time and place for all things, boy. This is not the time, and it is certainly not the place."

"I had no idea there was a history between you," said

Jasaray. "How interesting. However, I fear we are neglecting our other guests. Come, Bane, and sit with your friends."

Jasaray led him back to the two Rigante warriors, then turned away and strolled across to speak with Rage.

"What was that about?" asked Bendegit Bran, leaning in and speaking softly.

"He is my enemy," Bane told him. "It is a personal matter."

"You always were good at making enemies, Bane," said Fiallach.

Bane looked into the man's hostile gaze and smiled suddenly, feeling the tension drain from him. "There was a time I would have gladly killed you. There would not have been a moment's regret. I am older now and a little wiser." He took a deep, calming breath and returned his attention to Bran. "Why are you here?"

"The emperor invited Connavar to send ambassadors for talks. The king agreed. We have been here ten days, but there have been no talks so far. But what of you, Bane? How are you enjoying life here?"

Bane shrugged. "I am wealthy, but I miss the mountains. When I have accomplished what I have set out to do, I will come home."

"You'll not be welcome," said Fiallach.

"I never was," said Bane.

Bane was silent most of the way home and sat back against the leather seat of the open carriage, staring out over the city streets. Beside him Rage was also quiet, lost in thoughts of his own.

As the carriage moved out onto the main avenue leading to the hillside and the eighteen-room villa, a small commotion broke out in the crowd some way ahead. Lanterns had been lit, and in their glare Bane saw armed knights dragging several men and one woman from a doorway. Someone in the crowd shouted "Burn the traitors!" but mostly people stayed silent, watching the prisoners being hauled away.

"They won't succeed," Rage said, as the carriage moved on.

"Who won't?" asked Bane.

"The knights. Nalademus. Religion is a strange creature. It

thrives on persecution. After three years of burnings, hangings, and torture there are probably now more followers of the tree cult than there were at the start."

"That seems to make no sense," said Bane.

"I agree, but it's true. Religions that die away are those absorbed by society's rulers, not those damned by them."

"Why would that be?" asked Bane. "Surely the message is the same, but it comes without risk?"

"Perhaps that is part of the answer. We value little that comes without risk. But more important, once society absorbs and accepts a religion, the rulers set out to subtly change the message. It will happen here eventually."

"And people will accept this?"

"Of course. The tree cult does not believe in the taking of life. Killing is wrong, they say. In a few years some government-elected officer of the cult will say that it is not killing that is wrong but murder. He will cite the case of a man defending his family against attack or his daughter from rape. He will say, 'Surely the Source would not expect that man to sit idly by.' Most family men will find agreement with that argument. Then they will begin to talk of Stone as 'a great family' and the nations around us as 'hostile, barbarous, and evil.' There will then be justification for attacking them, on the grounds of 'saving the family of Stone.' " Rage laughed, though there was little humor in the sound. "It is like watered wine, Bane. In the right amounts it is tasty and good for the digestion and the heart. But if you keep adding water, all you end up with is the memory of the wine."

"You are a cynical man when sober," said Bane.

"I wish that I wasn't. I like much of what I have heard about the tree cult, about their caring for one another and their refusal to be drawn into the circle of hate. Did you know that on the night before their executions they hold prayer meetings at which they forgive their accusers?"

Bane smiled broadly. "It makes no sense to me. If a man hates you and seeks to kill you, then you must either run or kill him. There is no third way."

"You can befriend him," said Rage. "Then he will no longer be your enemy."

"Now you are joking, surely," said Bane. "You think I could befriend Voltan after what he has done?"

"Not from a position of hatred," Rage told him. "First you'd have to forgive him."

"Would you forgive him?"

Rage turned toward him. "I already have, boy. He is Cara's father, and because of him a child I loved killed herself." He patted Bane's shoulder. "The circumstances are different, I know. He did not set out to kill Palia, but the result was the same. I lost someone I loved. So did you."

"I'll forgive him," said Bane, his voice shaking with anger, "the moment he lies dead at my feet."

Rage fell silent, and the carriage moved slowly up the hill. A servant opened the wrought-iron gates before the villa, and the driver picked up the pace along the gravel path, hauling on the reins outside the main entrance. Rage paid him, and the two men strolled inside.

Cara came walking out to meet them. "Why are you not at school?" asked Rage, taking her into a hug and kissing her cheek.

"It is midterm, Grandfather. Are you not pleased to see me?"

"Always," Rage told her.

She swung to Bane. "And what about you, tribesman?" she asked him.

Bane smiled and looked at her. She was wearing an ankle-length blue silk gown gathered at the waist by a wide belt of gray leather stitched with golden wire. Her yellow hair was tied back except for two ringlets at her temples.

"You are looking beautiful, princess," he said, offering her a bow.

"No one calls me princess now. That's a child's nickname," she scolded him. "You think me a child?"

"Far from it," said Bane, keeping his gaze from her full breasts and the curve of her hips. "Welcome home, Cara."

"Walk with me in the garden," she said, advancing on him and hooking her arm into his.

"It used to be my arm," grumbled Rage.

Cara grinned at him. "I adore you, Grandfather, but there is something I want to talk to Bane about."

Lanterns had been hung on iron poles along the garden path, and the two young people walked slowly toward the circular fountain at the rear of the house. "Well, what is your news?" asked Bane.

Cara glanced back. "Let me show you something," she said, moving off to stand beside a yellow rosebush that was covered in blooms. "But first you must promise not to tell anyone."

"I promise," he said.

Cara knelt before the rose, scanning the flowers. "This one," she said at last, pointing to a fading bloom, its stalk bent, its petals falling. "Come and look."

Bane knelt beside her. Cara cupped her hands around the bloom and closed her eyes. Bane watched for a moment. The rose stalk stiffened, the bloom lifting. Slowly the dying petals swelled as if with new life. When Cara removed her hands, the rose stood proud, and its scent was magnificent.

"A clever trick," said Bane. "How is it done?"

Cara looked around to make sure they were alone. "I went to see the Veiled Lady. She touched my brow and told me that I had latent talent and that she had released it in me. I could be a healer," she said.

Bane felt a tightness in his stomach. "You shouldn't have done that," he said. "Don't you know how dangerous it is?"

"Of course I know," she snapped. "I went with three friends, and I was very nervous. But I heard her speak, Bane. I watched her heal people with a touch. It was extraordinary. Then she walked among us. She has a black veil, and you cannot see her face clearly, but I saw her hands, and they are young hands. I don't think she's much older than me!"

"You must not go again, Cara."

She stood up and dusted her gown. "I didn't expect you to be so cowardly," she told him.

He rose. "I am thinking of Rage and what it would do to him if you were taken, dragged to the arena, and burned at the stake."

"I'll be careful," she promised. "But I can't forget what I have seen and heard and felt. Standing here, I can feel the life in the garden, every plant and tree, every flower and shrub. I am part of it. You are part of it."

In the lantern light he looked into her face and suddenly saw Voltan there, the same cornflower-blue eyes, the set of the features. He stepped back suddenly.

"What is wrong?" she asked.

"Nothing. We should be getting back."

"Oh, Bane, you are such a disappointment," she said. "I have been longing to tell you. I thought, as a tribesman, you might understand what it is I have been feeling. I thought I could share it with you. I thought . . ." Her eyes showed sorrow as she turned away from him.

"What did you think?" he asked.

"I thought you might come with me to see her."

"Oh, Cara! I killed a man today. To entertain the crowds I plunged a sword into his heart. You think this Veiled Lady would want a gladiator close to her?"

"Maybe you wouldn't be a gladiator if you heard her speak."

"Then I don't want to hear her speak," he said.

"Go away and leave me alone," she told him, spinning on her heel and walking away.

Bane sat down on a nearby bench. The stitches in his side were painful and his rib was aching dreadfully, yet this was as nothing to the fear he felt inside. Cara had always been willful and headstrong, and now she had set herself upon a path that probably would lead to her death. Just like Lia.

A cold breeze whispered through the garden, a gentle reminder that winter was not far away. Bane sighed, remembering the last time he had sat with Lia in the house of Barus and the terrible events that had followed. Now it was happening again. He wanted to believe that this time he would not be powerless to prevent it, but he knew that was not so. If the knights came for Cara, there was little that he or Rage could do except fight and die, and this they would do.

Bitterness swept over him. All his life, it seemed, events had conspired to bring him pain: Connavar's continuing rejection, Arian's sad and untimely death, Lia's murder, Banouin's desertion. The only difference now was that Bane had advance warning of the tragedies to come.

He sat quietly for some while and then heard Rage walking

down the path. "Did you two have a fight?" asked Rage, sitting alongside him.

"Not exactly. We had differing views."

"She'll get over it," said the older man. "It is a beautiful night."

Bane glanced up at the stars. "Aye, it is. Tell me, do you miss Goriasa?"

"Sometimes," admitted Rage. "But Stone is good for Cara. I expect there will be suitors calling soon. She will be sixteen in three days."

"He'll need to be a strong man," said Bane. "Otherwise she'll eat him alive."

Rage chuckled. "I raised her to be independent and think for herself. I think maybe I did the job too well. Why did you mention Goriasa?"

"No reason. It just came into my mind."

"Ah," Rage said softly. "I thought maybe you'd heard about Persis."

"What about him?"

"He and Norwin were arrested two months ago. They have been brought to Stone for execution."

Bane swore. "I like him," he said. "He's a good man."

"Did you know he finally made a success of Circus Orises? He organized the Gath games, running events, horsemanship, wrestling. He filled the stadium. The last I heard, he was rich again." Rage shook his head. "Whatever possessed the man to join the cult? He wasn't stupid. He must have known the risks."

"It is imperative that we move swiftly," said Voltan, keeping his voice low even though the windows were closed, with heavy velvet curtains drawn across them. "The war in the east is won. At least ten Panthers will be returning to Stone within the month."

Naladeмus sat at his desk, his huge head resting against the top of the padded chair, his arms folded across his stomach. Eyes closed, he listened intently to Voltan's report. "How did such a disaster happen?" he asked.

"Stupidity," hissed Voltan. "Instead of using our money to hire mercenaries or weapons, Dalios paid a huge dowry to a

rival king in order to marry his daughter. Then he spent a further fortune on a huge wedding feast in the capital. All the
nobles were invited. Gods, it is sickening! The idiot had
all his generals attend. Barus heard about the feast and led
three Panthers on a quick raid. They sacked the capital, captured Dalios, then brought up the main army and crushed all
opposition."

"Captured Dalios?" snapped Nalademus, surging upright.

"Do not concern yourself, my friend," said Voltan. "I had
him poisoned. No one knows of our involvement."

"Someone always knows," said Nalademus. "And you are
right. We must move swiftly. Once the Panthers are back in
Stone, Jasaray will be invincible again."

"Leave it to me, my friend," said Voltan. "Jasaray will be
dead within the week."

"An accidental death," insisted Nalademus. "Otherwise
there will be another civil war."

Fiallach followed Jasaray and Bendegit Bran through the
elaborate maze, his irritation growing. Bran was chatting
amiably with the emperor and seemed unconcerned that
every turn and channel looked exactly like the last. The eight-
foot-tall walls of greenery pressed in on Fiallach, and he was
sweating heavily. Clasping his hands behind his back, he followed the two men and fought to quell a sense of panic.

At last they emerged at the center of the maze, where several benches and tables of stone had been placed around a
large marble pool. Fiallach sucked in a deep breath. From
there he could at least see the walls of the palace building
with its balconies and windows.

Jasaray sat down, beckoning the tribesmen to join him. "I
had this constructed after one of our western campaigns," he
said. "It is copied from a design I found in a captured city."

"What is the point of it?" asked Fiallach.

"For me it is a representation of life," said Jasaray. "We
wander through it, always wondering where we are going and
rarely able to go back and put right past mistakes. I come here
most nights and wander the maze. It helps me think."

"It makes me want to walk through it with an ax," muttered
Fiallach.

"It does have that effect on some people," agreed Jasaray.

Suddenly, from close by, there came a terrifying roar. Fiallach spun around, his hand moving to his empty knife belt.

"Be calm," said Jasaray. "My animals are being fed. There is no danger. I shall show you them later." The morning sun cleared the palace roof and shone directly down on the seated men. "I am sorry to have kept you waiting so long," said the emperor, "but there have been many pressing matters demanding my attention." Trailing his hand in the pool, he splashed a little water to his face. "It is my hope," he said, "that we can come to some agreement with the Rigante people."

"What kind of agreement?" asked Bran.

"A union of friends," said Jasaray. "Stone has been fighting wars for thirty years now, some against foreign enemies, some between ourselves. It is time, I believe, for a period of stability and calm. Armies, as I am sure you are now aware, are costly. Connavar has fought three civil campaigns during the last two years against rebel tribesmen from the Norvii and the Pannone. And why? Because he needs to tax the people to pay for his standing armies. And as each year passes without them being needed, the populace grows more disenchanted. Here in Stone we see Connavar's armies and wonder if they will be used against us, and therefore we also tax the public to pay for soldiers. It is very wasteful for both of our economies."

"What do you suggest?" asked Bran.

"I suggest a close treaty between our nations that will allow us both to reduce the size of our forces. The war in the east is costing us dearly, and we are beginning to have trouble with some of our northern neighbors, notably King Shard of the Vars. He also has standing armies now, and there have been several skirmishes with our troops."

"Shard is a powerful enemy," agreed Bran. "My first taste of battle was against the Vars twenty years ago. Shard invaded the north of our lands and linked with a Pannone army against us."

"And Connavar defeated him," said Jasaray. "I believe your father was killed in that campaign."

"He died, yes," said Bran. "His heart gave out after the battle."

"War brings many tragedies," said Jasaray. "I despise it."

"Then why are you so good at it?" asked Fiallach.

"A fair question and one to which there is no answer. I was a scholar and a teacher. I was brought into the army to organize supplies and help with logistic matters. It then transpired that I had previously undiscovered skills in the area of tactics. In life, I have discovered, men gravitate toward what they are good at. I am a good soldier. That does not mean, however, that I enjoy the slaughter and the bloodshed. I do not. It is extremely wasteful. I have no desire to lead an army into the lands of the Rigante. The borders of the Stone empire are large enough. Further expansion would be dangerous. That is the message I want you to convey to Connavar."

"Let us assume for a moment that we agree on this," said Bran. "What are you offering—in material terms—for this agreement, and what do you require?"

"Full access for our merchants, unhindered passage for our merchant ships, freedom to continue our settlements in the lands of the Cenii, constructing roads and towns and so forth. In return I will offer twenty thousand in gold to help with the costs of reducing the army and returning the soldiers to the land or other skills and trades."

"And we are to trust you?" snapped Fiallach.

"Trust your eyes," Jasaray replied, with no hint of anger. "I am a man approaching seventy. Do you truly believe I want to embark on another campaign, sleeping in tents, marching in rain and snow? If I were hungry for such activities, would I not, even now, be in the east, leading my armies against our enemies? People change as they grow older. Look at you, Fiallach. Do you still yearn for battlefields and cold beds?"

"I can still fight as well as ever."

"That's not what I asked."

Fiallach sighed. "No, I don't. I want to watch my grandchildren grow."

"Exactly. It is time for us all to do that. Connavar is preparing for an invasion that will not happen. Cogden Field was his great victory, and I take nothing away from that. Indeed, I felt some pride in that I had a part in training him for warfare. But Cogden is now almost two decades in the past. I will have my clerics draw up provisional agreements for you to take to

Connavar. I will then await your reply." Jasaray rose. "Come, let me show you my pets."

Fiallach's heart sank as they entered the maze once more, but this time Jasaray moved swiftly through it, emerging from an entrance to the west. Here there were many large cages containing animals from all over the empire: a giant black bear, two lions, three sleek panthers, and, set apart from the others, another lion, but this one bearing the most curious markings. Its tawny body was covered in dark stripes. Fiallach could not understand why anyone should wish to paint a lion in such a way and said this to Jasaray.

"It is not paint or dye," said the emperor. "It is a tiger, and these are its natural markings. Bigger and faster than a lion, it has prodigious strength. One blow from the paw can crush an ox skull. One bite would sever a man's leg."

"Why do you have them here?" asked Bran.

"Once the war in the east is won I shall donate them to one of the circuses, and the crowds will watch them being hunted and slain."

"How far has this creature traveled?" asked Bran.

"Over two thousand miles. It was quite a feat, keeping it alive."

"I can imagine," said Bran. "The cost of getting it here alone must have been enormous."

"Indeed it was."

"And all so that people can watch it being killed? Now that seems wasteful, Majesty."

"Perhaps," agreed Jasaray. Then he smiled. "But it would be an unwise ruler who did not spend a little money to keep his subjects happy. A contented people rarely see the need to overthrow their emperor."

Regrets, Voltan would often say, were only for the weak. This was, he believed, an unarguable truth. Strong men achieved; lesser men failed and in failing would blame external forces for their failure. Luck was against them, or they were the victims of malicious sabotage from those envious of their skills. Weaklings, all of them! Yet despite this iron belief Voltan had never been able to break free of the one great regret of his life.

Dressed now in a simple hooded toga and sandals, he moved

through the late-afternoon shadows to the entrance of the cata-combs and the rock tunnels that snaked under Agra, the fourth hill of the city. A young man was standing at the entrance, watching him as he approached.

"Good evening, friend," said the man.

"Good evening to you," said Voltan, drawing his hands to-gether and making the sign of the tree.

"Enter and be blessed," said the man.

Voltan moved inside the darkness of the tunnel. Ahead he could see torches in roughly made brackets on the wall as the tunnel widened into a high, arched chamber. It was cool there, and Voltan made his way past a series of jagged stalagmites jutting up from the ground, joining the crowd waiting pa-tiently in the torchlight.

Agents of the temple had located the hiding place of the Veiled Lady, and she would be arrested the next day. Every-thing was coming together. By the week's end the fading em-peror would be replaced by Nalademus, the tree cult would begin to wither, and Voltan would be placed in charge of the army. At thirty-seven his destiny awaited, a golden prize mere inches from his grasp.

Curiously, he felt no excitement, no sense of fulfillment or satisfaction. This was irritating in the extreme, yet it had al-ways been this way. Contentment and happiness were always just a little way ahead. I will be happy when I am Gladiator One, he had thought. On the day he had attained this, he had felt a surge of achievement and deep pleasure. It had passed within an hour.

Voltan eased his way through the crowds and sat down on a rock, wondering yet again why he had come to this place. What do you expect to find? he asked himself. A group of fools filled with a death wish listening to an idiot who would be burned within days. He sat quietly among the almost dead, thinking through the arrangements for the assassination of Jasaray. No plan was foolproof, but satisfied that he had con-sidered all the potential hazards, he relaxed. He felt the crowd stir and rose to his feet.

At the far end of the chamber a young woman in a pale blue gown and a black veil had entered, flanked by three white-

haired men. The crowd raised their arms above their heads.
Voltan copied the movement.

"May the Source guide you and bless you and receive you,"
they chanted.

The woman also raised her hands, touching the palms, then
opening her arms toward the crowd in a gesture of embrace. "What do we see in this world around us?" she asked
them. "What do we see in tree and stream, in mountain
and valley? What do we feel when we gaze upon the stars
and the silver moon? What do we experience when the
warmth of the sun touches our skin?"

"Joy!" chorused the crowd.

"And when a friend takes us into an embrace, or a child
smiles, or we receive an act of unexpected kindness?"

"Joy!"

"From which deep well does that joy come, my friends?"

"From the Source!" they cried.

"From the Source of All Things," she said. She fell silent for
a moment and stood with her head bowed. The crowd settled
down, seating themselves on the ground or jutting rocks and
broken stalagmites.

"There is so much evil in this world," she told them. "It is
governed by men whose spirits have been charred by the
smoke and fire of their greed and their lust. We should pity
these men, for they are empty now and upon their deaths will
walk the Void, lost and frightened, never to see the bright and
shining light, never to know the joy of paradise found. Their
momentary lives will flicker out as an eternity of regret
beckons. They think themselves great men. They see their
lives as full of glory and riches. Not so. The reality is that they
are—as we all are—seeds in the soft earth. We cannot see the
sun or the awesome beauty of the sky. We lie in the ground,
and we yearn for what we cannot see. The men of evil believe
the dirt is all there is, and they embrace it, drawing it around
them like a blanket. For them a belief in a sun they cannot see
is foolishness, so they wait under the earth until they rot.
Those of us with faith have a desire to grow. And we do grow,
my friends. We put out roots of love and kindness, and we
move up through the dirt, and we will see the sun and the sky.
The men of evil will not. So when they drag you from your

homes, pity them. When they tie you to the stakes, forgive them. Their lives are as nothing, worthless and dead."

She fell silent again. Then she began to move among the crowd, laying her hands upon their heads, whispering blessings. Voltan moved back to stand behind a tall stalagmite, but slowly she was moving toward him. He had a long dagger hidden in the folds of his toga and glanced quickly back along the tunnel. If she exposed him, he would kill her and run. He did not want it to happen. Nalademus would be furious if she was not taken alive.

Most of the crowd were on their knees, so Voltan crouched down, head bowed. He heard her approach and felt her hand upon his head.

"I forgive you," she whispered, then moved away, returning to stand before the crowd.

"I must leave you soon," she told them. There were cries of "No!" but she stilled them with a gentle gesture. "I will be taken," she said, "and led out to face the jeering mobs and the stake of fire. I know this. I have seen the vision. But do not fear for me. It will happen because I allow it to happen. And if the Source decrees that it is my time to leave this earthly existence, then I welcome it." An eerie silence settled upon the group. Some began to weep.

"There is a man here . . ." she began. Voltan tensed and eased his hand inside his toga, curling it around the hilt of his dagger. ". . . a man who does not understand the mysteries of life or the meaning of joy. For this man I have a message. Go from here to the marketplace of Stanos and stand by the stall with the yellow canopy. You will not have to wait long, and you will learn a great truth. And now, my friends, I must say farewell. May the Source bless you and keep you." She turned and walked slowly from the chamber.

Voltan stood very still. The crowd began to file past him, and he joined them. There were several exits, and soon he found himself wandering down through the narrow streets below the hill and walking toward the Stanos district. He moved warily. It was surely a trap, and she would have agents ready to spring upon him as he reached the stall with the yellow canopy. He did not fear them. He was Voltan, and even with a dagger he could kill any who attacked him.

There were few people in the marketplace, and many of the stallholders were packing up their wares. Ahead he could see the yellow covering above a stall selling jewelry items, mainly of green jade. Scanning the people close by, Voltan approached the stall. None of the men he could see were armed, and most were strolling with wives or lovers. He stood at the stall, looking down at the items on display.

A young woman, her hair blond and her eyes pale blue, approached and began examining a tray of pendant earrings. There was something about her that touched a chord in the former gladiator, and he wondered if he had met her before.

"Excuse me," he said. She looked up at him, and his mind slipped back through the years to a moment in a courtyard when he had said farewell to a tearful girl.

"Yes?"

"Have we met?" he managed to say.

"I do not believe so, sir."

"My name is Voltan, and I . . . sense that I should know you."

"I am Cara," she said with a smile, "and believe me, sir, I would remember."

"Where are you from, Cara?"

"I live with my grandfather."

"Perhaps I know him," he said. "Perhaps I saw you when you were a child."

"Perhaps you did," she agreed. "My grandfather is a famous man. He was Gladiator One, and he now trains the fighters of Circus Occian."

Voltan felt as if he had been struck above the heart. "Your grandfather is Rage?"

"Yes. Do you know him?"

"We have . . . met."

"Then you should come and see us. We live in a large villa now. But we have few guests."

"Perhaps I will," he said, unable to take his gaze from her blue eyes. She gave him another smile.

"And I have seen you before, sir. An hour ago." Lifting her hands, she drew the outline of a tree in the air. Then she smiled again and swung away. He watched her walk from the marketplace.

Swiftly he returned to the temple and sent a servant to fetch the file on the man Rage. In the fading light he read through it, then pushed the papers across the desk. Rising, he walked to the window and watched the dying sun fall behind the hills.

He had been nineteen when he had left Stone to join the eastern campaign with Panther Nineteen. Palia had wept and begged him to stay, but thoughts of warfare and glory had filled him. Once on campaign he had found himself thinking of her often and the times they had shared. Not just the carnal times but the moments holding hands beneath the trees or sitting arm in arm on the bench beneath the rose bower. He still held the memory of the scent of her hair.

Voltan had been away a year and on his return had rushed to the house of Rage, praying that Palia had taken no other lover. He had been greeted by strangers who had told him that Rage no longer dwelled in Stone but had moved to a distant part of the empire after the suicide of his daughter. Voltan had stumbled away, bereft and lost.

He stood now in the darkness, remembering the girl by the stall, her bright smile and blue eyes. Voltan's throat felt tight, and there was a weight in his chest.

"I have a daughter," he whispered.

He remembered the sign she had made, and for the first time in his life fear touched his heart.

Tomorrow would see the greatest cull in the city's history. Close to a thousand names had been gathered from agents, spies, and informers. The lists had already been dispatched to the hunt teams, and Voltan had no way of knowing whether Cara had been named. He heard a tap at the door, and a figure slipped into the darkness.

"All is ready, lord," said the man. "So do we kill the emperor tonight?"

"Aye, tonight," said Voltan.

◇ 9 ◇

THE ACQUISITION OF power, Jasaray had always said, was not without risk. This thought came to him as he opened his eyes and felt pain at his temple. Lifting his hand, he found a lump there, the skin split. He was lying beside the marble bench at the center of his maze. He struggled to sit, remembering the man who had stepped from the shadows and struck him. I should be dead, he thought. Dragging himself up, he groaned as fresh pain throbbed from his skull. Perhaps he believed he had killed me, he thought, sitting down on the bench. It made no sense.

As he sat down, he saw that his pale toga was drenched with blood. I have been stabbed! Wrenching the garment open, he examined his chest and belly. In the moonlight he could see no wound, and there was certainly no pain except from the pounding in his head.

Think, man!

Jasaray calmed himself. He had known for some months of the peril he faced as Nalademus and his knights grew in power. Yet with his armies in the east he had been unable to confront his old friend and force the issue, and so he had waited patiently, giving Nalademus more and more power while at the same time organizing subtle troop movements, bringing several loyal Panthers closer to the city. The first of them was camped only five miles from Stone, ready to march upon his order. At this moment Jasaray wished he had given that order, but he had decided to risk another few days. Then he could march nine thousand soldiers into Stone, arrest Nalademus and Voltan, and disband the Stone knights.

"It could prove a costly delay," he said aloud.

Why am I alive? And where is the assassin? Why had he been struck but not killed? And whence had come this blood?

Jasaray had been walking alone in the maze. His attacker had been waiting there, armed with a cudgel. Not a knife or a sword. Was the man merely a fool, or would he return and bludgeon Jasaray to death?

At the far edge of the maze the tiger roared. Did that signal the return of the killer? Jasaray pushed himself to his feet and left the open center of the maze, moving into one of the darker lanes. The assassin would have to be very good to find his way to Jasaray now.

The tiger roared again. This time the sound was closer. It must be a trick of the maze, thought Jasaray, the sound distorted by the tall, thick bushes. He walked on a little way, but the blow to his head had left him dizzy and weak, and he sat down on a small wooden bench set in an arch cut into a hedge.

He should have brought the soldiers in and taken a chance on surprising Nalademus, he thought. Foolish man! Timing is always the key to success. You waited too long, Jasaray, he told himself grimly. But I am not dead yet. If I can get to my guards and send a message to the Panther commander . . .

He heard the tiger growl again. This time the beast was definitely close. Jasaray froze as the sound of padding paws and heavy breath came to him from the other side of the hedge.

Realization came instantly. The blood on the toga! It was not his. It had been smeared there to attract the tiger.

Swiftly, his pain forgotten, Jasaray wrenched the robe from his body and threw it to one side. Then he ran down the lane, cutting left and right.

Never before in his life had the Scholar known panic, and even now, in his terrible fear, he had to acknowledge the sheer genius of this plan. The emperor killed by a wild beast while walking in his maze. Nalademus, as first minister, would naturally take power and swiftly appoint his own men to command the Panthers. Little risk of civil war and no one to blame except perhaps some poor animal handler who had failed to lock the cage properly.

Oh, it was sweet.

From somewhere behind he heard the tiger roar again. This

was followed by the sound of rending cloth. Jasaray ran on, heading for the eastern exit. He forced himself to slow as he neared the archway and, dropping to his belly, inched himself forward to peer around the hedge. The archway was blocked by a wooden frame, and he could just see the shadows of waiting men beyond it. Rising to his feet, Jasaray moved back into the lane. All four exits would be blocked.

Jasaray smiled suddenly and shook his head. So this is how it ends, he thought. The man who created the Panthers is butchered by a tiger. "It is almost droll," he whispered.

Bane's eyes flared open, and he surged upright. The bedroom in the west wing of the palace was moonlit and silent. Bane glanced across at the bed in which Rage slept, close to the balcony. The big man was sleeping soundly on his stomach, one arm hanging over the edge of the mattress, the other curled around a pillow.

It had been a long evening, sitting at the farewell dinner with Jasaray, Bendegit Bran, Fiallach, and Rage. The talk had been mostly of politics and treaties, and even when it had veered away from such mind-numbing topics Bane had remained uncomfortable, wishing he was somewhere else. Anywhere else, in fact. For they had spoken of Connavar, of his life and legend and greatness. Bane had swallowed his anger. At one point the elderly emperor had turned to him.

"Have you met the king?" he asked.

"Briefly," answered Bane. "I won a race. He presented the prize."

Jasaray looked closely at him, then turned his attention back to Bendegit Bran. "My agents tell me that King Shard is once more building a great fleet," he said. "Is Connavar aware of this?"

"We are all aware of the threat," said Bran. "Shard hates Connavar and has promised to cut off his head."

"What is the source of this hatred?" asked Jasaray.

Bran glanced at Fiallach. "You were there, my friend. Perhaps you should tell the story."

The giant yellow-haired warrior nodded, and Bane saw a look of sorrow touch Fiallach's grim features. "A raiding party of Vars, led by Shard, sacked my settlement. It was a ransom raid, and they were seeking to capture a young woman named Tae. She was the daughter of a powerful laird, and Shard believed he could extract a great amount of gold for her. He was probably right. Most of the warriors of the settlement had been lured away before the raid. We were in the woods some fifteen miles away, hunting a lion. But Connavar was close by, and he trailed the raiders and freed Tae."

"He did this alone?" said Jasaray.

"Aye, alone," agreed Fiallach. "It is a source of great shame to me that I was not there."

"How did he accomplish this feat?"

"The raiders had split up to confuse any chasing force. Connavar killed the men with Tae, then led her deeper into the woods. One of the men he killed was Shard's brother. Shard made a blood pledge that day to avenge the death."

"Great men always make enemies," said Jasaray. "I was saddened to hear of the death of Tae, which, as I recall, was also the result of a blood feud. Why has Connavar never re-married?"

The tribesmen had looked uncomfortable at the question, and it was Bran who finally answered it. "He is wedded to the cause of the Keltoi, Majesty, and has no time for personal pursuits. Much like yourself."

"Indeed so," said Jasaray, and the talk had returned to treaties and closer ties between races and cultures.

By the time the emperor had ended the evening Bane had almost lost the will to live. He and Rage had returned to their quarters. The older man had taken to his bed immediately. Bane had drunk a little wine and had sat on the balcony, gazing at the stars. Then he, too, had slept.

The nightmare had been violent and terrifying.

Bane's heart was still hammering, but the nightmare was receding now, falling through his memory. He recalled that Banouin had been in his dream. His friend was trying to tell him something, but Bane could not remember what it was. Something about a vision! A vision of demons hunting him? Then he remembered the night back in the house of Barus in Accia when Banouin's screams had awakened him. He had run to his friend. "The walls are alive!" Banouin had shouted, his face gleaming with sweat. "And there is a demon hunting you, Bane. Ah! I see him. Talon and claw. He is coming for you."

What else had he said? In the quiet of the room Bane pictured again that scene. "You were walking through . . . through corridors, but the walls were alive and writhing. You were carrying a short sword, and there was a man with you, an older man. And a demon was stalking you. A terrible beast of incredible speed and strength."

Rising from the bed, Bane walked to the balcony. It was cool now, a fresh breeze blowing in from the sea. He glanced down at the emperor's private gardens and the moonlit maze. He saw a movement. It was the emperor. He was naked and moving swiftly along one of the lanes. Bane smiled. It was an oddly comical sight. Still, he thought, if a man ruled an empire as mighty as that of Stone, he could behave as he liked. Bane yawned and cast his gaze around the gardens. Then he saw another movement. He blinked. It had been so swift that he could not quite believe what his eyes had registered.

A striped beast had padded across the clearing in the center, then disappeared from view. Bane focused his gaze on the spot. Lanterns had been lit throughout the maze, and he wondered if what he had seen actually had been a trick of light and shadow. Then he saw the beast again. It was massive—and it was hunting.

Bane ran back into the room and roused Rage from sleep. "The emperor is in danger," he said.

"What?"

"There is a beast hunting him in the maze."

Bane moved out onto the balcony, glancing down at the fifteen-foot drop to the grass below. Then he climbed over the top, hung from his arms, and fell to the grass, rolling as he struck. He came to his feet just as Rage dropped alongside him. The older man landed with a grunt. Neither man had any weapon. Only the royal guards were allowed to walk armed within the palace.

They ran around the western perimeter of the maze— straight into four armed men. Two of the assassins carried short swords, the other knives. The first swordsman ran at Bane, lunging his sword toward the other man's chest. Bane sidestepped, grabbed the man's wrist, and head-butted him full in the face. Holding to the wrist, Bane twisted it savagely. The man cried out, the sword spinning from his grasp. Rage caught it, leapt forward, and killed the second swordsman, slicing the gladius through the man's throat. A knifeman ran at Bane, who ducked and then threw himself at the man. They fell together. Bane sent a right hook into the knifeman's jaw. The last of the assassins turned to run. Rage hurled the gladius, which plunged into the man's back. Bane hit his own assailant twice more, then rose. The man he had disarmed was running back into the palace.

A wooden barrier had been placed across the maze entrance. Rage pulled it clear.

"Be careful," said Bane. "The beast was a lion of some kind. And big!"

Rage dragged the gladius from the back of the dead assassin and tossed it to Bane. Then he scooped up the second sword, and the two men entered the maze.

"How in heaven's name will we know where we're going?" asked Rage. "All the lanes look the same."

"Just follow me," said Bane.

"You are bleeding, boy," said Rage. "Did he cut you?"

Bane glanced down at his pale tunic. Blood was seeping through the cloth. "No. My stitches broke. It is nothing."

He began to lope along the lane, Rage close behind him. He turned left, then right, picturing in his mind the maze as he had seen it from the balcony. Vorna's magic had been unable to help him with his reading and writing, but she had told him that nature always finds a balance. "You have a wonderful memory, Bane, much keener than most men's. You will find it far more useful than the ability to decipher script," she had said.

His side was hurting as he ran, the tunic sticking to the inflamed flesh. Suddenly a growl came from close by. Bane swerved away from the sound, which was emanating from the far side of the hedge. The tiger roared and began lashing at the hedge with its great paws. Bane stood very still. The hedge was at least three feet thick, and though the branches were thin, there were hundreds of them. It would take even a creature such as this a little time to tear a way through.

In the bright moonlight Bane could not yet see the beast.

Then a massive paw slashed into view, splintering wood. As the branches parted, Bane saw—for a moment only—the face of the tiger and found himself staring into baleful golden eyes. Raised on its hind legs, the beast paused in its furious assault upon the hedge and stared back at the man. Time froze as Bane's gaze locked to those terrible eyes, and he felt the power of the beast, the strength, the energy, and the terrible hunger. Then the moment passed. The tiger let out a ferocious roar and crashed its huge frame at the hedge, which bent inward.

"Time to leave," said Rage.

Bane nodded. "In a moment," he replied. Then he called out: "Jasaray! It is Bane. Make for the center! We will meet you there."

The two men ran on. From behind them came the sound of wood splintering as the tiger crashed through.

Two more turns to the left and one to the right, and the two warriors emerged into the center of the maze. The naked Jasaray was there, standing very still, his hands clasped behind his back. He seemed very calm. Bane ran up to him. Jasaray took a deep breath and closed his eyes.

"We are here to help you, Majesty," said Rage. "Not kill you."

Jasaray opened his eyes and gave a thin smile. "That is gratifying to hear," he said, his voice showing no fear.

The tiger emerged from the lane entrance, its huge head swaying as it walked. Bane looked into its yellow eyes, then he and Rage moved a little apart. The tiger watched them as it padded closer. The tail suddenly twitched, and it charged at Bane.

The Rigante stood his ground. As the tiger leapt, he dropped to one knee, ramming the gladius into the beast's belly. The tiger struck him, smashing him to the ground. Bane could smell the tiger's fetid breath, and the fangs were inches from his face. Throwing up his left arm, he struggled to hold the beast at bay. Rage ran in, hurling himself to the beast's back and circling his arm around the throat, hauling the head back. Then he stabbed the tiger in the side, plunging his blade deep.

The tiger reared up and swung on Rage. Bane, weaponless now, surged to his feet and cast around for a weapon of any kind. His own gladius was wedged deep in the body of the tiger. The creature's tail twitched again, and it leapt at Rage. The old gladiator stood his ground. Bane threw himself at the tiger, his shoulder hammering into the beast's side. Rage darted forward, lancing his sword into the creature's neck. It twisted and lashed out at Bane. The Rigante hurled himself to one side, but not swiftly enough. Talons raked his shoulder, spraying blood into the air. The tiger was unbelievably fast. Even as Bane fell, it was upon him. Rolling to his back, Bane smashed his fist into the tiger's head. It was like striking rock. Fangs lunged for his face. Once more he threw up his arm, and his elbow lodged against the beast's throat, holding back the attack. Rage stabbed it again. The tiger's body spasmed. It gave a coughing roar, and blood pumped from its mouth. Yet still it bore down on Bane. The Rigante struggled to hold it back. With his right hand he reached down. His fingers curled around the hilt of the gladius jutting from the tiger's body. With all his strength he rammed the blade deeper.

The tiger ceased to struggle. Bane found himself once more staring into those golden eyes. For a heartbeat it was as if their spirits touched. Then the head sagged. Rage dragged Bane clear. The young Rigante knelt beside the tiger, laying his hand upon the creature's flanks. It was still breathing. Bane felt the weight of a great sorrow touch him.

"I am sorry, my friend," he said, stroking the fur. "You traveled a long way to die here."

The tiger's head twitched, and for a moment it seemed it would rise. Then the light faded from its eyes.

Rage knelt beside the younger man, examining the cuts on his shoulder. "They're not too deep," he said, pulling Bane to his feet.

"There are assassins at the perimeter," said Jasaray. "I do not know how many."

"Three less than there were," said Rage. "Let's get you back into the palace."

"First let us take time to think," said Jasaray. "The entrance you came through was guarded, yes?"

"Yes, Majesty," said Rage. "We killed three, but one escaped."

"There are two other entrances. We must assume they are also guarded. We must also assume, since so many assassins gained access to my private grounds, that some of my guards have been turned against me." Jasaray sat down on the marble bench and gazed down at the dead tiger. "It is time to smoke out the termites," he said. "But first we must clear my grounds of traitors." He looked at Bane. "Can you still fight?" he asked.

"I can fight."

"Then let us seek out the other killers."

Jasaray led Bane and Rage toward the first of the exits. As they came to it, they saw that the tiger's cage had been wedged between the hedges. Rage moved close to the bars and peered out. There was no sound or movement from beyond the cage. He and Bane pushed it clear. Three men ran from the shadows. Rage killed two in as many heartbeats. Bane blocked a knife thrust from the third, kicked his legs from under him, and then, as he fell, slashed his gladius through the man's throat. Jasaray stepped from the maze. "Nicely done," he said.

The third entrance was blocked by two upturned tables. There were no assassins there. Slowly they circled the maze. The grounds were empty.

An hour later Bane and Jasaray climbed a narrow, hidden staircase that ended at a locked door.

"Are you sure you want to do this?" whispered Bane.

"Life without risk is no life at all," Jasaray replied. He flicked open a latch, and the two men stepped out into the corridor some thirty feet away from Jasaray's private apartments. Three guards stood outside the emperor's rooms. As Jasaray stepped into sight, they momentarily stood and gaped, then snapped to attention. Jasaray, now wearing a pale gray tunic and sandals, advanced toward the guards. Bane stayed close to him, his sword in his hand.

"It has been an interesting evening," said Jasaray. "Has anyone been inquiring after me?"

The first of the guards licked his lips nervously. "We thought you were asleep, Majesty," he said. His gaze flickered to the blood-smeared Bane.

"I have not been asleep," said the emperor. "I have been

struggling to avoid the attentions of a hungry tiger and a group of armed assassins running free in my grounds."

The door to the apartments opened, and Voltan moved into sight. He was wearing his black and silver armor and carrying a gladius. "You are a hard man to kill, Majesty," he said. The guards stepped aside and drew their swords but made no attempt to attack or restrain Voltan.

"You are a thorough man," the emperor said softly. "How many of my guards have you turned against me?"

"These three only," said Voltan. "You chose well with the others. Singularly loyal and dreadfully dull."

Bane stood silently by, ready for the attack. Jasaray seemed unconcerned. "You might have waited until my death before invading my apartments," he told Voltan. "It is such bad manners."

"My apologies, Majesty," Voltan answered with a smile. "I wouldn't want to be considered rude. But I thought a dozen men and a tiger would be enough. Are you ready to die now?"

"I think no man is ever ready to die, Voltan. Tell me, how will you make it look like an accident now?"

Voltan laughed. "I do so admire bravery," he said. "You always were calm in the face of danger. I shall kill you quickly and then slash the skin to give the appearance of claw wounds. Clumsy, I know, but you have left me with little choice. You will be given a state funeral, and thousands will walk behind your coffin weeping. I don't doubt more statues will be raised to you, and men will speak for a generation about your greatness." Suddenly he leapt forward, his sword snaking out. Bane blocked the blow, pulling the emperor behind him. Almost in the same move the Rigante sent a slashing riposte. Voltan leapt back from it, then chuckled. "I have no time," he said, "to give you another lesson. Kill him," he told the guards. The men spread out and advanced.

At that moment there came the sounds of running men, booted feet pounding on the stairs. Scores of soldiers came into sight, weapons drawn, filling the corridor from both ends. Rage moved into view.

Jasaray, his hands clasped behind his back, looked at the treacherous guards. "Put down your weapons," he said, "and your deaths will be clean and swift. Hold to them and I will see that your eyes are burned out, but not before you have seen all your relatives and friends, loved ones, and children slaughtered." His voice was not raised, but venom dripped from every syllable. The three guards, their faces gray, released their weapons, which clattered to the floor.

Voltan stood alone now, sword in his hand. "Clever, clever Scholar," he said. "I underestimated you."

"Most men do," said Jasaray. "Put down your sword."

"Perhaps I would prefer to die fighting," said Voltan.

"Of course you would," said Jasaray. "And I will arrange it—if you give me evidence against Nalademus. I will let you die, sword in hand, in the arena, before the crowds. Otherwise I will order my men to take you alive. Your legs and arms will be hacked off, and you will be released to end your days begging for food as a cripple in the streets. Make your choice!"

"I could just kill you and be done with it," said Voltan, his pale eyes gleaming.

"You could," said Jasaray, "but my order would still stand. Can you see yourself begging for crumbs?"

Voltan stood very still for a moment, then tossed his sword to the floor. Soldiers ran forward, pinning his arms and leading him away.

"Wait!" he said as they came alongside Rage. "I need to speak to this man." The guards glanced back at the emperor, who nodded permission.

"What do you want?" asked Rage.

"Orders have been given to arrest cultists. Hunt teams will set out at dawn. Get Cara away from the villa."

"Cara?"

"She is one of them. She was with the Veiled Lady yesterday."

"Thank you," Rage said softly.

The guards led Voltan away. Jasaray summoned an officer. "Secure the palace. Relieve all the guards and send them to their barracks. Let no one know what has happened here tonight. And find me a scribe. I need to send several messages."

"Yes, Majesty," replied the man.

"And fetch a surgeon for my young friend here."

The officer saluted and moved away. Jasaray pushed open the door to his apartments and gestured for Rage and Bane to follow him inside. The emperor seated himself on an elegant couch that was beautifully yet simply made and covered with polished black leather. He leaned back against an embroidered cushion and closed his eyes.

"You must be tired, Majesty," said Rage. "Perhaps we should let you rest."

Jasaray gave a thin smile. "Not a night for rest. Come, seat yourselves." He glanced at Bane. "There are towels in the rear chamber. Cover your wounds. I do not want to get blood on my furniture."

"Might I ask a question?" inquired Rage as Bane went off in search of towels.

"Of course, my friend."

"If you suspected Nalademus of treachery, why did you allow him such power?"

Jasaray thought about the question. "The answer will be difficult for you to comprehend. You are an honorable man. You do not seek high office or power. Men who do are ruthlessly ambitious. They have great belief in themselves. This is what makes them so effective. Men like that are necessary. No empire can grow without them. They mirror nature, my friend. In the wolf pack there can be only one leader, but around that leader are a score of other males seeking to replace him. I do not blame Nalademus for his treachery. What condemns him is that he failed. Now he will suffer the consequences. However, the man I choose to succeed him will also be utterly ambitious. He, too, will one day seek to overthrow me. It is the ambition of such men that gives Stone its vitality and purpose."

"What you are saying is that you surround yourself with future traitors," said Rage. "This is a perilous way of life, Majesty."

Bane returned, a white linen towel draped over his shoulder. At that moment a scribe entered, carrying some thirty sheets of blank paper and a small box containing pens and ink. The man bowed low. Jasaray rose and walked to his desk by the window. "You have done me a great service, gentlemen," he told Bane and Rage. "I shall not forget it. Come to me tomorrow and ask of me anything. I will grant it. But for now return to your rooms. I will send the surgeon to you."

Bane was tired as he made his way along the corridor and down the stairs to his own apartments. He had reached the door before he realized Rage was not with him. Inside several of the lanterns had guttered and gone out, but one was still gleaming brightly. There was a jug of oil in one of the closets, and Bane refilled and relighted the lanterns before settling himself down on the bed. He was tired now, and the wound in his shoulder burned like fire. An army surgeon entered, followed by Rage. The surgeon, a small, balding man, peered closely at the talon wounds.

"These need cleaning," he said. "The claws of big cats carry some kind of poison. I've seen it before on campaigns."

"Not the claws," said Bane, "the fangs. Rotted food clings to them, and this infects wounds."

"Rotten food," the surgeon said scornfully. "Where do you tribesmen get such ideas?"

"A better question might be why we do not suffer infected wounds," said Bane. "Just stitch it. The flow of blood will have cleaned it."

"On your head be it," said the surgeon.

The wounds took eleven stitches, and the surgeon also added two stitches to the torn wound in Bane's side. "You need to rest for at least two weeks," he said. Bane thanked him, and the man left.

Rage sat down on the bed. "Well," he said, "it may not be the way you planned it, but Voltan is now under sentence of death. Your quest is over."

Bane looked into the old gladiator's dark eyes. "It will be over when I walk across the arena sand and cut his heart out."

Rage sighed and placed his hand on Bane's uninjured shoulder. "You are a fine and brave man, a brilliant swordsman and fearless in combat. But you can't beat him. He is a freak of nature, big and yet lightning fast. I understand why you needed to see him dead. He killed someone you loved. But he is dead, Bane. Why throw away your life on someone whose fate is already decided?"

"Because I swore I would kill him. I have lived for nothing else."

"I am sorry you feel that way, boy." He fell silent for a moment. "You never had a father, and I never had a son. I think that in some small way we have filled a gap in each other's lives. Like any father, I do not want to see my son die needlessly. Think on what I have said."

The dungeon walls were damp, the air fetid and clammy. It had been built to house twenty prisoners at the most, but more than fifty were wedged into the dank, airless room. Norwin sat hugging his knees in the corner. Beside him Persis Albitane sat quietly, his face and clothes filthy, a large red abscess on his neck, his face marked with bruises, a swelling, angry lump over his right eye. Norwin reached out and gripped his friend's arm. No words were exchanged, but Persis gave a weary smile.

The former slave closed his eyes, recalling the day he and the others had been taken while at a prayer meeting in the woods north of Goriasa. Soldiers had rushed in, carrying clubs and cudgels. Some of the thirty cultists had tried to run, but they had been caught and beaten badly. Then they had been bound and hauled off to spend the night in Goriasa's jail. The following morning they had been brought en masse to the court of magistrates, where a Crimson Priest had been sitting in the chair of judgment. Norwin had looked around and seen the public gallery packed with people. Some of them he knew were cultists like himself. Others were simply there for the dubious entertainment of seeing men and women sentenced to death.

The prisoners had been herded to stand before the Crimson Priest and told of their crimes against the state. One man tried to speak, but a knight cuffed him on the ear, splitting the skin.

"Silence!" roared the Crimson Priest. "This court has no wish to hear the filthy words of traitors."

"Why, then, is it called a court?" came a voice from the gallery. The words hung in the air. Norwin glanced up at the priest and saw the shock on his face.

"Who spoke?" he shouted.

"Persis Albitane," came the response. Norwin was stunned. He looked back to see fat Persis rise from his seat. "I am a citizen of Stone," said Persis, "with full rights and privileges. I see before you at least seven people I know. All are citizens. How dare you suborn the law! In the earliest articles of the city it was laid down that every citizen would have the right to speak in his own defense and to have others speak for him. You make a mockery of Stone justice."

The silence in the courtroom was almost palpable. Norwin looked back at the priest. At first it seemed his anger would explode, but then his eyes narrowed and he leaned back in his chair. "Step forward, Persis Albitane," he said. "Step forward and speak on behalf of these traitors."

Persis did so, easing his large frame past the silent spectators and moving to stand before the chair of judgment.

"I do not know all the defendants," he began. "But those I do know have been good citizens and have never spoken against the emperor or sought to bring ills upon the empire. This man," he said, pointing to Norwin, "is my former slave. He is as good a man as any I have met. I have never known him to lie or to steal or to show malice against anyone. His crime, as I understand it, is that he and others chose to walk quietly into a wood for the purpose of praying together. To call this a crime is a travesty of justice."

"It is not called a crime. It is a crime," said the priest. "Cultists have been named as traitors by the Stone elder himself, and these views have been enshrined in law. Merely to be a cultist ensures the sentence of death. Are you a cultist, Persis Albitane?"

Persis stood very still, and Norwin saw him draw in a deep breath. "Had you asked me that question a few moments ago, I would have told you—with all honesty—that I have never been a cultist, that I have never attended any of their meetings. But as I look at you and the evil you represent, I realize I was wrong to avoid them. I was not a cultist, but you have convinced me that I should be. And I thank you for it, priest."

"Condemned out of your own mouth!" shouted the priest. "And you will die with these other traitors." Surging to his feet, his face almost as crimson as his beard, he gazed malevolently at the public gallery. "Does anyone else here wish to speak on behalf of these enemies of Stone?"

No one did, and the prisoners, including Persis, were herded back to their cells. They were held for three days, then transported in chains to Stone. Norwin and Persis had been separated for most of the journey and had been reunited only that day, being transported from the dungeons under the Stone temple to this place beneath the arena of Circus Palantes. One of the guards had taken great delight in telling them of their fate. "Your teachings say you are to be a light to the world," he told them with a wide grin. "And tomorrow you will be. You will be dressed in oil-soaked rags and nailed by your arms and legs to tall posts set around the arena. Then you will be set afire, my dears. And you will scream and burn."

"You are a sad man," Persis told him. "And I pity you with all my heart."

The guard swore and ran at Persis, punching his face and knocking him to the ground. Savagely he kicked the fallen man, then turned and strode from the dungeon. Norwin helped Persis sit upright. "Oh, my friend, what have you done to yourself? You shouldn't be here."

"No one should be here, Norwin."

"Why did you speak up for us? Did you hear the voice of the Source?"

"I heard no voice," said Persis.

"Then why?"

Persis leaned his head back against the cold rock. "I have no idea except that I felt ashamed when I saw what was happening." He forced a smile. "Anyway, you would have missed me."

"Aye, I would have," Norwin said sadly. "You are a good man, Persis. A better one than you know."

Slow hours passed. The prisoners did not talk to one another but sat listlessly, each lost in his or her own thoughts. Then the door opened, and a young woman was hurled into the dungeon. She landed heavily, striking her head on the floor. Persis and Norwin moved to her side as she struggled to sit. She was young and dark-haired, her face bruised and swollen. Long streaks of blood had stained the back of her dress, and Norwin saw the marks of a whiplash across the top of her shoulders.

"Don't look so holy now, does she?" sneered the guard. "Without her veil she's just another doxy. Should have heard her scream as the lash fell."

Persis cradled the woman to him, careful to avoid touching her mutilated back. She lapsed into unconsciousness, her head resting on his chest. There was no water in the dungeon to clean her wounds, no bandages to bind them. But Persis held her to himself and whispered soothing words to her. She curled up against him like a child, and he stroked her hair.

After a while she opened her eyes. "Who are you?" she whispered.

"Persis Albitane. Rest now."

"I will rest soon." He helped her sit, and she slumped against him, her strength all but gone. "I do not know you, Persis Albitane," she said.

"Nor I you. It doesn't matter now."

She fell asleep again. Norwin sat gazing at her in the torchlight. "She is so young," he said. "Little more than a child."

In the far corner a man began to chant a prayer. One by one the others joined in. When it had finished there was silence in the dungeon once more, but a sense of calm had settled upon them.

"I wish I had time to learn about the cult," said Persis. "It would be nice to know what I was dying for."

"You'll have plenty of time to learn, my friend," said Norwin. "After the burning."

Nalademus had not slept. He had stalked his apartments throughout the night, his mood alternating between ecstasy and fear. Now the dawn light was bathing the city, and he was tired and irritable. Where was Voltan? Why had he not brought news of Jasaray's death?

Pushing open the doors to his balcony, Nalademus stepped outside. The air was sweet and cool, the city stretching out before him, pale and beautiful. This was his day, a day of glory and cleansing. Sixteen months of planning and the collection of thousands of names. Today would see the cultists utterly destroyed, and with them the increasingly feeble Jasaray.

His knights were marching from the barracks, hundreds of them. He watched with pleasure as they moved out into the city, column after column, the officers carrying lists naming traitors. They would be hauled from their beds and dragged back to the temple. There would be too many for the dungeons, so they would be herded into the barracks square before being transported to the various circus arenas for execution. More and more of his knights filed out of the barracks. Nalademus watched them with pride. From tomorrow the people of Stone would march toward destiny.

But where was Voltan?

Nalademus stared out along the deserted avenue, hoping to see the lord of the Stone knights riding toward the temple. He swore loudly and moved back inside the apartment. One of the lanterns began to gutter, and oily black smoke sputtered from the wick. Nalademus blew it out. On the table were the remains of the previous night's meal and an empty jug of wine. He picked up a piece of bread. It was stale now, and he hurled it to the floor. His huge stomach rumbled. Calling one of the guards, he sent the man to fetch him some food, then slumped down in a wide leather chair, his anger growing. Voltan had been growing increasingly arrogant of late. Soon it would be time to dispense with his services. Not yet, though. With Jasaray's death there was still the risk of civil war.

The guard returned with a plate of cold meats and a fresh jug of wine. "Send Banouin to me," said Nalademus, taking the plate and stuffing a handful of ham into his mouth. Moments later there was a rap at the door, and the slim, dark-haired Rigante entered.

"My heart is pounding," said Nalademus. "Prepare me a tisane."

"The emperor is alive," said Banouin, his voice soft, almost sorrowful. Nalademus jerked, his great head coming up, his eyes peering at the younger man.

"What do you know of this?"

"Everything, lord. I am a seer. Among my people I would have become a druid. Last night I had a vision. It was one I first had several years ago. My friend Bane was moving through strange corridors, the walls alive and rustling. A beast was stalking him. There was an older man with him, a man I did not know. Now I do. His name is Rage. Last night a group of killers tried to murder the emperor by releasing a wild beast into the maze in his garden—a huge creature, a striped lion. It had been starved for some time. One of the assassins felled the emperor with a blow to the head, then smeared him with blood and left him for the lion. Fortunately for Jasaray, my friend Bane and his comrade Rage entered the maze and killed the beast. Then Jasaray summoned his loyal guards, and Voltan was arrested."

Nalademus sat stunned, his mind struggling to grasp what the boy was saying. "If this happened last night," he said, "why have the emperor's guards not come for me?"

Banouin walked past him and stared out over the balcony, where the last of the knights were marching out into the city. Nalademus heard the sounds of marching feet, and his heart stuttered. Jasaray knew of today's cull. He was waiting for the temple to empty.

Nalademus stumbled out onto the balcony and shouted at the departing troops. "Come back!" he yelled. They did not hear him. He stood for a moment, his thick fingers gripping the stone of the balcony rim, his knuckles white. Then he looked into the calm face of the young man beside him. "What can I do, Banouin?"

Banouin sighed. "I am going home, lord. Back to my people. I should never have come here."

"Help me!"

"No one can help you." Banouin turned away and moved toward the door. Nalademus lunged out, grabbing Banouin's arm.

"It was you!" screamed Nalademus. "You betrayed me!"

Banouin lifted his hand and touched Nalademus lightly on the chest. The Stone elder's restraining hand spasmed open, and Banouin continued to walk toward the door. Nalademus took a deep breath, ready to shout to the guards to kill the boy, to cut him down before his eyes. Banouin looked at him, and Nalademus found his throat constricting. Then the Rigante was gone.

Nalademus, his heart beating wildly, lumbered out onto the balcony. He felt dizzy and nauseous. Out on the avenue he saw a unit of foot soldiers marching toward the barracks, the morning sunlight shining on their silver armor and white plumes. They were Jasaray's Royal Guards.

Nalademus stepped back, trod on his crimson robe, and fell to the floor. He scrambled to his knees, then ran to the dining table. Picking up a knife, he sawed at his fat wrist, but the blade was too blunt.

The Royal Guards came through the gate.

Nalademus tore open the door to the outer corridor. There were two of his guards there. "Give me your sword," he ordered the first.

"My sword?"

Nalademus grabbed the hilt of the man's gladius, wrenching it clear of the scabbard. From below came the sounds of a commotion and voices raised in anger. Nalademus moved slowly back into his apartment and gazed around at the rich hangings and decorations, the shelves lined with tomes, the golden goblets. Through the balcony window he could see the white and perfect glory of the city.

He fell to his knees and reversed the sword. Wrenching open his robes, he placed the blade against his chest, the hilt against the floor. Then he threw himself forward. The hilt slipped, the blade merely slicing through the skin above his sternum and lodging under his collarbone. Hands grabbed him, hauling him to his feet. "No!" he wailed. "No!"

During the four days that followed the arrest of Nalademus and the ending of the power of the Crimson Priests, wild celebrations broke out in every district. Thousands of cultists were freed from prison, returning to their homes. Many Crimson Priests shaved off their beards and fled the city. Others waited defiantly, continuing their duties, sure that the furor would soon die down. Most of them were arrested, summarily tried, and put to death quietly.

The prisoners in the dungeons below the arena of Circus Palantes knew nothing of the great events in the city above. They were the last to be freed and, when the dungeon doors were opened, believed they were to be taken for burning. Many cried out, begging for their lives.

"Silence!" thundered the guard. "You are to be freed on orders of the emperor."

The prisoners huddled together, unwilling to believe him. Surely, they thought, this was just an attempt to lull them into walking obediently to their deaths. A white-robed councillor stepped into the doorway, holding a scented handkerchief to his face to mask the stench from within.

"What the guard says is true," he told them. "Nalademus

has been arrested and condemned, and you are all free to go to your homes, wherever they may be."

Persis Albitane heard the words and felt an enormous wave of relief surge through him. He struggled to his feet and turned to help the Veiled Lady stand. Her face was ghostly white and gleamed with sweat. Her flesh was hot to the touch, her eyes fever-bright.

"Leave her where she is," said the guard. "She's not to be freed."

"Why?" asked Persis. Most of the cultists had filed through the doors, anxious to be clear of this dreadful place. They had left without a backward glance at the woman. At last only Norwin and Persis remained with her. "Why?" Persis asked once more.

"Not for me to know," said the guard. "Now be on your way."

"She is sick and needs help," said Persis.

"Stay with her, then." The guard sneered. "I don't mind if you die with her."

"They cannot stay," said the councillor.

Persis knelt by the stricken woman. "I am so sorry," he said.

Her eyes cleared momentarily, and she smiled at him. No words were spoken, but her hand reached up and stroked his bearded face. As her skin touched his, Persis felt a great warmth begin to flow through him. The searing agony of the abscess on his neck disappeared, and all the pain from the bruises and cuts on his face and body faded away. Still the warmth grew, as if the sunlight were seeping through his skin, filling his veins with bright light. And with that light came a vast understanding that transcended any intellectual learning. His gaze locked to hers, and tears fell from his eyes. Her hand fell away.

Persis Albitane reached out and stroked her hair. He felt the power move within him. The three men remaining in the cell stood in astonished silence as they saw a pale light glowing around the dying girl. The dreadful, pus-covered whip wounds sealed themselves and healed without scars. The skin of her face began to glow with health, all her bruises disappearing. The light faded, and Persis rose. He looked into the eyes of the guard.

"Don't hurt me," said the man, backing away.

"How could I hurt you more than you are hurting your-self?" Persis asked him. He glanced back at the young woman. She smiled at him and gestured for him to go. "Do you have her veil?" asked Persis. The guard nodded dumbly. "Then fetch it for her. And find her some clean garments and food. Will you do this?"

"I will. I promise," replied the guard, still terrified.

"Then may the Source bless you," said Persis. With one last look at the woman in the cell he took Norwin by the arm and walked along the dungeon corridor and up the steps toward the light.

Nalademus was put on trial before Jasaray's council. The main witness was Voltan, who told of the murder plot and also admitted that temple funds were being used to help Stone's enemies in the east and prolong the war. Just before sentence Nalademus was allowed to speak. He at first railed at Jasaray, who was not present, accusing him of weakness and divisive policies, undermining the great destiny of Stone, but when sentence of death was passed, he collapsed and was carried from the chamber.

Bane sprinted up the hillside, hurdling a fallen tree, then slowed to an easy run as he entered the woods. The wounds on his left shoulder and side were healing fast. Rage had re-moved the stitches the previous day. The two men had at first exchanged only a few words.

"You are still angry with me," said Bane as Rage snipped the last stitch, pulling clear the thread.

"Not angry," said Rage, "disappointed."

"I think you are wrong. I can beat him."

Rage shrugged. "That is not the point. You no longer need to fight him, to risk throwing away your life. It is not about re-venge now or justice. It is just vanity. He defeated you, and now you must prove that you are the better man. Life should be worth more than that, Bane."

The words echoed in his mind as he ran. He could not ex-plain the depth of his feelings to Rage or the despair he had felt through most of his young life. Lia had been the rainbow after the storm, the one great chance to change his destiny. When Voltan had killed her, he had planted a seed of hatred in

Bane's heart, a seed that had flowered and grown. Not a night
had passed without Voltan's face hovering in Bane's mind as
he slipped into sleep. Not a morning had broken without a
thought of the merciless gladiator and the blade that had sent
Lia's soul hurtling from the world. For more than two years
now the hatred had eaten away at him, and Bane believed it
would pass only when he faced the warrior eye to eye, sword
to sword. It was the Rigante way.

Dipping his shoulders, Bane powered up yet another hill,
then onto a winding path that flowed down into a wooded
valley. A low mist drifted across the bracken, and Bane
slowed his run, unable to see the ground ahead. The last thing
he needed now, a day before the fight, was to twist his ankle
on some hidden root or stone. Ahead he saw two men hauling
the trunk of a dead tree toward a slope. One was old, with only
one hand, and the other was in his teens. They were struggling
with the trunk. A broken branch had wedged itself against a
buried rock. The one-armed man chopped off the branch with
a hatchet, and they began to pull once more. Bane joined
them, grinned at the old man, then took up the end of the
rope. The trunk moved more easily now, and they hauled it
down the slope to a clumsily built cottage beside a stream.

"My thanks to you," said the old man. "We would have
made it, but by heavens, it was quite an effort."

"You are Bane," said the slim, dark-haired youngster. "I
saw you fight Dex."

The older man moved in closer and peered at Bane. "Aye,
you have the look of a swordsman," he said, his voice less
friendly.

"Is it true you are to fight Voltan?" asked the youngster.

"Aye, it is true."

"I hope you make him die slowly!"

"That is enough!" roared the old man. "I don't want to see
any man die slow, not even foul creatures like him. There has
been more than enough killing already."

"How can you say that?" asked the young man. "He was
one of those who murdered our friends, took them for
burning. He deserves a painful death."

The older man sat down on the fallen tree, pulled clear the
leather cup that covered the stump of his left wrist, and

scratched at the scarred and puckered skin. He glanced up at Bane. "As I said, our thanks to you. Do not let us keep you from your training."

Bane stood for a moment, then ran on, heading back up the slope and off onto an old deer track. As he reached the higher ground, he saw the city below him, glistening in the early light. His legs were tired now, his calves burning.

The bathhouse at Circus Occian was open, though the water was not yet heated, and Bane moved through to the new open-air training area designed by Rage. Several of the younger gladiators were already there, hoisting weights under the supervision of Telors. Bane stretched out his aching muscles, then did some light work on the climbing ropes, hauling himself up to the top of the frame and down several times.

Telors joined him. "Not too much, now," he said. "Save something for tomorrow."

"You think I am being foolish?"

"It is not for me to say. Men do what they must. Personally I'd have asked the emperor for a mountain of gold and my own personal whorehouse." Telors shrugged.

"You've seen him fight," said Bane. "Rage does not believe I can take him."

"Vanni regrets saying that. He wouldn't have wanted to say anything to make you doubt your abilities. He was hoping he could talk you out of the contest."

"What do you think? Give me the truth."

"I can't give you the truth, Bane, only opinion. I once saw a big soldier, fully armed with breastplate, shield, and sword, brought down by a boy carrying a makeshift wooden spear. When a man fights, anything can happen." He gave a rueful smile. "And I'm not going to stand here and tell you how good Voltan is—not the day before you fight him. I can tell you how good you are. You are a match for almost anyone. You have the speed, the strength, and most importantly the heart. I'll be with you tomorrow. I'll put a fine edge on your sword, and your breastplate will gleam with oil."

"Breastplate? It is a death bout."

Telors looked uncomfortable. "The emperor has suspended the usual rules. Voltan will fight without armor of any kind."

"Then so shall I. It is to be a duel, not an execution."

"I thought you'd say that," admitted Telors. "It does you credit. Rage would have said the same."

A servant called out that the water was heated, and Bane moved back inside.

The bath was sixteen feet long and nine feet wide. Steam was rising from the surface of the water, carrying the scent of lavender. Bane stripped off his clothing and slipped into the water, ducking his head and swimming to the far end, where he sat on a ledge, resting his head on the rounded brass rail surrounding the bath. Tension eased from his muscles.

He lay in the water for some time, then toweled himself dry and wandered to the massage room, where an Occian slave rubbed oil into his skin and worked on the muscles of his legs and upper back. Bane dozed for a while. When he awoke, he found he was alone. The slave had placed warm towels over his body and had left him sleeping. Rising, he went to his locker, put on a fresh tunic and leggings, and walked barefoot back into the bathhouse. Leaving his training clothes with a slave for washing, he tugged on his boots and walked out into the sunlight.

It was a beautiful day, and he strolled along the avenues back toward the villa. Most of the celebrations were over, but there was still an air of elation over the city. At the villa the gardeners were at work, weeding the flower beds, and Bane saw Cara, dressed in a pale green dress, walking among the roses. A dark-haired and handsome young man was walking with her. Cara saw Bane and waved. He strolled over to them. "This is Maro," said Cara. "He is the son of the general Barus." Bane shook hands with the man. "He has come to see Grandfather," continued Cara, "but he is still out on his run."

"He must have taken the western route," said Bane. "I have not seen him today."

"Maro and I are to be married," said Cara.

"If your grandfather agrees," put in Maro.

Bane smiled. "I am sure he will—if that is what you desire, princess. However, I am hurt. I always thought you would save yourself for me."

"You are too old," she said with a mocking grin. "And not handsome enough."

Bane put his hand over his heart. "Women are so cruel. Be warned, Maro!"

He bowed and walked away. Cara ran after him, taking his arm. "You and Grandfather should end this quarrel," she told him.

"We have not quarreled," he said.

"You do not look me in the eye anymore," she said suddenly. "Why is that?"

"Nonsense," he said, forcing himself to meet her gaze. Her eyes were bright blue and pale. Voltan's eyes. He looked away. "Your guest is being neglected," he added.

"Have I done something to offend you, Bane?"

"Not at all." He felt awkward standing there.

"Are you still planning to fight tomorrow?" she asked him. "Yes."

"I met him, you know. Voltan. I met him in the market-place. I liked him. Oh, I know people say he is evil, but I saw him at one of our meetings. The Veiled Lady touched his head and blessed him. So he can't be all bad."

Bane sighed. "I do not know if he is all bad. He killed someone I loved. He will die for that, not for some . . . political intrigue."

"He will die anyway, Bane. We all do. It is a shame that you cannot forgive him."

"Some things cannot be forgiven."

"I do not believe that."

"That is because you have never suffered," he said, a note of anger in his voice. "It is so easy for people like you, living in luxury, servants attending your every need. What is there to forgive? A cook makes your porridge too thin? Oh, I forgive you. But the women of the Gath who saw their babes plucked from their arms by Stone soldiers, their little heads smashed against the walls of the houses, they know what suffering is. Do they forgive? I saw Voltan plunge his sword into the heart of the woman I loved. He laughed as he did it. And you ask me to forgive? Look around you! Everything you have here—everything in this city—is built on the blood of slaughtered people. Maybe one day they will forgive you. But I doubt it." Furious now, he strode away from her.

As he reached the front of the house, he saw two men walking along the gravel path. "Persis!" he shouted, and went to meet them. Both were dressed in filthy clothes that stank horribly.

"It is good to see you, my boy," Persis said wearily. "Is there somewhere we can cleanse ourselves of this dungeon aroma?"

"Of course. Follow me."

Persis was too large and Norwin too small for any of the clothes in the house to fit them, so while they were bathing, Bane sent a servant to the market to purchase fresh garments. Cara and Maro, who had seen the men arrive, came to Bane as he waited in the east-facing main living room. "Was that Persis?" she asked.

"Yes. They were freed yesterday, but with no money and no friends here they sought us out."

"I am glad that they did. I shall get the cook to prepare them some food." She moved away, and Maro remained. Bane gestured him to a chair.

"I know a friend of yours," said Maro. "Banouin."

"He is not a friend. He is someone I once knew."

"Oh. I did not realize. He speaks of you fondly."

"I have always preferred fond deeds to fond words," said Bane. "How is he?"

"He left the city this morning. He is going home. I shall miss him."

Bane had no interest in talking of his former friend and changed the subject. "How did you and Cara meet?"

Maro smiled. "I suppose it is safe to say it now, but I saw her at one of the Veiled Lady's gatherings. Afterward we talked and . . ." He spread his hands. "I grew to love her. I shall be nineteen in three weeks. We plan to wed as soon after that as her father will allow."

"She is a fine girl."

"I know that."

"What are your plans?"

"I shall become a soldier, like my father."

"A soldier?" queried Bane. "I thought you cultists did not believe in war."

"I am not a cultist. I have attended their meetings, and there is much about their philosophy that I admire. But this is not a perfect world, and there are many dangers in it. I am perfectly willing to offer love and generosity of spirit to all I meet, but there will be a sword at my side in case the generosity and love are not reciprocated."

Bane nodded agreement. "How does Cara feel about this?"

"How do you think?" Maro responded with a grin.

◇ **10** ◇

"**C**AN I COUNT on your support?" Jasaray asked Bendegit Bran as the two met for the last time on the steps of the Imperial Palace. Fiallach was waiting with the horses and the ten-man honor guard that was to accompany them to the city gates.

"I have much enjoyed our visit, Majesty," said Bran, "and it was a great privilege to meet you. I thank the gods that you survived the assassination attempt and am honored that it was a Rigante warrior who aided you on that fateful night. I shall report faithfully to my king everything you have said, and it is my hope that the days of enmity between our peoples are at an end."

Jasaray took his arm and walked with him down the steps. "Wars are sometimes necessary and often inevitable," said the emperor, "but Stone has enemies far closer to home than Connavar of the Rigante. Tell him this and assure him of my good wishes."

Bran bowed, then stepped into the saddle. Fiallach also bowed. Jasaray looked into the warrior's eyes. "I think you will be glad to be heading home," he said. "I fear that city life does not suit you."

"I have a longing for the mountains," admitted Fiallach.

"Caer Druagh is said to be very beautiful," said Jasaray.

"If you visit us as a friend, I will take you riding in the countryside, the high woods and the valleys," promised Fiallach.

"That would be most pleasant," said Jasaray.

Bran touched heels to his mount, and they rode slowly from the palace, the silver-clad honor guard marching behind them. An hour later they cleared the gates and took the horses into a light run across the western hills. Drawing rein at the top, Bendegit Bran gazed back at the city of Stone.

"You look troubled, my friend," said Fiallach.

"Indeed I am. War is coming, Fiallach."

"But Jasaray said—"

"It doesn't matter what he said. He acts like a scholar and a man longing for peace, but he lives for war and conquest. I knew it when we saw the tiger in his gardens. Can you imagine at what cost they caught the beast and transported it thousands of miles? And for what? So that Jasaray could send it into the arena to be killed for sport, so that the mob of Stone could glimpse more blood. Is this the act of a scholar? No, he has won in the east and destroyed his enemies at home. Now he will seek to win the mob's approval with a war against the only enemy ever to have defeated a Stone army."

"But what about his talk of King Shard and his growing army? Surely Shard is a greater danger to Stone. He wouldn't have to cross the sea to fight Jasaray. His armies could march into Stone territory within days."

"Indeed they could," agreed Bran. "But it is my belief that Jasaray and Shard have made an alliance. Come the spring, Shard will invade in the north, Jasaray in the south. We will have a war on two fronts."

Swinging his horse, Bran headed west.

Fiallach rode after him. He respected Bran more than any other man except perhaps Connavar. Bran was more than a general, and even the king deferred to him on matters of strategy and tactics. His mind was sharper than daggers, his skills in battle almost mystical. Connavar often said that Bran could read a battle the way other men read simple script.

"It is a shame that the bastard saved him," Fiallach said, as they angled their mounts down the slope and onto the wide western road.

Bran glanced at the giant warrior. "Bane's act was heroic. I can't fault him for that."

"I can," Fiallach said with feeling. "He is no good, Bran. Born of treachery, he carries it in his blood."

"I have heard this argued of bastards before," said Bran, "and I do not believe it. Bane carries the blood of Connavar in his veins. By Taranis, he even looks like him! He has courage and strength, and he deserved better than the treatment my brother gave him. It saddens me that you hate him so."

"I do not wish to hear you criticize Connavar," said Fiallach, anger creeping into his voice.

"Kings are not beyond criticism, my friend. In truth, I also blame myself. I should have gone to Conn a long time ago and argued Bane's case. I did not, and it shames me. My father raised me to believe that love of family was the first duty of a Rigante. I have lived by that with my own children. Bane is my nephew, and I should have embraced him as such."

"He would have spurned you," Fiallach said sadly, "as he spurned me. When he was a youngster—around thirteen, I think—I sent him an invitation to come to Seven Willows and spend the summer with us. He wrote me an insulting reply. That insult alone shows his nature. He'll get no second chance from me."

"That is curious," said Bran, "for Brother Solstice told me that Bane never could master reading and writing. It seems odd that he should have written to you."

"Well, he didn't actually write it," said Fiallach. "Braefar wrote telling me what Bane had said. But it is the same. He said he had no wish to spend any time in my company and did not regard me as family. Had he been a man then and not some callow boy, I would have killed him for his impertinence."

Bran shook his head. "It never ceases to surprise me how often Braefar's name figures in misunderstandings, disagreements, and quarrels."

"You think he lied to me? That is ridiculous! What would be the point?"

"I cannot answer that," said Bran. "I have never understood it. There is a deep well of bitterness in him, and I think he takes pleasure in creating the same bitterness in others. It is like a game to him. I'll tell you truly, Fiallach, I do not know what Bane might have said, and it could be that Braefar reported it truthfully. It is just that I have come to view my brother and his motives with great suspicion."

"I think you do him an injustice," said Fiallach. "He has always been most courteous to me. His only complaint has been that Connavar does not offer him work more suited to his talents. Braefar is a clever man, but he commands no regiments and is restricted to running Three Streams and the border lands with the Norvii."

"I am glad that you like him," said Bran. "Let us leave it at that."

Bane's mood was somber as he sat in the sword room beneath Circus Palantes. Telors was close by, gently honing the edge of the Rigante's gladius. A towering figure moved into the doorway. For a moment Bane thought it was Rage, for the light of a powerful lantern was behind him. The man stepped inside, and Bane saw it was Brakus, Gladiator One. He glanced up at the golden-haired man. Brakus moved past him to a locked cabinet on the far wall, took a key from the pocket of his leather jerkin, and inserted it into the lock. Bane saw him remove two leather-covered flasks and a small scroll wrapped in ribbon. He was a big man, larger than Rage, but he moved with the same catlike grace.

He made to leave, but Telors spoke up. "Ignoring old friends, are we now, Brak?"

The gladiator paused, then grinned. "By heavens, Telors, when did you grow that disgusting foliage? I remember when you were young and handsome."

Telors chuckled, and the two men shook hands. "I heard you and Vanni were training the Occian fighters. You've done a good job."

"It's good to be back," said Telors. "I thought you'd be retired by now. You must have a mountain of gold already."

Brakus shrugged. "I keep promising myself that each fight will be the last. But then some arrogant young fighter steps out of the shadows, telling me I'm old and how he's going to kill me. Pride takes over then." He looked across at Bane. "You want to tell me how old and tired I look, boy?" he asked.

"You look strong and fit to me," said Bane.

Brakus nodded. "Indeed I am. Tell me, what made you want to take this bout? You're famous enough without it, and Voltan will prove no easy meat."

"It is personal," put in Telors. "Voltan killed a friend of his—a woman."

"Oh, I see. Well, good luck to you, Bane. Perhaps we'll meet again."

"I doubt it," said Bane. "This is my last fight. Tomorrow I'm heading for home."

Brakus smiled. "Then all my notes on you will be wasted." He walked to the doorway, then turned. "You have a habit of clenching your left fist before an attack. Voltan will spot that quickly."

"Thank you. It is a habit Rage has warned me of. I can't seem to lose it."

"Voltan is very fast on the riposte. Lose that habit today or you won't be going home." He swung to Telors. "Good to see you, my friend. I'm having a small gathering to celebrate my birthday in three days. Come up to the house. Bring Vanni with you."

"I'll do that," said Telors. Brakus left, and Telors went back to honing the blade.

"I thought Rage would come," said Bane.

"Aye, well, you know what he thinks."

"I know. He thinks I'm going to die. He's wrong."

"He's been wrong before. We all have." Telors glanced at the marked candle on the shelf and gauged the time. "Less than an hour before the fight. How do you feel?"

"I'm fine." Bane sat and gazed around the room. It was a far cry from the sword room at Circus Orises. Brightly painted frescoes adorned the walls, and there were niches inset, holding busts of the greatest heroes of Palantes. Bane scanned them. "Where is Rage?" he asked.

"Palantes removed the bust when Rage was disgraced."

Bane settled back. Before a fight he had never had difficulty emptying his mind of all other worries, but this day was different. Memories and thoughts crowded him, each vying for attention.

Suppose he were to die today, who would care? His friend Banouin had deserted him, his father had never acknowledged him, and now Rage had not even turned up to watch him face his toughest test. He glanced at Telors. He liked the man, but they were not close. If Bane's body was dragged from the arena, Telors would shrug and go back to the villa, have a few drinks, say nice things about him, and get on with his life.

Suddenly Bane felt alone, and in that moment fear began to grow inside him. What have I done with my life? he wondered. What have I achieved? He shook his head. These were not good thoughts before a death duel, and he rose and moved to the table, lifting a leather-covered flask and breaking the wax seal to pull forth the cork. All the gladiators prepared their own drinks, sealing them with wax so that no competitor could drug them before a bout. Lifting it to his lips, he drank deeply. The crushed-fruit drink slipped down his throat like silk. "Not too much," said Telors. "You won't want to be bloated."

Bane sat back down. He had dreamed the previous night that the Morrigu had come to him. He had awoken to the rustling of the wind through leaves and the whispering of branches. Sitting up, he saw that his bed was now in the middle of a small clearing surrounded by oaks. The Morrigu was sitting on a tree stump.

"Satin sheets," she said. "How rich you have become."

A black crow swooped over the bed and settled on a branch close to the Morrigu.

"What do you want of me?" he asked.

"Considering the foolishness you are engaged upon, I think it more apt to ask what you might require of me."

Bane rose from the bed and took a deep breath. He could smell the cool air flowing from the mountains. "I would have wished only one thing from you, Old Woman. I would have wished to save Lia's life. Now there is nothing. I will win tomorrow or I will die."

"Yes, yes," she said, "you could not save your love. Life can be like that, Bane. But what of your own life? If you ask me, I will grant you the strength and speed you need to defeat Voltan."

"I already have that."

"No, you don't. Vanni told you that. Voltan is bigger, stronger, and faster. He is more deadly. Ask me!"

"No!"

"Is it pride that stops you?"

He thought about the question. "Perhaps it is, but I won't use magic against him. I want no help. I will face him as a man on equal terms."

"How noble," she said. "Do you believe for a moment that Voltan would do the same?"

"I am not responsible for what Voltan does or does not do. I want him to pay for Lia's death and to know that is what he is dying for."

"And what will this achieve, Bane? Do you think he will care? Do you think that it will create in him the merest speck of remorse?"

Bane shook his head. "It is not about him. It is about me. When I have killed him, I will know peace."

"Ah, I see. It is all about Bane. Not about Lia or the evil of Voltan. Just Bane."

"Yes, it is about Bane," he said angrily. "And why should that not be so? Who has ever fought for me? I have always been alone. I loved my mother, and I think she loved me when I was a child. But as I grew, every time she looked at me, she saw Connavar. And she withdrew from me." He laughed, the sound hollow, causing the crow to flap its wings. "Where are my friends and loved ones? The one friend I thought I had deserted me when he thought me dying. Yes, it is indeed about Bane. If I die tomorrow, who will mourn for me?"

"Who indeed?" she answered. "Well, if I am not needed, I shall not remain. Return to your bed, Rigante. Sleep."

It had been a curious dream, born no doubt of his fears, but it haunted him still.

"Time to loosen those muscles," said Telors.

Two soldiers in silver armor moved into the sword room. "The emperor commands your presence," the first told Bane.

"He needs preparation time," said Telors.

"Come with us," said the second man, ignoring Telors.

Bane pulled on a shirt of black silk and followed the guards through the underground corridors and up a flight of steps to the second level. Out in the open he glanced around and saw that the stadium was full, rank upon rank of citizens waiting for the afternoon's entertainment. Circus Palantes could seat almost thirty thousand people, but hundreds more were standing in the aisles.

"Big crowd," said the first guard.

"Don't get too swell-headed," said the second. "They've mostly come to see the Veiled Lady burn. They're wondering if she'll work a miracle and fly away into the sky." He gave a harsh laugh. "Some hope."

"I thought all the cultists had been freed," said Bane.

"Not her. She'll be burning alongside Nalademus. Good joke, eh? Wonder what they'll have to say to one another as they're raised up above the pyres."

The guards moved on, climbing to the third level and the guarded entrance to the Royal Enclosure. As Bane was ushered inside, he saw Jasaray sitting alone. The emperor was wearing a white robe and a long purple cloak. Upon his head was a wide-brimmed hat of woven straw, shielding his face from the sun. "Come in and sit, my boy," said Jasaray.

"I thank you, Majesty," said Bane, "but I must prepare for my fight."

"All in good time," he said.

At the edge of the arena a trumpeter sent out a long single note. The crowd settled down. From the western end of the arena a swordsman stepped from the gate, advancing across the sand. The crowd booed and jeered. Bane looked down and could scarcely believe what he was seeing.

The swordsman was Voltan.

"I must go, Majesty!" he said.

"Wait!" commanded Jasaray.

"But I am to fight him. You promised!"

"Indeed I did, young man. And I keep my promises. However, I did not promise that you could fight him first."

The gate at the eastern end of the stadium opened, and another swordsman made his way across the sand. Stripped to the waist and wearing a leather kilt, he drew a red silk scarf from his belt and tied it over his bald head.

It was Rage.

At first Bane could not believe what he was seeing. "Why?" he whispered.

"I wondered that myself when Rage first asked me," said Jasaray. "It was the night of the tiger. I had told you both that you could ask of me anything. Rage stayed behind and said that he wanted to be the first to fight Voltan. Then, the following day, you came to me. That is when I had my answer. I think you know it, too."

Bane felt sick. Leaning forward, he gripped the rail above the enclosure balcony. Yes, he knew. Rage was doing this for him. And the older man's words flowed back into his mind in letters of fire.

"You never had a father, and I never had a son. I think that in some small way we have filled a gap in each other's lives. Like any father I do not want to see my son die needlessly."

Shame swept over the younger man. His selfish desire for personal vengeance had put at risk the only man who had truly befriended him. His mind swam with the enormity of the moment, and all the bitterness and self-pity of his youth began to melt away, the rejections and the loneliness, the hurts and the disappointments. All became as nothing compared to the sacrifice this man was making for him. Rage knew that Bane could not beat Voltan and knew also that old as Rage was, he could wear the man down, tiring him, perhaps wounding him, before his duel with Bane, giving the younger man a greater chance of survival.

"I didn't want this," said Bane.

"I expect not," agreed Jasaray, "but it is a magnificent gesture." There was pride in his voice, pride and a note of astonishment, as if, though sensing the greatness, he could not quite understand the motive.

The emperor rose, removed his straw hat, and waved it in the air. A trumpet sounded, and the two fighters touched swords in salute. Then they circled. Voltan attacked first with terrifying speed, but Rage blocked and parried, sending a riposte that forced Voltan to leap back. The crowd fell silent as the two men fought on. Few among the thirty thousand could appreciate fully the level of skill they were observing, but all knew they were watching two extraordinary fighters. They sensed that this epic duel would go down in history and that in the years to come they would tell their children and grandchildren of the day they saw Voltan and Rage duel to the death in the arena of Circus Palantes.

Bane watched the fight, caught between amazement and horror. Rage had been right. He could not have beaten this man. For all his size Voltan moved with awesome speed. His footwork was perfect, keeping him always in balance, whether leaping to attack or defending desperately. The pace of the fight was almost inhuman, the two men locked in a combat that was almost a dance. Bane watched unblinking, his breathing shallow and fast. His mouth was dry, his knuckles white as he clenched the rail. Whatever happened this day, he knew he would be changed forever by Rage's sacrifice. Never again would he complain about life and its unfairness. On this one hot afternoon he had been given a gift worth more than all the hurts he had ever suffered.

Voltan's sword sliced across Rage's chest, sending a spray of blood into the air. Bane groaned, the sound swamped by a great cry from the crowd. Voltan leapt in for the kill. The old gladiator swayed to the right. His blade lashed out. Voltan threw himself back, but not before Rage's sword had ripped open a wound above his right hip. The two men circled more warily now. Rage had been cut across the top of his chest, underneath the right collarbone, the blood streaming down over his belly. Voltan's wound was also bleeding heavily, staining his kilt and flowing to his thigh. The two men came together again, blades clanging and clashing. As they closed, Voltan suddenly threw a punch that caught Rage on the temple, knocking him back a step. Rage rolled with the blow and managed to parry a disemboweling thrust. They circled again.

The fight was less furious now, more measured as each man sought out a weakness in the other. It was no less tense, and the crowd was unnaturally silent. For Bane it was as if time had slowed. He stared at Voltan, trying to see a weakness, a tell, anything that would indicate an opening for Rage. But there was nothing. Voltan was the most complete fighter he had ever seen.

And Rage was tiring. Despite his fitness and the endless hours of exercise that had created it, age was beginning to tell now. Voltan could see it, too, and slowly the fight became more cat and mouse. Voltan blocked a sudden lunge, and his riposte cut Rage's shoulder. Another attack saw Rage almost stumble. Voltan's sword snaked out, the blade glancing from Rage's temple as he threw himself aside. Blood was on the older man's face now.

Voltan tried a feint, followed by a lunge to the heart. Rage parried it and sent a return cut that struck Voltan's left bicep, slicing open the skin. Suddenly the pace picked up again, both men hacking and slashing, blocking and moving. Bane knew Voltan was seeking to exhaust his tiring opponent, and he was succeeding. Rage's sword arm did not have the same speed as before, and Voltan's blade found a way through, stabbing the older man in the left shoulder. Rage backed away. Bane could see his great chest heaving as he sucked in air. Voltan, though bleeding profusely, did not seem to be suffering.

A commotion began in the stands to the right of the Royal Enclosure. Bane glanced around to see Telors pushing people out of the way, clambering over a low wall, and grabbing a large padded drumstick from a surprised drummer. Hoisting the huge drum to the wall, Telors began a slow, steady beat that boomed like distant thunder around the arena.

Out on the sand the two fighters paused momentarily as the drum sounded.

Voltan was more tired than he appeared. His years as a Stone knight had been wonderfully fulfilling, but an arena duel required the kind of specialist training he had not undertaken for years. His sword arm felt heavy. His opponent was even more weary, however, and Voltan would at least take pleasure in killing him. He had always wondered how good Rage really was. Now he knew, and deep down, he was glad they had not fought earlier. The old man's reflexes were surprisingly sharp, as was the speed of his counters.

The sun was high and hot, and a heat haze was rising from the sand. Voltan circled the older man. "What made you want to fight me?" he asked. Rage did not reply. "Too weary to talk, old man?" sneered Voltan. Rage merely smiled. Irritated, Voltan leapt to the attack. Rage parried. Voltan struck out with his left fist. Rage swayed away from the blow and thundered a left hook into Voltan's jaw. Voltan rolled with the blow and spun away as Rage's gladius hissed through the air. As Rage rushed in for the kill, Voltan parried a thrust and lunged. The blade struck Rage's belt buckle and glanced away.

"Lucky, lucky!" said Voltan, seeking to unsettle his opponent. But Rage remained focused, not bothering to reply. In his movements, however, there was a growing exhaustion.

"Not much strength left now, Rage," said Voltan. "How does it feel to know you are going to die?"

Still no response, and Voltan began to feel a growing irritation. He had always found a way to unsettle opponents, to make them rash or careless, to dismantle their concentration. But not Rage. It was as if he were fighting a statue made flesh, a creature without feelings or emotions.

Even so, Voltan was winning. It was just a question of time. As they circled, he noted that Rage's sword was a little lower than before, as if its weight were dragging it down. The old man was also breathing heavily. "Perhaps you should rest a little," Voltan said conversationally. "Step back and catch your breath." As he spoke he attacked, almost taking Rage by surprise. The old man's sword came up more slowly than before, and Voltan's blade slid by it, glancing off Rage's ribs and ripping the skin. Rage spun on his heel, turning full circle, and lashed out. Voltan only partly blocked the cut, and the blade sliced the flesh of his shoulder. He leapt back. Rage did not follow up his attack, and Voltan grinned as he realized the old man had come at last to the end of his strength.

Then the drum sounded. Voltan blinked and glanced to the crowd, locating the black-bearded Telors.

As the beats sounded out, the crowd, knowing of Rage's legend, began to clap their hands in time to the booming drum. Voltan returned his attention to Rage and saw that the old gladiator was standing straighter now, and in his dark eyes there was a gleam where before there had been only weariness. Voltan swore. It was going to take longer to kill the old bastard now.

Rage took one deep breath, then advanced. "Cara sends her love," he said softly, his voice friendly and warm.

For a moment only Voltan froze. Then Rage was upon him. Voltan parried desperately, but Rage's sword tore into his belly, ripping up through a lung and out through his back. Voltan sagged against Rage, letting go of his sword and resting his head on his killer's shoulder.

"Clever . . . move," he whispered.

"It needed to be, boy," said Rage, lowering him to the ground.

The crowd erupted in applause, and a burst of cheering filled the stadium.

"I . . . think . . . they're glad to see me die." Voltan forced a smile. "You should . . . get those wounds stitched."

"I'll wait awhile," said Rage.

Voltan lay quietly for a moment. There was no pain, and he felt curiously at peace. "Does . . . Cara . . . know about me?" he asked.

"No. Nor will she. She's a fine girl, though, strong, courageous, and loyal. Any man would be proud to be her father."

"I would have been . . . had I known."

Voltan's head rolled to the side. He found himself staring at the two execution stakes erected at the center of the arena, rising like spikes from mounds of oil-soaked brushwood.

"She forgave me," he whispered. But Rage did not hear him.

Bane sagged against the railing as Rage rose from beside the dead Voltan. The old gladiator raised his sword in salute to the emperor, then strode from the arena, thunderous applause ringing in his ears. Slaves ran out to grab the dead Voltan's heels and drag his body across the sand.

From the far end of the arena came a troop of soldiers, leading out two figures. The first was Nalademus. As he saw the stake, he began to struggle, throwing himself to the ground. Soldiers hauled him up and dragged him toward the pyres. He screamed and shouted, and the crowd jeered.

A little way back came the Veiled Lady. She was small and slim, her pale blue dress gleaming with oil. Two soldiers were holding her bare arms, but she did not struggle and walked with her veiled head held high.

"Burn them! Burn them! Burn them!" chanted the crowd.

"I suppose," said Jasaray, "that I should offer you another wish, since Rage has robbed you of your revenge. Ask and it shall be given to you. You want Voltan's estates or other lands? Chests of gold, perhaps?"

Bane was staring down into the arena. "I'll take her," he said softly. "Give me her life."

"What? You know her?"

"No."

"Then think again, Bane. She is the heart of these cultists, and if I pardon her, there will be a riot."

"You said I could ask anything, Majesty," Bane reminded him.

Jasaray's face hardened. "At this moment I am your friend, Bane. Emperors are good friends to have. If you persist in this, you will become my enemy and there will be no place for you in Stone or any of the lands of Stone. Why make me your enemy for a woman you do not know?"

Bane stared down at the woman and listened to the baying of the crowd. While Nalademus screamed and begged, she merely stood, shoulders back, aloof and proud, the jeering of the crowd washing over her. "She has courage," he said softly. "And with all due respect, Majesty, I think her life is worth far more than your friendship."

Jasaray rose from his seat and walked to the balcony's edge. The guards holding the prisoners were waiting for his signal. He pointed to the woman, beckoning the guards to bring her forward. He swung to Bane, his expression calm but his eyes angry. "Go down and collect your prize," he said. "You have two days to leave Stone—never to return."

Bane bowed and walked from the enclosure.

In the arena Nalademus was dragged screaming to the stake. Bane ran down the aisle to the lowest level, climbed over the wall, and leapt the twelve feet to the arena floor. He approached the guards holding the woman. "The emperor has granted her freedom," he said. The guards glanced up at the tall, stooping figure of Jasaray, who nodded to them. Instantly they released the arms of the Veiled Lady.

A single trumpet sounded, and the flames were lit beneath Nalademus. His terrible cries were pitiful, and the crowd hooted and yelled abuse at him. The Veiled Lady turned toward the tortured man and raised her hand. The Stone elder's head came up, and he stared through the rising smoke at the frail woman in blue. His screams ceased, and he rested his head back against the stake. Rising plumes of smoke covered him.

"What did you do?" whispered Bane.

"I took away his pain," said the woman.

Without his cries of agony there was no entertainment for the crowd, and they began to shout for the Veiled Lady's death.

Bane took her arm and led her across the sand toward the gate to the sword room. Her clothes were slick with lantern oil, the smell sweet and pungent. She walked silently beside him, saying nothing. Once the mob realized she was not going to burn, they began to yell and scream. A fight broke out in the western stand. Soldiers moved in to quell it. Seats were ripped from the stone, and someone hurled a cushion at the Royal Enclosure. More and more soldiers poured into the stands. Bane reached the sword room and ushered the Veiled Lady inside.

Rage was sitting there, a surgeon stitching his wounds. His face was gray, and he was holding a blood-covered towel to the wound in his chest. The Veiled Lady moved to his side. Taking the towel from him, she dropped it to the floor, then laid her slim hand upon the bleeding gash in his chest. The wound closed instantly. The surgeon stood by astonished, for where there had been an open cut, bleeding profusely, there was now a long white scar, perfectly healed. She did the same for the cut on his temple and the wound in his shoulder. As Bane watched, he saw the color return to Rage's cheeks.

"I thank you," said Rage, taking her hand and kissing it.

"And I thank you, Vanni," she said, "for without your sacrifice I would have burned." She turned slowly toward Bane and lifted her veil.

He gasped and almost fell back. "Sweet heaven!" he whispered. His limbs began to tremble and shake, and he sank onto a bench seat.

The Veiled Lady was Lia.

The door burst open, and Telors ran in, followed by the gladiator Brakus. "There is a riot outside," said Telors. "Mobs are gathered at every exit. They are shouting for her death. And the soldiers have been withdrawn."

Rage heaved himself to his feet and reached for his sword. "There will be no need of weapons," said Lia. "Trust me!" Rage stood still for a moment, then turned his attention to Bane, who was sitting slumped on the bench.

"Are you all right, boy?"

Bane ignored him and stared straight at the young woman in the glistening robes. "I saw you die," he said. "I saw his sword cleave your heart."

Lia sat beside him, taking his hand. "I remember being stabbed by Voltan and then my eyes opening in a wagon. The surgeon Ralis was beside me. The next face I recall was of an old woman, hooded and veiled. It was a dream. We were walking in a forest, a place of exquisite beauty. There was someone else there, a shining figure whose face I could not see. The shining figure reached out and touched the wound above my heart. The wound healed, and I felt something flowing into my veins. It was as if all my life I had been a dry well, and now the water of life was filling me. When next I woke I was in the house of Ralis, and he told me that the old woman had come to the death house and saved me."

"Why did you not come to me?" he asked, gripping her hand tightly.

"Ralis told me you had been killed. Two days later I boarded a ship for Goriasa. When next I heard of you, it was as a killer in the arena, a man of blood. We took different paths, Bane. When I saw my father killed, I wanted an end to violence and set out to achieve it. When you saw me struck down, you wanted blood and vengeance and death."

"I love you," said Bane, tears in his eyes. "I have thought of you every day since last we met."

"And I love you. Nothing will change that."

"Then you will come with me to the mountains as first we planned?"

She did not answer at first, and in the silence Bane knew that he had lost her a second time. "I cannot be a wife to a man of blood. I will continue my work," she said. "Not in Stone, for another has taken my place. But I shall journey and preach. I shall find people who yearn for the spirit, and I will share with them the joys I have learned."

"I tried to save you," said Bane. "I just was not strong enough then."

"You did save me," she whispered. "I am sorry, Bane. I am sorry for both of us."

Moving to his side, she put her arms around him. He drew her in and kissed her cheek. "Where will you go?" he asked.

"To the far north. There is a tribe there who dwell in the White Mountains. I will bring the Source to them."

"I have heard of that place," said Brakus the gladiator.

"Even the Vars shun the area. The tribes of the White Mountains are ferocious. Some even say they eat the hearts of their enemies."

Lia smiled. "Then they have great need of what I will bring to them." She walked toward the door.

"The crowd will tear you apart, lady," said Telors. "We will come with you."

Lia shook her head. "No one will see me, and no one will harm me. Not yet. May the Source bless you all." With that she walked from the room toward the distant sounds of the rioting crowd.

Bane sat very still, his mind spinning. For more than two years he had lived with but a single thought: to avenge the murder of Lia. He had trained hard, eschewing all the comforts and pleasures of youth. Not for Bane the joys of the Occian whorehouse or the wild and boisterous gatherings organized by the circus. Invitations from beautiful women, both married and unmarried, to attend them in their private chambers were politely refused. Each night as Bane took to his bed he saw Voltan's face and pictured the day he would bring justice to the killer.

Now he sat in the silence of the sword room, staring down at the marble floor.

Rage moved to the seat beside him. "Talk to me, boy," he said, putting his arm around the younger man.

"It was all for nothing," whispered Bane.

"We should leave here before the mob ransacks the place," said Telors. "Having lost the Veiled Lady, they may turn on you, Bane. They saw you lead her from the arena."

"Get dressed," Rage said softly. "We'll go back to the villa and talk. Come on." Taking Bane's arm, he drew him to his feet. Still in a daze, the young Rigante stripped off his gladiator's kilt and greaves and pulled on black leather leggings and a tunic shirt of thick blue wool edged with silver thread. Belting his sword around his waist, he started to follow Brakus, Telors, and Rage out of the room. The surgeon who had been treating Rage when the Veiled Lady had healed him took hold of Bane's arm.

"Which goddess is she?" he whispered.

Bane shrugged the man away and caught up with the others. They walked up into the deserted arena and along the wide corridor to the eastern exit. The gates were open, and Bane could see the huge crowd outside. Brakus moved out first, followed by Telors and Rage. The three men formed a screen ahead of Bane, but someone in the crowd yelled out: "There he is! It's the savage who freed her!"

The crowd surged around them. Someone pushed Brakus, and his fist lashed out, sending the man spinning from his feet. Just as the scene threatened to turn ugly, Rage raised both of his arms in the air.

"Silence!" he bellowed. The voice was commanding, and the crowd obeyed him. Rage waited for several heartbeats for the noise to subside. "The emperor pardoned the Veiled Lady," he said. "And she is gone from this place. None of us know where. Now let us pass!" Instantly he moved forward, and the crowd parted for him. Brakus, Telors, and Bane walked through the mob, crossed the square, and hailed a passing two-horse carriage. As Bane sat down, he caught a glimpse of a woman in a pale blue gown walking through the crowd. No one noticed her or looked in her direction. Seeing him, she waved, then crossed the avenue and walked into a side street.

Half an hour later the carriage arrived at the villa. Persis Albitane and Norwin were waiting for them at the front gate. Bane, Rage, and Telors stepped down from the carriage. Brakus leaned over.

"An interesting day," said the golden-haired gladiator. Telors grinned and shook his hand. "I'll see you both, I hope, at my birthday celebrations." Gesturing the driver to move on, Brakus settled back in his seat, and the carriage trundled away.

"Good man," said Telors to Bane. "I'm glad you didn't have to fight him."

Bane said nothing and walked toward the villa. Persis tried to speak to him, but Bane eased past and went upstairs to his room, where he stood at the window, staring out over the bay.

Rage found him there some minutes later. "It was not for nothing," Rage said quietly. "Had you not been in Stone, she would have died. You have tortured yourself for two years because you did not have the strength to save her. Yet now you have."

Bane turned from the window. "She thanked you, my friend. And she was right. I saved her by default, because the emperor offered me a second wish. Had Voltan killed you, I would have fought him, and she would have died. My need for vengeance would have killed her, and I would never have known."

"It didn't happen, though," Rage pointed out. "You are a man, Bane, and a man makes choices and lives with the consequences. I heard what she said to you about different paths. Yes, all gladiators can be criticized for those we have killed in the name of glory, or sport, or the pursuit of fame and riches. But the men we fought were also pursuing those goals and stepped before us willingly. There was no malice on either side. You did not ask Voltan to change your life by attacking those you loved. His was the evil. Your actions since then would be understood by every hero who ever walked the earth." Rage sighed, then sat down on the bed. "You know, I have listened to the preachings of the cultists, and I like a lot of what they say. Indeed, I even believe in that greater power they speak of. There is no room in my heart for hatred, and—as they preach—I will offer the open hand of friendship to all those I meet. But if men broke into my house and offered harm to Cara or the servants, I would cut them down without a moment's remorse. And had I been you, back in Accia, I would have crossed the world to find the man who brought death to those I loved. Now throw that weight from your shoulders, man! The girl is alive. We are all alive."

"I thank the gods for that," said Bane. "With all my heart." He looked at Rage. "I will never forget what you did for me. It will live in my heart forever."

"You are not angry, then, that your vengeance was denied?"

"Angry? Oh, Rage, I could not be farther from anger. When I watched you both, I knew what you had been trying so hard to tell me. He—and you—are a different breed. I have never seen such focus, such power. I would have died out there. I know that with certainty. I could never be that good."

"That's not true," said Rage. "You are what . . . nineteen? You have yet to reach the peak of your strength and power. In five or six years you will be faster and deadlier than both of us." He laughed suddenly. "All those young gladiators out there should rejoice that Bane is no longer one of them. Have you given thought to what you will do now? There are many merchant ventures into which you could put the riches you have made. You can become fat and lazy."

"I'm going home, my friend," said Bane. "The emperor has given me two days to leave Stone."

"So much for the gratitude of rulers, eh?" muttered Rage.

Bane shrugged. "He is a cold man, and I should have expected no less. I'll return to Caer Druagh. I need to see the mountains and to feel the grass under my feet. Why not come with me, show me how to run a farm?"

"Perhaps I'll visit, but Cara is to be married in four months, and I'd like to see that. I'd also like to watch a great-grandchild grow. I hope it is a boy. Girls are wonderful, but I think I need a little variety." He rose from his seat and drew Bane into a hug. "You know, maybe you should find your father and make your peace with him."

For the first time Bane kissed Rage's cheek. Then he drew away. "I have no father. If I could choose one, it would be you."

"That is good to hear, and I thank you for saying it. Now, before we become mawkish, let's go down to the others and eat. I am famished."

"One last thing," said Bane. "Will you be getting drunk tonight?"

Rage chuckled. "Probably. I don't like to kill—even evil men like Voltan."

"Then let's drink together. We can talk about the stars and the spirits and ramble on about the meaning of life."

"Sounds hideous. We'll do it," said Rage.

Snow was swirling across the plain as the young druid crouched at the foot of a standing stone watching the wind scattering hot cinders from his tiny fire, leaching the heat away from his frozen body. Hunched against the cold stone, Banouin felt the weight of failure dragging him down. Four times now in the last six months he had tried to free the ghosts of Cogden Field, but on each occasion they had ignored him and continued their senselessly ferocious battle.

The last time he had tried reasoning with the shade of

Valanus, pointing out to him that Cogden had been fought in bright sunlight, whereas now only the moon shone down upon the battlefield. Valanus had laughed and gestured toward the sky. "There is the blazing sun," he cried. "And the sky is blue. I have no more time for this, demon. Come, lads. One more charge and the day is ours."

The wind died down, and the shivering Banouin added dry sticks to the fading blaze. Flames licked out, and he held out his hands to the fleeting warmth.

The king had allowed him this one last attempt—three weeks leave of absence. And he had failed. Tomorrow he would have to return to Old Oaks as he had promised.

"I care for these souls," said Connavar, "but in truth I care for the living far more. The information you supply on Jasaray's troops is vital to us. No one else has your talent, Banouin. You are the eyes of the Rigante."

All this was true, but the ghosts of Cogden Field were like a dagger in Banouin's soul. The land cried out to be freed of this nightly slaughter. Grass no longer grew upon the plain. Not a single weed could be seen on the dead brown earth. Banouin glanced out from behind the stone. The ghosts were still fighting on a field of snow. Despair flowed over him.

The armies of Stone were gathering across the water, and already four Panthers—twelve thousand men—had crossed the narrow strip of sea and were camped in the lands of the Cenii. Many among the Cenii had joined the army as scouts for the campaign all knew would come in the spring—the push north into the lands of the Norvii and then the Rigante. More battles would be fought, and more souls would continue their eternal fighting, draining the spirit from the land.

"I must find a way," said Banouin. Brother Solstice always said that the truth has a power all its own, yet he had tried the truth on those martial spirits and they had ignored it. What more can I do? he wondered.

"Morrigu!" he shouted. "Where are you?"

There was no answer, though the wind picked up and scattered his fire. Banouin sat miserably, his sheepskin cloak tugged around him, the hood low over his face. He recalled the first time he had come to this circle of stones, with Bane. It seemed so long ago now, another time in another world. He had been heading toward his dream, and his heart had been light and full of hope.

Banouin missed Bane and wished with all his heart that he had gone to him in Stone and asked forgiveness for deserting him. Now Bane was back in the mountains, and still he had not sought him out. He had come home rich and had acquired land bordering the Narian Forest, twenty miles southwest of Three Streams. The land had been sold cheaply, for there were many outlaw bands in the area and the last two owners had been killed by them. Connavar had sent troops into the forest to root them out, but the area was colossal, and his men saw no one. Many people in Three Streams had laughed when Bane had bought the land, knowing that his cattle would be spirited away, his houses ransacked.

They were not laughing now. His cattle were feeding on the best grass, and not a single robber had appeared to trouble him. "He is in league with the outlaws," they said, and their dislike of him grew. Bane made no attempt to win them over.

Then the Sea Raiders had landed a small force near Seven Willows. Fighting men were gathered to oppose them. All men knew that Bane was a great fighter, and a rider was sent to him. He told the man to leave his property. "When the Sea Raiders attack my land, I shall kill them," he said. "And I will ask no help from you."

Dislike became open hatred then, and men talked of how he had killed Forvar and the two friends of Fiallach. "He is a mad dog," they said. "He should be driven from the land."

A delegation went to Braefar, urging him to take action. Braefar, while agreeing that Bane was a disgrace, pointed out that he paid his taxes promptly and that those taxes were used to fund Connavar's army. "He has broken no law," said Braefar, "and paid weregild to the men he slew after his mother's death. However, if you wish to sell him no feed for his cattle, no supplies for his men, no shoes for his horses, that is up to you."

This they did, and Bane was forced to send for supplies from the Pannone to the north at a far greater cost. Even so, his venture thrived. When lung blight destroyed half the king's herds and reduced many farmers to near poverty, Bane's cattle escaped the disease. People were then forced to buy from him, and his prices were high.

The saddest part of all for Banouin was that he knew that most of the people who hated Bane were good people with kind hearts. They were reacting to a man who wanted nothing to do with them, much as they had once reacted to Banouin. Bane no longer helped with the barn building, or attended the feast days, or joined the hunts, or trained with the militia. His every action was seen—mostly accurately—as a slight on the Rigante as a whole.

Under pressure from their families, most of the young men who worked for him had quit his service, and he now employed outsiders, Wolfsheads or runaways: men who—like Bane—wore no cloak of allegiance. Bane's cloak was black and without adornment. Not once had he worn the checkered blue and green colors of the Rigante.

Banouin shivered. The winter cold was seeping through his boots and leggings. He stood up and stamped his feet. I should not hate the winter, he thought. When it is gone, war will come.

Jasaray would come from the south, and King Shard of the Vars had gathered more than three hundred ships, ready to lead an invasion in the north. The days of blood were drawing near. And here I sit, thought Banouin, worrying about the lost souls of an earlier conflict.

"Morrigu!" he shouted again.

He heard movement and stared out into the night. A horse was plodding slowly through the snow, the rider hunched in the saddle, his head hooded. The rider eased his horse into the circle of stones and flicked back his hood.

"You still don't know how to place a fire, idiot," said Bane.

The warrior stepped down from the saddle, tethered his mount, took a large bundle of dry wood tied with thongs from the back of his saddle, then walked to the far side of the circle, where one of the giant stones had cracked and fallen. Swiftly he prepared a fire against the stone. Taking a burning branch from Banouin's small blaze, he lit his own, which crackled into life. Shielded from the worst of the wind, the fire burned hot and bright, warmth reflecting from the stone. Bane sat down, gesturing Banouin to join him.

"I would have built it here," said Banouin, squatting down. "But I can see the battle from this spot, and it grieves me."

"Are they fighting now?" asked Bane.

"Yes."

"Let me know when it is over."

"Why?"

"I will help you release their souls."

"You are not a mystic. How can you help me?"

"You never did know how to talk to fighting men," said Bane. "I do."

"The Morrigu sent you, didn't she?"

"No. Your mother came to my farm. She asked me to help you." He looked directly into Banouin's eyes. "Vorna has always been a friend to me. I help my friends where I can."

Banouin looked away. "I am sorry about what happened in Accia," he said.

"Pah, it is in the past. Forgotten."

"Is that true?" asked Banouin, hope flaring.

"Of course it is not true," snapped Bane. "I was trying to be polite. Now tell me about this battle of souls."

"What is there to tell? They fight eternally the battle of Cogden Field, not knowing that it is over and gone. Their spirits are trapped here, caught in a web of hatred and violence. I have tried talking to Valanus. He hears me but does not believe what I tell him."

"And why is it important to you that he believe you?" asked Bane.

"It is the land, Bane. It suffers as they suffer. All life is being drained from this place, like a stain that grows and grows. There must be an end to it. The dead must know peace."

"Why should they be any different from the living?" asked Bane. "When do we ever know peace?"

"You still sound bitter."

Bane laughed with genuine good humor. "Ah, you misread me. I am no longer the man you once knew. I found a friend in Stone, a great friend, a man who risked his life for me. That changed me. I am more content now. I care nothing for Connavar and his rejection of me or for the dislike of my fellow Rigante. I live my own life, answerable to no man."

"Like a leaf in the breeze," said Banouin. "The Rigante are your people."

Bane shook his head. "My people are the twenty men who work for me and the friends who have stood by me: Vorna, Rage, and Telors. The rest of you can rot and die. How is the battle faring?"

Banouin glanced back and shuddered. "It is at its height. It will go on like this for an hour or more, then start again." Bane added more sticks to the blaze. Banouin watched him. His hair was still long, a tight yellow braid hanging from his temple, but he had grown a golden beard now, trimmed close to the chin. He seemed larger across the shoulders.

"Mother told me that Lia was alive and that you rescued her," he said.

"Aye, I rescued her."

"I am glad."

"Well, that is good to hear."

"Please don't hate me, Bane. What I did was cowardly and wrong, but I am trying to make amends with my life."

"Druid's robes suit you," said Bane. "Men say you are a great healer and a prophet. I am pleased for you. And I do not hate you. I have no feelings for you at all, neither hatred nor love. You are just a man I know."

"But we were friends once, weren't we?"

"I don't think that we were. Anyway, it is immaterial now. How is the king? I understand there was yet another attempt on his life."

"Yes. Two Pannone attacked him while he was hunting. Killed his horse and wounded him. The wound was not deep, and I healed it."

"One cannot blame the Pannone," said Bane. "They didn't ask to be overrun by the Rigante."

"Most Pannone believe in the king," said Banouin. "As do most Norvii and the other smaller tribes now under his banner. But there will always be those who yearn for the old days."

Bane laughed. "By the old days you mean the time when they were free to make their own decisions and not pay taxes to a foreign king?"

"He is not a foreign king," said Banouin. "He is a Keltoi, fighting to preserve our ancient way of life in the face of a terrible threat."

Bane shook his head. "Does it not seem strange to you that the act of protecting that way of life is altering it beyond recognition? Citizens of Stone pay taxes. The Keltoi never did. The Rigante, Pannone, and Norvii crossed the water centuries ago to find a land where there would be no kings. They thrived as free peoples. There were no armies. When enemies threatened, every man took up arms to defend the land. There were no tax gatherers, no clerics, and a few simple laws. What freedoms do we have now? If I were to hold this conversation in Three Streams, I would be arrested as a malcontent."

"Without the unity forged by Connavar this entire land would be under the godless rule of Stone," said Banouin.

"As it probably will be one day, anyway," said Bane.

"Not as long as Connavar lives."

"Then may he live long," said Bane.

The two men lapsed into silence, each lost in his own thoughts. The snow began again, heavy and fast, large flakes spluttering on the campfire. Bane lifted his hood back into place and leaned back against the fallen stone. Banouin fed the fire and occasionally glanced back at the silent battle. It was nearing its end. He nudged Bane, who came instantly awake. "Give me your hand," he said, lying down next to Bane.

"Why?"

"If you are to help me with the ghosts, you must be as a ghost. Give me your hand and I will draw your spirit from your body."

Bane did so and felt a cold rush of air sweep over him, as if he had dived into a winter lake. He shuddered and rose to stand naked alongside the spirit of Banouin.

"How do you wish to be clothed?" asked Banouin, who was apparently wearing a pure white druid's robe.

"Can it be anything?" asked Bane.

"Anything."

"Then dress me as a Stone officer with gilded breastplate and helm." Even as he spoke he felt the armor settle upon him. A bronze reinforced kilt appeared around his waist, and two bronze greaves nestled against his calves.

"Where is the sword?" asked Bane.

"You think you'll need one?" countered Banouin.

* * *

The two ghostly armies began to form on opposite hilltops as Bane and Banouin strode out across the field. Bane glanced down. His booted feet made no marks on the snow, and he could feel no hint of the winter winds. The two spirits made their way toward the silent Stone ranks, which shimmered in the moonlight. Bane stared in wonder at the soldiers before him. They seemed to have been carved from mist, translucent in the moonlight. The sounds of faraway commands came to them.

"Panther Three, form up. Rank seven, at the beat!"

A drum sounded, its slow ponderous beat echoing across the field. Bane saw the troops shuffling into formation in ranks of seven. He and Banouin continued to walk up the hill. The spirits of the Stone soldiers ignored them, continuing their battle preparations.

As Bane came within thirty feet of the first line, he halted. Then he cried out in a loud voice: "Appius, where are you?"

Now the spirits noticed him, and he felt their cold stares upon him. "Appius!" he called again. Then: "Oranus, where are you? Speak to me, Oranus!"

The first line parted, and an officer stepped from it. He was tall and handsome, his breastplate intricately engraved, as were his greaves, helm, and wrist guards.

"It is Valanus," whispered Banouin.

"Appius!" yelled Bane again.

"Who are you?" demanded the officer, coming closer, sword in hand.

"I am Bane, son of Connavar the King."

"Nonsense! I know Connavar. He is a young man, little older than you."

"Appius!" shouted Bane.

"He is not here!" snarled Valanus. "Now tell me what you want and why you are dressed in the armor of Stone. Speak or I will cut you down."

"Why is Appius not here?" demanded Bane. "Is this not Cogden Field? Is Appius not your second in command?"

Valanus stood very still, confusion in his face. "He is gone," he said at last.

"Gone?" echoed Bane. "How can he be gone? The battle is not yet started."

"He is gone, damn you! What do you want?"

"The Rigante are charging!" hissed Banouin.

Bane ignored him and kept his gaze locked to Valanus. "Then where is Oranus?" he said. "Is he not your aide? Where is Oranus?"

"What trick is this?" shouted Valanus.

"It is no trick," Bane told him. He glanced at Banouin. "Dress me as a Rigante warrior," he said. "Quickly now!"

Instantly the armor of Stone disappeared, replaced by a swirling pale blue and green checkered cloak and a shining mail shirt.

Swinging on his heel, Bane waited until the advancing Rigante were close. "Connavar!" he shouted. "Let Connavar show his face!" The charge slowed. "Fiallach! Where are you? Bendegit Bran, let us see you! Govannan, come forth!" Bane walked to meet the advancing men, still calling out the names of their generals. The spirits slowed to a walk, then began glancing nervously around. A Rigante noble pushed his way to the front of the line.

"Why do you call for Connavar?" he asked. "Are you an agent of the enemy? Do they seek a truce?"

"Where is Connavar?" asked Bane.

The man hesitated, then looked around, scanning the ghostly ranks. "He is not with us," said the officer.

"How can that be?" Bane asked him. "This is Cogden Field. It was here that Connavar the King won his greatest victory. Fiallach rode with him, as did Bendegit Bran and Govannan." Bane looked into the man's face. He was not young. His hair was thinning, and his features showed the deep lines of his advancing years. "Maccus also rode with them," said Bane, remembering the stories. "Maccus, who was more than sixty and who led a charge that broke the left wing."

"I am Maccus. I remember that charge."

"It was a moment of great glory," said Bane. "So why are you here now?"

"Here . . . ? I am here to fight the enemy."

"Why do you fight without Connavar? Without Fiallach and the others?"

"I do not know. But I do know the enemy is before us."

The spirit of Valanus advanced to stand alongside Bane. "What is happening here?"

"One more charge, lads. One more charge and the day is ours," said Banouin softly.

Valanus looked as if he had been struck. He swung on the young druid. "Why do you say that? Why those words?"

"Were they not the words you used before that last, courageous assault?"

"Yes . . . no. The battle is not yet fought."

"Look around you, soldier," said Bane. "Here is Maccus, who died leading a charge against your wing. A spear tore open his throat." He swung on the elderly Rigante. "You remember that spear, Lord Maccus?"

"I remember."

"If a spear tore open your throat on Cogden Field, why are you still here?"

"I . . . I do not know."

Banouin stepped in close to the Rigante general. "Someone is waiting for you, Lord Maccus. She has waited a long time. All men know the story of your love for your wife. When she died, you were bereft. She waits for you now in a far better place than this."

"Then . . . I am . . . dead?" said Maccus. "The spear was not a dream? I remember lying on the ground, unable to breathe. I remember . . ." His spirit faded from sight.

"We are not dead!" screamed Valanus. "This is a Rigante trick."

"You are all the dead of Cogden Field," cried Banouin. "And you have fought this battle a thousand times since. You are shades, ghosts, spirits. That is why Connavar and Appius are not here. They lived beyond the battle. Think! All of you, think! Remember the day, the awful slaughter. Remember how you died!"

Valanus backed away. "I cannot lose again," he said. "I am a Stone general. We do not lose. I will fight on. I will have victory." One by one the shades of the Rigante faded away. Valanus ran at them, waving his sword. "It is not over!" he screamed. "Come back, you cowards! Come back and fight!"

Banouin began to cry out toward the milling soldiers of

Stone, speaking this time in Turgon. "Be at peace, soldiers!" he shouted. "You died valiantly, but you do not have to die again and again. Let this be an end. Move on from here. Seek out the better place that awaits you!"

Valanus swung and saw his own force vanishing. "Soldiers of Stone!" he called out. "Hold your ground. One more charge . . . one more . . ." His voice faded away.

And he stood alone.

Bane approached him. "You fought bravely, Valanus. Your name is known through all the world. Go now and find peace."

"I am not dead!" screamed Valanus. "This is Rigante magic! My men will come back! Get away from me. I shall wait for my men!" He spun on his heel and ran, his fleeing form lost in the swirling snow.

Bane awoke back in the stone circle. Banouin added fuel to the dying fire. Bane sat up and began to rub life into his cold hands.

"I had not thought of crying out for the living," said Banouin. "That was clever. I thank you."

"It was nothing," said Bane, rising to his feet and moving toward his horse.

"Are you leaving now?" asked Banouin.

"Of course. I did what I came for."

Banouin stood miserably by as Bane saddled the gelding. "Will you ever forgive me?" he asked.

Bane sighed. "I forgive you, Banouin. That is no lie. I wish you well."

"But you cannot forget what I did? Put it aside."

"No, I cannot forget." Bane stepped into the saddle, swung his mount, and rode from the circle.

◇ 11 ◇

THE WINTER WAS the harshest in living memory. Rigante cattle, already decimated by the lung blight, died in the hundreds, and but for the king's granaries, deaths from starvation among the tribes would have numbered in the thousands. Even so, in some remote areas cut off by blizzards, whole communities suffered losses, mainly among the old and the very young. In some parts people were even eating the bark from trees to fill empty stomachs.

The people of Three Streams suffered enormous hardships, for Braefar had not kept the granaries full, instead selling off surplus grain to the Cenii during the autumn. Connavar stripped him of the title of laird and installed Govannan in his place.

For Bane, with a farm in the lowlands, the winter was not as deadly. He and his men had baled enough hay to feed his winter herds, and his losses were few. Govannan came to him at midwinter and bought cattle to feed the population of Three Streams. Bane demanded and received top price for his beef, paid in gold.

As the weather worsened, he sent another thirty steers to the settlement, this time without charge.

A revolt began in the lands of the northern Pannone, led by a Pannone noble named Guern. Several of the king's granaries were ransacked and looted. Connavar sent out his Iron Wolves to put down the rebellion. Guern, however, avoided any direct military clashes. He and his men went into hiding, then gathered together to strike at remote outposts. Bendegit Bran was put in command of the Wolves and lured Guern and his band into a trap. Scores were killed or taken, but Guern escaped.

The situation might still have become critical, for the ransacking of granaries led to greater starvation among the Pannone. Guern could have increased his popularity by distributing his stolen grain. Instead, he chose to sell it to raise money for armor and weapons. Connavar shipped in supplies from the lands of the Ostro and the Gath to feed the Pannone, and the revolt died in its infancy. Even so, the cost had been enormous, and food supplies were severely depleted.

Then, on the first day of spring, in Connavar's fortieth year, three hundred long ships beached near Seven Willows on the eastern coast, and fifteen thousand Vars, led by King Shard, invaded the lands of the Rigante. Simultaneously in the south the emperor Jasaray, leading eight Panthers of twenty-four thousand men, came ashore in the lands of the Cenii.

Bane guided his horse carefully up the icy hill and reached the crest. He paused there, staring down at the lowlands and the endless sweep of the Narian Forest. Nestled against its eastern border was the long rectangular stone-built farmhouse, with its two barns close by, and a dozen small roundhouses that served as quarters for his men. The steeply dipping road ahead was pitted and icy. He dismounted and led the horse on the long walk home. Bane's hood was topped with snow, and sharp shards of ice had formed in his beard.

The first day of spring, he thought. What a mockery.

The horse slithered on the ice as Bane picked his way down the slope. The man's feet were cold and numb, his fingers frozen even in the rabbitskin mittens. Smoke was coming from the two chimneys of the main house, and Bane pictured himself sitting before a warm fire. He moved slowly, anxious not to begin sweating with overexertion. Sweat would become ice on his skin under the thick tunic, jerkin, and cloak. It would make him drowsy and weak. It would fool him into thinking the temperature was rising and thus kill him. It was vital, Bane knew, to resist the pull of the cold, the siren song of a winter death.

As he walked, his mind wandered, thinking back to Banouin and the freeing of the spirits. He wished he could forget all that had happened between them and embrace his old friend as once he had. But it was not in his nature. He had loved Banouin as a brother and had risked his life for him. Yet in his own hour of need Banouin had deserted him, and no amount of soul-searching could erase that deed from his memory. Banouin's friendship was part of the past, never to be rediscovered. The thought saddened him, as did the emotional withdrawal from his Rigante heritage.

Bane stumbled and pushed himself to his feet. He felt warmer now and knew he was in great danger. The last slow ten miles had taxed his strength and stamina. He was tempted to climb to the saddle and ride but resisted that desire. The trail was too treacherous, and his horse deserved better treatment than that. He walked on, his mind full of daydreams and remembrances. He was a small child again at the Riguan Falls, and he and his mother had been swimming in the twilight. She had lit a fire and cuddled him close.

Back on the hillside Bane blinked and looked around. He was sitting on a boulder. Why am I not walking? he wondered. With a great effort he rose. Weariness was upon him now, and he contemplated a short rest and sleep. That will bring back my strength, he thought. Fool! Get to the farmhouse, he told himself. You are dying here!

His legs felt numb, and his limbs were trembling uncontrollably. The sun was dropping behind the mountains, the temperature plummeting, though Bane could no longer feel it. He had pushed hard during the last week but had always been careful to make his night camp early, before cold and exhaustion stripped his life away. But today he had thought to make the last eighteen miles in one long haul. It had been a mistake. Through bleary eyes he looked at the distant farmhouse. He was still half an hour from his goal, and his strength was all but gone. At some point he must have let the reins go, for the horse was plodding on farther down the trail. Bane staggered after it.

Twice more he fell. The second time saw him roll over and over until he came up against a snow-covered rock. He grunted with the pain of impact. Pushing his arms beneath himself, he tried to rise. He was hot now and very sleepy. He swore and heaved himself to his knees. "I will not die here," he said, his voice slurred.

"No, you won't," said a deep voice. A large hand took hold

of Bane's arm, drawing him up until he sat on the boulder. Bane blinked and saw a flask being offered to him. He took it and sipped the contents. The fire of uisge flowed through him. He looked up into the red-bearded face of Gryffe, his lead herdsman. The outlaw grinned at him. "You're weak as a three-day puppy," he said.

Bane drank again and tried to push the stopper back into the flask. The task was beyond him. Gryffe took the flask, stoppered it, and tucked it into the pocket of his jerkin. "Let's be getting you to a fire," he said, throwing Bane's arm around his neck and hauling him upright.

Twenty minutes later, his ice-covered clothes removed and his body wrapped in a warm blanket, he sat before a log fire. It was excruciating. His skin felt as if hot needles were being pricked into him constantly. He drank more uisge, but Gryffe took the flask away. "It's good to take a little when cold, but not too much."

Gryffe's woman, the plump and plain Iswain, appeared from the kitchen, carrying a dish of thick meat broth. "Eat!" she commanded. "You need some proper warmth in your belly."

Bane did so and after a while began to feel better, the pins and needles wearing off. Iswain pulled the blanket clear of his neck and began rubbing warmed oil into the skin of his shoulders, arms, and upper back.

"Thank you," he said, taking her callused hand and kissing the knuckles.

"That's enough of that!" said Gryffe. "You'll spoil the wench!"

"Do you good to learn some proper manners," said Iswain, lifting the blanket back over Bane's shoulders. She moved around to squat in front of Bane, looking deeply into his eyes. "I think you'll be fine now," she told him. "A good night's rest will help. You are lucky not to have frostbite. 'Twas a foolish thing to do!"

"You tell him, girl!" said Gryffe.

Bane smiled and gazed into Iswain's plain features. "I could have been here earlier," he said, "but I wanted to be mothered by you."

She gave a gap-toothed grin. "Like all men you are an idiot," she told him. "I'll get you more broth."

"I am full," said Bane.

"You'll do as you're told," she said sternly. "I've known men come in from the cold and then die in their beds. You'll sit by this fire and eat until I tell you otherwise."

"Aye, he will," put in Gryffe. "And if it please you, I will have some of that broth. I was in the cold, too."

"No more for you," said Iswain. "I have no taste for fat men, and already your stomach is straining your belt."

"That's my winter covering," argued Gryffe. "Protects me from the cold. Like a bear."

"Aye, well, it is spring now," she told him, "and time for bears to wake up." She walked out into the kitchen.

Bane settled back in his chair. "What's been happening?" he asked.

"Ah, we'll talk in the morning," said Gryffe. "You'll be in no mood for all the boring details now."

"Bore me," said Bane.

Iswain returned with more broth. Bane took it, ate a few spoonfuls, then looked at Gryffe. "Talk to me," he said.

Gryffe swore, then glanced up at Iswain. "The man asked you a question," she said.

"Lorca and his gang came out of the forest three days ago and drove away twenty steers and a good old bull. Boile and Cascor tried to stop them, reminding them of the agreement they had with you. Lorca said he was renegotiating that agreement. Cascor tried to argue. Lorca accused him of disloyalty, and they killed him."

Bane finished the broth, then laid aside the wooden dish. "I'll find Lorca tomorrow," he said.

"He has more than seventy men with him now. I think that's why he needed the extra beef. It might be wiser to let it pass."

"The beef I can afford to lose," said Bane. "But no one comes to my home and kills one of my men without facing the consequences."

Grale sat quietly in the doorway of the roughly built roundhouse, listening to the arguments among the group of men squatting by the central fire. He had not been with Lorca's band long enough to have a say in the debate. Asha, one of the camp's three whores, came and sat next to him. Her dark hair was matted and filthy, her clothes ingrained with dirt. "You look in need of a little company," she said.

He looked into her dark brown eyes. They were lifeless. "That is kind of you. Maybe later."

"If you have no coin, you can pay me another time, after a raid."

He turned toward her. "Come back in a little while, dear heart," he said. "Once the sun is down."

She moved away. Grale rubbed at the empty socket of his left eye. Sometimes it still pained him, and he would wake at night stifling a scream as he recalled the druid cutting free the mutilated orb and sewing shut the lids.

"We don't need Bane," he heard Lorca say. "It is not as if he is popular among the Rigante. We could move on the farm, gather the herds, and drive them to Pannone land. There has been starvation there, and beef prices are higher than ever before."

"I'll grant that," said the outlaw known only as Wik, a thin, sour-faced man who looked puny alongside the hulking figure of Lorca, "but what would we do then? Leaving the farm as it is means we get a constant supply of food. Bane has been fair in all his dealings with us."

"Fair?" sneered Lorca. "We supplied the men to work the cattle. We guaranteed him freedom from attack. And for what? One-tenth of his profits. Does that sound fair?"

The listening Grale wondered if any of the six men around the fire would state the obvious: that Lorca had broken the agreement by raiding the farm and killing one of Bane's men. It did not surprise him when the subject was not raised. Lorca was a man of unpredictable mood, given to sudden acts of random violence.

"What about the men in Bane's employ?" asked Valian, a short stout man with greasy blond hair and a drooping mustache.

"They are our men, Val," Lorca told him. "But if any of them have lost sight of that, they can become worm meat like Cascor."

"I think some of them will object," put in Wik. "I was talking to Gryffe the other day. He likes Bane, and he likes his new life as a herdsman. He's even talking of marrying Iswain the next time a druid comes by."

"How sweet!" Lorca sneered. "He plans, I suppose, to spend the rest of his life shoveling cow turds while his wife pops out more mouths to feed. Well, a pox upon Gryffe and any other fool who goes against us. We have seventy-three men here and more joining us each month. More than enough to handle Bane and any who stand with him."

Grale gazed around the huge clearing with its forty crude roundhouses. Men and women in ragged clothes were everywhere, sitting—as was he—surrounded by squalor and stench. By the stream a woman was washing out several blankets, beating them with a rock, perhaps trying to kill the lice that infested them. At the far hut he could see Asha, on her knees, a large bearded man rutting with her in full view of everyone. No one took any notice. Grale's heart sank. He gazed down at his mutilated left hand and remembered the days before a Stone gladius had slashed away three of his fingers. He had been a man then, a hero. Even through his pain he had joyed in the victory at Cogden Field. If anyone had predicted that years later he would be sitting in this foul place, listening to men talk of robbery and murder, he would have laughed aloud. He was not laughing now.

A man came running into the camp. "Riders coming!" he shouted. Instantly every man within earshot ran into his roundhouse, emerging with a weapon. Some carried daggers, others swords or axes.

Lorca surged to his feet. "How many?" he asked.

"Two! Bane and Gryffe."

"Two, you miserable piece of goat shit? You alarmed the camp for two?"

At that moment Bane and Gryffe came riding through the trees. Grale smiled as he remembered the first time he had met Bane, several years before, in the clearing where the mystic lad had reminded him of Cogden Field and days of glory.

The two riders drew up close to Lorca and dismounted. Bane was carrying a long hunting lance, and a short sword hung at his hip. He moved past Lorca without a word and walked to Lorca's hut. Once there he reversed the lance and placed the haft on the frozen ground. Then he rammed it deep into the earth.

"What are you doing?" asked Lorca. "I have no need of a lance."

What happened next was so sudden that all the men in the clearing just stood in shock. Bane swung toward Lorca, his short sword flashing into his hand. Before the outlaw leader could react, the blade slashed into his neck, crunching through the vertebrae and slicing clear. As Lorca's body started to topple, Bane struck again. This time the head rolled clear. Bane lifted it by the hair and carried it to the lance. Raising the head, Bane rammed it down over the iron point and stepped back. The lance quivered from side to side, blood oozing from the severed head and spilling to the ground. Then he walked to the decapitated corpse, cleaned his sword on the dead man's clothes, and sheathed it.

The men and women of Lorca's band stood staring at the head on the lance. It was as if a spell had been cast over them. Grale cast his gaze over the group.

"Does anyone else here wish to renegotiate our agreement?" asked Bane, his voice cold.

The thin figure of Wik was the first to react. "What if we do?" he asked.

"You'll get the same response I have just delivered to the dear departed Lorca."

"You think to kill all seventy of us?" asked Wik, gesturing his men forward.

"Do I need to?" asked Bane, moving in close to Wik. "Have you not fed well through this winter? And what will you do when I am dead and gone? Seventy men, you say. And why do you have such numbers now? It is because there is food here and many of those who joined you were starving at home. Without my farm and my cattle how many will remain, Wik? Twenty? Less?" Suddenly he laughed. "I am through talking," he said. "Make your decision." His sword flashed once more. Wik jumped back. The powerful figure of Gryffe stepped forward, a broadsword in his hands, to stand beside Bane. Grale read Wik's intent. Pride was strong in the outlaw leader, and he was about to order his men to attack.

"Wait!" shouted Grale, striding forward into the group. "What he said makes sense. We have a constant supply of food, and when he sold his cattle to Govannan, he brought us a tenth. Or, to be more precise, he brought Lorca a tenth. We made an agreement with him. Lorca broke it. And Lorca paid for his treachery. Let that be an end to it."

"You have no say in this!" stormed Wik. "You are not the leader here."

"No, I am not," said Grale. He swung and pointed to the head on the lance. "He is! Shall we ask him for his views? I say we should call for a show of hands." He raised his voice. "How many here want to see our food supplies ended?" No one raised his hand. "Then that should settle it," he said, turning and walking back to his roundhouse.

For a moment there was silence, and in that silence the tension eased. The seventy outlaws, weapons ready, awaited an order from Wik. Wik looked at Bane and shrugged. "Most of us were not in favor of Lorca's actions," he said. "Cascor was a good man and did not deserve to be cut down. Does our agreement still hold?"

"Of course. Though I'll need a man to replace Cascor for the spring gathering."

Wik nodded. "I'd offer him to you," he said, gesturing at Grale, "but he's only got one good hand."

"I'll take him," said Bane. "If he wants to work for me." He grinned. "Maybe he'd prefer to stay here and become leader."

Wik scowled, then laughed. "You are an unusual man, Bane. What made you think you could ride in here, kill Lorca, and ride out again?"

"I didn't expect to ride out," admitted Bane. He glanced around at the waiting men. "You'd better start thinking of limiting your numbers," he added. "Either that or start a new tribe. No way will you be able to feed many more than this."

"I have been thinking the same," agreed Wik.

The twin invasion was proving a logistic nightmare for Connavar and his generals. Fiallach was sent south with a thousand Iron Wolves and six hundred horse archers and ordered to gather fighting men from the Norvii.

"Do not," Connavar urged him, "seek a direct clash with

Jasaray. Avoid a major battle at all costs, no matter what the enemy tries to do. Instead destroy his cavalry and his scouts."

"You can rely on me, Conn," said Fiallach.

"I do rely on you, my friend. But Jasaray is a cunning and pitiless enemy. He will stop at nothing to force you into combat."

Meanwhile Bendegit Bran was gathering troops from all over the north, ready to march against Shard and his fifteen thousand Sea Wolves.

At Old Oaks Connavar faced a growing problem. The five thousand inhabitants of Seven Willows and the surrounding areas had been evacuated before the invasion, thanks to the uncanny talents of Banouin, who had seen Shard's ships set sail. Although the Rigante had therefore been spared losses, it meant that the food stores around Old Oaks—already low— were now almost gone. To lessen the drain on resources a large number of women and children were sent to settlements farther west and south, where granaries and warehouses were still stocked with food.

The king's mother, Meria, and the wives and younger children of Bendegit Bran and Fiallach were among several hundred people who traveled south to Three Streams in the second week of spring. They traveled with an escort of twenty Iron Wolves led by Finnigal, Fiallach's eldest son. It was his first command, and he tried to hide his disappointment at being offered such a lowly task. He had begged to be allowed to ride with his father or, if not that, to assist Bran and the northern army. However, the king himself had decided his role, and now he would miss both battles.

"Is this a punishment?" he had asked the king.

Connavar had shaken his head. "You are a good and brave soldier, Finn, and deserving of no punishment. There are outlaws and robber gangs in the area surrounding Three Streams. Your presence will deter them from raids. You think I would punish a man by asking him to protect my mother and the wives and children of my closest friends?"

"No, sir. It is just that I will miss the fighting."

Connavar had laughed then. "Spoken like the son of Fiallach. My boy, you are seventeen years old. There will be plenty of time for battles. Trust me on this."

Finnigal twisted in his saddle and looked back along the line of wagons. The ancient tracker Parax was seated alongside Meria in the first, and it was Meria who held the reins and urged the horses onward. The old man was slumped in his seat, his head on his chest. Finnigal rode back to the wagon.

"Shall I get one of my men to take over?" he asked Meria nervously. The king's mother was a stern woman, her tightly braided hair the color of iron, her green eyes cold and hard.

"You think I am incapable of driving a wagon?" she asked him.

"No, lady, of course not."

"Then be about your business, Captain Finnigal."

Bendegit Bran's five-year-old son, Orrin, peeped out from under the canvas canopy. "Are we there yet, Uncle Finn?" he called out.

Finnigal's mood rose as he saw the straw-haired youngster's freckled face. "Not yet," he answered with a grin. "Soon. How is Ruathain?"

"He's sleeping again," said Orrin. "He's very hot."

Finnigal swung his horse and cantered ahead of the wagons. Ruathain was dying, and it was hard to take. Only last year the seventeen-year-old had been as wide-shouldered and powerful as a young bull. Now he was all bone, a shadow of what once he had been. His eyes were sunken, the skin around them bruised and dark, and his face looked like that of an old man. Finnigal shivered, remembering that he, too, had succumbed to the yellow fever but had recovered within weeks. Not so poor Ruathain.

An hour later, just before dusk, Finnigal crested the last hill above Three Streams and gazed down on the settlement. It was here that his father and mother had met. It was here that Connavar the King had been born. He glanced back. Maybe here Meria would learn to smile again, he thought. Then he laughed at his own stupidity. If Meria were ever to smile, her face would crack apart under the strain of it.

Sixty miles to the east four of Shard's long ships beached in a secluded bay, and 250 raiders waded ashore.

Their leader, Snarri Daggerbright, was a veteran of many raids. A hulking figure with deep-set eyes and a misshapen mouth—the result of a kick from a horse some years before, that had smashed out his front teeth and crushed his nose flat against his skull—Snarri relished this mission. Shard's informant had assured him that almost all the fighting men would have been moved either north to face Shard or south to resist Jasaray. That left only the old men and the women. Snarri felt his blood rise at the thought of the Rigante women and the days ahead of blood and rape and cleansing fire.

He marched his men across the sand and up into the woods, halting at the tree line to scan the surrounding land.

"Where do we strike first?" asked Dratha, his second in command.

Snarri pointed to the west. "Three Streams."

"There must be closer settlements," said Dratha.

"Aye, there are, but Shard says that Connavar's mother, the lady Meria, will be there. It is also where Connavar was born. Kill her and put Three Streams to the torch and it will lash the Rigante bastard with whips of fire."

It was a source of sadness to Vorna the Witch that no matter how great the magic, it could never change a human heart. Not the heart that was merely a giant muscle propelling blood through capillaries, veins, and arteries but the invisible heart at the core of every human soul.

Vorna sat at her window, watching the refugees leave their wagons and be welcomed into the homes of the people of Three Streams. Meria and the brood of children and women with her went to the old house that the first Ruathain had built, and soon smoke from the hearths drifted up from the chimneys. Vorna watched as two soldiers helped the boy Ruathain from the wagon. His legs all but crumpled beneath him, and they carried him into the house.

When the wagons had arrived, Vorna had been standing by the first bridge. She had seen Meria driving one wagon, but her old friend had turned her head away as the wagon passed. It had hurt Vorna deeply. There was no reason she knew of that would cause Meria to treat her with such discourtesy. Had she not saved Meria's son from certain death? Had she not, through her magic, kept her husband, Ruathain, alive long after his heart should have failed?

She trudged back to the house, placed a kettle on the stove, and made herself a mug of chamomile tisane.

There had been a seed of bitterness in Meria's heart ever since her first love, Varaconn, had died. She had then married Ruathain, and the bitterness had flowered, causing the marriage to founder. Then, when near tragedy had brought them together again, Meria had seemed a changed woman. She had laughed often and was carefree, her green eyes alive with hopes and dreams. Then Ruathain had died in the first great battle against the Vars. Meria had not laughed since.

Yet why she should shun one of her oldest friends was a mystery to Vorna and a source of grief, especially when one of her grandchildren hovered at the point of death. Meria knew Vorna was a healer, yet such was her apparent hatred that she would let her grandson die rather than come to the one person who might save him. Vorna sipped her tisane and moved away from the window. Banouin, she knew, had tried to heal Ruathain, and for some days he appeared to have succeeded. But then the boy had suffered a relapse, his fever returning.

"I cannot understand it," Banouin had told his mother during a spirit visit. "It seems as if the disease is emanating from within his own body, as if it is at war with itself. Every time I heal an injured organ, it begins to wilt again worse than before."

Vorna had been able to offer no clue but had thought about the problem deeply for weeks afterward. Knowing that the boy was being brought to Three Streams, she had hoped to be able to examine him herself, floating her spirit through his bloodstream, seeking to identify the cause of his illness. She knew now that she would not be asked for help.

"What did I do to you, Meria?" she asked aloud. "What crime have I committed against your family?"

A sharp rapping sounded at the door. Vorna put down her mug and called out for the visitor to enter. A young soldier pushed open the door. He was tall and well formed, his long dark hair hanging between his shoulders in a tight braid. Vorna smiled, seeing both Gwydia and Fiallach in the boy's features. "Welcome, Finnigal," she said.

"You know me, lady?" he asked her.

"You look like your father," she said, "tall and strong, with the same ferocious glare."

He grinned. "Most people say I take after Mother," he told her.

"There is that, too. What can I do for you, soldier?"

"I have been asked to contact the man Bane to purchase more cattle to feed the refugees. I understand that you are his friend and that my request might be better received if I went to him in your company."

"Come in and sit," she told him. "May I offer you a drink? Ale, uisge, or a calming tisane?"

"The tisane would be pleasant," he said, removing his sword belt and cloak.

"Would you like it sweetened?" she called from the kitchen.

"Aye, lady. I have a sweet tooth."

She returned with a mug and passed it to him. Then she sat opposite him. "Bane is your cousin. Why would you need my help to speak to a member of your own family?"

"My father dislikes him, and though I have not met Bane, I wondered if he would refuse my request because of the bad blood between them."

"Put your mind at ease, Finnigal. Bane would never see children go hungry because of his quarrel with Fiallach."

"It sounds as if you like him."

"Indeed I do. His treatment by his own family has been shameful." She saw his face harden. "Reserve your judgment until you have met him, Finnigal."

"I do not judge him," the young man told her. "I do not know him. The lady Meria says he is—as his name shows— accursed. Ill fortune will follow any who seek his company. She says the blood of a bastard is thin and that at heart, all bastards are treacherous and mean-spirited."

"Ah, well, I bow to her judgment," Vorna said coldly. "She knows more about mean-spiritedness than any person I have ever met."

Finnigal rose. "I did not come here to listen to slanders against the king's mother," he said. "Will you aid me with Bane?"

"No. You will not need me. Treat him with respect and he

will agree to your request. Be warned, though, young man: If you offer him any discourtesy, you will pay for it dearly."

"I was raised to offer courtesy to all people," said Finnigal.

"Then you will have no problem with Bane," she said.

Finnigal offered a slight bow, strapped on his sword belt, looped his cloak over his shoulders, and left the house.

Vorna sat quietly, seeking an inner calm that continued to evade her.

Gwenheffyr had always been reserved, a quiet child who had grown into a shy woman. Her gentle nature radiated harmony, and no one had ever known her to raise her voice in anger. As a child she had been often ill and on three occasions had come close to death. "She will not be long-lived," some had said. "She is too delicate."

Slim and small, her dark hair emphasizing the paleness of her features, Gwen had been seen as a fragile creature. It had surprised all who knew her that she had given birth to three lusty babes.

She sat now at Ruathain's bedside, little Orrin beside her. Her youngest child, Badraig, was asleep in his cot close by. "Why doesn't he get better?" asked Orrin, peering at Ruathain's face, which was eerily pale in the lantern light and damp with sweat.

"I am sure that he will . . . soon," said Gwen, putting her arm round Orrin and kissing his head.

Orrin took hold of Ruathain's skeletal hand and began twisting the white gold and moonstone ring on his brother's finger. "It will fall off soon," said the boy.

Gwen nodded, and tears began to form. She took a deep breath. "Time for you to sleep, little man," she said.

"I'm not tired, Mam," argued Orrin.

"Then just lie down for a little while, then come out and join us by the hearth," said Gwen, leading Orrin to the second bed. The little boy climbed onto the bed and slid his legs under the covers.

"I won't sleep," he said.

"Then I'll see you soon by the fire," she told him, leaning down and kissing his cheek. Rising from the bedside, she took a last look at Ruathain and walked out of the room.

Meria was sitting by the fire, a white shawl around her shoulders. Gwen moved past her to the door and pulled on a pair of shoes. Then she took a cloak from the peg by the door.

"Where are you going?" asked Meria.

"I thought," Gwen said softly, "that I would ask Vorna to tend Ruathain."

Meria glanced up, her features hard. "To what point?" she asked. "Her son has great talent as a healer—far greater than hers. If he could not heal the boy, then calling upon her would be a waste of time."

"Even so . . ."

"And she is no friend to our family," snapped Meria. "I would not wish to see her invited to my home. Let us speak no more of it."

Gwen sighed, replaced the cloak on its peg, and moved to the chair opposite. For a while she looked into the fire, thinking of how strong and healthy Ruathain had been before this dreadful illness. Sadness swept over her. "I think he is going to die," she said, tears in her eyes. "Vorna might know of some remedy . . ."

"I said we will speak no more of it!"

Gwen sat very quietly, Meria's anger causing her to tremble. She had always hated raised voices and argument. Closing her eyes, she thought of Bran and wondered how such a warm and compassionate soul could have sprung from a harsh and unfeeling woman like Meria. Gwen wished she could have known Bran's father, the first Ruathain. Men still spoke of him with fondness and talked of his love of family and his affinity with children. Meria had never once hugged Gwen's sons or shown any genuine affection toward them. It was a mystery to Gwen. Opening her eyes, she glanced across at Meria. The older woman seemed to be dozing. Gwen rose from the chair and moved back into the bedroom.

Orrin was fast asleep, his thumb in his mouth. Ruathain was lying very still, his skin gleaming in the lantern light. She stroked his brow. The skin was hot, but he seemed more comfortable. Gwen sat down beside him, holding his hand.

She was still there two hours later when his breathing grew more shallow. Suddenly his eyes opened. He looked at Gwen and gave a smile. She felt him squeeze her fingers.

Then he died.

* * *

Bane could not sleep. Throwing back the covers, he climbed from his bed, pulled on a knee-length tunic of pale gray wool, and walked out into the main room. The fire was almost dead, and he blew it to life, adding fresh fuel. The events of the day would not leave him. Riding into Lorca's camp had been an act of almost suicidal stupidity, and he was angry with himself. Had it not been for the crippled warrior Grale, he would now be dead, his body dumped in the forest, food for foxes and worms.

From the back bedroom he could hear Gryffe snoring. The sound was somehow comforting, although, in a way he could not quite fathom, it left Bane feeling isolated and alone. He sat quietly, feeling the heat of the fire wash over him. Truth to tell, he missed Rage and Telors. All the time he had been in Stone he had thought of the mountains and forests of Caer Druagh with a fondness covered by the warmth of the word "home." Yet now that he was here, the same warmth touched him when he remembered Rage. It was as if contentment were always somewhere else, floating before him like a wraith, ever beckoning, never found.

He heard the gentle creak of a bed board and then the soft padding of feet on the rugs of the floor. Bane glanced up to see plump Iswain move into the room, carefully and quietly pulling shut the bedroom door behind her.

She walked over to him. "Shall I fetch you something to eat?" she said, keeping her voice low.

Looking into her round and friendly face, he met her gaze. Her dark eyes seemed sorrowful in the firelight. "Are you all right?" he asked her.

"Aye, I am fine. I could prepare a tisane."

"No. I need nothing."

They sat in silence for a little while, Iswain taking up the iron poker and prodding at the burning logs.

"Talk to me," he said softly. "What is troubling you?"

She took a deep breath and seemed about to speak. But then she shook her head. "Everything is all right now. My man is asleep in his bed. There is food in the larder and no enemies close by. Who can ask for more than that?"

"True," he told her.

"Gryffe says that the next time a druid passes, we will walk the tree. He says that when the summer is here, he will buy me a ring and that one day we might have a farm of our own. He is a good man, Gryffe."

"I know that."

"Do you?" she asked, her voice accusing. "Do you really?"

"Of course. Why do you doubt me?"

"He is asleep in his bed," she said again. "But he might have been lying dead beside you today and not snoring beside me. You took him to a place of death. You did not tell him what you planned. You just rode in and killed Lorca. And my man stood beside you. Did you think of him at all?"

Bane was silent for a moment. "No," he said. "I did not."

"I thought not." She sighed. "He was an outlaw, a nithing! You gave him back his self-respect. I love you for that, Bane. But my man is worth more than to die for your pride."

"I told him I was going alone, Iswain, but he would not hear of it."

"Of course he wouldn't," she snapped. "Are you blind? Can you not see what you mean to these men you have brought from the forest? Do you not know what your trust has done for them? All of them have been branded worthless. They have been cast out from their tribes and their communities. They came—in the main—to consider themselves worthless. Then you came along and lifted them. You treated them like men again. You valued them, trusted them, and they in turn value you. Why do you think young Cascor died? He was not the bravest of men, but he stood up to Lorca on your behalf. And why? Because his chieftain had ordered him to protect the cattle."

"I am no chief, Iswain, no laird or leader. These men are not my serfs or slaves. They are here as long as they choose to be, and they work for coin."

"Pah! Have you no understanding of the nature of men? You think Cascor died for five copper coins a month? You think my man stood beside you in Lorca's camp for his two silvers? You are the king here, Bane. And a king—though he has power—also has responsibility for those who serve him. I love Gryffe . . ." Her voice faltered, and he saw tears falling to her cheeks. "There, it is said! Iswain the whore is in love!

And Iswain wants the ring that Gryffe has promised her even though it be iron or brass. Iswain wants the little farm."

Reaching out, he took her hand. "I am sorry, Iswain," he said. "You are right. These men have shown me loyalty beyond the payment I give them. I will remember what you have said. I promise you that."

Wiping away the tears, she took hold of his hand in both of hers. "You brought me out of the forest, too, Bane," she said. "I didn't mean to scold you."

He smiled. "You scold away whenever you feel the need. There must always be honesty between us, Iswain. I value that greatly. Now go back to bed."

"Are you sure you don't want a tisane?"

"I am sure."

Rising, she kissed his cheek and left the room.

Some minutes later, in warm leggings and fur-lined boots, a black cloak over his shoulders, Bane walked out into the night. There were dark patches on the hillsides where the snow was melting, and there was a warmth in the air that promised the final death of winter. The sky was lightening, the dawn awakening.

He trudged across the snow, past the new corral and the roundhouse barn and the silent huts of his workers. On the far hills he could see around a dozen of his steers. Several had risen and were cropping the new grass.

A gray-muzzled hound moved into the open and padded across to him. Bane patted its head and stroked its scarred flank. The hound sat down beside the man, and when Bane moved off toward the woods, it went with him. The hound had appeared some weeks before, half-starved, several old wounds on its side weeping pus. The herdsman Cascor had taken it in and fed it, cleaning its sores with a mixture of wine and honey.

Reaching the woods, Bane looked back at his farmhouse and the silent forest beyond it. He felt calmer, more at peace than ever before in his life. It was a good feeling, and he clung to it.

The wind picked up, whispering through the branches above him. His cloak billowed out, alarming the hound, which yelped and fled several paces from him. Then Bane heard his name on the whispering wind and spun around. There was no one close by.

"Bane!"

"Who is there?" he called out, advancing beyond the tree line into the wood. In the east the first rays of the morning sun had turned the sky to pale gold. Bane walked on.

A crow swooped by him, settling on a twisted branch. Cocking its head, it watched the warrior. "Where are you, Old Woman?" Bane called. "Show yourself!"

There was no response, but the crow flew from the branch, angling its flight deeper into the wood. Bane swore softly and followed, the hound padding at his heels. Some fifty paces farther on the crow was waiting, perched on a boulder beside a deep rock pool. Bane scanned the trees for signs of the Morrigu.

"Is this some game we are playing?" he called out.

The muddy water in the pool began to bubble and steam. A mist rose from it, coalescing into a large, glimmering globe that hung motionless in the air above the pool. Bane watched it. The mist flattened until the globe became a shining shield the color of polished iron. Sunlight touched it. For a moment only the shield was transformed into a mirror, and Bane saw himself reflected in it. Then his image faded. At first he thought the mist was clearing. It peeled back from the center, creating a ring that hung in the air. Inside the ring Bane could see blue sky and drifting clouds. He stepped closer and found himself staring at a sheltered bay. Four long ships were beached there. The scene shifted, and he saw two hundred or so Sea Raiders marching across the snow-covered land. They became smaller and smaller as if Bane were flying higher and higher above them. He could see the Druagh mountains now, mist clinging to the slopes. And in the distance, some sixty miles from the raiders, was the settlement of Three Streams.

Bane's heart began to beat faster, and he drew in a sharp breath. How soon would the raiders reach the settlement? Two days? Three? Was it sixty miles or less? Panic touched him.

The scene in the ring of mist changed again, and he was looking down upon the settlement. Hundreds of people were gathered on the hillside, and Bane saw a body, wrapped and tied in a blanket, being lowered into a deep grave. He recognized most of the people there: His grandfather, Nanncumal the Blacksmith, was standing beside his daughter, Gwydia. Neruman the Tanner was present, as was the forester Adlin. A woman with a harsh face stepped to the graveside, throwing a handful of dirt down into the hole. Beside her a dark-haired young woman covered her face with her hands and wept while a little straw-haired boy clung to her dress. Around twenty soldiers were close by, dressed in the chain mail and iron helms of Connavar's Iron Wolves. Some way back from the crowd, a dark shawl around her shoulders, her silver-streaked hair blowing in the breeze, stood Vorna.

Slowly her image grew larger, as if Bane were approaching her. "Vorna!" he called.

She spun and gazed up directly into his eyes. He heard her voice echo inside his head, though her lips did not move. "Bane? Where are you?"

"I am in the woods near my farmhouse."

"How are you doing this?"

"I do not know, Vorna. The Morrigu's crow is here. But that is not important now. Listen to me: There is a large force of Sea Wolves heading toward Three Streams from the east. I think they are at least three days away, but they may arrive sooner. How many soldiers are there with you?"

"Twenty. They are led by Finnigal, Fiallach's son."

"Twenty will not be enough—the raiders are ten times that number. You must convince people to leave the settlement and strike west toward my farm and the Narian Forest. Load all the food you can onto wagons and burn the rest. Leave nothing for the raiders. I will come to you as soon as I can. Can you do this? Can you convince them?"

"Not all of them," said the voice of Vorna in his mind. "There are more than eleven hundred refugees here, many of them older people or women with young children. Without proof of invasion many of them will choose to stay in the shelter of the community rather than risk walking out into the snow and the cold. But I will do what I can."

The vision faded. The mist ring disappeared. The crow cawed and flapped its wings, rising higher and higher above the trees until Bane could see it no more.

The young warrior ran back to the house, waking Gryffe

and sending him into the forest with orders to find Wik and bring him and all the other outlaws to the farm.

"Why would they come?" asked the bleary-eyed Gryffe.

"Tell Wik there is gold to be had for every man. He'll come. But tell them to come ready to fight."

The first person Vorna approached was young Finnigal, calling out to him as he walked from Ruathain's funeral. The soldier hesitated, unwilling to be drawn into conversation with her, but then strolled over to where she stood.

"What do you want of me, lady?" he asked, his voice coldly polite.

"Walk with me," she commanded, then moved away from the crowd toward the first bridge. He strode alongside her.

"I have little time for idle chatter," he said. "There is much to be done."

"I think you will find you have less time than you think," she said, walking out onto the humpbacked wooden bridge and pausing by the rail to stare down into the rushing water below. Chunks of white ice floated beneath the bridge, thumping against the foundations. Only a few days earlier the stream had been frozen solid, village children playing upon it.

Vorna swung toward the tall soldier, her dark eyes holding to his gaze. "You stood beside the grave of your friend and recalled a time when both of you were hunting. Ruathain's horse stumbled, hurling him into a thornbush between two jagged boulders. He rose laughing and scratched, and you pointed out to him that had he struck the boulders, he would now be dead. He told you he planned to live forever. Is that not so?"

He stepped back a pace, his face blushing. "I did not know you were a mystic," he said. "It is most discourteous to enter a man's mind in that way."

"Indeed it is," she said, "and I apologize for it. But it was necessary, Finnigal, so that you would give credence to what I have to tell you. And believe me, I have spent many years keeping this gift secret, and only something of the greatest import would cause me to reveal it." She glanced back at the crowd making their way to their homes. One elderly woman, almost crippled by arthritis, was being supported by two soldiers. Vorna sighed.

"Tell me what you have to say," said Finnigal.

"There are Sea Wolves to the east of us. They are heading for Three Streams."

"What? That is not possible!"

"It is true, Finnigal. Two hundred, perhaps more. They will be here within three days."

The young man swung toward the east, scanning the land as if expecting to see the raiders marching over the hilltops. "Two hundred?" he whispered. "Are you sure?"

"I am sure."

"Why here? There are settlements closer to the sea."

"I do not know. What I do know is that they are coming. We must organize a withdrawal, head west for the Narian Forest. The raiders will be carrying their own supplies. They will not have the food to follow us far."

Finnigal stared back at Three Streams. "We have around sixty wagons. There is no way to transport all the villagers and refugees. Narian is . . . what? . . . twenty miles or so. The weather is breaking, but the land is still frozen. We couldn't make it in a day, which means a night out in the open. And when we get there, what shelter would we have for the elderly and the very young? Gods, woman, many would die of the cold."

"More will die if they stay here," she said. "We should head for Bane's farm. He has outbuildings and several barns, and within the forest there are sheltered clearings."

"And outlaws," said Finnigal. "Murderous cutthroats who will prey on the weak."

"That, too," she agreed.

Finnigal stood silently, and Vorna knew he was calculating the amount of time it would take a rider to reach Old Oaks, gather reinforcements, and head back. More than a week. And then only if there were reinforcements to be had, considering that the king and his main force had left for Seven Willows to confront Shard and his fifteen thousand Vars. Finnigal turned his gaze to the south. His father would be a hundred miles away by now, preparing to defend against the armies of Stone. Fear tightened his belly, and he licked his lips nervously.

"I do not like the choices," he said softly. "To leave will mean deaths from the cold and the destruction of Three Streams. To stay will bring great slaughter to those I am pledged to protect."

Vorna saw the torment in his eyes. "I know this is hard for you, Finnigal. This is your first command, and it calls for great strength. You have that strength. I know this."

He smiled at the compliment, but his face was pale and strained. "Time, I think, to call the village elders together."

Within the hour the thirty elected elders were seated in the great roundhouse built by Braefar. They listened in stunned silence when Finnigal told them word had reached him of a Vars force to the east, but the silence ended when he suggested an evacuation. The first to voice a protest was Nanncumal the Smith. "If they are sixty miles away, what makes you think they are coming here?" he asked.

Finnigal glanced to where Vorna was seated at the back. "It is my belief," he said at last, "that we are in great danger. I believe they plan to sack the settlement."

"You believe?" put in the black-bearded forester Adlin. "No disrespect to you, Finnigal, but you are young and inexperienced. Why should we risk the lives of our people because you believe they may be coming? There are at least five other settlements closer to the coast."

"Yes, there are," agreed Finnigal, "but this is the richest, and the Vars will know there are few troops left to guard the area, added to which Three Streams is the birthplace of the king and as such is a place dear to his heart. Yes, there are risks in leaving. I know this, and it grieves me. The risks if we stay are far greater."

"You say that," put in Neruman the Tanner, a skinny, round-shouldered man, "but what of Lorca and his outlaws? Lorca is a vile creature who lives for rape and pillage. You are suggesting we walk blithely into his domain."

Others of the elders began to shout questions. Lady Meria stepped into the center of the circle, raising her hands for silence. "I would like to know," she said, "how this word reached you, Captain Finnigal. What was the source, and how reliable the information?"

Vorna could see that the young man was taken aback by the question. He had not mentioned Vorna's vision, and she was grateful for his effort to maintain her secret. But now Vorna rose from her seat. "I told him," she said. Heads turned toward her.

"Ah," said Meria, "and how, pray, did you come by the news?"

"In a vision," said the former witch.

"I see," Meria said with a sneer. "You have a bad dream, and the whole of the settlement must rush out to die in the snow or be slain by outlaws? Your powers were lost years ago."

"Aye, they were," said Vorna, her anger rising. "Lost to save your son, you ungrateful bitch!" She strode through the seated elders until she stood no more than a few feet from Meria and Finnigal. "You all know me," she continued. "I have healed your wives, your husbands, and your children. I have delivered your babes. I am Vorna, and I do not lie. Nor do I have bad dreams. I tell you that the Sea Wolves are coming. I urge you to evacuate this settlement."

"And I say," stormed Meria, "that she is deluded. And I, for one, have no intention of quitting my home on a madwoman's fancy."

"Nor I," said Nanncumal.

Others joined in, and the arguments began again. Voices were raised, and the meeting descended into a shouting match. Vorna looked at Meria and saw the glint of dark triumph in her eyes.

"How did you become such a vile and spiteful creature?" said Vorna. Then she strode from the roundhouse, the sounds of discord ringing in her ears.

By evening the meeting was over, the situation unresolved.

Gwen was glad when Meria left for the meeting, for she found the older woman's company unsettling. She radiated disharmony. Gwen did not like to think ill of anyone and had tried hard to like her husband's mother. It was terribly difficult. Meria had only one passion in her life: the love of her eldest son, Connavar. Her utter focus on this one object led her to largely ignore her other two sons. Braefar had suffered the most. Gwen felt sorry for the man. Now in his late thirties, he had never married and she saw, as no one else had, how desperately he needed his mother's affection. And he was the most like her, even down to the bitterness that endlessly corroded his finer qualities.

Gwen held baby Badraig to her breast, feeling the warmth of his body against hers. The boy was sucking hard, and she winced at the sudden sharpness of pain in her nipple. "Gently, gently," she whispered, stroking the crown of his head. Her thoughts turned to Bran. No bitterness there, no jealousy at his brother's rise to fame and the crown. She pictured his broad face and felt a fresh outpouring of sadness. He would be distraught to learn of Ruathain's death even though they had both known it was coming. Gwen's eyes welled with tears, and she blinked them away. Badraig had finished feeding now, and his head flopped against her as he slept. Gwen rose from the rocking chair and took him to his cot, laying him gently down and covering him with a soft woolen blanket. Transferring her gaze to the bed, she saw that Orrin was still sleeping. The boy had complained of feeling unwell, and Gwen had guessed it to be from the grief and tension of the funeral. Better for him to sleep than to sit by remembering the day.

Returning to the main room, she glanced around the well-crafted walls, the shelves, and the cabinets. There was a feeling of peace here and contentment that must have come from Meria's first husband, Ruathain. It certainly had never emanated from Meria herself. Gwen's own house at Golden Rocks was like this, built with care and filled with objects that spoke of love and devotion. On the far wall of the main room at home there was a piece of polished oak carved into a heart, bearing her name. It was the first gift Bran had given her, eighteen and a half years earlier. They had met at the Samain Feast. Gwen, being shy, had sat herself away from the crowd, and Bran had seen her and wandered over. Watching the golden-haired young man heading for her, Gwen had felt fearful. She had wished for no company and turned her head away, hoping he would pass by. But he had not.

He had halted before her and asked politely if he could sit. Her shyness had at first made speech impossible, so she had merely nodded. The dancing had begun by the fire, the music of the pipes blaring out.

"Do you dance?" he asked her. She shook her head. "I like to dance sometimes," he said, his voice soft, almost musical. "Last week I was riding in the high hills above the loch, and the setting sunlight kissed the waters, turning them to gold. I felt like leaping from my pony and dancing with joy."

"And did you?" she found herself asking.

"Aye, I did. A proper fool I must have looked, cavorting over the grass. My horse stood watching me, and I could see in his eyes that he thought me mad. But then, he is an old horse, and he views the world with great cynicism."

"How does one tell if a horse is cynical?" she inquired. He was sitting beside her, looking back toward the fire. This made Gwen feel a little more at ease, for she did not like to be stared at. His profile was very fine, and she saw in his face a gentleness often missing from Rigante men.

"Well," he said at last, "my horse and I have many conversations. I tell him of my hopes and dreams as I ride, and he listens. Occasionally, when I speak of my more romantic beliefs, he will toss his head and snort. That is his way of telling me that the world is not as I would wish it to be."

"He sounds very wise, your horse."

"Indeed he is."

They sat in silence for a while, and Gwen was surprised to find that his company was not at all intrusive. He applied no pressure, was not inquisitive. He merely sat, completely at ease, watching the fire dancers as they leapt and twirled. She wanted to ask his name, but that would have meant initiating a conversation, so she, too, watched the dancers.

After a while he spoke again. "Do you know the land to the east of Golden Rocks, where the woods back onto cliffs of sandstone and the river widens?"

"Yes," she told him. "It is very pretty there."

"I plan to build a house there. I plan to build it with stone."

"Stone? Why would you have a house of stone?"

"I want it to last. I want my children and my children's children to come there and know the joy I experienced. I intend to have large windows facing west so that the setting sun can shine on my hearth. I mentioned this to my horse, and he did not snort once."

"Then you must do it," she said. "One should never ignore the advice of a wise horse."

He laughed then, and she smiled. Never before had she made a joke, and though it was not a particularly good one, it was a breakthrough for Gwen. She wished he would tell her his name.

"Do you have other wise animals?" she asked him.

"No. I have a very stupid hound. We call him the Old One. He does not like other dogs but will pad across the meadows in the early morning, ignoring all the rabbits. They are so used to him that they carry on feeding as he passes by. He likes rabbits. One of my other hounds—a young rascal named Piga—took off one morning on a rabbit hunt. The Old One charged at him, nipping his shoulder and driving him from the meadow. Then he sat down, and all the rabbits came back out of their burrows and began feeding again. I am very much mocked by my fellows for the antics of the Old One."

A redheaded woman approached them. "There you are," she called. "Come, Bran, as the master of the feast you should be at the table."

He waved at her. "That is my mother, Meria. Commanding, isn't she? Well, I must go and do my duty." He rose and strolled away.

Gwen found that she missed his company even as he began the walk back to the feast tables. Suddenly he turned and strolled back. "Come," he said, holding out his hand. "We can dine together."

Fear flickered once more, but she took his hand and he raised her to her feet. They were married five weeks later.

Now, as she gazed around the house in which Bran had grown to manhood, Gwen felt only sadness. Her son had been so strong, so quick, and so full of life. It amazed her how swiftly that strength had evaporated. And now he was gone.

The door opened, and Meria strode in. "Can you believe the stupidity of that woman?" she said. The calm atmosphere disappeared in an instant.

"Which woman?" asked Gwen, returning to her chair.

"Vorna. She had a dream that Sea Wolves were coming across the land to Three Streams and that we should all just leave and run away into the wilderness. I'm sure some people will. Idiots, all of them."

"It is said she once had great power."

"Aye, she did. But not anymore. Now she is merely willful."

"Why do you hate her so?" asked Gwen.

"She befriended the bastard Bane, the man who has sworn to kill Connavar. Can you imagine that? Such treachery. She should have been hanged!"

Gwen said nothing. She walked back into the bedroom, anxious to be away from Meria and her radiated unpleasantness. Orrin was still sleeping. It had been over four hours now, and he rarely slept so long in the daytime. Gwen sat beside the bed and gently shook his shoulder. "Time to wake, little one. I shall toast some bread for you."

He did not stir. Gwen rolled him onto his back. His eyes were dark-ringed, his skin gleaming with sweat. "No!" she whispered. Then she cried out: "Orrin! Orrin!"

Meria came into the room. "What on earth is this noise about?" she asked. Then she saw the still figure of the child. "Oh, no!" she said, rushing to the bedside. "It cannot be!" She placed her fingers on the child's throat, feeling for the pulse. "He is alive," she said. "But his heart is racing!"

"It is just like my Ru," cried Gwen. Meria said nothing. The evidence was all too clear.

Gwen gathered the child in her arms and lifted him from the bed.

"What are you doing?" Meria asked.

"I am taking him to Vorna."

"I forbid it!" shouted Meria, storming to her feet.

"I have one dead son," replied Gwen. "I will not lose another because of you."

She carried Orrin out into the dusk and across the field to the house of Vorna.

◊ 12 ◊

Vorna laid the comatose child on her own bed and looked
up at the mother, seeing the terrible fear in her eyes. "Go to
the kitchen," she said. "Boil some water for a tisane."

"He cannot drink," said Gwen.

"No, but we can. Go. Do it now while I examine him."

"Please don't let him die!" said Gwen, dissolving into tears.

"I will do what I can. Go. Make some tisane for us. I take
mine unsweetened. You will find chamomile in the blue jar
beside the oven."

Turning away from the woman, Vorna laid her hand on the
boy's head. Closing her eyes, she allowed her spirit to flow
into the child. He was dying. Of that there was no doubt, the
organs of his body close to collapse. At first Vorna could find
no reason for his condition, and she flowed deeper, her spirit
merging with the blood streaming through his veins. His kidneys were the greatest source of concern, and Vorna concentrated her power there, strengthening the tissue. Even as she
healed the organs, she felt them come under fresh attack. It
was just as Banouin had told her concerning his treatment of
Ruathain. Every time an area underwent healing, it almost
immediately began to weaken again.

Orrin's laboring heart suddenly gave out. Vorna sent a burst
of energy into it. It flickered, then began to beat once more.

Vorna honed her concentration, flowing yet deeper into the
bloodstream. Now she could feel the vital elements within
the flow. Still she could detect no sign of disease. The liver
began to fail, and Vorna strengthened it. Then the kidneys
weakened once more, and she boosted them with fresh energy. She was tiring now, and still there was no clue to what
was killing the child.

Vorna withdrew from the boy. His color was a little better, his breathing easier. Gwen returned to the room, carrying mugs of tisane. Vorna saw her spirit soar as she looked down upon her son.

"Do not get your hopes up, Gwen," Vorna said sternly. "I cannot yet identify the source of his sickness. Sit quietly by and do not in any circumstances speak to me unless I ask you to. You understand?"

"Yes," Gwen said meekly.

Vorna gazed at the child's waxen skin. Think, she told herself. Whatever is causing this is powerful indeed, yet why did he not succumb earlier? If it was a sickness, surely he should have caught it from Ruathain far sooner than this. As should the mother and any others with close contact with the boy. Therefore, it was not like the plague or any contact-borne sickness. Yet there had to be a link.

The boy's heart stopped again. Vorna's spirit eased once more through the skin, sending a bolt of energy to the stricken organ. Orrin's body convulsed, then the heart began again.

Vorna withdrew and turned to Gwen. "You say the sickness began only today? No indications before this?"

"None. He has always been healthy. Aren't you going to do something?"

"I am doing something, Gwen. Stay calm."

Vorna returned her attention to the child. The surface of his skin was hot, his body battling to bring down the fever temperature. Vorna flowed deeper, once more repairing the liver and kidneys. She had never come across anything like this before. It was as if the disease were continually invading the child.

For another hour she fought on, but she was tiring rapidly. Pulling back from his body, she slumped in her chair and sipped her cold tisane. Whatever had killed Ruathain was now destroying his brother. Again she turned to Gwen. "How long was Ruathain sick?"

"Almost a year now. At first he just felt weak and had no appetite. He would sleep all the time. Then, as the months passed, he grew weaker and weaker. He rallied when Banouin tended him, but only for a while. Why has it struck Orrin so savagely? He looks now like my Ru at the end."

"Orrin is younger. Perhaps that is the key. Perhaps a strapping lad can fight off this . . . this malady with more strength than a child. But there is a link here that we must find. Otherwise he will not last the night."

Closing her eyes, she entered his body again, but this time, instead of joining the bloodstream, she floated just below the surface of his skin, helping to ease out the fever. When she reached the area of his chest, she felt a sudden burning that caused her to flee to the sanctuary of her body. Rising from her chair, she moved to a tall chest under the window on which lay some balls of thread and a long pair of scissors. Returning to the bedside, she cut open the little boy's tunic.

Upon his chest lay a ring of white gold with a moonstone at the center. Orrin had hung it around his neck with a long leather thong.

"What is this?" asked Vorna, cutting the thong and lifting the ring clear.

"It is Ruathain's ring. Orrin must have taken it as a keepsake to remind him of his brother."

Vorna laid the ring upon the floor, then returned to the child. Now, as she flowed through him, healing the tortured tissue, there was no secondary attack. Orrin's heartbeat grew stronger, his fever abating.

Vorna covered him with a blanket. "He looks a little better," said Gwen.

"He is well," Vorna told her. "The evil is gone from him." Lifting the ring on the end of her scissors, she examined it. It was beautifully crafted. "Where did Ruathain acquire this?" she asked.

"Meria gave it to him. It was originally a gift for Connavar from a Stone merchant, but the king does not wear rings, so Meria gave it to Ru. Why do you ask?"

Vorna walked to the kitchen, returning with a flat length of black slate that she laid on the chest by the window. Lifting a lantern from a bracket on the wall, she placed it alongside the slate, then dropped the ring onto the gleaming black surface. As Gwen watched, Vorna held her hand over the ring and whispered a word of power. The temperature in the room plummeted, and upon the slate ice formed instantly. The moonstone glowed bright, then cracked open. Gray fluid oozed from the stone, spreading out across the slate. Vorna snapped her fingers, and the temperature rose once more. Gwen stared at the ruined ring.

"It is poison," said Vorna, "distilled by a mistress of the craft. She split the stone, hollowed out the center, and made many imperceptible holes through the surface. Then she filled the center with poison, remade the stone, and set it within this ring of white gold. Once the moonstone touched human skin, it would slowly seep its poison into the blood. It was obviously meant to kill Connavar."

"Then all I had to do to save Ru was remove the ring?" said Gwen. "Oh, sweet heaven!"

"Do not blame yourself, Gwen. You could not know. The fault is not yours."

"Yes, it is," said Gwen. "I wanted to come to you and ask you to tend my son. But I did not. Had I done so, my Ru would still be alive."

"Mam!" said Orrin. "Mam!"

Gwen went to the bedside. "Hello, my little one," she said, wiping the tears from her eyes. "Are you all right?"

"Yes, Mam. I was sitting with Ruathain, and there was this bright light. And I woke up." He looked around. "Where are we, Mam?"

"You have been sick, little one, but Vorna healed you. This is Vorna. Say thank you."

"Thank you, Vorna," he said obediently.

"It was my pleasure, young man."

Orrin's eyes closed, and he fell asleep. Gwen brushed the hair back from his brow and kissed him tenderly. "I don't have the words to express my gratitude," she said. "What can I do to thank you?"

"Leave here tomorrow with those heading west," said Vorna. "For death is coming to Three Streams, and my powers can do nothing to prevent it."

It was more than four hours after Bane had seen the vision before the first of the outlaws walked from the forest. In that time Bane ordered a steer slaughtered and a fire pit dug, and as the men made their way toward the farmhouse, the smell of roasting beef filled the air.

The first to arrive was the slender, round-shouldered Wik, and with him were some forty men, mostly armed with long-bows and daggers. Bane greeted them, and Iswain began to cut meat for them. There were not enough plates, but Iswain had gathered sections of broken black slate, which she had stacked on a long trestle table. "How many still to come?" asked Bane.

Wik shrugged. "Valian is scouring the other small camps. Maybe another sixty. Maybe less. What is this about?"

"Let's talk inside," said Bane.

The two men wandered into the farmhouse. Bane did not know Wik well, but his impression was not a good one. Wik was a man who lacked the appetite for work of any kind. Lazy and untrustworthy, he would sooner live in squalor and semi-starvation for months in the hope of one good robbery than labor for his daily food. What he possessed, in Bane's opinion, was an animal cunning and an ability to gather to him like-minded souls. The man was not unintelligent, but neither was he as bright as he believed. Bane watched as Wik's dirty fingers tore at the rich meat.

"Well?" asked the outlaw leader, juices flowing to his wispy brown beard.

"I want to hire you and your men," said Bane. "For five days."

Wik belched. "You have anything to drink here?" he asked. "Ale or uisge?"

"Uisge would be good."

Bane took a jug from the cupboard and poured a generous measure into a clay cup. Wik downed it in one swallow. "Hire them for what?" he asked.

"To fight. Why else?"

"Who are we to fight?"

"Sea Wolves. They are heading for Three Streams."

Wik finished his meal and licked his fingers. "How many Sea Wolves?"

"Two . . . maybe three hundred."

Wik laughed and shook his head. "Are you insane, man? We will have maybe a hundred men. Lazy turds most of them. Aye, and cowards among them."

"But you are no coward," said Bane.

"I am not an idiot, either. Where are Connavar's soldiers? Where are those famed Iron Wolves?"

"There are twenty of them at Three Streams; the rest are near Seven Willows ready to take on the Var king and his army."

Wik thought for a moment. "Then we should be sacking Three Streams first. Twenty soldiers my men can take."

"I plan to offer every one of your men two gold pieces for five days work."

Wik's eyes widened. "Man, that's a fortune! You have that much gold here?"

"Of course I do not," said Bane. "But it is close by, buried and waiting. You I will offer ten gold pieces."

"You are richer than I thought, Bane. What in the name of Taranis are you doing living in this place? You could have a palace!"

"I am where I wish to be. What you must consider is where you wish to be."

"What does that mean?"

"It is very simple. Among the people at Three Streams are relatives of the king. His mother is there, as is the wife of Bendegit Bran and her children. The man who saves them from the Sea Wolves—and that is you, Wik—will be offered great rewards. Your crimes will be pardoned, and it is likely you will have more gold than you can spend. No more sitting in the mud of a forest camp. You will have the palace you desire."

Wik thought for a moment. "A dead man has no need of a palace. I fought the Sea Wolves once, when I was still a Pannone. Evil bastards, but they can fight. No give in them."

"Riches and fame do not always come easily," said Bane. "Ask yourself how many times in your life you will be offered the chance to save the king's mother and be a hero into the bargain. At the very least you will come out of this with ten gold pieces, plus two for every man who dies."

"I'll have some more uisge," said Wik. Bane poured another measure, which disappeared even faster than the first. "What is your plan?"

"I am hoping the people in Three Streams will evacuate the settlement. We will form a rear guard behind them. We will not tackle the Sea Wolves head on but fight and move, wearing them down."

"No pitched battle, then?"

"Not if it can be avoided."

Wik pushed his cup toward Bane, who filled it. "And what if you're killed, Bane? How do we get our money then?"

"I will see to it that you are all paid whether I live or not."

"Oh, and I just trust you on this, do I?"

"Aye, you do, Wik. But as a gesture of good faith I will give you five gold pieces in advance." Bane unhooked the pouch from his belt and tipped the contents to the table. The five heavy golden coins rolled across the wood. Wik stared at them for a moment, then scooped them up. Dropping four into his own pouch, he drew his dagger and cut into the fifth, examining it closely. Then he added it to the others.

"Are we agreed?" said Bane.

"Aye, we are agreed. We'll defend the people of Three Streams for five days."

By dusk more than ninety outlaws had assembled by the corral. Wik and the stocky Valian moved among them. Finally Bane walked out, wearing breastplate and helm, two short swords hanging at his side. Climbing onto the trestle table, he called the outlaws forward.

"You know me," he said. "I am Bane. You know also that I have promised two gold coins to every man who marches beside me for these next five days. I hope you are not insulted by this, for you are all Keltoi, and I know many of you would willingly march for nothing against a savage enemy threatening the lives of Keltoi women and children. The reason I make this offer is simple. The soldiers of the king are paid when they fight for the king. And for the next five days you are all soldiers of the Rigante. So do not spurn the gold, my friends. Just earn it! We will leave two hours before the dawn."

Leaping down from the table, Bane strode back to the farmhouse. Gryffe joined him there. "That was nicely said," he observed. "However, most of them wouldn't pull their mothers from a pit unless she paid them first." Bane grinned and moved inside. Iswain was waiting there.

"So now you are all soldiers of the king," she said, her voice sorrowful.

"Gryffe will remain here," he told her, "and make arrangements to feed those who have fled from the settlement."

"What?" roared Gryffe.

Iswain's eyes blazed. "How dare you insult my man!" she thundered. "I will stay here and make arrangements for the refugees. The other women from the camp will help me. You'll not shame Gryffe by going without him."

Bane raised his hands. "My apologies to you both," he said. "It was not my intention to offend anyone. Nothing would delight me more than knowing Gryffe was at my side. But I thought—"

"What did you think?" Gryffe asked angrily. "What possible reason could you have to leave me behind?"

Bane caught Iswain's eye and saw the fear there. If Gryffe knew she had approached Bane about putting her man in danger, he would be even more angry. "I was thinking," said Bane carefully, "that I needed someone I could trust to look after the farm and the cattle. And that, of course, was disrespectful to you, Iswain, for you are more than capable." He swung toward Gryffe. "No insult was intended, my friend. Of that you can be sure. It lifts my spirits to know I'll have you with me."

"Ah, none taken," Gryffe said, with a grin. "I'll sharpen my sword." He wandered off to the rear of the house.

"You misunderstood me," Iswain said softly. "What I was trying to say this morning was that I didn't want my man put in pointless danger. But he is a man—and a good, brave man. There is nothing pointless about helping women and bairns in danger."

"I stand rebuked," Bane told her.

"Just try to bring him back safe," she said. "And do not worry about the farm or the refugees. I'll take care of things."

Bane leaned in close. "There is something else you can do," he said. "At the back of the first barn there is an old chest containing a few items I brought back from Stone. Underneath it, about two feet down, I buried another chest. This one is full of gold pieces. If for any reason I do not make it back, dig it up and pay every survivor the two gold pieces I promised them. The rest—and there won't be much left—you can keep."

"You trust me with that much gold?" asked Iswain.

"Of course I do," he answered with a smile.

"Ah, Bane," she said, leaning in to kiss his cheek, "you are a fool sometimes, but I do love you."

In the gathering darkness Gwen trudged back to the house of Meria. She had left Orrin sleeping peacefully in Vorna's bed, and now, her shawl wrapped around her, she felt her emotions clash. The death of Ru and the saving of Orrin had come so close together that she no longer knew what she felt. Sadness and joy warred within her. What she did know was that had little Badraig not been back at the house, she would have asked Vorna if she could stay the night. The last person she wished to see now was the hard-faced Meria.

Gwen was not a vengeful person, and there was no thought in her of punishing Bran's mother. She just wished she could be heading anywhere else than back to this house of disharmony. She considered collecting Badraig and returning to Vorna's, but there was a great deal to pack for the next day's journey. With a heavy heart she approached the door, pushing it open.

Meria was sitting by the fire, but she surged to her feet as Gwen entered. "Is he dead?" she asked fearfully.

"No. Vorna healed him."

"But . . . she has no powers now."

"I saw her hold her hand over the poisoned ring, and ice formed under her fingers. The ring cracked and broke. I think she has powers still, Meria." Gwen walked past the older woman.

"What are you talking about? Poisoned ring? What poisoned ring?"

"It doesn't matter," said Gwen. "Orrin is healed and well and sleeping. Let us leave it there. I am very tired."

"I want to know what happened in that house," said Meria, stepping in front of Gwen, who sighed and walked to the chair by the fire. She sat down and told Meria all that had happened, of how Orrin must have taken Ruathain's ring and how he had looped it around his neck.

"Vorna thinks the poisoner planned for the ring to kill Connavar. It was a slow-acting poison, which is why it took so many months to kill my Ru."

"I don't believe it was poisoned," began Meria.

"Stop it!" said Gwen. "I am not a fool, Meria. When that moonstone cracked open, I saw the foulness that seeped from it. I could see then that the stone had been hollowed. As soon as it was removed from around Orrin's neck, he strengthened and was quickly well. What you believe or do not believe is up to you. I know what killed my son. It was no one's fault— save the murderers who intended harm to Connavar. No one set out to rip Ruathain from the world. And I do not blame you for giving him the ring." She rose from the chair. "That is all there is to say except that I shall be leaving tomorrow, with my sons. I believe Vorna when she says the raiders are coming. All who stay here will die, and I have seen too much death lately."

Meria stood very still, and Gwen saw the hardness ease from her face, and for a moment she regained a semblance of what must have once been great beauty. "I stopped you from bringing Vorna to this house. I killed my grandson."

"Not wittingly," said Gwen. "And I could have disobeyed you." She left her there and went to the bedroom. Badraig awoke as she entered. Gwen lifted him from his cot and held him close.

For Finnigal the new day was a continuing nightmare of frustration and nearly boiling anger. It had begun reasonably, with many of the refugees leaving their homes at dawn and harnessing their wagons. The first argument broke out within minutes, when Finnigal saw several people loading large chests onto the back of a wagon. He strode over and told them that only people and food would be leaving that day, since there were insufficient carriages. The man, an elderly Rigante merchant, berated him soundly and refused to unload them. Finnigal tried to reason with him but finally ordered two soldiers to remove the chests and carry them back into the house. The merchant, white-faced with fury, then refused to leave

Three Streams, saying that if all his money was taken, he would be better off dead, anyway.

And that was just the beginning. Rows broke out, and another refugee, a large Pannone woman, struck one of his soldiers. Finnigal did his best to calm matters, but as he was all too aware, his nature was similar to that of his father, Fiallach, and anger was never far from the surface. Yet he struggled on, trying to do his duty, forcing himself to stay calm. After more than two hours, as the first of the wagons finally began the journey to the west, Finnigal's head was pounding. Then the rain came in a slashing torrent that turned the hillside to mud, and many of the heavier wagons became bogged down. People clambered from the wagons, slithering and sliding, slowly pushing them up the hill.

Finnigal, his mail shirt and clothing drenched, rain seeping under the iron neck guard and soaking his undershirt, trudged through the mud to the house of Meria. Lady Gwen and her children had already left, and he found Meria sitting comfortably by a blazing fire, working on a piece of embroidery. "Almost time to leave, my lady," he said.

"Then leave. I shall not be traveling with you."

Finnigal stood his ground. "Your action is undermining my authority, lady. Hundreds of townsfolk are staying merely because you do. And if you stay, then my soldiers and I must stay, which means there will be no one to defend the refugees from outlaws."

"Are you done, Finnigal?" she asked. "For there is a mighty draft from that open door, and I have no wish to catch a chill."

Furious, he turned and walked back into the rain.

By noon the storm had ceased, but the trail west had become a quagmire. Fewer than six hundred of the eleven hundred inhabitants of Three Streams had so far left the settlement, and only twenty wagons remained. Many people were leaving on foot, carrying sacks of food and spare clothing. But more waited.

The sun broke through the clouds, momentarily lifting Finnigal's spirits, but the feeling was short-lived. People suddenly came streaming back down the hillside, dropping their provisions, shouting and waving. Finnigal removed his iron helm the better to hear them. "Outlaws!" he heard one man cry. "Hundreds of them. Flee for your lives!"

Finnigal swore and shouted for his sergeant, a twenty-year veteran named Prasalis. The soldier came running from the direction of Nanncumal's forge. "Gather the men," ordered Finnigal.

"Here they come, sir," said Prasalis, drawing his sword.

Finnigal strode out along the main street and past Eldest Tree, a colossal oak. He saw a man wearing a gleaming iron breastplate and helm leading the outlaws. The panic on the hillside eased as the advancing men showed no intention of attacking. Prasalis moved alongside his young captain. "I make it a hundred and three," he said. The Iron Wolves ran to line up alongside Finnigal, swords drawn.

The outlaws approached, and Finnigal found himself staring open-mouthed at their leader. As he came closer, he looked more and more like Connavar! It was uncanny. Even the eyes were the same, one green and the other tawny gold. There was no doubting who he was: the bastard Bane. None of the outlaws had their weapons drawn. Even the archers had removed their bowstrings in a bid to keep them dry.

"What do you want here?" demanded Finnigal.

Banc smiled. "Relax, Captain. We are here to help you."

"I need no help from a scurvy—"

Bane raised his hand. "Say nothing more, Captain," he advised. "Come, walk with me." Turning away, Bane strode toward the forge. He did not look back to see whether Finnigal was following.

"If there's the first sign of trouble, attack them," Finnigal told Prasalis. Then he moved after Bane, who was waiting by the forge fence.

"If you have come here to rob—"

"Shut your mouth, boy," snapped Bane, "and listen to what I have to say. There are two hundred Sea Wolves close by, and we have no time to bicker with one another. Now, it is my intention to open Nanncumal's armory and get mail shirts, swords, and bucklers for my men. Then we will help you evacuate the settlement and put ourselves under your orders for a rear guard. I have sixty bowmen and forty other men who will fight with sword or ax. That gives us at least a fighting chance of protecting the refugees. You hear what I am saying?"

"I expect your price will be high for this," said Finnigal. Bane's eyes grew cold and hard, and Finnigal felt the onset of fear.

"Aye," said Bane, "my price will be high. Now, do you have a scout in the east?"

"Of course."

"Then he should give us at least some warning when the raiders are close." Bane scanned the settlement. "Why are so many people still here?"

"Lady Meria refused to leave. Others have followed her lead."

"Is that so? We will attend to that presently. But first I will arm my men. Be so good as to advise yours to put away their weapons and continue with the evacuation."

Finnigal reddened. "Is this what you meant about putting yourself under my orders?"

Bane paused, and when he spoke, his words surprised the young officer. "You are quite right, Captain. How do you wish to proceed?"

Finnigal suddenly felt foolish and a little ashamed. If the Sea Wolves were coming, he would need every fighting man he could find. He looked at Bane and saw the contained anger in the man. "This has been a tense day," he said by way of an apology. "Take your men into the forge and arm them." Turning to his men, he called out: "Put away your swords and continue with the evacuation."

Leaving the bowmen outside, Bane led the others through to the rear of the forge and the armory beyond. The bald, stooped figure of Nanncumal stepped in front of the doorway.

"What are you doing here, Bane?" he asked. "Bringing more shame upon the family?"

"Naturally," said Bane. "However, we have little time for debate, Grandfather. The enemy is coming, and I need armor and weapons."

"You are letting him do this?" Nanncumal asked Finnigal.

"I have instructed him to do it," said Finnigal. "Bane and his men are now under my orders."

"This is madness," persisted Nanncumal. "These men are robbers and killers."

"Stand aside, Grandfather," Bane said softly.

"Do it!" roared Finnigal. Nanncumal took a step to the left, and Bane went by him into the armory, his men trooping after him. Finnigal approached the elderly blacksmith. "They are pledged to protect the refugees, and we badly need them, sir," he said.

"But there are no Sea Wolves close by," said Nanncumal. "Lady Meria insists that Vorna is mistaken."

"I hope she is right," said Finnigal, "but I do not believe that she is."

From inside the armory came the sounds of whooping and laughter.

"Do you know," asked Nanncumal, "how much that armor is worth? Each mail shirt costs ten ounces of gold, and you are giving them away. You will have to answer for it."

"I doubt that," said Finnigal. "I am charged with protecting Lady Meria. If she stays, I stay. So it is likely that by dusk today I shall be dead."

The old man looked at him, and his expression changed. "You are a good man, Finnigal," he said. More laughter came from inside. "I'd better see what they are taking."

Finnigal nodded and returned to the main street.

The evacuation was continuing at an even greater pace now, and Finnigal smiled. Many of the people had dismissed the fears of a Var force approaching, but they had no wish to remain in a settlement where a hundred outlaws had gathered.

Prasalis approached him. "This may not be wise, sir," he said. "I know some of those men. The thin bowman by the wall there is Wik. He's a cold killer. He'd slit his grandfather's throat for a bent copper coin. Then there's the Norvii, Valian. The king has warrants out on him for rape and murder. There are at least a dozen others with no belly for a smash-skulls-or-die skirmish."

"As matters stood this morning," Finnigal told him, "we had twenty men and some fifty middle-aged volunteers facing a force above two hundred strong. Now we have 170 men. Some of them may be cowards, but they are here, Sergeant."

"And what if it is all a trick, sir, and they have come to rob and kill?"

"Then I will have made a dreadful mistake. I don't, however, think that will prove to be the truth. I looked into Bane's eyes. I do not think him treacherous."

"Just because he looks like the king doesn't mean he will act like him," Prasalis pointed out.

"By the gods, I actually feel like a soldier," said Gryffe, holding out his arms and admiring the sleeveless mail shirt. He chuckled, then gazed up at the sword rack on the wall. He swung to Nanncumal. "No battle-axes?"

"No axes," replied Nanncumal. Gryffe lifted down a longsword.

"This will do," he said.

"It will not do," said Nanncumal, striding forward and snatching it from Gryffe's hand. "This is a rider's weapon. Do you know nothing? It is blade-heavy and meant to be swung downward from the saddle." Replacing the sword, he pushed past several other outlaws and took down a longsword with a leather-covered grip and curving quillons. It was some eight inches shorter than the first blade. "Here, numbskull!" he said. "Feel the balance of this!"

Gryffe took it. "I have to admit it feels better," he said.

Nanncumal sighed. "You expect these men to stand up to Sea Wolves?" he asked Bane. "The Vars are born ready to fight. They are utterly ferocious. Gods, man, you know this. You've fought them yourself!"

"You are right, Grandfather," said Bane. "We'll send a messenger to the Vars asking them to wait for a week while we find better men to oppose them." He smiled as he said it, and the old man suddenly chuckled. Then his expression hardened.

"I had believed . . . hoped that this story of the Vars was some nonsense dreamed up by Vorna. But it's not, is it?"

"No, it is not. Would you help my men choose suitable weapons? I need to see Finnigal."

"Aye, I'll help them. I can't help feeling it will be like measuring a hound for a hat—an interesting but pointless exercise."

"A plain speaker, isn't he?" said Gryffe.

Bane nodded and left the forge. Finnigal was standing beneath Eldest Tree. Hundreds of Three Streams dwellers were trudging past him, heading for the west.

"I have scouted some possible areas for ambushing the Vars," said Bane. "Perhaps you'd like to ride out and see them for yourself."

"No need," said Finnigal. "I won't be coming with you."

"How, then, will I learn of your orders, Captain?" Bane asked with a smile.

Finnigal laughed, but there was little humor in it. "You won't. You'll take command. Since your arrival quite a few of the good folks of Three Streams have reconsidered their decision to stay in the settlement, but not Lady Meria and some fifty others. My men and I will stay and fight the Vars. With luck we'll reduce their numbers by at least thirty. Also, since some of those staying are young women, the Vars will probably dally here awhile before giving chase."

"This is daft, man," said Bane. "Compel them to leave."

"How does one compel the king's mother? She is not a soldier and therefore not under my command. Be serious, Bane. The old lady has made her decision. I can say nothing to sway her."

Bane stood silently for a moment. "That is a terrible waste of twenty good men," he said. "However, perhaps there is an alternative. It will require you to trust me. Later on—if there is a later on—you can berate me publicly."

"What is your plan?"

"Best that you do not know. Then there can be no question of collusion. I suggest you take your twenty riders to the top of the hill to examine the ground beyond for possible fighting sites. In the meantime I will organize the evacuation."

The soldier removed his iron helm and pushed back his mail hood. "Lady Meria," he said, "has gone to the roundhouse with the others who are remaining. Some of them have changed their minds, and she is seeking to strengthen their resolve." He shook his head. "Ah, well, Bane, I think I'll take a ride with my men."

"First have them bring a wagon to the roundhouse," said Bane.

Finnigal walked away, and Bane returned to the forge. His men were gathered outside. All of them now wore breastplates and helms and were carrying swords and round wooden bucklers, edged with iron.

He called Wik to him. The outlaw leader had no mail shirt, but was carrying a longbow and a quiver of arrows. "Take the men to the brow of the hill and wait for me there," said Bane.

"So far it is the easiest gold I've ever earned," said Wik.

"The day is not over yet," Bane reminded him.

Keeping Gryffe, the stocky Valian, and the crippled Grale with him, Bane returned to Eldest Tree and waited until two Iron Wolves drove the last wagon to the roundhouse. The men climbed down and mounted their horses. Finnigal and the seventeen other riders came into view, and the troop rode off toward the west.

"Time to pay my compliments to a dear relative," said Bane. "Grale, you get ready to drive the wagon. You two come with me."

Bane walked across to the double doors of the roundhouse, Gryffe and Valian just behind him. Throwing open the doors the three men strode inside. A large number of people were gathered at the center fire, and Lady Meria was talking to them. She fell silent as Bane approached. He looked into her eyes and saw both anger and astonishment.

"Grandmother, how nice it is to meet you at last," said Bane.

"Get out of my sight!" she shouted. It surprised him that after the first glance she did not look at him but turned her face away.

Bane grinned, then scanned the faces of the crowd. Most of them were elderly, but there were some young women with small children by their sides. "The Vars will be here soon," he told them. "The old ones they will kill, and the babes and toddlers. The young women they will not kill. Not immediately. But when they are finished with them, they will cut their throats. That is the Var way with prisoners they cannot take home as prizes."

"There are no Vars," said an old man. "Lady Meria has assured us—"

"If Lady Meria is right, then you will all spend a few uncomfortable days and nights in open country. If she is wrong, you are all dead," said Bane.

"You will leave now!" commanded Meria. "You are not welcome here!"

He bowed. "As you command, lady, so shall it be." Stepping forward, he ducked down, threw his arm around Meria's hips, and hoisted her to his shoulder. She shouted and rammed her fists against his lower back. Ignoring her, he swung toward the outraged crowd, many of whom had risen to their feet. "When the Vars come," he thundered, "have the courage to kill the children quickly." He started to walk away.

"Where are you going with her, you brute?" shouted a middle-aged woman.

"To safety, lady. I suggest you all follow us."

With that he carried the struggling Meria out of the round-house and lowered her to the back of the wagon. "Understand this," he told her, his voice cold and hard. "If you run, I shall catch you and tie you to the wagon. You have lost a little dignity today. You will lose far more if I have to drag you through the mud and tie your hands and feet."

"You will pay for this with your life!" she hissed.

The crowd began to move out of the roundhouse and cluster around the wagon. At that moment an armored rider came galloping from the east. His horse thundered over the second bridge, and he brought it to a stop before the round-house. "Where is Captain Finnigal?" he called.

"He is on the hilltop, scouting the ground," said Bane. "Have you sighted the Vars?"

"Aye, two hundred of them. They're right behind me."

"Bara's teeth, man, how far east did you ride?"

"The captain said to go no more than a mile. So I waited on Giant's Tooth until I caught sight of them."

Bane swore long and loud. Had the man been sent farther east, he would have seen the Vars earlier and the news would have given the civilians greater incentive to evacuate Three Streams. But there was no point in hammering such a truth home now. Bane addressed the crowd. "We can take fifteen of the oldest and most infirm in the wagon," he said. "The rest of you better run for your lives."

The Vars had marched just under sixty miles in three days, but there was little sign of weariness among them. Snarri Dagger-bright marched at the head of his little army, his second in command, Dratha, beside him.

"One more mile," said Snarri, licking his misshapen lips. The rain had eased, the sun now shining brightly through a break in the clouds. Snarri had never been this deep into Rig-ante territory before. The lands were lush and fertile, unlike the rocky slopes of his home. The cattle they saw were, de-spite the harshness of the winter, already fattening well on the new grass. Snarri thought of his farm, which was more stone than soil, the crops withered and thin. Seeing this verdant land made him realize more than ever why Shard was deter-mined to conquer it.

Snarri glanced back at his men, their mail shirts gleaming in the sunlight. On the first day of the march the Vars had been uneasy. Despite the assurances from Shard they scanned the horizon, constantly expecting to see a Rigante force. By the second day they were more relaxed. Snarri promised them women and plunder and a rich harvest for the gods of blood.

"I've never had a Rigante woman," Dratha said on the second day.

"Hellcats, every one of them," Snarri told him. "Unless you beat them unconscious, it takes three men to hold one down. They'll scratch, punch, kick, and bite. You get no pleading from them, and they stare at you with murder in their eyes. Ah, but it is an experience to treasure."

Dratha considered this information. "I thought old Lars had a Rigante wife once."

"Nah, she was Perdii. Softer. Once he got her back from the raid, she settled down well. Lars said she only needed the lash a few times. After that she was fine. But I knew a man tried to take a Rigante woman for his wife—snatched her on a raid. Nothing but trouble. Ran away three times. He lashed her, beat her, broke her arm if I remember. She cut his throat one night, then she cut off his balls and nailed them to the door."

"I remember that," said Dratha. "I was about ten. Didn't she jump off a cliff or something?"

"Aye. We had her cornered, but she ran to the cliff top and leapt. Three hundred feet she fell. Tide was out. Not a pretty sight when we found her." He laughed. "But prettier than she would have looked had we taken her alive. No, take my ad-vice, Dratha. When we get to the village, find a married woman with a small child. They'll do anything to protect their young."

At the base of the last hill Snarri called a halt and gathered his men around him. "Three Streams is just over the rise," he told them. "We go in fast and hard, kill every man and old woman you see. The younger women will be taken alive and bound. No pleasures to be taken until the settlement is secure. Does everyone understand that?" He looked around into the stern faces of his fighters. No one spoke. "Good. Now, there is one older woman who must be taken alive. Her name is Meria. She is around five and a half feet tall, with long silver hair and green eyes. Kill no old women with green eyes. Take them and bind them."

"What about soldiers?" asked a man close by.

"A troop of twenty Iron Wolves traveled with Meria. They need to be taken out first. Two more points to remember: A few of the villagers will run into the hills. Do not pursue them. Concentrate on those left in the settlement. And second, no plundering until I give the word. When all the Rigante are dead—save maybe a few women for later pleasures—we will loot the homes. We will then divide the spoils evenly and equally. Are there any other questions?" Again no one spoke. Snarri drew his sword. "Then let us begin the slaughter," he said.

He led the way up the steep hill. The rain had made it treacherous, and as they pushed on, it became more so. One man at the rear lost his footing in the newly churned mud, slipped, and slid on his backside all the way to the foot of the hill. The Vars hooted and jeered, and shamefaced, the warrior scrambled up to join them.

Snarri reached the top of the hill and saw a column of fleeing refugees heading toward the west. He swore loudly. A wagon packed with women was moving slowly up the hillside opposite. One of the occupants was a middle-aged woman with silver hair. She was wearing a fine gown edged with gold. Snarri swore again. "First share of the loot to the men who capture that wagon," he shouted. Drawing his longsword, he set off down the hill, the Vars streaming behind him.

* * *

The four horses were straining to drag the wagon up the muddy incline, the iron-shod wheels sinking deeply. Bane, Gryffe, and Valian pushed from the back, but slowly the wagon ceased its upward movement.

"Everyone off!" yelled Bane. He glanced up at the hilltop some forty paces ahead. "You'll have to make it on foot." People began to clamber down. One elderly woman slipped and began to slide. Gryffe threw himself down, catching hold of the woman's dress. For a moment they both slid, then Gryffe clawed at the mud. His hand hit a buried stone, halting the slide. Valian moved back to help the woman to her feet. Three hundred yards away the Vars had entered the settlement and were racing toward the hill. Freed of the extra weight, the wagon surged forward. An old man stumbled close by. Bane lifted him to his feet and helped him up the slope. At the top Bane called out for the bowmen to line the crest. He looked at Wik, who was very pale, his eyes wide and frightened.

"Do not shoot until they reach the hill itself," yelled Bane. "They'll not be able to come up it fast. When you've emptied your quivers, fall back."

"Damn right we'll fall back!" said Wik, licking his lips nervously.

"The rest of you line up behind the bowmen!" shouted Bane. The outlaws shuffled into line. Bane swung to Gryffe. "You think they'll stand?" he whispered.

Gryffe shrugged. "No way to tell. But I will!"

Finnigal and his nineteen Iron Wolves had tethered their horses some fifty feet back from the hilltop. He led his men forward and glanced down at the charging Vars.

Bane moved in close to the young officer. "You mind a word of advice, Captain?" he asked, keeping his voice low.

"I'm listening."

"Spread your men through the line. Some of the outlaws are looking terrified. Having Iron Wolves among them will stiffen their resolve."

"That's good thinking," agreed Finnigal. He grinned suddenly. "I'm feeling a little terrified myself."

The Vars reached the foot of the hill, and a bloodcurdling

roar erupted from them. Wik was standing, bow bent, staring down at them. Bane saw that his hands were trembling.

"Take aim and shoot on my command!" shouted Bane. The fifty outlaw bowmen drew back on their bowstrings. "Now!"

Fifty shafts slashed through the air. Many of the Vars were carrying iron-rimmed shields, and most of the shafts slammed into them or bounced from iron helms. One man fell, an arrow through his forehead. Several others were hit in the legs or arms.

"Again!" yelled Bane. "Hit them with everything!"

The second volley was far more deadly than the first, for the charge had slowed as the Vars labored up the slippery hillside. Now, as men fell, they slid into the paths of those following, knocking them down or causing them to lower their shields. By Bane's reckoning at least twenty Vars were down. "Keep it going!" he bellowed.

Volley after volley hit the climbing men. As the Vars came closer, the volleys became more ragged, many of the shafts flashing over their heads or into the ground. "Steady now!" shouted Bane. "Steady!"

As the enemy came closer to the hilltop, Bane saw that the width of their line would allow the Vars to encircle the defenders. Moving back from the crest, he shouted for his men to spread out along both sides.

Suddenly Wik dropped back, turned, then sprinted away from the crest. He still had several arrows in his quiver. The other bowmen saw him run, and they, too, scrambled back behind the mail-shirted warriors.

"Forward!" yelled Finnigal, drawing his sword. At the center of the line Bane drew his two short swords and advanced.

The Vars reached the crest. Bane leapt forward, spearing one blade through a man's throat and slashing the second across the face of the warrior beside him. Both men fell back, impeding those behind. Gryffe, with a bellowed battle cry, hurled himself at the Vars, swinging his sword double-handed. It smashed into a hurriedly raised shield, but such was the force of the blow that it knocked the bearer from his feet.

The air was filled with the sound of clashing blades, the screams of the wounded, the ugly snarls and grunts of the fighting men, the snapping of bones, and the rending of flesh.

Slipping and sliding on the treacherous ground, the Vars could not at first make use of the weight of their numbers to force a way through. But then Snarri and Dratha got a foothold on the crest. Snarri lashed his sword against the un-protected thigh of a defender. Blood sprayed out, and the man fell. Snarri pushed past him. Dratha, following, hammered his single-bladed ax through the man's skull. Other Vars streamed over the hilltop.

Ahead Snarri could see the silver-haired woman. She was standing by the wagon, watching the battle, and she was close enough for Snarri to see her green eyes. He and Dratha moved toward her.

Bane, seeing the breach in the line, dropped back and ran to fill it. He killed two Vars and kicked out at a third who had just reached the crest. The man slipped and fell, rolling back into his fellows. Gryffe raced to join Bane. A sword blade rammed into his side. The mail shirt stopped the blade slicing into his flesh, but Gryffe felt a rib snap under the impact. Dropping his sword, he lunged at the Var, punching him full in the face. Then he grabbed him at the throat and groin, heaved him into the air, and hurled him into a group of Sea Wolves about to clear the crest. Sweeping up his blade, Gryffe gave a great shout and threw himself at the charging men. His sword hammered against an iron helm, splitting it in two, the blade crushing the skull beneath. Finnigal and two Iron Wolves joined him and closed the breach.

As Snarri and Dratha ran at the woman by the wagon, a slim warrior moved to stand before her. Snarri saw that the man was middle-aged, with only one eye. The Var leader leapt to the attack. Instead of jumping back or parrying, the one-eyed man ducked under the sweeping blade and sent a deadly thrust at Snarri's face. The huge Var swayed away from the thrust and kicked out, catching the one-eyed warrior in the knee. The Rigante stumbled. Dratha stepped in swiftly, bring-ing his ax down on the man's shoulder. The snapping of bone followed, and the Rigante cried out. Then he surged to his feet, the ax still embedded in his flesh. Dratha tried to leap back, but the warrior's sword opened his throat in a bloody spray. Snarri swung his longsword at the Rigante's neck but mistimed the stroke, the blade clanging against the man's helm, knocking it from his head. Dazed, the Rigante tried to turn, but Snarri's reverse sweep smashed his skull to shards.

Another fighter loomed before him. Snarri blinked. The man was wearing an iron breastplate, helm, and greaves styled in the Stone fashion, and he was carrying two short swords. His face and arms were spattered with blood. Snarri attacked, but the warrior moved like quicksilver, blocking his thrust and spinning into him. The Rigante's shoulder struck Snarri in the chest, knocking him back. He struggled to recover his balance only to see, in the last heartbeat of his life, a silver blade flash before his eyes. It struck his jaw, glanced down into his neck, and ripped through bone, tendon, and vein. Snarri was already dead as the second blade hit his neck from the other side, severing the head completely.

Back at the crest of the hill the fighting was chaotic and furious. Of the 200 Vars who had made the charge only around 110 had made it to the crest. Of these, more than half were down. But so were many of the defenders. Gryffe, blood-covered now, was still fighting furiously, as was Finnigal. But they had been pushed back. Bane charged into the fray, his gladiatorial skills raising the spirits of the defenders as he cut down Var after Var.

Finnigal went down. A Sea Wolf carrying a battle-ax loomed over him. Bane leapt at him feetfirst, hurling him to the ground. Finnigal rolled and smashed his sword across the man's face. The captain climbed to his feet to see Bane launch himself at three Vars. Half-stunned, Finnigal staggered to his aid.

At that moment men began to rush past the dazed soldier, throwing themselves upon the Vars, stabbing them with hunting knives and daggers. It was the bowmen who had fled the field earlier. Catching his breath, Finnigal watched as they ripped into the exhausted Sea Wolves. He glanced around to see the outlaw leader Wik draw back on his bowstring. The shaft tore through the chest of a tall, wide-shouldered Var, his body pitching back over the hill and sliding all the way to the bottom. More arrows followed, and some of the surviving Vars began to run back down the hill. On the hilltop the remaining Vars were still fighting furiously. Bane ran at them,

Gryffe and Valian just behind him. Finnigal tried to follow, but a great weariness settled on him and he sat down heavily.

The fighting was over within a few minutes, his sergeant Prasalis knocking the last Var to the ground before braining him with several vicious blows. Prasalis looked around, saw Finnigal sitting alone, and ran over to him.

"Are you hurt, sir?" he asked, kneeling down.

"Aye, but I'll live . . . I think," said Finnigal. Blood was streaming from several cuts to his legs and upper arms, and there was a gash on his brow that was dripping blood into his eyes. Prasalis pulled a cloth from his belt and wiped the gash.

"There's nothing too deep, and your skull isn't cracked."

"How many did we lose?" asked Finnigal.

"I'll find out, sir," said Prasalis, moving away.

Bane, his swords sheathed and his helm discarded, walked over to where Wik was standing, staring down over the settlement. The outlaw had an odd expression in his face that Bane could not read.

"Good to see you," Bane said with a smile. "Thought you might have left us."

"I did leave you," said Wik. "I was pissing myself with fear."

"Then why did you come back?"

Wik shrugged. "I've been asking myself the same thing. The other five gold pieces, I expect."

"Nonsense," said Bane. "You came back because you're a man. Don't belittle yourself. How do you feel?"

"Truly? I feel sad, and I can't tell you why."

Bane placed his hand on the man's shoulder. "We saved hundreds of lives today. We stood our ground, and we won. But I feel sad, too." He smiled. "And I don't know why, either. We'll talk later. For now let's see to the men."

Prasalis returned to Finnigal and helped the captain to the wagon. "We'd better get those wounds stitched," said the sergeant, "or you'll bleed to death."

"What are our losses?"

"Eleven of our men and sixty of the outlaws dead or dying. The Vars lost 164 men. The survivors fled to the east."

Finnigal leaned against the side of the wagon. He saw

Bane walk over and stand beside the body of a dead outlaw. "Who was he?" called out Finnigal.

"His name was Grale," said Bane. "I almost killed him two years ago. A friend of mine told me that he was once a hero, that he had fought bravely at Cogden Field." Bane glanced across at the silent figure of Meria. "He died for you, lady," he said. "I hope you have the grace to remember his name."

From the hills to the west came the refugees from Three Streams. Vorna and a group of the women began to move among the wounded, tending them.

Bane called Gryffe and Valian to him, then walked over to Finnigal. "With your permission, Captain, I'll take some men and pursue the Vars, keep them on the move."

Finnigal reached out and shook Bane's hand. "I appreciate everything you've done. I never was in command, but I'll not forget your courtesy. Go on! Give chase. And then come back and we'll have a drink together . . . Cousin."

◇ *13* ◇

THE GLOOMY ESTIMATE of Prasalis of sixty outlaws "dead or dying" would have been accurate but for the arrival of Vorna. Eighteen of the men with mortal wounds were brought back from the brink, as were three of the badly wounded Iron Wolves. There were no survivors among the Vars, for the outlaws moved among the wounded, killing all who still breathed. The folk of Three Streams stripped the dead of their weapons and armor, and according to the orders of Finnigal, the forty-two outlaw dead were buried in a mass grave, the bodies of the Vars burned on a massive funeral pyre. Bane and his twenty riders returned to the settlement at dusk, having hunted down the fleeing Vars and killing all but three who escaped into the woods to the west. Bane did not stay in Three Streams but rode back to his farm.

In her home Vorna dozed in her chair by the fire, dreaming of past days when the sun seemed brighter, the world infinitely less perilous. Her husband, Banouin, was by her side, and they walked the hills close to the Wishing Tree woods. These were the days after she had brought Connavar back from the dead, after his fight with the bear, days when the lands of the Rigante were largely peaceful and good men like the mighty Ruathain, Banouin, and the Long Laird seemed immortal, everlasting.

But nothing lasts, thought Vorna, coming out of her doze. Even the mountains will one day be gone, vanished under ice or swallowed into the depths of the ocean. She thought of the men she had healed this day. Merging with them to mend their injuries, she had touched their souls. Many among the outlaws were dark and twisted, yet on this day a bright spark had flickered in them. She wondered if those sparks would catch, the light growing within them, or whether they would burn out quickly, leaving the men much as they had been before.

There was, she knew, such a small distance for a man to walk between good and evil. Connavar the King was considered a good man, devoting his life to the welfare of all Keltoi on this side of the water. Yet once, blinded by rage and despair, he had ridden into a Pannone village and butchered men, women, and children. Sadness touched Vorna then, and her eyes filled with tears.

"No point crying for what is already past," she told herself aloud.

There came a knock at the door. Vorna took a deep breath. She knew who had come to her house and was not relishing the visit. "Come in, Meria," she called.

The king's mother moved hesitantly into the firelit room. In the gentle flickering light she looked younger, more like the woman Vorna had once known. But she is not that woman, Vorna reminded herself.

"I hope you do not mind me calling so late," said Meria.

"What is it you want?" asked Vorna, keeping her voice neutral.

"I . . . wanted to thank you for saving my grandson."

"Sit yourself," said Vorna, knowing that answer was not the whole truth.

Meria removed her pale green and blue checkered cloak and sat down in the chair opposite. Folding the cloak carefully, she rested it over her lap. "I have been foolish, Vorna," she said, not looking at the witch but staring instead at the flames of the fire. "In all my life I have only truly loved one man. My Varaconn."

"But not Ruathain," Vorna said harshly, "who died for you?"

"No," admitted Meria. "Not Ru, who deserved better." She gave a deep sigh. "It is said that the people of Stone have three words for love. I do not know what they are, but Brother Solstice explained them to me once. There is love of family or friends, there is the fierce and protective love we have for our children, and there is the all-consuming erotic love burning with the flames of devotion and adoration. It is perhaps wrong to say that I did not love Ru. For I loved him as deeply as one would a big brother. But Varaconn was my love and my life. When he died, a part of me—perhaps the best part of me—was laid to rest in the earth beside him." The fire was burning low, and Meria leaned down to add a log to the flames. "I thought I had remembered his face, the contours, the smile. I had recalled him as looking like my Connavar save that his hair and beard were golden. But I had not, Vorna. Over the years I had forgotten."

"Then you saw Bane," said Vorna.

"Aye, I saw Bane. And in him I saw Varaconn. It was as if he had stepped through a gate in time. Oh, Vorna! What have I done with my life?" Tears began to fall. "I let my grandson die. I almost doomed the settlement. I have become a harridan, unloved by all. But worse, far worse, I turned my back on Connavar's only son."

"Yes, you did these things," Vorna said coldly, "and they cannot be changed. All our deeds have consequences, and we must face them. You are now facing yours."

Meria brushed away her tears. "You are not making this easy for me, Vorna."

"No, I am not."

"Do you hate me so much?"

"I do not hate anyone," Vorna told her. "Once we were friends, and I treasure those memories. Now we are not. I can live with that. It interests me to know why you chose to end that friendship."

"I was wrong to do so," said Meria. "It was weak of me and petty. It happened after I learned of Ruathain's death at the great battle. Brother Solstice told me that Ru had a diseased heart and that you had been tending him. He said that you had warned Ru not to fight. But I did not know of his condition. You recall my son's *geasa*?"

"Of course. I prophesied it. He will die on the day he kills the dog that bites him."

"Exactly. And Conn was bitten by a dog. The hound's teeth locked on to Conn's wrist guard and did not break the flesh. When I told Ru, he said that this was not a true bite. I took no notice. I was so terrified that Conn would be killed in the following day's battle that I urged Ru to go with him and defend him. I told him—may the gods forgive me—that he had once promised to defend Varaconn and had failed and that he must not fail again."

"And he did not fail," said Vorna. "He fought all day alongside Connavar. His heart gave out only after the battle. But why did this cause you to hate me?"

"I did not have the courage to blame myself for his death," said Meria, "so I convinced myself that had you told me of his condition, I would never have sent him into battle. Thus his death became your fault, not mine. And then, when you befriended Bane, my hatred grew. I look back at what I have become and I am ashamed, Vorna."

"Then change," said Vorna, "but know this: It is too late."

"Too late? What do you mean?"

"It is too late for you to forge a relationship with Bane. He needed you as a babe, as a toddler, as a child. He does not need you now. Nor does he want you."

"But you are his friend, Vorna. You could explain to him . . ."

"What would I explain to this twenty-year-old warrior who has grown to manhood despised and rejected by his family? He needs no explanations. He knows. He watched his mother die before her time, weighed down by the contempt of others who blamed her alone for Connavar's loss. Now he is a man and because of the disappointments of his childhood has no desire for familial affection. Your time to build a relationship with Bane has long gone. If you truly desire to change, then let that change show with those children who might yet benefit from it, your own grandchildren, Orrin and Badraig."

"Then you will not help me?" said Meria, her face hardening, her green eyes gleaming in the firelight.

Vorna laughed. "Now that is the Meria I know."

Meria slumped back in her chair, the light of anger fading from her eyes. "I suppose that it is," she said. "But I don't want to be her anymore. Tonight I tried to cuddle Orrin, and he ran away from me. He was frightened."

"These things take time," said Vorna, her voice softening. She rose from the chair. "I will make some tisane, and we will talk of happier days."

* * *

Three days passed with no news of the great battle being waged between the Rigante and the Vars near Seven Willows. The people of Three Streams went about their business, but they were fearful. What if Connavar was to fail? What if, after they had defeated a few hundred Vars, ten thousand were to appear in the distance? Scouts were sent out to watch the eastern horizon, and people left many of their clothes and belongings packed, ready for flight.

On the morning of the fourth day a rider came galloping over the hills. As he came closer, they saw he was one of Bendegit Bran's horse archers, his silver mail shirt gleaming in the sunshine, his bow tied to his saddle. His horse thundered over the first bridge and down into the settlement center. People ran from their homes, anxious for news. He waited until more than fifty were gathered, with still more pouring in.

"Victory!" he shouted. "The Vars are defeated, their king slain."

A huge cheer went up, and word spread fast through Three Streams. Men and women gathered around the rider. His horse became skittish and reared. People fell back then. The rider calmed his mount and leapt down from his saddle, leading the nervous horse to the corral alongside the forge. "Where is Lady Meria?" he asked. Men pointed to her house, and the horse archer strode across the open ground, a huge crowd following. He turned to them. "I will give a full report at the roundhouse in an hour. First I must deliver messages to the king's mother and to the wife of Bendegit Bran."

He left them then and walked to the front door of the house. It was open, and Gwen was standing in the doorway.

"Is Bran alive?" she asked.

The rider removed his black leather helm and bowed. "He is alive and well, my lady. I am Furse, son of Ostaran, and I have a letter for you." Opening the pouch at his side, he pulled forth two wax-sealed letters. He gave the first to Gwen.

Meria emerged from the kitchen, flour on her hands. "I heard the shouting," she said. "I take it my son has won another great battle?"

"Indeed he has, Lady Meria."

"Gwen, fetch our guest a cup of ale. He must be thirsty after such a ride. Then he can sit and tell us all the news." Meria looked at the rider closely as Gwen moved past her into the kitchen. He was slender and not tall, his pale hair cut short after the fashion of the men of Stone. "Do I not know you, young man?" Meria asked.

"You do, lady. I am Furse. My father—"

"Ah, yes, Ostaran the Gath. I like him. He makes me laugh. Sit you down, sir."

Gwen returned with a mug brimming with ale. Furse thanked her and drank deeply. Then he sat and gave a wide smile.

"We smashed them," he said. "Bendegit Bran organized the deployments. It was his strategy. We took them on three sides, forcing them up onto the Hallowed Hills. Then Connavar led the Iron Wolves against their left flank, splitting their force. They fought hard, these Vars, but it was an easy victory. They tried to hold to the hilltops, but we drove them off. At the last King Shard tried to lead his men in a charge, attempting, I think, to break and run for their ships. But Bran had thought of this, and my father's horse archers cut them off.

"Ah, ladies, but the finish was glorious. Shard—a mighty man and fully six and a half feet tall—stood alone upon a narrow bridge. His men were dead or fleeing the field, but he stood brave and strong and taunted us, calling for a champion to fight him man to man. Three he killed before King Connavar rode up. Shard saw him and called out: 'At last a foe worthy of my blade.'

"The king drew his sword and stepped out to meet him. The battle was brief, ladies, but wondrous. When Shard fell, the king knelt by him. I was one of those close by, and I moved in to hear what passed between them. Shard spoke, but the words were whispered, and I did not catch them. Then Shard reached up and took the king's hand. I heard Connavar say, 'And on that day there will be no hatred between us.' Then Shard died."

"What were our losses?" asked Meria.

"More than two thousand slain, my lady, and at least five thousand wounded. As I said, these Vars are tough men. The king ordered a day of rest, but after that the army will be heading south to face Jasaray. Our scouts tell us that the army of Stone numbers thirty thousand and three thousand cavalry."

"My son will defeat them," said Meria. "It is his destiny."

"Yes, lady," said Furse. Then he remembered the letter he carried. He passed it to Meria. "I fear the contents will sadden you. I will allow you to read it in private." He rose, but Meria beckoned him to seat himself.

"If my sons are alive and we have a victory, I can think of nothing to sadden me," she said. Breaking the seal, she held the letter at arm's length, squinting to see the large script. She finished the letter, then leaned back in her chair, eyes closed.

"What is it?" asked Gwen. Meria merely shook her head, rose from the chair, and walked from the room. Gwen turned back to Furse. "Do you know what was in the letter?"

"I believe I do, lady. There were Pannone rebels among the Vars, perhaps three hundred or so. They were led by Guern, a noble from the far north. He and seven of his men escaped, but we will find him." Furse looked away. "But there was another with them. He was spotted fleeing the field. Our outriders could have taken him, but they were so surprised that they held back." Furse sighed. "It was the king's brother, Braefar. He was with the enemy."

Wik drained another cup of uisge. He had hoped to get drunk, but the alcohol seemed to have little effect on him. The sixty survivors of the hilltop battle had not returned to the forest but were camped at Bane's farm, sharing the roundhouse huts of Bane's workers. Wik himself had been offered, and had accepted, a room in the main building. The next day Bane and Gryffe had carried a chest from one of the barns and paid each man the sum promised. Wik himself had been given more than one hundred pieces of gold, the extra five he had been promised plus two more for each man slain. It was more gold than Wik had seen in his thirty-one years. He gave it away, distributing it equally among the survivors. The act amazed him, and even now, a day later, he could not imagine why he had done it. The sense of sadness that had followed the battle had not left him, and even the alcohol could not numb it.

Bane found him sitting in the hayloft of the first barn, staring out over the hills. The young warrior, carrying a fresh jug of uisge and a lighted lantern, climbed to the loft and sat beside the outlaw chief. The sun was dipping below the mountains, and the land spread out before them was glowing in its fading light.

Bane hung the lantern on a peg, then filled Wik's cup and his own. "If we had stayed in Three Streams," he said, "they'd probably have thrown a feast for us."

"A pox on their feasts," said Wik.

Bane laughed. "I have never seen you this sour," he said. "Are you this way after every heroic act?"

"How would I know?" countered Wik. "This was my first."

"Then what ails you, Wik?"

"I wish I knew." He glanced at the man beside him. "That chest was almost empty by the end, Bane. Are you a poor man now?"

"I've as much left as you," he answered with a smile.

"Then what a pair of fools we are," said Wik. The far hills turned to gold for a moment with the last blazing light of the dying sun. "Ah, but that was pretty," he said as darkness fell. "You know that most of the men who died were newcomers? They weren't really outlaws, just poor folk who had no food in the winter. Some were Pannone, others Norvii. There was even a Cenii lad. Yet they put on the armor you gave them, and they fought like . . . like . . ."

"Heroes," said Bane.

"Aye, heroes." Wik hawked and spit through the opening. "And for what? People who wouldn't have given them a crust of stale bread if they were dying of starvation. I saw Boile go down. They damn near hacked off his arm, and he carried on fighting. He was a stupid man, was Boile. And he was frightened of the dark. Last summer his hut burned down because he left the fire blazing." Wik laughed. "He came running out with his leggings ablaze." His smile faded. "What in the name of Taranis was he doing standing his ground like that?"

"Why did you come back?" asked Bane.

Wik shrugged. "I have no idea whatever. Did you see Grale defending the king's mother? Ah, of course you did. You killed the second of them." Wik shook his head. "Part of me wishes I'd never listened to you, Bane. I should have stayed in the forest. I knew who I was there."

"Who were you?"

Wik thought about the question. "I was nothing, though I didn't know it. Now I do."

"So what will you do? Go back to the forest?"

"I haven't made up my mind." Wik suddenly shielded his eyes from the glare of the lantern and looked out of the opening. "Riders coming," he said. "Soldiers!" He swore and clambered to his feet. He swayed and almost pitched from the loft, but Bane caught him.

"I don't think they've come to arrest you," said Bane. "Sit here. I'll see what they want." He climbed down the wooden steps and walked from the barn. Some of the other outlaws had seen the soldiers, and Bane saw that they were nervous. He calmed them and ordered them to continue the preparations for the feast he had arranged.

There were some thirty soldiers, all dressed in the black and silver armor of the Iron Wolves. But at their head rode a man in a patchwork cloak. Bane felt his stomach tighten. Moonlight shone down, and Bane stood his ground, his eyes fixed on the king of legend. He was a big man, wide-shouldered, his long red and silver hair unbraided, his white-streaked beard cut close to his chin. He rode easily, sitting tall in the saddle. Bane felt his anger rise but forced it down.

The riders came down the hill, skirted the paddock, and drew to a halt. The king stepped down and approached the waiting warrior. Bane looked into his odd-colored eyes, the mirror of his own. "What do you want here?" he asked.

"We need to talk," said Connavar, moving past him and striding toward the house. Angry now, Bane followed him.

Connavar pushed open the door and walked into the main room. Gryffe and Iswain were sitting by the fire. They both rose as Connavar entered. The huge red-bearded warrior stared at the newcomer, then recognized him and bowed. "It's the king," he hissed to Iswain.

The plump woman folded her arms across her chest. "Not my king," she said.

Bane walked in. Connavar removed his cloak and swirled it over the back of a chair. Then he moved to the fire and warmed his hands. Gryffe glanced at Bane, who signaled for them both to leave the room. They did so. As the door shut behind them, Bane spoke. "Make this brief," he said, "for you are not welcome in my house."

Connavar straightened from the fire and turned. "That is understandable," he said, "and believe me, it is not my wish to be here."

"Then why come?"

"Two reasons. I have brought gold for the outlaws who helped Finnigal defend Three Streams. I understand you have promised them two coins each. I will double that and repay you. I expect no one else to suffer a loss for defending my family."

"You intend to pardon them for their crimes?"

"Is that the price they asked for their aid?" queried the king, contempt in his voice.

Bane gave a cold smile. "They don't need anything from you, you arrogant bastard! No more do I. Keep your gold and choke on it! What I did was not for Meria or the good folk of Three Streams. It was for Vorna. It was for friendship. As for the outlaws, yes, they came because I promised them gold, but they stayed and died because they were men. Now speak your piece and then get out!"

Connavar's eyes blazed. "Beware, boy. My patience has a limit."

"As indeed does your gratitude," said Bane. "I expected no thanks from you. I expected what I have always received from you: nothing at all. I had thought, however, you would have gathered these men who fought for you and thanked them. For without them your mother would be dead and your beloved Three Streams a pile of smoldering ash."

For a moment he thought the king was going to attack him, such was the fury in the man's eyes. But Connavar stood very still, and Bane saw him struggle to remain calm. "There is truth in what you say, Bane," he said at last. "And I am at fault here. Gather your men, and I will speak to them. The other matter can wait until later."

Bane had no need to gather the outlaws. Word had spread that the battle king had come to the farm. The fabled Demonblade was among them. As Connavar strode out into the open, they were huddled just beyond the front door. They fell back and opened a path as he walked through to the fire pit. Men gazed at the patchwork cloak made up of the symbols of five tribes: the pale blue and green of the Rigante, the black of the Gath, the yellow and green of the Pannone, the blue stripes of the Norvii, and even the red circle on yellow of the southern Cenii. The cloak alone said it all: This man was beyond tribal dispute. This man was the high king of the Keltoi.

The flames from the fire pit shone on his breastplate and greaves, glittering red on the rings of his mail shirt. The men stood in silence as he moved among them.

Gryffe came out from the house and moved alongside Bane. "Gives you the shivers, doesn't he?" he whispered.

When Connavar spoke, his voice was low and deep, but it rumbled like thunder in the silence.

"Two days ago," he told them, "we fought a mighty battle against the Vars. Twelve thousand Rigante, Pannone, and Norvii against fifteen thousand Sea Wolves. The grass of the field was red with blood, and the streams ran crimson. Great heroism was seen on that day—on both sides! Men of courage and valor, men who carried mountains on their shoulders. We were outnumbered, but we were fighting for hearth and home, fighting to protect our women and our children. That is the nature of a true man.

"But you, my friends, were not fighting for your loved ones or your homes. You stood against a foe who was not your enemy. You fought for those who were not your kin. I was told in Three Streams that you fought for gold. I have seen men who fight for gold. At the first reverse they break and run. Yet many of your number gave their lives on that hilltop. They did not run. They did not plead. They fought! You fought! And in doing so you saved the life of my mother, the wife and children of my brother, Bendegit Bran, and the son of my dearest friend, Fiallach. I am proud of you all, and to each of you I offer my thanks.

"Every one of my soldiers receives payment for his services, and you on that day of courage were my soldiers. I have therefore brought gold for each of you. And with it I offer you a pardon for all crimes committed before this day. Where is the man Wik?"

"I am here," said Wik, striding out of the group.

Connavar offered his hand, and Wik shook it. "In two days," said the king, "I ride south to face the greatest enemy of all. I need good men, Wik. Will you join my horse archers?"

"I will," said Wik.

"Good man." Connavar raised his voice. "Any of you who wish to ride with us are welcome. I will supply the horses and the armor, the bows and the shafts. All I ask in return is that you bury those shafts in the hearts of Stone."

A cheer went up, but Wik raised his arms to quell the roar. "It was Bane who led us, Lord King. It was Bane who held the line. What does he receive?"

"Anything he desires of me," replied the king. Another cheer went up. Connavar walked back through the crowd and into the house. Bane followed him, pushing shut the door.

"A fine speech," he said. "It even sounded sincere. I don't doubt they'll now ride into hell for you. Now, what was the second reason you spoke of?"

"You and I must ride to the Wishing Tree woods. Tonight. Alone."

Bane laughed. "And why would I do this?"

"Vorna came to me. She said it was of the utmost importance. Believe me, Bane, I do not want to ride with you. I have never wanted any part of you to touch my life. But Vorna is my friend, and I owe her more than I can ever repay. If you do not wish to ride with me, I will go alone."

Bane was silent for a moment. "And Vorna asked for me to ride with you?"

"Aye, she did."

"Then I will go." He looked into the king's face. "You know, for a long time I wanted to speak with you, to win your respect. And when that proved impossible, I wanted to kill you. Not anymore, Connavar. To me you are just another selfish and arrogant man heading for the grave. You will get there soon enough without my help."

"Are you ready to ride?" asked the king.

"I am ready," said Bane.

* * *

Vorna made her way slowly up the hill toward the Wishing Tree woods. It was an hour before dawn, and the gnarled oaks seemed sinister and threatening in the moonlight. Humans had long avoided the woods, for this was the realm of the Seidh, and the perils within were well known to the Keltoi.

In the past brave heroes had ventured into this dark place. Most had never returned, and one who had was aged beyond all reason. He had entered as a young man, proud, tall, and strong. The next day he had returned as a mewling old man, toothless and tottering, his brain—like his strength—all but disappeared.

Vorna paused before the tree line and sat down on a flat stone. The wind was chilly there, and she wrapped her thick black shawl around her shoulders, lifting the rim over her head. Only one other Rigante, to her knowledge, had walked these woods unscathed: the child Connavar. Vorna sighed. What did the Morrigu want of her now? she wondered. And why did she require both Connavar and Bane?

Closing her eyes, Vorna reached out with her mind, calling upon the Seidh goddess. There was no response. She tried to contact the Thagda, the Old Man of the Forest, the tree man who had aided Connavar in distant days past. Nothing.

Vorna shivered. The wind was bitter, and she yearned to walk into the wood, to sit with her back to a huge oak and block the cold ferocity of this icy breeze. With a single word of command she could have a fire burning, but the wind would blow it away in an instant, she knew.

Slowly and coldly time drifted by. At last she heard the sound of horses pounding on the hillside. Vorna stood and saw the two men riding toward her. This close to Wishing Tree her powers were heightened, and she felt the tension radiating from them and knew that their ride had been a silent one. Sadness touched Vorna. Two good men, kind and brave, held apart by guilt and sorrow, grief and rage.

Connavar drew to a halt before her and stepped down from the saddle. "Well, we are here, Vorna," he said. "What is it you need of us?"

Bane leapt lightly to the ground, moved in close, and embraced the witch. "You are cold," he said, rubbing her back. Removing his black sheepskin cloak, he draped it over her shoulders. Vorna shivered with pleasure at the weight and warmth of it. She turned to Connavar.

"I require nothing of you, Conn, my dear," she said. "The call came from the Morrigu. She came to me in a dream. She said she would meet us here before the dawn."

"Then where is she?" asked Bane.

"I do not know. I have called to her, but she does not reply."

"I have no time for these games," said Connavar. "There is much to do, and time is short. I will wait a little longer, but if she has not come, I will leave."

"She told me to remind you," Vorna said gently, "that you once asked a gift from her and that one day she would call upon you to repay it. This is the time!"

Before Conn could reply there came the flapping of wings from the woods. All three looked around, expecting to see the Morrigu's crow come swooping out of the dark. But then silence fell once more.

"There is something wrong here," whispered Vorna. "I cannot sense her presence."

"Obviously something more important came up," Bane said lightly.

"You may be right," Vorna said softly, "but not in the way that you might imagine. The Morrigu may sometimes appear to be capricious, but she does not lie. She told me that it was vital for the future well-being of the Rigante that you both come to her. Something is wrong," she said again.

She stood in silence. Beyond the woods the distant snow-covered peaks of Caer Druagh began to gleam with the promise of the dawn.

"I am going into the woods," Vorna said suddenly. Conn stepped in close, placing his hand on her shoulder.

"That you must not do," he said. "You will die there, Vorna!"

"I have walked these woods before," she told him.

"Aye, but never uninvited. You told me that even for you entry to these woods without first being called by the Seidh would mean death. Is that not so?"

"Yes, it is so. There are spells that need to be laid aside. Even so, I must make the attempt."

"I'll come with you," said Bane. "I always had a wish to walk these woods."

"Do not be foolish, boy," Connavar said angrily. "This is a magical place, and mortals are not welcome here. You are young and strong. In a few hours you could come stumbling from this place white-haired and stick-thin."

"You think I should leave my friend to face the dangers alone?" Bane asked him coldly.

"Neither of you should enter," insisted Conn. "The Morrigu said she would be here. She is not. The fault is not ours!"

"I must go," said Vorna. "I know this. In all my years I have never felt this strongly about anything. I know in my heart that I must walk these woods. And walk them in faith!"

"But I cannot, Vorna," Conn said sadly. "For the first time in many years I am afraid. To the south is an enemy who will destroy everything we hold dear. All my life I have been preparing for this moment. Can you understand that? I have put aside love and family and all pleasures of the flesh. For twenty years I have labored to give us just one fighting chance of preserving our way of life. If I risk myself now, all may be lost!"

"Then wait here, my dear," said Vorna. "Bane and I will see what is wrong." She turned away from him and, taking Bane's hand, began the walk to the trees. Bane drew one of his swords, but Vorna placed her hand on his wrist. "Put it away," she said. "There is nothing beyond that can be fought with iron."

He sheathed the blade. As they approached the trees, a mist seeped up from the damp earth, forming a wall. Vorna paused, her heart beating fast. "Hold fast to my hand," she whispered, then walked into the mist. It was colder than ice, and it swirled up over their shoulders, clinging to their faces. Blind now, they moved slowly onward. Bane stretched his arm out to the front, moving it back and forth. He could not see his fingers. Neither could he see Vorna, though he felt the warm touch of her hand upon his. Inch by inch they eased their way into the wood. Bane's outstretched hand touched the trunk of a tree, and they moved around it. Time passed, and neither of them had any sense of direction. Vorna stumbled, for the cold was intense, and felt her legs growing numb. Bane pulled her upright.

"This," he said, teeth chattering, "was not the best idea you ever had."

Vorna put her arm around his waist. "I fear that is true," she said. She slumped to the ground. Bane knelt beside her. "It is not over yet," whispered Vorna. "Wait and see."

"It would be nice to see," Bane told her.

They huddled together. Vorna took off Bane's heavy sheep-skin cloak and curled it around the freezing man's shoulders. She spoke a word of power to make a fire. As the flame sprang from her fingers, the mist settled around it, extinguishing it even as it was formed.

"I see something," said Bane. "To the right."

Vorna strained to peer into the mist. Then she saw it: a tiny flicker of light. "Over here!" she called. The light froze in place momentarily, then slowly moved toward them.

The mist parted before it, and they saw Connavar the King advancing into the wood, his Seidh sword held before him, the blade gleaming brightly. The mist receded from it, the gnarled trunks of the old oaks looming out of the gray.

As the last of the mist disappeared, Connavar thrust his sword back into its scabbard. Vorna climbed to her feet and looked into his scarred face. "I knew that you would come," she said. "And do you know why? Because this is the way of life you have been defending, a friend standing by a friend, ready to risk life for the sake of another. This, my dear, is Rigante!"

"Let us find the Old Woman," he said gruffly. But even as he spoke, he put his arm around Vorna and kissed her brow.

The three companions moved farther into the wood. On the ground ahead of them lay a dead bird. It was large and black, the skull above its beak bare of feathers. Bane knelt by the bird. "It is the Morrigu's crow," he whispered.

"Bring it with us," said Vorna.

Bane lifted the bird. He was surprised by the weight. "It is heavier than a puppy," he said.

Vorna walked on, Connavar beside her, Bane following. There was no wind there, the temperature much higher than it was on the hillside. The companions came to a downward slope. "I remember this place," said Connavar. "This is where I came as a child."

Vorna halted in her walk and closed her eyes. "She is close."

They moved on, splashing through a shallow stream and on up a steep slope. Vorna stepped from the trail and pushed her way through the undergrowth to a small clearing. The Morrigu was sitting propped against a tree. Ivy had grown over her legs and had covered one arm. There was moss upon her cloak, and a spider had woven a web from her veil to the tree trunk. Vorna ran to her side.

"How does a goddess die?" whispered Bane.

"She is not dead. Not yet," replied Vorna, laying her hands on the veiled head. A low, feeble groan came from the Morrigu, and her ivy-covered arm twitched.

"Where is my Bab?" she whispered. Vorna swung to Bane.

"Bring her the crow!" Bane knelt on the other side of the Morrigu and laid the dead bird in her lap.

The Morrigu tried to move her arm. Connavar crouched down and ripped away the ivy. Slowly the old woman's hand came up until it rested on the black feathers of the dead crow. She sighed then. Once more Vorna placed her hands on the head of the goddess, sending healing power surging into her. It was little more use than a drop of water to someone dying of thirst.

"I should have passed the gateway long before this," said the Morrigu, her voice a tiny whisper they had to strain to hear. Then her head sagged back against the tree.

"Gateway?" queried Bane.

"Many of the Seidh have already crossed over," said Vorna, "seeking other worlds where magic is still strong. I don't know why she remained so long."

"Where is this gateway?" asked Connavar. "Perhaps we could carry her there!"

"I do not know," said Vorna. "I have not been so far into these woods before."

"Can you not merge with her?" asked Connavar. "You did this once before to save me."

"Merge with a Seidh? I do not know if I could or whether my body or my soul could withstand it."

"It . . . could not," whispered the Morrigu. "And you cannot take me to the gateway. It is guarded by a creature no human can overcome."

Vorna took hold of her hand. "Show me the gateway," she insisted.

A flicker of light glowed from under the skin of the Morrigu's hand and flowed along Vorna's arm. The witch stiffened and cried out. Then she sagged into the arms of Connavar. "Oh, the pain," she whispered. She sat very still for a moment as the burning agony in her head receded. She glanced at the Morrigu, who was once more unconscious. "The gateway is close by," said Vorna. "No more than half a mile to the southeast. It stands within a golden circle of stone. There is a path to it known as Piare la Naich, the Walk of Life. She must be carried along it, her body passing between the two tallest stones. But I saw the monster there. It is hideous and scaled. In some respects it is like a bear, though the talons and teeth are longer and the hide is tougher than leather. You heard what she said: No human can overcome it. What is it that we should do?" she asked Connavar.

The king sighed. "She gave me a gift once, and I have not repaid her. A man should always pay his debts. I will carry her to the gateway, and if necessary I will cut the heart from the beast."

"I fear you will not be able to carry her alone," said Vorna. "A moment ago I lifted her hand. She appears slender and frail, but her body weight is several times that of a grown man."

Connavar pushed his arms under the unconscious Seidh and strained to lift her. "It is as if she is anchored to the ground," he said. He looked at Bane. "Will you help me?" he asked simply.

"Why not?" answered Bane. "It is not every day you get to see a king fight a demon bear."

The two men crouched on either side of the goddess and prepared to lift her. At that moment a glow began beneath the Morrigu's veil. Flickering lights swept along under her skin.

"Release her!" yelled Vorna. But it was too late. Both men began to glow as if fire were burning within them.

* * *

Bane opened his eyes. There was something strange about his vision. He blinked, trying to clear his head. He could see better than ever before. No, not better, he realized. Wider! From this position he could see the trees behind him and before him. How peculiar, he thought. He tried to rise, and pain pricked him. Startled, he tilted his head and looked down. It was not the sharp brambles in which he was trapped that stunned him, causing his heart to flutter wildly. It was the fact that when he looked down, he saw not his own body but the pale legs of a white fawn. Panicked now, he struggled to rise. The thorns cut deep into his legs and flanks. He tried to call out but heard only a frightened bleat. His back legs kicked at the brambles, and he half rose, then fell back. One of the brambles snapped and whiplashed across his face, cutting into the soft skin of his long neck. Then he saw the boy at the edge of the brambles. He was around ten years old, red hair framing a pale, freckled face. He drew an old bronze knife. The child advanced into the brambles, which wrapped themselves around him, tearing his tunic and cutting his skin. For a moment Bane thought the child intended to kill him, and his fawn's body struggled wildly. The child spoke: "Be still, little one. Be still and I will help you."

The voice was soothing. The fawn that was Bane looked into the strangely colored eyes of the child. It is Connavar, he thought. The boy slowly cut away the brambles and lifted the fawn clear.

The world spun, and darkness fell over his vision. When it cleared, he was still being carried, but this time at some speed. He was lying in the arms of a young man who was running awkwardly over the hills. Bane became aware of his own weakness. His arms were thin, lacking muscle and power, and he could not feel his legs at all. His head turned, though he did not will it to do so, and his eyes saw a huge black bear lumbering across the hills in pursuit. Blood was on its snout. And it was gaining. Bane was now looking up into the straining face of the young man carrying him. It was Connavar, young and beardless. His teeth were gritted, his breath coming in ragged gasps. Bane heard a voice and realized it was coming from his own mouth. "Put me down. Save yourself."

The runner stopped, and Bane felt himself being lowered

gently to the grass. The young Connavar drew a dagger and faced the charging beast. "Oh, please run!" Bane heard himself say.

"I'll cut its bastard heart out!" said Connavar, and leapt to face the beast.

Bane watched in silent horror as the bear's talons ripped at the frail body of the young warrior, its teeth crunching down on the shoulder. He fought to the last before being thrown aside like a bloody rag.

The darkness fell again, and when his eyes next opened, his body exploded with agony beyond enduring. He almost blacked out with it. Indeed, he wished he could black out. He was lying facedown on a long table, his wounds bandaged, fire burning through his veins. He saw Vorna sitting beside him. She was younger, but her face showed her exhaustion.

"How are you feeling?" she asked him.

"Better," he heard himself say.

"You will take time to heal, young man."

"I must be strong by the time of the feast," he said. "I am to wed Arian." Bane felt the surge of love and need within the youngster, but he saw also the sadness in Vorna's eyes.

"You must rest now," she ordered him.

Bane-Connavar was sitting upon a pony. He was very tired and weak. Crowds were lining the way, cheering and clapping, and he saw that he was riding into Three Streams. His body was still ablaze with pain, but his head turned back and forth, seeking out the golden-haired girl he had dreamed of for so long. Bane felt his anguish when Connavar realized she was not among those cheering him.

He was helped from his pony, and Bane saw Meria and Ruathain. They helped him to a bed and laid him upon it. The scene shifted and became dark, and from the darkness came a voice: "I suppose you haven't heard about Arian. She married Casta at the Feast of Samain."

A groan came from the stricken youngster, and Bane felt sorrow engulf him.

"I'm sorry, Conn. I tried to tell you that she didn't care for you," said the voice.

Bane felt the grief and with it almost a seeping away of the will to live. All that saved the young man was a seed of anger, which flowered in his heart like a rose tipped with acid.

"Bane! Bane!" The voice seemed to come from far away, and he felt Vorna's hands on his shoulders, dragging him back from the body of the Morrigu. He groaned and sat down upon the earth. Then he looked across at the still figure of Connavar, crouched over the Old Woman. Bane rolled to his knees and rose unsteadily. Staggering to the king, he dragged him back and laid him on the grass.

"What happened?" Bane asked Vorna.

"Her spirit flowed into you. I thought it would kill you."

Bane rubbed his hands over his eyes. "I saw things, Vorna. I watched Connavar fight the bear. I saw . . . him, in the cave, speak to you about my mother."

"He loved her very dearly," she said softly. "They were to be wed."

"I know. She . . . betrayed him."

"Do not think of it as betrayal," she said. "Arian was a fey and troubled woman. She needed someone to lean on, to keep the darkness at bay. Everyone thought Conn would die. This terrified Arian, so she wed Casta. But all this is in the past now. Let it go."

The king grunted and sat up. "We will need to make a stretcher," he said. "I could not go through that again."

"What did you see?" Vorna asked.

"We must cut poles," said Connavar, "and thread them through Bane's cloak. It is the strongest cloth we have. I believe it will take her weight."

He pushed himself to his feet. Vorna moved to stand before him. "What did you see, Conn?"

"Too much," he told her. Drawing his sword, he walked away into the trees, returning with two stout lengths of wood. Taking his dagger, he chopped twigs and leaves from the lengths. Then he spread Bane's sheepskin cloak upon the earth and cut a series of slits along both sides before sliding the poles through them.

"We've still got to lift her onto it," said Bane.

"Aye," agreed Connavar. "Let's do it quickly."

Laying the stretcher alongside the Seidh, they took up their positions and heaved her onto it. This time there was no flickering light. Bane and Connavar gathered up the stretcher and followed Vorna toward the southeast. It was heavy going, and both men were sweating profusely as they climbed down the last hill. Before them, in a large clearing, was a circle of standing stones shining golden in the dawn light.

"I can't . . . see any beasts," grunted Bane, his muscles aching.

"Not yet," said Vorna.

Slowly they approached the circle. Once more a mist swelled beneath their feet, swirling over the stones, rising higher and higher, blocking the sunlight. Then the mist thickened, growing blacker and darker, forming a dome of night over the stones. At the center of the circle, beside a long flat altar, a glowing form appeared. Bane and Connavar carried the Morrigu to the edge of the circle and gently laid her down. A low growl came from the creature by the altar. Bane drew his sword and let out a long, low breath. As Vorna had described, the creature was almost eight feet tall, its body covered with silver scales. Its long arms ended in wickedly curved talons. Bane looked into the beast's face. It had a long snout, almost like a wolf, yet with teeth like dagger blades.

"I'll take it from the left, you from the right," said Bane, turning toward the king. "What are you doing?"

Connavar had unbuckled his sword belt and was now removing his breastplate and chain mail, his wrist guards and greaves. "Are you going to fight it naked?" asked Bane.

"I am not going to fight it at all," said Connavar.

"Then what is your plan?"

Connavar knelt beside the stretcher and pushed his arms under the Morrigu. With one enormous heave he staggered to his feet, his knees almost buckling under the weight. He took one faltering step, then another, and crossed the circle past the tallest stone. The beast lumbered toward him. Bane ran into the circle, ducked under a sweeping talon, and lashed his sword against the creature's belly. The sword bounced clear. Something struck Bane in the chest with terrible force, lifting him from his feet and hurling him from the circle. He landed heavily but rolled to his knees in time to see Connavar staggering toward the altar. The scaled beast loomed above him, sending out an ear-piercing roar. The king ignored it and reached the altar, laying the Morrigu and her crow upon it.

As her body touched the stone, the dome of darkness disappeared. Sunlight touched the scaled beast, and it began to shrink and fade. Bane climbed to his feet and, Vorna beside him, walked into the circle. The Morrigu's body began to tremble violently. A flame burst from her chest, setting fire to the cloth of her dress. Fire sprang from her fingers, the flesh falling away dry and stiff, like shards of clay. The veil caught fire, peeling back from her face as flames roared up from her eyes. Brighter and brighter she burned, and the three onlookers stepped farther back from the altar, shielding their eyes.

The fires died down swiftly, but the terrible brightness remained. "Turn away," came the now-powerful voice of the Morrigu, "for you must not see the gateway open." They obeyed her. Then her voice came again. "I have always loved this world, which the Seidh named Tir na Nogh. I have cherished the belief that it will one day feed the soul of the universe from which it sprang. You spoke, Connavar, of spending twenty years seeking to protect the Rigante way of life. I have spent ten thousand years on ten thousand worlds seeking to protect life itself. Life is spirit. One cannot exist without the other. Deep in their hearts the Keltoi understand this. The people of Stone, save for the few cultists among them, do not. I have seen the fall of worlds and the conquests and desolation caused by the armies of lust and greed. Here Stone is the great enemy. On other worlds it is Rome, or Cagaris, or Shefnii, or Pakalin. The names change; the result of the evil remains the same: the death of spirit, the death of worlds." Her voice faded for a moment, then she spoke to the king. "Twenty years ago you asked a gift of me, and I told you there would be a price. That price is a simple one: When your brother calls upon you, do as he bids no matter what else is pending, no matter the time or the greatness of events. You understand? Do as he bids."

"Which brother?" asked Connavar.

"You will know. Do you accept this price?"

"I said that I would," said Connavar. "I will keep this promise—as I should have kept another promise all those years ago."

"That is good," said the Morrigu. "And now to Bane. Will you offer me a gift?"

"What can I offer you, lady?"

"In eight days, on the night of the hunter's moon, you will return to this circle?"

"What then?"

"Whatever you choose. And now . . . farewell."

The light faded. Vorna turned and saw that the altar had disappeared.

"A simple thank you would have been pleasant," said Bane.

Connavar pulled on his mail shirt and breastplate and buckled on his sword belt. Bane approached him. "How did you know the beast would not attack you?" he asked.

"I, too, would like the answer to that," said Vorna.

Connavar knelt and put on his bronze greaves. "The Morrigu took a great risk with us," he said. "She could have made it to the gateway a week ago, as her energy was fading. Instead she stayed where she was in the hope that we would come for her. I read it in her mind. She tried to close her thoughts to me, but by then she was too weak." He straightened. "I always thought of her as a malicious creature, but the depths of her love for this land and its people are beyond belief."

"Yes, yes," said Bane impatiently. "She was a sweet and loving woman. But the beast . . . ?"

"The creature no human could overcome? It was a lesson, Bane. A good man tried to teach it to me many years ago. You cannot overcome hatred with more hatred. Sometimes you have to surrender in order to win. There are only three possibilities when faced with an enemy: run from him, fight him, or make him your friend. The creature in the circle was created to respond. Attack it and it will come back at you with twice your strength. I ignored it. And it, true to its nature, ignored me."

"You sound sad, my dear," said Vorna, moving to his side.

"Oh, that it were only sadness," said Connavar. Then he walked away from them.

Two days later, at the head of ten thousand Iron Wolves and three thousand horse archers, Wik among them, Connavar rode south. The main body of his foot soldiers—just over twenty-five thousand men—had already begun the march under the generalship of Govannan. Hundreds of baggage wagons followed the army, which stretched over nine miles of country. The folk of Three Streams watched them go.

Bane emerged from the roundhouse as the king passed. Connavar saw him and raised a hand in farewell. Bane acknowledged it with a brief wave. Then he mounted his horse and set off to the west and his farm.

Vorna was standing by the forge as the army moved south. She watched Connavar until he was a distant golden figure on the hilltop horizon, then turned away and walked slowly to her house.

Meria was waiting for her there. "It is a fine army," said Meria. "They will prevail."

Vorna saw the fear in her green eyes. "Let us hope so," she said.

"It is Conn's destiny to defeat them," said Meria. "All his life he has known it."

Vorna had no desire for company, but she stood politely, waiting for Meria to come to the point of her visit. "Conn came to see you yesterday," said Meria. "How did he seem?"

"He was . . . thoughtful," Vorna told her.

"Ever since the night he spent at Bane's farm he has been withdrawn. Did they argue? I see that Bane has not ridden south with the army."

"They did not argue," said Vorna, "and he did not spend the night at Bane's farm. He and Bane came with me to the Wishing Tree woods."

Meria sighed. "He did not tell me." She forced a smile. "But then, he did not tell me the first time he ventured into those woods. Did he meet with the Seidh?"

"Yes."

"Did they give him a talisman against the armies of Stone?"

"In a way."

"It is foolish, I know, for me to worry so. Conn is forty years old. Not a child to be protected. It is just . . ." Her eyes brimmed with tears. "It is just the way he said farewell to me." Meria looked into Vorna's dark eyes. "Have you seen the future?"

"No."

"But you think he will come back?"

Vorna turned away and stared at the towering, distant slopes of Caer Druagh. There were storm clouds shrouding the white peaks. "I have not seen the future," she said. "But Conn has. He is a man of great courage, and he will face his destiny as a king should."

"Did he tell you what is to be?"

"You already know in your heart what is to be," said Vorna. Meria closed her eyes, and tears fell to her cheeks. She let out a soft cry and sagged against the wall of the house. Vorna put her arms around her. "Come inside," she said.

Meria shook her head. "No . . . I will go home. Gwen and I are taking some children to the Riguan Falls." She glanced at the sky. "I had hoped it would be sunny. You think the storm is heading this way?"

"No," Vorna said gently. "It is moving east."

"The falls are beautiful," said Meria, wiping away her tears. "Ruathain and I used to swim there. I remember the first day Conn leapt from the high rock into the pool. He was only five." She bit her lip and turned her face away. "It does not seem so long ago, Vorna. I look at the house sometimes, and I expect little Bran to come scampering into the yard and to see Connavar and Wing playing on the hillside." She fell silent, her eyes turning to the marching army. Then she sighed. "Now Bran is a general, Wing is a traitor, and my Conn . . ."

Head bowed, tears streaming, Meria walked away across the meadow.

Banouin's spirit floated high in the sky above the Rigante army while his body lay in a small wood to the north, Brother Solstice sitting beside it. To a casual onlooker the young druid would have appeared to be sleeping. Instead he was tasting the freedom that only a mystic could ever know: no yearning from the flesh, no hunger, no passion, no anger. To soar free of the body was unlike any other experience in

Banouin's life, and he could not describe the exquisite joy of
it. It was, he once had told Connavar, like seeing the sun dawn
after a night of fear and trembling. But that was a pale and inadequate description. It was said that in the far north the sun
shone for six months without cease, and then night would fall
and darkess would remain throughout autumn and winter.
Perhaps, thought Banouin, the people who dwelled there
would understand the analogy better.

He gazed down at the army. They were traveling in four
columns, and it seemed to Banouin, from this great height,
that the columns resembled immense serpents slithering over
the hills. Farthest south was Connavar and his ten thousand
Iron Wolves. Sunlight glittered on their mail shirts and helms,
giving the snake the appearance of scales. Behind and a half
mile to the west came the horse archers, followed by heavily
armored infantry. A long way back were the baggage and
supply wagons, hundreds of them, drawn by oxen.

Banouin flew to the south, covering more than twenty
miles in a few heartbeats.

The soldiers of Stone were building their nightly fortress, a
massive undertaking involving the creation of ramparts ten
feet tall set in a great square with sides close to half a mile in
length. This daily feat of engineering was a tribute to the
skills of Stone and the cold, calculating genius of Jasaray.
Every morning three Panthers, nine thousand fighting men,
would leave the fortress and march a specified distance into
enemy territory, usually around twelve miles. An advance
guard of mounted officers would mark out the next night
camp, using colored stakes to signify the placement of the
general's command tent, the officers' area, the section where
the troops would pitch their tents, and sectors for latrines,
baggage wagons, and picketing for horses. Once the Panthers
arrived, the first and second would take up defensive positions around the site of the camp, while the third would begin
to dig the enormous square trench, throwing up earth to form
the walls of the fortress.

It was a colossal undertaking and had been planned with
great precision. If an enemy attacked the advance guard, they
would fall back toward the previous night's fortress. If an

enemy force struck at the center of the line as the army moved from fortress to fortress, the Panthers would fold back and encircle it. If the rear of the line came under threat, they would withdraw in order to the new fortress. Banouin gazed down, watching the soldiers digging. If Connavar's cavalry looked like a serpent, then from here the soldiers of Stone were termites, working tirelessly in the earth.

There was, of course, a serpent. The lines of Jasaray's marching army extended back over the full twelve miles to the previous night's camp. The last of the wagons and the three Panthers guarding them were yet to leave. Banouin floated closer to the marching men, flowing along the lines until he saw Jasaray. The emperor was riding a gray horse and was chatting to a group of officers. Sadness touched Banouin's spirit, for riding just behind Jasaray was Maro, the son of Barus, his friend from the university.

Banouin withdrew once again to a great height. Better not to see faces, he thought. Better not to think of the thousands of individuals on both sides who were moving inexorably toward pain, mutilation, or death.

The young druid estimated the size of Jasaray's force, then flew back to his body. He opened his eyes. Brother Solstice was sitting quietly nearby, dozing, his back against a tree. He awoke as Banouin sat up. "How far?" asked the older man, yawning and stretching.

"Just over twenty miles. There are twelve Panthers but few mounted scouts."

"Twelve? That's not good," said Brother Solstice.

Banouin rose and walked to his horse. During the past thirty years Stone armies had defeated enemies boasting ten times their number. Their victories had been won by awesome organization, discipline, and the fact that the soldiers of Stone were not militia, drafted into battle from their farms to fight, but professional soldiers who trained daily, obeying orders instantly without question. Their close-order skills were legendary, and previous Keltoi armies had been crushed by them with ease. Jasaray himself had destroyed the Perdii across the water using only five Panthers, fifteen thousand men. And the Perdii army had mustered more than a hundred thousand warriors.

Connavar would take the field with around half that number, facing 36,000 battle-hardened Stone veterans led by the greatest general of them all. Banouin shivered at the prospect.

Heeling his horse forward, he rode from the wood to make his report to Connavar.

◇ **14** ◇

BROTHER SOLSTICE WAS a big man. In his youth, it was said, he had been a bonny fighter, wide-shouldered and immensely powerful. Now, in middle age, he had added weight to the hips and belly, and that made his choice of a mount all the more unusual. Brother Solstice rode a fat donkey and had to lift his legs to keep his feet from dragging on the ground. He did not mind the jokes of the men in marching columns as he rode past but gave them a cheery wave and a smile. "Horses," Brother Solstice was fond of saying, "make a man proud. Druids should avoid such temptations."

"You don't avoid ale," Banouin had once pointed out. "Or uisge or fine food."

"Ah, but then, no one is perfect," Brother Solstice had told him.

As he rode now behind Banouin's tall horse, Brother Solstice was in a more somber mood. It was not just the news of Jasaray's army, though that was enough to make most sane men somber. Rather, it was the demeanor of the two principal generals of the Rigante, Connavar the fighting king and Bendegit Bran the strategist. Conn had always been a serious man, deep-thinking and focused. Now he seemed strangely withdrawn, as if he carried a burden he could share with no man. And Bendegit Bran, well loved by the men for his good humor and lack of arrogance, had become moody and short-tempered. The death of his son had hit him hard. Like his father before him, Bendegit Bran was a family man, and by that Brother Solstice meant a man to whom family was everything. Bran had adored his son. Brother Solstice felt for him, but there were larger issues at stake here. One distracted general could result in a costly mistake. Two distracted generals

spelled disaster, and not only in issues of strategy. Brother
Solstice could feel the growing unease in the army. Many
among the Keltoi had misinterpreted Bran's grief as fear of
the advancing Jasaray. That in itself would not affect the outcome of the battle, for the army looked to Connavar for
overall leadership. He was their talisman, the undefeated
warrior king who had already smashed one army of Stone.
This was the man who carried the magical Seidh sword that
could cut through armor. As long as he rode at the head of the
army, the hearts of the fighting men would be inspired.

Connavar had always been somewhat withdrawn, and therefore the men had not noticed the subtle change that had come
over him. But Brother Solstice had.

He followed Banouin through the ranks of marching men,
cracking jokes with a few who mocked his donkey. By the
time the two druids reached the front of the line, the Iron
Wolves had already picketed their horses and the king's tent
had been erected. Inside Connavar was seated on a rug at the
center of the tent, his senior generals around him. Govannan,
his hair prematurely silver, sat to his right, and beside him was
Ostaran, the Gath warrior who had joined Connavar twenty
years ago after the fall of his homeland across the water. Bendegit Bran sat to the king's left. Only Fiallach was missing. He
and his men were ranging far to the south, attacking the
enemy's supply lines.

Banouin made his report about the size and disposition of
Jasaray's forces. Connavar listened, then questioned the young
druid for several minutes. Bendegit Bran said nothing. Brother
Solstice watched him. He was not concentrating, and his blue
eyes had a faraway look. Connavar seemed not to notice his
brother's malaise. Osta and Govannan cast nervous glances at
him but offered no comment.

"Anything else you can think of which might be useful?"
Connavar asked Banouin as the druid finished his report. Before he could answer, Brother Solstice spoke, his voice low.

"The regiment of flying dragons may prove difficult to
overcome. What do you think, Lord Bran?"

Bran blinked, his shoulders straightening. "Yes," he said.
"We must consider that."

An uneasy silence followed. "How many men are facing

us, Lord Bran?" asked Brother Solstice. "Where is their army now?"

Bran's eyes narrowed. "Who are you to question me?" he said.

"Who am I, you insolent puppy!" thundered Solstice, his voice booming. "We are discussing the future of all we hold dear. Twenty miles away is an enemy who will destroy our way of life, take thousands of our women into slavery, and butcher the children who are too young to be sold for profit. Who am I? I am the man who sees a general so obsessed with his own personal grief that he will bring about the destruction of his people!"

"How dare you!" stormed Bran, surging to his feet.

"You want to sit in a corner and weep?" said the druid. "Go home. Shed your tears. Cuddle your wife. Get her to dry your eyes. And leave the fighting and the planning for those who have the stomach for it!"

Bran rushed at him. Brother Solstice made no attempt to defend himself. Bran's fist crashed against his bearded chin. The druid staggered, then placed his huge arms behind his back. Blood flowed from his split lip, staining his black and silver beard. He looked into Bran's eyes. "Now that you have woken up," he said, "perhaps our leading strategist can tell us where the enemy lies and what strength he brings to the field."

"Get out of here, you fat bastard," shouted Bran. "Or I'll kill you where you stand!"

"That's enough," said Connavar wearily. "No one is going to be killed here. Sit down, Bran."

"You heard what he said to me."

"I heard. And you should take note of it." He turned to Osta and Govannan. "Leave us for a while, my friends. Come back in an hour and we will continue our planning. You, too, Banouin."

Brother Solstice turned to leave with the others, but Connavar called him back. "Sit," he said, passing a cloth to the druid. Brother Solstice held it to his lip and dabbed the blood from his beard.

Connavar waited until the generals and Banouin had left the tent, then turned to the still-angry Bran. "Brother Solstice spoke the truth," he said. "The Rigante are relying on you to develop a strategy to defeat the armies of Stone. And here you sit, having daydreamed through the most vital reports. You have lost one son, and I grieve with you. But I am the king, and all the Rigante are the king's children. I will not see my children destroyed because one of their generals could not put aside personal grief at a crucial time."

"I can't do this," said Bran. "I can't stop thinking about Ru. I'll head for home tomorrow."

"We need you, Bran," said Connavar.

Bran shook his head. "You taught me everything I know," he told his brother. "And with you at the head the Stone army will be beaten. I am sure of that."

"I may not be here," said Conn, keeping his voice low.

"What?"

Brother Solstice saw the shock register on Bran's face. The younger man crouched down beside his brother. "What madness is this? Of course you will be here!"

"I hope that is true, my brother," Conn told him. "I have seen two futures. In one I am betrayed and die before the battle. In the other I lead a charge against the enemy. These were no dreams, Bran. The images came to my mind when I touched the Morrigu. Both are true, though I know not how this can be. What I do know is that if you leave, the Rigante die. Everything I have lived for, struggled for, suffered for will be dust. You want focus? Think on that. If that is not enough, do not picture dead Ruathain in your mind. Picture instead the man who sent the ring that killed him. Picture Jasaray."

Bran bowed his head, then looked up at Brother Solstice. "I am sorry, my friend, for striking you."

"Forgiven and forgotten," said the druid. "Perhaps you should find Banouin and listen to his report a second time."

Bran nodded, then turned to Connavar. "You won't die, Conn," he said. "You are destined to ride against Jasaray. Nothing will stop that."

"Nothing will stop my destiny," agreed Conn. "Are you back with us now?"

"Aye."

"Then do as the brother bids and seek out Banouin. We will talk more later, when Govannan and Osta return."

Bran rose and left the tent. Brother Solstice remained. "Tell me of these two futures," he said.

Connavar told him of the rescue of the Morrigu and her passing from the world. "In the first vision I am lying against a golden rock, my lifeblood seeping from me. I know the great battle will be fought the following day. I feel despair that I will not be there to fight it. Enemies lie dead on the ground close by. Then a young boy climbs down from a nearby tree and runs into the circle of stones. All goes dark then, and I know that I am dying."

"And the second?" asked the druid.

"I see myself on a tall horse, my armor shining bright, my helm in place. I draw my blade and hold it aloft. Fiallach is beside me. The great battle is under way, and together we lead the charge down the slope."

"Perhaps these were not true futures, merely signs of what could be," said the druid. "They cannot, after all, both be true. You cannot die before the battle and fight in it thereafter. It seems to me that the most obvious choice of action is to avoid circles of stone."

Connavar reached into his tunic and pulled forth a folded piece of parchment. "This was brought by messenger to me this morning," he said, handing it to the druid.

Brother Solstice took the parchment and opened it. There, in Braefar's flowing script, was the message: "My dear brother, we have suffered a great misunderstanding. I have spoken to Guern, and he agrees that the time has come to settle our differences. We will meet you at the Circle of Balg tomorrow at dusk. If you have any love left for me, come alone, Conn. I assure you that there will be no treachery." It was signed "Wing."

"He must think you stupid," said Brother Solstice.

"Yet I will go," Conn told him. "The Morrigu asked me to make her a promise. She said, 'When your brother calls upon you, do as he bids no matter what else is pending, no matter the time or the greatness of events. You understand? Do as he bids.' I broke a promise once, long ago, and have lived with the shame and grief of it ever since. This promise—though it breaks my heart—I will keep."

"Then take a troop of men with you."

"How can I, my friend? He bids me to come alone."

"Oh, Conn, you know Braefar. He has always been weak, his actions inspired by jealousy for all you have achieved. His envy of you became malice years ago."

"I know that," said Conn sadly. "It was after I fought the bear. He and Govannan were there, but it was Govannan who rushed to my aid. Wing just stood there, terrified. He was young, he had no weapon, and he froze. No one blamed him, but he saw contempt in everyone's eyes after that. He was always trying to prove to me that he was worthy, and he tried so hard. He was so desperate for acclaim that he took risks, many of which failed."

"I know, Conn," said Brother Solstice. "We all know. Had he been any other man, you would have dismissed him years ago. How long has he been in league with Guern and the Sea Wolves?"

"More than a year. Jasaray sent him money to help finance a rebellion among the Pannone. One of the few projects Wing handled with care. He recruited Guern and supplied him with coin and weapons. The two of them were made for each other, both bitter, eaten alive by envy. Guern was related to the old laird, but when he died, I sent Bran to govern the north." Conn poured himself a cup of water and drained it. He looked soul-weary, thought Brother Solstice. "I did not know they had linked with Shard, though I suppose I should have guessed it. Wing began to believe that I was the source of all his misfortune, that his life would have been blessed had I never been born. He may even be right in that. I don't know anymore. What I do know is that Wing, when young, was a bonny lad. He loved me then. I was his big brother, and he would follow me everywhere."

"Men change," said the druid. "Weak men cannot deal with guilt or shame. It always has to be the fault of another when they fail. If they fail continually, they see themselves as victims of some great conspiracy."

"Ah, well," said Conn, "it will all end tomorrow."

"It must not end!" said Brother Solstice. "What you are

planning is foolish. Perhaps the Morrigu intended you to refuse."

Conn smiled and shook his head. "I do not understand all she had planned, my friend. But I know if I fail to keep this promise, the Rigante will fail in their war with Jasaray. I cannot explain it. I saw so much . . . I saw Jasaray in many guises, on many worlds. He won every battle he fought. I saw visions of horror beyond belief, of worlds dying, the air poisoned by towers belching poisons into the air, of dead trees, their leaves scorched, and fertile lands turned into deserts. I saw men with gray faces and frightened eyes living in cities of stone, scurrying like ants from day to day. In truth, I wish I had never touched her!"

"You think these visions will come to pass in the lands of the Rigante?" asked the druid.

"I do not know. I only know what I must do. And that is ride to the circle. Alone."

"They will kill you, Conn. I know this Guern. He is charismatic, and men follow him, but he is a vile creature and there is no honor in him. He is big—almost as big as Fiallach—and he can fight. He's killed several men in blood feuds. And he will not be alone. You will be."

"I have always been alone," said Conn. "I think we all are."

Bane saddled a chestnut mare, then walked back into the farmhouse. Gryffe and Iswain were waiting in the main room. "When will you be back?" asked Gryffe.

"Some day," Bane told him. Reaching into the pocket of his black, sleeveless jerkin, he produced a rolled parchment. "I made this deed in Three Streams the day the army moved out. It has been witnessed by three elders." He handed it to Gryffe. "It deeds the farm and all the cattle and land to you." He grinned at the surprise on Gryffe's features. "You are no longer Wolfshead, Gryffe. You are a landowner."

"I don't understand," muttered the red-bearded warrior.

"He's not coming back," said Iswain. She moved in to stand before Bane. "Why are you doing this?"

He shrugged. "I have a need to wander, Iswain."

"It is more than that," she said.

"If it is, then I choose not to talk about it. You said you and

Gryffe were dreaming of a place of your own. Somewhere to raise children, to watch sunsets as you grow older. This is a good place, and I think you will be happy here."

"We are happy here," said Iswain. "And we would both like to see you happy."

He drew her into an embrace and kissed her plump cheek. "When I come back, we will have a feast and I shall regale you with my adventures." He turned to Gryffe and thrust out his hand. Gryffe ignored it and stepped in, drawing Bane into a bear hug.

"I shall hold half of all profits for you, man," he said. "And when you want to come home, this farm will be waiting for you." Releasing him, Gryffe smiled. "We'll have taken your bedroom, mind. It's bigger than ours, with a better view." The smile faded. "You take care, Bane. Hear me?"

"I hear you, big man." Gathering up his saddlebags, Bane walked from the house. Settling the bags into place, he stepped into the saddle and rode away without a backward glance.

It was a bright morning, and he rode steadily east, crossing the hills and valleys until he reined in some four hours later on the hilltop overlooking Three Streams. It seemed so peaceful now in the spring sunshine, no hint at first of the bloodshed and valor, no echo of clashing swords and screaming men. Bright yellow flowers had bloomed along the slopes. Bane looked around the scene. A cast-off shoe lay in the grass close by, surrounded by flowers, and beyond it was a broken sword blade already pitted with rust.

From the woods came three boys, running and laughing. They were carrying wooden swords. Seeing Bane, they paused. Bane waved at them, then heeled the mare onto the slope. He rode down into the settlement, past Eldest Tree, the colossal oak, and on to the forge, from where he could hear the steady beat of a hammer on iron. Dismounting, he tied the mare's reins to a fence rail and walked into the forge. Nanncumal was watching an apprentice boy thumping his hammer on a red-hot section of iron. The old man glanced up as Bane entered. Together they walked out into the sunshine. Nanncumal ran a cloth over his bald head, mopping up the sweat. He saw the saddlebags on Bane's mare. "Where are you heading?" he asked.

"Across the water."

"For what purpose?"

Bane shrugged. "Perhaps it is to find a purpose," he said.

Nanncumal sat down on a long bench seat. "You did well here, boy," he said. "People won't forget."

"They will or they won't," said Bane, seating himself beside his grandfather. "It doesn't matter to me."

Nanncumal looked away. "I didn't do right by you, Bane. It grieves me to say that."

"Long ago and far away," said Bane. "Forget it."

"Easy to say. I loved my Arian. She was a good girl until her sister died. They were children, sharing a bed. Little Baria was five years old. She had a fever, and her heart gave out in the night. Arian awoke and found her dead beside her. She was never the same after that: terrified of the dark and of being alone. When Conn was savaged by that bear, Arian almost went mad. I tried to talk her out of marrying Casta. It was not a good match. But she was convinced Conn would die, and she clung to Casta as if he were life itself." The old man sighed.

"We don't need to talk about this," said Bane. "Mother is dead. Nothing can change that."

"I'm talking about the living," said Nanncumal. "I'm talking about you and . . . Connavar."

"I don't need to hear it."

"Maybe you don't, maybe you do. But I need to say it, so humor me, Grandson. I know that you have always believed Connavar took your mother by force. It is not true. Arian told me herself that she seduced him on that day, hoping to win him back. She knew deep down that he had never stopped loving her. The Seidh had warned Connavar never to break a promise or great tragedy would result. He had promised to take his new wife riding. Instead he stayed for many hours with Arian. When he returned, he found his wife had been murdered while he had been taking his pleasure. Connavar was insane with grief. He destroyed the murderer's village, slaughtering any who came within sword reach. In his madness he killed women and children that day.

"When you were born and Casta saw your eyes, he knew Arian had been unfaithful and cast her out. She came home to me. I went to see Connavar and told him of his son. We drank uisge long into the night, and he talked of his sorrow and of his love of my daughter. Much of it I won't repeat. But he also talked of the people he had killed and of how no amount of good deeds could wash away his guilt and no punishment could be great enough to ease his pain. I asked him if he would consider taking Arian to wife and acknowledging you as his son. He said that his heart yearned for exactly that. His love for Arian burned as brightly as ever, and every night since he had learned of the birth he had longed to ride to her and lift his son into his arms. But he could not. This was the punishment he had placed upon himself: never to wed, never to sire children. He told me that he would never set eyes upon Arian again. And he never did. There, it is said. He was not punishing you, Bane. He was punishing himself."

"Why are you telling me this, Grandfather?"

The old man shrugged. "You are a good boy with a good heart, but I know you came to hate Connavar. I thought the truth would help lance the boil."

Bane leaned over and kissed his grandfather's cheek, then rose. "I must say farewell to Vorna," he said.

Nanncumal climbed to his feet. "And I'd better get back to the boy before he sets the forge or himself on fire." They stood for a moment, then Nanncumal reached out and shook Bane's hand. "I doubt we'll see each other again," he said.

"Who knows? I may be back within a year."

Nanncumal nodded, though he knew it was not the truth. "I hope so, Bane."

The younger man climbed to the saddle and rode off across the settlement. He saw Meria with a young child, sitting on a porch seat before her house. She looked up. Her hand flickered as if she would wave, but then she looked away.

Vorna was not at home. Bane waited for an hour, then mounted up and set off toward the Wishing Tree woods.

The king had slept badly, the night haunted by dreams. Not all of them were bad, but even those filled him with sorrow. When young he had believed himself as immortal as the mountains. He had looked upon older people as being from a different species. Now, in his fortieth year, he found himself looking back on that young man with a sense of bewilderment. It was not as if he had not known he would one day grow old and then die. Yet despite the knowledge there was some deep instinct in him that denied its truth. He had been young, the future stretching out eternally before him. He remembered when he and Wing had last traveled with Ruathain to sell cattle in the south. Men had talked of an earth maiden who dwelt in the town, a woman of enormous beauty and great skill in lovemaking. When the boys had seen her, they had been shocked beyond belief. She was old. Older than their mother, she was well past thirty. Conn remembered thinking, How could she let such beauty slip away? Such a stupid thought, as if anyone chose to let time erode his health and strength and dignity.

Conn sat up. His lower back ached from a night on the floor of the tent, and his neck was stiff. He stretched and groaned. The dawn sun gleamed on the eastern side of the tent, illuminating the interior. Conn glanced at the armor tree bearing his mail shirt, breastplate, and helm and the patchwork cloak Meria had made for him all those years ago.

"If you are to be the king of all Keltoi on this side of the water," she had said, "you cannot ride around the countryside in the colors of the Rigante. You must wear something that signifies that you are above tribal divisions." He had at first laughed at the garment, for it had seemed then truly ugly, with clashing colors and symbols, crafted from cloaks from five tribes. Now he viewed it differently. Meria had been right. The cloak had become a talisman, drawing the tribes together.

Conn poured himself some water. The memory of the dreams was strong upon him. He had seen his stepfather, Ruathain. He had been standing by the shore of a lake, his arm around the shoulder of the dead grandson who bore his name. Conn had called out to him, but Ruathain had not seemed to hear him.

Sitting alone in his tent, Connavar the King thought back over his life, seeing again the great days of victory and freedom, the bleak times after the deaths of Banouin, Tae, and finally Ruathain. He had loved Tae, though never with the all-consuming intensity of his feelings for Arian. Even after all these years guilt for that lack lay heavy on him. She had deserved better from him, he knew, but love was not a matter of choice. A man did not—could not—say: This woman is worthy of love, and therefore I will love her with all my heart. A man loved passionately or he did not. It was that simple.

Conn's eyes felt gritty and tired. Bran, Govannan, and Osta had been in the tent well into the night, discussing strategies to use against Jasaray's forces. Bran had worked out a battle plan. It was a good one but fraught with danger. The Rigante center would be manned by fifteen thousand untrained tribesmen, with ten thousand heavy infantrymen placed on the left and right wings. Both flanks would be protected by the Iron Wolves and the horse archers.

"We will draw Jasaray in toward the weak center," said Bran, "and engage him there."

"We'll not be able to hold him," pointed out Govannan.

"Exactly. I will set the center in a bow formation, the wings behind the front ranks. The Stone front lines will push us back. The heavy infantry, under you, Govannan, will hold their positions. As the Panthers drive us back, our lines will become crescent-shaped. Then I will signal the heavy infantry to close in from the left and right. The Iron Wolves, having dispatched or driven away Jasaray's cavalry, will turn on the rear of the Panthers."

"The plan has merit," said Connavar. "Such a double envelopment will hem his troops in, making it almost impossible for them to change formation. But it relies on Jasaray reacting the way we desire. Should he identify the danger early enough, he will spread out his lines in an advancing square. Then, when we try to crush their formation, he will repel us with ease."

"And what of his archers?" asked the Gath general Osta. "There are a thousand skilled bowmen marching with him."

"I know," said Bran. "Each man carries a quiver of thirty shafts. We must force Jasaray to use them early on our center. Otherwise our cavalry charge will be cut to pieces, the Iron Wolves destroyed."

"And what avenue of escape is there should this strategy fail?" asked Govannan.

"None," said Bran. "I will be with the center, and our backs will be to the river. If we cannot crush Jasaray in this one engagement, we will be destroyed utterly. This, my friends, is a win or die battle. I can think of no other way to overcome the Panthers."

"Neither can I," said Connavar.

"I am not a strategist," said Osta, "but it seems to me that the center will take appalling losses. What if they break and run? Half of them will be Norvii and Pannone. We don't know them."

Connavar laughed. "Most of my men did not know the Gath when you rode with us at Cogden Field. They know you now, Osta, my friend. The center will be manned by three tribes. Not one man among them would wish to be seen, by a rival tribesman, running away. They will hold."

Now, in the dawn, Conn found himself worried about the plan. It was simple and could be devastatingly effective. However, the tribes were not facing an ordinary general. He recalled the battles against the Perdii twenty years earlier, when he had stood beside Jasaray. The man had been cool, anticipating every move of the enemy and countering it swiftly, decisively, murderously. Conn shivered.

Moving from the tent, he saw Govannan and several others swimming in a nearby lake. It lightened his spirit, and he walked over to join them, stripping off his tunic and plunging into the cold water. But even as he swam, he thought about his brother Braefar and the meeting he would have with him later that day. Brother Solstice was convinced that Wing and his new friends would seek to kill him. Conn believed this to be true but held to the vision he had glimpsed in the mind of the Morrigu. He would lead the charge of the Iron Wolves the next day, and he would end once and for all the threat of Stone. His whole life had been in preparation for this one charge, and surely, he reasoned, not even the most capricious of gods would rob him of the day.

With smooth, strong strokes he swam to where Govannan was washing his silver hair. Coming up behind him, Conn flicked the general's legs from under him, dunking him into the water. Govannan came up sputtering and threw himself at Conn, and the two men fell below the surface. Govannan came up first. As Conn surfaced, he was pushed under once more. This time it was Conn who came up sputtering. "Is that any way to treat your king?" he asked. Govannan laughed and lunged at him again. Conn swayed, caught Govannan by the arm, and twisted him. The general flopped to his back. Before he could go under the water again Conn drew him up. "It is too beautiful a day to be spent fighting with you," he said.

The two men waded toward the shore. Just as they were about to emerge from the water, something sharp bit into Conn's calf. With an angry cry he looked down and saw an otter attacking him. His hand lunged into the water, grabbed the creature, and hauled it clear. Then he flung it with terrible force. The otter struck a tree and flopped to the ground, its neck broken. There was blood in the water. Conn climbed to the bank and examined the wound. It was not deep.

"Damn, but these water dogs can be a nuisance," said Govannan, kneeling by the king.

Conn sat very still, all color fading from his face.

"Are you all right?" asked Govannan, concerned.

"I am fine," said Conn. "Is the creature dead?"

Govannan moved to the tree and nudged the otter with his foot. It did not move. He picked it up. "Aye, it is dead."

Conn rose from the ground and walked back to his tent.

Otters had many names among the tribes; "water dogs" was the most common, but in the old high tongue they were called "hounds of the riverbank."

All his life Conn had been fearful of his birth *geasa*. Vorna had told his mother he would die on the day he killed the hound that bit him. It was that prophecy that had led Meria to urge Ruathain to stand beside him in the first battle against Shard, for Conn had killed a dog that had fastened its teeth to his wrist guard. Having survived the battle, Conn had believed the *geasa* to be broken. Now he knew different. All his life he had avoided close contact with dogs and hounds.

Back in his tent he bound the wound in his calf. "If today is the day, so be it," he said aloud.

Then he donned his armor.

Banouin had also spent a fitful night, and his spirits were low as the dawn came. Brother Solstice, with whom he shared a small tent, saw the strain in his eyes. "Do you fear the coming battle?" he asked the younger man.

Banouin shook his head. "No, it is not fear but sadness. I have been thinking of the thousands of young men who will lose their lives, men on both sides. And for what, Solstice? What ultimately will be achieved by this coming violence? Surely man, with all his intellect, can find some other way to settle disagreements without more seeds of hatred being sown, more souls to haunt a battlefield."

"It would be pleasant to think so," said Brother Solstice. "Yet harmony is often achieved by violence. Forest fires are terrible, but without them the forest itself would not survive. The deer rely on the wolf to cull the herds, eliminating the weak, ensuring that the food supply will be adequate for their survival. If the Source had decided upon a world without violence, it surely would not have created the hawk and the lion."

Banouin thought about it for a moment. "Is it your argument, then, that the Source in some way desires this coming conflict and the slaughter which accompanies it?"

"I am not arrogant enough to even guess at the answer to that, my friend. My heart is heavy with the thought of the dead to come. But I tell myself that evil must always be countered. We did not ask the soldiers of Stone to invade our lands. We did not request them to enslave our women and butcher our children. So what are we to do? Allow them to achieve their aims? When a man sits by and allows another to kill and rape and plunder, then he is as guilty as the offender."

"According to that argument," said Banouin, "you should be carrying a sword and shield tomorrow."

Brother Solstice smiled. "Believe me, my boy, were I standing close to a mother and her child and a soldier of Stone was advancing on them, I would take up sword and shield. I am not as holy a man as I would wish to be."

"Then you accept that holy men should avoid violence no matter what lives are threatened?"

"I do accept that we are pledged to uphold the sanctity of life," said the druid. "And I revere those men who can live by such a code. I am not—yet—one of them."

Banouin pushed open the flap of the tent and stepped out

into the early-morning sunlight. Cookfires had been lit all over the valley, and thousands of soldiers were moving around, some tending to their horses, others sharpening weapons or playing dice bones. Brother Solstice dismantled the tent, and Banouin helped him fold the canvas and then roll it.

"In Stone," said Banouin, "there was a group known as the tree cult. They believed in nonviolence, and they were killed in the thousands. Not once did they raise their hands against their killers. And they won, for they are now accepted among the citizens."

"I have heard of them," said Brother Solstice, "and I admire them enormously. My first spiritual teacher—a wonderful old druid named Conobelin—told me that you can change the minds of men by argument or debate but cannot change their hearts by the same means. Hearts are changed by actions." Brother Solstice tied the rolled tent. "You say the cultists won, though I might debate that. But why did they win? As I understand it, Jasaray arrested and executed Nalademus. Why was he able to do that? Because two men with swords saved him from both traitors and a wild beast. And in saving him and gaining a victory for the gentle cultists, we now have a Stone army ready to destroy our lands and butcher our children. Is that what the Source desired? A man could drive himself insane seeking deeper meanings within such complex events." Brother Solstice stood silently for a moment, staring around the valley and the shores of the lake. "I find that it helps," he said at last, "to focus one's mind not on the evils but on the greatness of man, on the power of his love rather than the nature of his hatred. Love of family, love of friends, love of land. The Rigante are a fine people, Banouin. I hold to that. We seek not to enslave our fellows but to live with them. We do not make war on our neighbors. But when war comes to us, we fight. Not a man here among these thousands does not wish he could be somewhere else. He is here to defend those he loves, and in that there is nobility of purpose."

Banouin shook his head. "The Morrigu talked of feeding the spirit of the land. She said that man alone among the animals has the talent to do this. Every kindly thought and deed, every moment of compassion and forgiveness is like a raindrop of spirit to the earth. But war? War is a torrent of dark rain that poisons the earth, bringing us one tiny step closer to the death of the world."

Brother Solstice put his hand on the younger man's shoulder. "Yes, it is, my friend. It is vile. But when the fighting is over, you and I will move among the wounded and heal them as best we can. And we will—if it pleases the Source—watch them return to their farms and their lands and hug their wives and their children. We will see them smile at the infinite beauty of the sunset and dance on feast nights with all the joy of life. And we will hope that they will put aside hatred and teach their children to love their friends and neighbors so that future generations can avoid wars and thus replenish the spirit of the earth. It is all we can do."

"But first comes the slaughter," Banouin said softly.

"Aye, first the slaughter."

In the hour before dusk Bane rode to the edge of the Wishing Tree woods. The mare refused to cross the tree line, shying back as he tried to heel her forward. She then stood still, her flanks trembling. Bane dismounted and stroked her neck. "I have no wish to enter, either," he told her. Trailing the reins, he left her there and walked into the shadow-shrouded trees. There was no mist, but as he walked Bane thought he could hear whispers on the wind and felt eyes upon him.

He followed the trail down to where they had first seen the Morrigu, then continued up the slope opposite, coming at last to the circle of golden stones. A young man was sitting on a rock close by. He was slender and golden-haired, his face gentle. Beside him, resting against the rock, was a golden shield of fabulous workmanship. The rim was shining steel, the center like a spider's web of golden wire flowing around a gray, shimmering stone the size of a man's fist. The young man looked up and smiled as Bane approached.

"She said you would come," he said, his voice low, almost musical.

"And I did," said Bane. "Who are you?"

"I am . . . was . . . Riamfada. Will you sit awhile?"

"My horse is waiting beyond the woods, and I have a long

way to travel. So can we make this brief? Tell me why the Morrigu asked me here."

"Your mare is already wandering back to Three Streams, from where it will be returned to the farm you gifted to Gryffe and Iswain," said Riamfada. "Should you decide to travel to the coast, I can send you there through the portal and save you weeks of journeying." Riamfada lifted a slender hand and gestured toward the stones. The air rippled, and Bane found himself staring down a sloping hillside at the port of Accia. The air rippled once more, the vision disappearing. "Sit for a while," said Riamfada. "I have long desired this meeting."

"Who are you?" asked Bane again. "Or perhaps that should be, What are you?"

"Once I was human like you." He smiled. "Well . . . not exactly like you. My legs were crippled, and I could not walk. But I was Rigante, and I dwelled in Three Streams. I died there before you were born, on a feast night, surrounded by my friends. The Seidh brought me here to dwell among them."

"And now you are Seidh?"

"No, you cannot become Seidh. But those of us who were once human have been taught certain . . . skills, shall we say, involving the manipulation of matter. It is probably simpler to say we have learned magic."

Bane reached out and touched the young man's arm. It was solid, the flesh warm to the touch. "You are no ghost, then?"

"No, not a ghost."

Bane sat down on a flat rock. "So why am I here?"

"To make a choice. As I said, I can speed your way to the coast or beyond if it pleases you. Once I could have transported you to Stone itself, but they tore down the circle that stood on the fourth hill to make way for a bathhouse and a market. But I can send you to a circle some twenty miles northeast of the city."

Bane laughed. "The Morrigu would not have brought me here merely to save time on my travels. What is it she requires of me?"

"She requires nothing, Bane. She asks for nothing. I was told merely to present you with alternatives."

"And these are?"

"You can travel where you wish, to any of the circles around the globe of the world."

"Is there a circle in the White Mountains?"

"The White Mountains of Varshalla, north of the land of the Vars?"

"Yes," said Bane.

"Indeed there is. But why would you wish to go there? The tribes worship the gods of blood, and the word among them for a stranger is the same as the word for an enemy. Even the Vars do not travel there."

"Someone I love is there," said Bane. "I would like to see her again."

"Then I can send you there," Riamfada told him.

Bane glanced down at the spiderweb shield. "Why do you need a shield?" he asked.

"It is not mine, though I crafted it. I made it for you, Bane, as I once made a sword for your father."

"It is a pretty piece, though one hefty cut would destroy it."

The young man lifted the shield and carried it to a nearby oak, hanging it on a broken branch. "Show me," he said.

Bane drew one of his short swords and walked to the tree. He lunged at the shield. The blade bounced away. He hacked and slashed at it, then stood back. There was not a single mark on any of the wires. Sheathing his blade, he lifted the shield and was amazed by its lack of weight. Slipping his forearm through the two leather straps, he hooked his fingers around the fist bar, then looked for buckles to tighten the straps. The leather slid around his arm, shrinking until the straps fitted perfectly. "How do I remove it?" he asked.

"Simply loosen your grip on the fist bar," advised Riamfada.

Bane did so, and the straps opened. "It is a wondrous piece. I thank you for it."

"I hope it proves useful," said Riamfada.

Bane sat down once more. The sun was falling behind scattered clouds, and the sky was molten gold above the mountains. "What is it you are not telling me, Riamfada? This is a battle shield, and though it may prove useful in the White Mountains, you did not craft it for that purpose."

"I have one more vision to show you," said Riamfada. He

gestured once more, and Bane saw the air shimmer and found himself staring at nine men sitting within a stone circle. He recognized Braefar, and his eyes were drawn to another man, a huge, hulking warrior with long, braided yellow hair. The scene shifted, and Bane saw a rider on a white horse in the distance.

"That is Connavar," said Bane. "Why are you showing me this?"

"The king is riding to his death," said Riamfada. "He knows that his brother plans to kill him. He knows he cannot survive."

"Then why is he doing it?"

"You were here when the Morrigu told him to agree to his brother's request. Conn promised that he would, and he is a man of honor."

"I see," Bane said coldly. "And you want me to rush through to his rescue. That is what this . . . this talk of alternatives comes down to. I am here to save the king."

"I wish that were true, Bane, for I love Connavar and can feel the heaviness of his heart. But you cannot save him. This is his destiny."

"Then why am I here?"

"To make a choice."

"Suppose I decide to find Lia. What happens to Connavar?"

"He dies alone."

"And if I step through to his aid?"

"He dies, but not alone. But know this, Bane. If you do step through, you will be faced with another choice, one that will probably see you die within a day."

◇ 15 ◇

Maro, son of Barus, watched as the unit slaves pitched the thirty tents of the junior officers. They worked efficiently and well, with a disciplined economy of effort that spoke of long practice. Maro, as junior duty officer in charge of the tents, felt entirely redundant. He scanned the scene but could find no fault with the work of the twelve slaves. When they had finished, he thanked them, cursing himself inwardly as he did so. He had been warned twice for such odd behavior but found it difficult to treat any human being with less than courtesy. Dismissing them, he wandered across the huge new compound. To the left Jasaray's personal slaves were assembling the mosaic stone floor of his command tent. Every one of the 2,307 stones was numbered, and some of the slaves had been assembling and disassembling this floor for more than thirty years. They, too, worked with diligence and speed. It was vital that the floor be completed and the huge tent pitched before Jasaray arrived with the center columns.

Maro was enchanted by the activity within the new fortress, as he had been enchanted on every occasion since the campaign had started. The power and ingenuity of Stone were never more apparent than in this daily ritual. Nothing was left to chance. Advance guards would pick out the land, flag officers would map out the camp, and the advance columns would put aside their armor to dig out the vast defensive trench. To the north and south parties of horsemen were dragging felled trees to the gate areas, where the trunks would be split and expertly crafted into strong gates. And all the while more Panthers were arriving, marching into the fortress and immediately setting about preordained tasks: the digging of latrines, the erection of rows of tents, the setting of cookfires.

Maro climbed to the northern ramparts and stared out over the rolling hills beyond. Somewhere out there was the Rigante army, the army that had destroyed Valanus and put a blight on the unblemished record of Stone conquests. According to the most recent reports, it numbered fewer than fifty thousand men—a tenth, men said, of the size of the force that had defeated Valanus.

The young man lifted his helm clear, pushing his fingers through his dark hair. The wind was cool and pleasant. His back was itching, but there was no way to scratch it through the iron breastplate he now wore. It had taken Maro weeks to become accustomed to the heavy armor, the wrist guards, and the greaves. He had felt for the most part like a fraud, a student pretending to be a soldier. It was harder for him than for most of the new juniors, for he was the son of Barus, conqueror of the east, and much was expected of him. In a way he was glad that his father had remained in Stone. It would have been embarrassing for his early mistakes to have been witnessed by Barus.

Thousands of soldiers were now inside the fortress, and Maro glanced back, picturing the grid plan and locating the area where his fifty men were stationed. Replacing his helm, he strode from the ramparts and crossed the compound to where the tents of his own section were situated. Having ensured they had been fed, he went back to his tent and began to compose a letter to Cara. There were four letters now in his pack. He had numbered all of them in the order they were to be read. Tomorrow he would ask again if his letters could be carried back to Accia. Only ten officers a day were allowed to submit letters home, for there were only two riders carrying dispatches, and Jasaray always insisted they ride light.

As he was writing, he heard a commotion beyond the tent and put aside his materials. Stepping outside, he saw that a group of cavalry had arrived. Many of the men were wounded. Maro stood in the sunshine and watched as the cavalry leader dismounted and glanced back at the men with him. There were around thirty horsemen. The insignia on the officer's breastplate showed that he was the commander of a hundred. Maro eased his way forward. The officer, a lean, middle-aged veteran, was talking to one of Jasaray's flag officers, the dour, laconic Heltian.

"They hit us from the woods to the east," said the cavalryman. "The Cenii scattered and ran almost immediately."

"Losses?" asked Heltian.

"I lost sixty-eight men," the officer told him. "They surrounded Tuvor, and I doubt any of his men survived. I recognized the old bastard who came to Stone. Fiallach, isn't it? He led them."

"Enemy losses?"

"Hard to say, sir. All was chaos as they struck. We thought the Cenii scouts would give us warning of any attack, but they either ran or were killed. The enemy was upon us in moments."

"How many?"

"I'd say around a thousand."

"Get your wounded to the hospital tents," said Heltian, "and then prepare a fuller report for the emperor when he arrives."

"Yes, sir," replied the cavalryman, saluting.

Maro was still standing close by when the cavalryman walked off and Heltian turned. The flag officer looked at him. "You have no duties, young man?"

"No, sir. My men have been fed, the tents pitched."

"You are the son of Barus, are you not?"

"I am, sir."

"And you listened to the report."

"Yes, sir."

"Tell me what you made of it."

Maro struggled to gather his wits, his mind racing back over the conversation he had overheard. "It seems that 168 of our cavalry have been killed by Fiallach's Iron Wolves."

"Go on."

"They were attacked from hiding, outnumbered five to one. The Cenii scouts proved ineffective." And then he had it. Realization struck him. "Our two cavalry units were riding too close together. Had they been at the regulation distance of . . . of two hundred yards . . . one of them should have broken free. And cavalry orders are to skirt wooded areas, out of bowshot range."

"Indeed so," said Heltian. "The officers were careless and

treated the enemy with disrespect. They learned a hard lesson as a result." Heltian turned away and walked off toward the northern gates.

Maro returned to his tent and his letter to Cara, telling her yet again how he missed her and their infant son. Then he described the lands of the Keltoi on this side of the water, the beauty of the mountains, the purity of the streams and rivers. He paused and thought of Banouin, wondering where his friend would be now. He was not a warrior and was unlikely therefore to be at risk in the coming battle. Then he thought of Bane the gladiator. Rage said he had come home to the mountains. It was probable that he was out there sharpening his swords. Maro shivered. The late-afternoon sun was giving little heat now.

There was no bed in the tent, but a canvas sheet had been pegged across the earth. Maro removed his breastplate and scratched his back. Then he stretched out, laying his head on a folded blanket. Back home Cara and their son probably would be in the garden, the boy asleep in a crib placed in the shade of the old elm. Maro closed his eyes and pictured them. As he did so, he felt a swelling of love for them both and an aching sadness that he was not with them.

Cara had been angry when he had left and had refused to say farewell. "You have allied yourself with evil," she had told him when he had announced his commission in the Twenty-Third Panther.

"It is not evil to defend one's city," he replied.

"This is our city," she said. "Where is the enemy army? I do not see it."

"The Rigante are massing men, and their agents have crossed the water, stirring up trouble among the conquered tribes, encouraging them to revolt against the rule of Stone. If we do not deal with them now, then in the future they could well have an army at our gates."

"Some men will always seek a reason for war," she said coldly. "Bane told me that the Rigante have never made war across the water and have no interest in acquiring the lands of others. They are not a greedy people. They do not lust for conquest and slaughter."

"Neither do I," he said.

"And yet you will invade their lands, enslave their women, and kill their men."

"You make it sound so base, Cara. Everywhere ruled by Stone knows peace and harmony. We are bringing civilization and culture to these people. Did you know that their druids sacrifice babies on their altars? They are a barbarous and uncouth people."

"Barbarous and uncouth?" she echoed. "Yesterday in the Great Arena five women were torn apart by wild beasts for the entertainment of the crowd. Don't talk to me of barbarous and uncouth. The Rigante have no arenas."

"This is an entirely different matter," snapped Maro. "It is typical of a woman to change the subject. The women you speak of were obviously criminals and thus subject to execution. Murderers, probably, deserving of all they received."

"You are a fool, Maro. And I hope you come to see that before it is too late."

In the weeks leading up to his departure she had not spoken to him. He hoped that his letters would soften her heart and that when he returned as a conquering hero, she would look more kindly upon him.

Braefar's head jerked around. Just for the briefest of moments he thought he saw two men on the outer edge of the stone circle. He blinked, and they were gone. Just a trick of the fading light, he thought, and settled his back against the golden column of stone. The wind was cool, and he drew his sheepskin cloak around him. The others had set a fire and were sitting in a circle around it, but Braefar had no wish to join them. In truth, he had no wish to be there.

If Connavar had not been so selfish, so hungry for power and praise, he thought, none of this would have happened.

Braefar stared down at the large golden ring adorning the third finger of his right hand. It had been a gift from Connavar upon his coronation, a princely gift. Of course, Bendegit Bran had been given a golden torque, Govannan a beautiful cloak brooch with a ruby center, and Fiallach a sword, the hilt entwined with gold wire, the pommel stone a beautifully cut emerald. Braefar had examined the gifts closely. His own golden ring had cost less than all the others. It had been a studied insult.

Braefar had been swallowing such insults all his life. Ever since the day of that accursed bear!

He could see it now, huge and black, its jaws dripping with the blood of the boys already slain back in the woods. It was charging at Connavar. The sight of the beast was awesome, and it froze Braefar's blood. Conn leaped at it, stabbing it with his dagger. Then Govannan ran in to help. It was all over so fast. One moment Conn was alive and strong, the next torn apart, blood sprayed all over the grass. The hunters had come then, plunging their lances into the beast. Only then did Braefar discover the power to move. They had all looked at him, thinking him a coward. They did not say it out loud, but they felt it. And Braefar's life had been cursed from that moment.

Conn had never forgiven him. He had said he had, but it had been a lie. He had spent the next twenty years punishing him, causing him to fail and look stupid in front of his fellows. Oh, how Conn must have laughed on each occasion. Braefar did not doubt the king had discussed his "failures" with Bran, Govannan, Osta, Fiallach, and the others. They thought he did not notice them laughing behind his back, but he noticed. Braefar did not have to see them to know. It was all so obvious, as were the grotesque plots to make him seem incompetent.

Conn had put him in charge of the northern gold mines, with a brief to improve the production and swell the treasury. Braefar had invented several tools for the men at the face. They had been a huge success. Then had come the cave-in. Braefar was accused of pushing ahead too fast with insufficient timber supports. Forty men died, and the mine was closed for four months. As if that was his fault! Get more gold, the king had said. Braefar had gotten more gold, doubling production.

Every role Conn ever offered him was tipped with poison. And all because of that bear!

That was why he had never been given a rank in the army. What a humiliation that was. It was like telling everyone, "Braefar is a coward." Even Bran had come to believe it after the misunderstanding in the first Pannone war twenty years

earlier. Conn had left Braefar in charge of gathering reinforcements while he marched off to face the highland laird
and the Sea Wolf Shard. Braefar had done exactly as he was
told, gathering men from all over Rigante lands. And he
would have marched to Conn's aid as soon as the reinforcements were fully gathered. But no, the fifteen-year-old Bran
had to be the hero, sneaking off and riding to the battle with
but a few thousand recruits, while Braefar had been rein-
forcing Old Oaks in order to protect the citizens in case of
disaster.

Naturally, no one saw it that way. Conn made sure of that.
Cowardly Braefar had failed in his task and would never be
entrusted with armed men again. Yet he had stayed loyal year
upon year. While Bendegit Bran ruled the north, and Fiallach
the east, Braefar had been thrown the bone of Three Streams.
That was when he found out who his true friends were. The
emperor Jasaray had sent agents to seek his advice. The emperor, they said, understood the brilliance Braefar had shown
on many occasions, not least the invention of stirrups, which
enabled cavalrymen to wear heavier armor and to maintain
balance during fights on horseback. The emperor would be
honored, they said, to count Braefar as a friend.

Jasaray had been a true friend. His agents had witnessed
Connavar making fun of Braefar, and they listed the numerous occasions when the king made slighting remarks.
Once Connavar had even claimed to have invented the stirrups himself. Jasaray was right, too, about the military expansion under Connavar's rule. It was costly and hugely
inefficient. The Rigante would prosper far better, Jasaray had
written, under the wiser rule of someone like Braefar.

Jasaray understood. He had complimented Braefar on his
actions during the first Pannone war. "Only a fool," he had
written, "would have marched with all his men, leaving his
citizens unprotected against a reversal of fortune in the first
battle." Braefar had memorized that line. Jasaray also had
pointed out that Connavar's domination of the Pannone was
against all Keltoi tradition, and he had, through his agents, introduced Braefar to Guern, the rebel Pannone warrior
seeking to throw off the Rigante yoke.

It had all been so exciting, planning and plotting in secret.

He would show Connavar that his strategic skills were greater than those of his little brother, Bran. He would also prove he was no coward when the time came by riding alongside Shard when the Sea Wolves invaded.

Braefar shivered at the memory as he recalled the wild, terrifying ride to flee the battlefield. Yes, he had been frightened out of his wits, but that also had been the fault of Connavar, for his brother had never offered him the chance to fight in battle. Had he done so, Braefar would have learned to overcome his fears. Well, he had overcome them now. He was waiting here with Guern and his warriors to kill Connavar.

To kill Connavar! The thought shook him.

All his life—until the last few years—he had worshiped his brother. Most of the mistakes he had made, though not entirely his fault, had come about by trying too hard to please him. "I loved you, Conn," he whispered.

He relaxed as he realized that Conn would never ride in alone to meet Guern. He would know it was a trap. He would send Fiallach and a score of Iron Wolves to arrest them all. Braefar knew what he would say when he was brought before the king: "So, Conn, you did not have the courage to meet us as we asked. Perhaps you are not such a hero, after all, sending your Wolves where you did not dare to go." It would be worth banishment just to say that phrase in front of Connavar's generals. Then he would head south and join Jasaray.

Guern called out to him. "Here he comes!"

Braefar's heart sank. On the far hillside he saw a single rider on a white horse, the sinking sun turning his armor to gold.

"Oh, no!" whispered Braefar. He scanned the hills for signs of the accompanying Iron Wolves, but slowly, as the rider approached, he realized that the man was alone. "Oh, Conn, why did you come?" he said.

Connavar the King rode into the circle. He was wearing a winged helm of bright silver, a breastplate embossed with the fawn in brambles crest of his house, and the famous patchwork cloak. At his side was the legendary Seidh sword with its hilt of gold. His full-faced battle helm was on the pommel of his saddle. The king dismounted and walked forward. He did not look at Braefar, who slunk back into the shadows of the stones.

Guern stepped forward. "Come and join us, Connavar. Let us talk of a new peace."

"You have not asked me here to talk," said Connavar, drawing his sword and resting the blade on the rocky ground, his hands on the golden pommel. "You have asked me here to die. Come, then, traitors. I am here. And I am alone."

The eight men around the campfire had stood as the king rode in. Now they drew their swords and formed a half circle around the golden warrior facing them. Despite their numerical advantage they were reluctant to attack. This was not a mere man facing them. This was Connavar, the Demonblade, the warrior king who had never tasted defeat.

Braefar watched the scene, and a terrible sadness filled him. Conn had never looked more magnificent than he did at this moment, whereas his enemies had become in Braefar's eyes small men with small dreams. Braefar had never wanted this. He knew it now. He drew his own sword, determined to rush in and aid his brother. Yet he did not. His legs would not obey him, and he stood, as he had all those years ago when the bear had attacked, and did nothing.

Suddenly two of the men rushed in. Connavar swung the Seidh blade in two slashing cuts. Blood sprayed into the air, and the men fell. The other six rushed in, hacking and cutting.

At that moment there was a blast of cold air, and the circle trembled. A bright light shone, and a warrior leapt from nowhere. Braefar blinked, his sword falling from his nerveless fingers. This new warrior carried a golden shield of incredible brightness. He rushed at the fighting men, smashing the shield into the face of the first and driving his sword through the ribs of a second.

Braefar looked down at his fallen sword. He wanted to stoop to pick it up, but his legs were trembling, and he feared he would fall if he tried. So he drew his dagger. The sound of sword blades clashing and the screams of dying men ripped through him, and he fell back against a stone column, squeezing shut his eyes and holding his fists over his ears. He could not shut out the sounds and instead forced his mind to remember happier times, when he and Conn, as children, had played on the slopes above Three Streams.

The sounds ceased, and Braefar opened his eyes. The new warrior—he saw now it was the bastard Bane—was standing alongside the king, holding his arm. Connavar's winged helm was lying on the ground close by, dented by a sword blade. There was blood on the king's cheek, dripping to his breastplate. There was more blood on his left arm. Braefar watched as Connavar loosened his breastplate. Bane pulled it clear. Then the king shrugged out of his mail shirt. Braefar saw two huge bruises on the king's left side, the skin gashed.

The trembling ceased, and Braefar tottered forward. Connavar saw him, and his expression changed. Braefar had expected—desired—anger. But there was only sorrow in the king's features.

"Why, Wing?" he asked.

"Why? For all the hurts and humiliations you have piled upon me."

"What hurts? I love you, Wing. I always have."

"I know how you have laughed at me all these years. Don't lie to me, Conn. I know."

"No one laughed," said Connavar. "Not in my presence. Where did you hear such nonsense?" He stepped in toward Braefar. "Let us put this behind us, Wing," he said. "There is a great battle coming . . ." He reached out to his brother.

"Don't touch me!" yelled Braefar, lashing out, the dagger in his hand almost forgotten. In that fraction of a heartbeat, with his anguish and anger paramount, Braefar tilted his fist. The blade slid between Connavar's ribs. The king grunted and fell back, blood streaming from the wound.

"No! I didn't mean . . ."

Bane drew his sword and advanced on the slender figure. "Leave him! Don't kill him!" said the king, and then he slumped to the ground. Bane stood for a moment, his cold eyes locked to Braefar's tortured face.

"Get away from here, you snake!" he hissed. "If I ever see you again, I'll kill you where you stand."

For a moment Braefar did not move. Bane's sword came up. Braefar turned and sprinted for the woods.

He ran and ran, legs pumping, heart racing.

*   *   *

Bane was stunned. He thought Riamfada's prophecy had been proved wrong. He and Connavar had killed the rebels, and the king had sustained but a few minor scratches and bruises. But now, as he looked down at the gray-faced man sitting quietly, his back to a column of stone, Bane knew he was dying. The dagger had plunged deep.

As the light faded, Connavar began to shiver. Bane removed his own cloak and draped it around Connavar's upper body. "Are you in pain?" asked the younger man.

Connavar coughed, and blood dribbled into his beard. "A little," he confessed. "Where is Wing?"

"He ran into the woods. Why did you want him spared?"

Connavar leaned his head back against the stone. He smiled. "He's my little brother," he said. "I've looked after him all my life."

"He's a treacherous dog, and he's killed you."

"I came . . . here to die," said Connavar. "That was the price the Morrigu wanted. I don't know why. She always made it clear that the defeat of Stone was . . . important. Without me . . ." He fell silent for a moment. "What are you doing here, Bane?"

"A friend of yours asked me to come. Riamfada."

"The little fish," said Connavar.

"Fish?" queried Bane.

"When he was . . . human . . . his legs were useless. Govannan and I used to carry him to the Riguan Falls. We . . . taught him to swim."

Bane looked into the pale face of the dying man. "He was the boy you were carrying when the bear attacked?"

"The same. The Seidh gave his spirit a home." Connavar groaned, his face contorting. "Damn, but this little wound is troublesome." He looked up into Bane's face. "I am glad you're here, Bane. It would have hurt my soul to die without . . ." He winced again, his body spasming.

"Don't talk," said Bane. "Just rest easy."

"To what purpose?" asked Connavar, forcing a smile. "When we lifted the Morrigu, I saw many things, and I shared moments of your life. When you won that race and came running toward me . . . You remember?"

"Of course I remember. You turned your back on me."

"I am sorry for that, Bane. When I saw you running ahead of the others, I was so proud, I thought my heart would break. But I couldn't stay. To have embraced you and acknowledged you as my son would have meant seeing your mother, and I had sworn never to cast eyes upon her again. If I had my life over, I would do so many things differently."

"You blamed her for your own shortcomings," Bane said, without anger.

"No," said the king. "I never blamed Arian. I loved her from the moment I first saw her. The fault was entirely mine. But I had to pay for my evil, for the slaughter of innocents and the death of Tae." The king lapsed into silence, and Bane thought he had died. The night grew colder.

A movement came from behind. Bane rose and whirled, sword in hand. A straw-haired boy in a faded tunic stood there. He looked startled as Bane swung on him. Bane put away his sword. "What are you doing here, boy?" he asked.

"I saw it," said the lad. "Wolves chased me, and I climbed a tree. I saw the fight and saw that man stab the king. Is he going to be all right?"

"Gather some wood for a fire," said Bane, then returned to Connavar's side. Reaching out, he touched the king's throat. A pulse was beating weakly there. Connavar's eyes opened, and he reached up, taking Bane's hand.

"I had a vision," he said. "I saw myself dying here, but I also saw myself leading a charge against the enemy. I didn't understand how both could be true. I see it now . . . I see it!" Once more he lapsed into unconsciousness.

The boy gathered wood and laid a fire close by. Then he found several pieces of flint, and Bane sat quietly, listening to the rhythmic strikes of the firestone. At last a flame caught in the tinder, and the wood began to crackle. The boy nursed it to life, then eased himself around to sit on the other side of the king. "He's not going to die, is he?" he asked.

"What is your name, boy?"

"Axis. The king came here once and gave my da a bull, for ours had died."

"You keep the fire going, Axis," Bane said gently. "We'll keep him warm."

"He is going to die, then?" said the boy, tears spilling to his cheeks.

"Yes, Axis, he is going to die. Tend to the fire."

Bane glanced down. The king's hand was still holding to his own. Bane felt the warmth in the fingers and saw the battle scars on the king's arm. Blood had ceased to flow from the wound in his side, but Bane knew that internal bleeding continued. He had seen wounds like this in the arena. It might take hours yet, but death was certain.

The moon rose above the stone circle. Bane looked around at the boy by the fire. "Go and check the horses the killers rode," he said. "Perhaps they had food. You look hungry."

"I am hungry," said Axis. "Shall I bring the horses into the circle? The wolves may still be close by."

"Yes, do that," said Bane.

The boy ran off and came back moments later leading three horses, which he tethered inside the circle. "The rest ran off," he said. Axis moved past the fire, gathering the reins of the king's white gelding, bringing that also close to the fire. Then he searched the saddlebags of the other mounts, coming up with several thick slices of ham wrapped in muslin. He offered some to Bane, and the two sat in silence as they ate. Time passed slowly. The boy Axis fell asleep by the fire, and Bane found himself thinking of the past, of his hatred for Connavar, of his yearning to be accepted and acknowledged. He had lived so long dreaming of the day he would kill this man whose hand he now held.

The king groaned again. Bane looked at his face and saw that his eyes were open. But they were not focused on him. "Ah, Wing," the king said, "don't look so sad. Everything will be all right."

"Connavar!" said Bane, squeezing the king's fingers. Connavar blinked and then looked at Bane.

"He came back," he said. "He is waiting for me."

Bane said nothing, for there was nothing to say.

"Put . . . my sword . . . in my hands," said Connavar, his voice fading. The blade was leaning against the stone behind the king. Bane lifted it, placing the hilt within reach. Connavar did not move. Carefully Bane opened his fingers, pressing them closed around the fabled hilt. The dying man gave a last sigh, then his head sagged, his body sliding into Bane's arms. For a little while Bane sat holding the king, feeling the weight of Connavar's head against his shoulder. Then he laid the body down.

Riamfada walked into the stone circle and knelt beside the body, leaning over and kissing the brow. He turned to Bane. "I thank you for being with him," he said.

"Why didn't you tell me about Braefar? I could have stopped him."

"I did not know exactly how it would happen, Bane, only that it would happen."

"I'd like to find him and kill him myself," said Bane.

"There is no need. Braefar is dead. He ran into the woods and slashed his own throat with the dagger that killed Connavar. Now he and his brother are together, and all the ill feeling is gone."

"Then it was Braefar the king saw as he was dying?"

"Aye, it was."

Bane rose.

"Have you made your choice?" asked Riamfada.

"I have, as I think you knew I would."

"Of course," said Riamfada. "You are the son of Connavar, and I would expect no less."

◇ **16** ◇

IN THE FAINT light of the predawn, as the breakfast trumpet sounded, Jasaray awoke from a light sleep. For the first time in years he had suffered bad dreams. He had been walking toward a torchlit parade being held in his honor. As the crowds cheered, he saw a shadow above him and realized it was a falcon flying through the night sky. He looked up, wondering what would force a sunlight bird of prey to take to the skies in darkness. Then it swooped down toward him, its talons rending his face.

Jasaray shivered at the memory. He had a slight ache in his back and groaned as he sat up. It had been some years since he had embarked on a campaign, and at sixty-five his body was complaining bitterly. His joints had throbbed since he had arrived at Accia during a thunderstorm, and his mood was sour.

Outside the command tent he could hear men moving about their chores, the stripping down of tents ready to be rolled and packed, the gathering at food lines for the bowl of hot meat broth and the hunk of bread, the rattling of harnesses, the banter of fighting men who knew that a battle loomed. These were sounds Jasaray had come to love with a passion that had been missing from every other aspect of his life. He had hoped that the campaign against the Rigante and their allies would lift his spirits and resurrect the joy of his youth, but that hope seemed doomed now. There was no way that the coming victory would really satisfy either the people of Stone or himself. The citizens were used to victories by Jasaray and his Panthers against overwhelming odds. Invincible Jasaray!

The emperor sighed. Who would have imagined thirty-seven years ago that the spindly lecturer in mathematics would become the greatest military genius of the age? Certainly not the man himself, Jasaray thought with a wry smile.

The twenty-eight-year-old whose coordination was so bad that he had never mastered either swordplay or the throwing of spears, who had never attended the military academy, found that his first rank in the army was that of a general. It had been wonderfully bizarre. The civil war was at its height, and the biggest problem facing those trying to save the republic concerned logistics and supply: food for the army, wagons, horses, weapons. In short, the Third Army of the Republic, under Sobius, needed a qualified quartermaster. In order for him to negotiate at the highest level, Sobius had made Jasaray a general. He had, as they hoped, proved a brilliant quarter-master, and the Third Army was never short of equipment or food. What it was short of, however, was intelligent leadership, and that led to the army's being routed by the rebels. In the space of three short days, with Sobius and his staff dead, Jasaray was the only general who could take the field.

And he had, fighting a stunning rearguard action, using tactics no one had ever encountered, marshaling his troops with a precision previously unheard of. Thus the man known with affectionate contempt as the Scholar won the war and saved the republic.

Within the next few years the increasingly powerful Jasaray wrote three manuals of combat that changed the face of war. His armies were well armed, well fed, and superbly disciplined, exchanging personal heroism for unit cohesion, brute strength for tactical brilliance. No Stone army under Jasaray had ever tasted defeat. In fact, the only stain on the military history of Stone had come at the hands of Connavar when the idiot Valanus had marched a pitifully small force deep into Rigante territory and been massacred.

Now that reverse was to be expunged from memory by a crushing victory, yet there would be little joy in it. Jasaray had hoped Connavar would be able to gather an army of at least a hundred thousand. Instead reports suggested that less than fifty thousand opposed him.

What a waste of time and energy, thought Jasaray, rising

from his bed and pouring himself a goblet of water. He should have sent Barus to subdue the tribes. And he would have done just that except for the unrelenting and increasing boredom he had suffered since becoming emperor. He could have blessed Naldemus for his treachery, which at least had provided a spark of excitement. The truth remained that the only real pleasure still to be had was on the battlefield, and Stone was running out of worthwhile enemies. Jasaray could have invaded the Rigante many times over the years, but he had reserved Connavar as a special treat, the last great opponent in an increasingly dull world.

Jasaray had followed his career with interest, remembering the young Keltoi who had served under him in the battles against the Perdii. A fine young man, brave and intelligent, yet with the mental strength to curb the wild, reckless excesses of his Keltoi nature. This day's battle, though its outcome was certain, would not be an easy one. And there would be no glory in it. Back in Stone they would hear of his victory and shrug. "Ah, well," they would say, "it was only a few tribesmen."

The tent flap opened, and one of his guards looked inside. Seeing the emperor awake, he called out, "The scouts are back, lord."

"Send them in."

Two Cenii scouts entered the tent, accompanied by the guards, who watched them warily. Both of the Keltoi were rough-looking men, sour-faced and surly.

"Well?" asked Jasaray.

"The Rigante are forming with their backs to the river," said the first. "They are manning a line of hills around a mile north of here."

"How many?"

The scout spread his arms. "A little more than you have here. I can't count that high."

The general Heltian ducked under the tent flap. Jasaray dismissed the scouts and told Heltian to have horses saddled.

Minutes later, dressed in a simple tunic and a hooded woolen coat, Jasaray, with Heltian and three junior officers, rode from the night fortress. Jasaray did not take a weapon. There were two reasons for this. The first was that having never mastered the sword, he would be useless in any physical encounter. The second reason, however, was far more important. The troops would watch their emperor riding out unarmed to view the enemy and say, "There goes the Scholar, afraid of no man." They would chuckle, and much of the prebattle tension would ease away.

Jasaray and his officers rode out onto the open land to the north until they spied the enemy forces ranged against them. Jasaray reined in. His eyes were not as sharp as once they had been, but vanity stopped him from admitting it. He turned to one of the junior officers. "Maro, describe their formation."

The young man gazed out over the distant ranks of tribesmen. "They have massed in the center, possibly some fifteen thousand men. I can see heavy infantry to the left and right of them but no cavalry or archers as yet."

"What does the formation suggest?" asked the emperor.

"I . . . do not know, lord," admitted the young man.

"What about you?" Jasaray asked a second officer.

"They expect us to attack the center and have reinforced it?" he suggested without confidence.

As the five riders studied the enemy, a long column of heavily armored riders appeared a half mile to the right, moving slowly along the hilltops. "That will be Fiallach and his Iron Wolves," said Jasaray. "They will bear watching. Can anyone see Connavar?"

"I see the king's banner," said Maro, pointing to the center of the enemy. Fluttering on the breeze was a pale blue cloth with a white motif.

"What are they doing now?" asked Jasaray, squinting toward the enemy lines.

"They are passing out food, lord," said Maro.

"A wise general knows that men fight better on a full belly," said the emperor. "Well, gentlemen, I think we have seen enough." Turning his mount awkwardly, he heeled it into a canter and rode back to the earth fortress.

Inviting Heltian into his tent, he ordered servants to bring them breakfast. While they ate, Jasaray pictured the battlefield. The land was flat between the hills, then steadily rising. Beyond the Rigante center was a wide, deep river, and that meant that Connavar had left himself without a natural line of retreat. "What do you think?" he asked Heltian.

The normally grim-faced officer smiled. "I'm glad you didn't ask me in front of the youngsters. I'm probably wrong, but it looks to me like they are preparing for a head-to-head, win-or-die battle. Nothing more."

"Yes, you are wrong," said Jasaray. "Connavar is a little more cunning than that. If that were the true situation, he would have placed his heavy infantry at the center. But no, they are, with the cavalry, on the flanks. Their center stretches for at least a quarter of a mile. To attack along its length we would normally adopt a five formation. It is Connavar's hope we will do just that and launch a major push against his center. Then his heavy infantry would move against our flanks, compressing our forces, making maneuverability difficult. Since his center is lightly armed, he would expect us to use our archers to thin their ranks, using up all their shafts. At that point the Iron Wolves would charge our rear, compressing us further. Surrounded, with no opportunity to change our tactics, we would be slaughtered like sheep."

"Then how do we proceed, lord?" asked Heltian.

"Exactly as they require. We will march in the five formation, close ranks ten deep, archers at the rear. As we approach their center, that formation will change into the full open fighting square, six deep, two Panthers in reserve. The archers will not loose a shaft until ordered by me. We will hold them for the charge of the Iron Wolves. Once the open square is fully functional, we will advance slowly against their center and crush them. If possible I want Connavar taken alive. He will be my trophy. We will take him in chains to Stone and execute him in the Great Arena."

"You make it sound like an easy day, lord," said Heltian.

"Oh, I don't doubt Connavar will have a few surprises for us. Either him or that brother of his, Bran. Clever man. I should have had him killed when he visited Stone."

"Do you want him taken alive, too, lord?"

Jasaray shook his head. "No. Kill him with the rest. No prisoners today, Heltian. No slave lines. Every Keltoi standing against us must die. When Valanus was defeated, the Rigante placed Stone heads upon spears at the border. Today we will plant a forest of heads so that all who dream of rising against Stone will take heed."

"Yes, lord."

Jasaray saw that the man looked troubled. "What is it, Heltian?"

"You are the Scholar, and I do not have your skills in strategy, lord. Yet it seems to me that to march into their trap is unnecessary. If we storm their right, pushing back their infantry, they will be forced to change their battle plan and be thrown into disarray."

"Ah, yes," Jasaray said, with a smile, "indeed they would be. But where's the joy in such a simple victory? The enemy will think they have us, and then, when we show that we know their plan, their hearts will break. Cruel, I know, but emperors must have their pleasures."

Bendegit Bran stood on the rising ground and watched as the columns of Stone marched out of the morning mist almost a mile to the south. Around him the volunteer forces from Pannone, Norvii, and Rigante stood their ground, fierce eyes observing the advancing enemy.

Bran had made no fiery speeches to these men or exhorted them to fight hard for their loved ones and their land. There was no need. They knew that this day's battle could change forever the lives of every Keltoi. They knew that if they failed, their wives and daughters would be enslaved, their children slaughtered. No, thought Bran, there was no need to inspire these men.

Although in truth he wished there was someone who could inspire him.

The death of his firstborn son had all but unmanned him, but the news Banouin had given him several hours earlier had been crushing.

Connavar was dead, killed by Braefar.

Even now Bran could scarcely believe it. Wing had always been a troubled soul, but Bran had never doubted his love for Conn or his own people. Yet he had in one dreadful thrust destroyed both his brother and the hopes of the Keltoi. Connavar's legend was such that he was worth ten thousand men in battle, for the troops would see him in his golden armor, and their spirits would soar like eagles. Even now Bran could see men scanning the hillsides, wondering when the king would appear.

Ahead, on the flat plain, the army of Stone continued its advance, the columns smoothly melding, the formation changing. Closer now, and Bran could see sunlight glinting on their helms and the great rectangular shields they carried. Their formation was, as he had hoped, the classic five, ten ranks deep along a wide front, their flanks defended by six Panthers, three on either side, stretching back down the plain and creating three sides of a square. Between the defensive lines Bran saw the Stone archers bringing up the rear. He gauged their numbers to be around a thousand.

Scanning the enemy force, Bran calculated their numbers. He reckoned Jasaray had brought ten Panthers, plus his archers: 31,000 fighting men. That meant he had left two Panthers to defend the night fortress, allowing himself room to withdraw to a position of safety if the battle should go against him. Against him Bran had marshaled just over forty thousand tribesmen, many of them untried in major battles. Despite the numerical superiority, the reality was that Jasaray had the stronger force. The real strength of the Keltoi army lay in the ten thousand Iron Wolves, eight thousand heavy infantry, and three thousand horse archers. These were battle-hardened, well-trained, and disciplined fighters. The rest were brave tribesmen who, left to their own devices, would be cut to pieces by the soldiers of Stone within an hour.

The wind changed, and the sound of drumbeats echoed across the field as the Stone army continued its march toward the Keltoi center. Bran signaled his archers to draw up behind the front lines. Hundreds of Rigante bowmen ran forward.

Three hundred yards away now, and a trumpet sounded in the enemy ranks. The soldiers of Stone halted their march, the formation changing again. Bran's heart sank, for the Stone line spread out into the open fighting square. Then they advanced once more. Bran's mind raced. They could still envelop the enemy, but to what advantage? Their only hope had been to compress them, destroying their ability to maneuver. This new formation was flexible, and Bran could see two

Panthers in reserve at the center, ready to plug any gaps that might develop.

Two hundred yards, and Bran could see the figure of Jasaray at the center of the enemy square. The emperor was wearing a simple unadorned breastplate of iron and an old battered helm. He was walking with his hands clasped behind his back and chatting to the officer beside him.

One hundred yards, and the drums picked up their beat. The advance quickened. Bran could feel the tension in the men around him, the beginnings of fear.

"Death to Stone!" bellowed Bran, drawing his sword and holding it high. A huge cry went up from the Keltoi, a roaring, releasing wall of sound that swept over the advancing ranks.

Fifty yards. Now Bran could see individual faces. "Archers!" he shouted.

The Rigante bowmen notched shafts to their bowstrings, drew back, and let fly. Bran saw four Stone soldiers run to Jasaray, locking their shields around the emperor. Most of the shafts clattered from shields and helms, but a few found gaps in armor and sliced into unprotected flesh. A score of soldiers in the front line fell. The advance continued. Volley after volley soared through the air.

Twenty yards, and Bran signaled a halt to the shooting. They had hit and injured some two hundred enemy soldiers, many of whom continued to march. Then the enemy shouted a battle cry and surged forward. The Keltoi leaped to meet them.

And the killing began.

Following Bran's orders, the Gath general Osta led his horse archers in a flanking attack against the enemy's right. With shields worn on the left arm, the right flank of an advancing army was always more vulnerable. But as Osta's five hundred riders bore down on them, the men of Stone merely spun on their heels, presenting their shields and blocking the first volleys.

Osta swung his men and galloped parallel to the enemy line, shooting as he rode. Beyond the shield wall Osta saw the Stone archers. Not one of them loosed a shaft. The attack having proved abortive, Osta signaled his men to return to the hillside. Once there, the Gath dismounted and walked to where Govannan was waiting with his heavy infantry.

"This doesn't look good," said Osta. "If we attack, we'll break on their shield wall like waves against a cliff."

"We'll wait for the signal from Bran," said Govannan, "then we'll smash that wall or die trying."

"Where in the name of Taranis is Conn?" whispered Osta, leaning in close.

Govannan said nothing. Before the king had ridden out the previous day, he had summoned Govannan to his tent. The white-haired infantry leader had expected a conversation about tactics. Instead Conn had poured him a goblet of wine. "I shall be gone for most of today," he had said. Govannan had seen that the king was in full armor.

"Where to?" he had asked.

"I cannot say."

"The battle is tomorrow, Conn. For the sake of us all, take no risks!"

"Some risks cannot be avoided."

An uneasy silence had developed. Govannan had broken it. "What is it that you wished to discuss?"

Conn had smiled. "You remember the bear?"

"How could I forget?"

"You and I were not friends then, yet you ran to my aid. I have never forgotten that, Van. As the beast tore into me, I saw you attack it, and in that instant I knew what it was to be Rigante. No matter how terrifying the enemy, we stand together and we do not run."

"Why are you saying this?" Govannan had asked, suddenly fearful.

Connavar had smiled. "I wanted to thank you for that day."

"Damn, Conn, but you are worrying me now. Where are you going?"

"To meet someone I love." He had offered his hand, and Govannan had shaken it. "I'll see you tomorrow."

The king had left the tent, mounted the gray horse Windsong, and ridden off toward the east.

"If he doesn't come, we're finished," said Osta, the words jerking Govannan back to the present. Govannan said nothing.

The fighting on the hillside was ferocious now. Hundreds of Rigante were down, and the Stone advance continued.

Fiallach rode down from the hillside, leading ten thousand Iron Wolves. Slowly they filed across the field, just out of bowshot of the enemy rear, forming up into five well-spaced lines, ready for the charge when the signal came.

The giant Rigante warrior longed to kick his horse into a run and thunder toward the hated foe, his blade scything through flesh and bone, and it took a great effort of will merely to sit and await Bran's signal. Especially now, with Bran's plan in ruins and hundreds of Rigante warriors being cut down by the advancing square.

Fiallach stared with undisguised malevolence at the enemy bowmen. Not one shaft had been loosed, and that meant the charge would take place under a rain of death, horses falling, men being trampled under iron-shod hooves. The horses' breasts were covered by chain mail, but their necks, heads, and legs were open to attack. The big man eased his shield from his left arm, hooking it over the high pommel of his saddle. His son, Finnigal, moved alongside. The boy should not have been here, but Vorna had healed him well, and he had insisted on riding beside his father. Fiallach scratched his silver-streaked beard. "Not long now," he said.

Finnigal removed his helm, running his fingers through his hair. "The losses will be fearful," he said. "We'll be riding into an iron-tipped hailstorm."

"Aye, and we'll ride through it," Fiallach said grimly. "This is the moment I have waited half my life for, to destroy once and for all the myth of Stone. And we will, boy."

"Where is the king?" asked Finnigal, echoing the question in every man's mind.

"He'll be here; don't you fret about that. You think Connavar would miss this battle?"

"He's missed it so far," muttered Finnigal.

Fiallach did not respond. The king's absence was a mystery and a worrying one at that. Many men had seen Connavar ride from the camp. By the evening Fiallach had sought out Bran, but he had had no idea where his brother had gone. All he could say was that he and Conn had worked on a strategy and that Conn had left the camp in midafternoon. Fiallach had then spoken to Govannan, who had told him of the conversation earlier, when Connavar had said he was going to meet someone he loved.

"Many men need a woman the night before a battle," said Fiallach. "It helps relax them."

"I think he was planning to meet Braefar."

"For what purpose?"

Govannan shrugged. "To forgive him, perhaps. Hell's teeth, Fiallach, I don't know. What worried me was that it sounded like a farewell."

"You must be mistaken," said Fiallach. "Conn would never leave us at such a time. Gods, man, this is Jasaray we are facing!"

"I hope you are right, my friend," said Govannan, "because without him we'll not succeed. Don't misunderstand me. Bran is a great planner, and you are a fighter beyond compare. But Conn brings his own personal magic. Every man fights harder when he is close. He inspires the men just by his presence."

"He'll be with us," said Fiallach.

But now the battle was under way, and there was no sign of the king. On the slopes far ahead the Stone advance had pushed halfway to the crest. Several thousand Rigante had been killed. Fiallach hefted his shield and slipped it over his arm. Signal or no signal, he would not wait much longer.

A huge cry went up from the right. The heavy infantry on the hillside was cheering wildly. Fiallach swung in the saddle. The lines parted, and Connavar the King came riding through, his golden armor ablaze in the sunlight, his full-faced helm in place, his patchwork cloak streaming in the wind. Upon his arm was a shining shield of gold that glittered so brightly that it seemed the sun itself was riding with him.

"What did I tell you?" said Fiallach, relief flooding him.

Jasaray, hearing the roar from all sides, looked around to see Connavar riding his white horse across the battlefield. He shivered suddenly, even though the sun seemed to shine brighter in the sky for a moment. The feeling was exquisite.

Jasaray thought about it for a moment, analyzing the sensation. This was fear, he realized. How excellent it was. Jasaray's whole body felt alive.

Ahead the advance slowed as the Rigante hurled themselves with renewed vigor at the soldiers of Stone. One Keltoi, half his face sheared away, grabbed at a soldier's shield, dragging it down. A second Keltoi warrior leaped forward, plunging his sword through the face of the shield bearer. The man fell back, and the Rigante thrust himself into the opening, slashing his blade through the throat of a second soldier even as he himself was cut down. The line closed, but the advance had halted. All along the line the Rigante fought with terrifying ferocity.

Heltian moved alongside Jasaray. The emperor glanced at him, and both men stared back at the Iron Wolves and the golden figure riding toward their center.

"A magnificent sight," said Jasaray. "Gaudy but magnificent nonetheless."

"Aye," agreed Heltian. "It makes the flesh crawl."

"He's a throwback to more ancient times," said Jasaray, "embodying the principle of heroic leadership and the days when kings and generals fought in the front line with their men. See how much better they fight now that they see him with them?"

Heltian gave a tight smile. "I'm not so anxious to see them fight better, lord."

Wounded men were being carried back from the front line and laid in the open square behind, where surgeons tended them. "They are still losing two, perhaps three, for every one of ours," said Jasaray. "They cannot sustain such losses for long."

Clasping his hands behind his back, he turned once more to survey the fighting. Because of the slope he could see Bendegit Bran some way above. He was standing beneath the blue and white banner. Now that he was closer, Jasaray noted that the white motif on the banner was a fawn trapped in brambles. How odd, he thought, that a fighting race should have such a motif. Then he recalled having seen it once before. It had been in his tent before the first battle with the Perdii, when he had summoned the young Connavar to meet with him. The fawn in brambles had been fashioned both on his cloak brooch and on the hilt of his sword. Curious, he thought. If we do take him alive, I shall ask him about it.

The Stone line began to bulge inward at the center as the Rigante not only held their ground but pushed back against their enemies. Jasaray signaled for another three sections of reserve warriors to bolster the line. The three hundred men hefted their shields, drew their swords, and marched into place smoothly. The line straightened. Jasaray swung his gaze to the heavy infantry on both sides of his force. It would be soon now, he thought. They cannot compress us, and they cannot hold the center. Connavar would be forced to signal the heavy infantry to advance in order to take the pressure away from his brother.

He turned to Heltian. "Drop back to the reserves and be ready to bolster the flanks. Leave two Panthers to close the rear of the square once the Iron Wolves charge."

"Yes, lord," said Heltian.

Even as the general moved back, Jasaray saw the man next to Bendegit Bran hoist the fawn in brambles banner and wave it from side to side.

The heavy infantry began to move. Jasaray had expected them to charge down the slope in the Keltoi manner, racing to their doom with all the enthusiasm of young men pursuing comely maidens. Instead they came slowly, shields at the ready. He saw then that they were not carrying the long-bladed swords so popular among the tribes but short stabbing swords like those of his own soldiers. This was cause for concern, for the Keltoi longsword was an inadequate weapon for close-quarter fighting, since the tribesmen had to open their ranks in order to swing the swords. Short swords meant they could fight shoulder to shoulder with their comrades, putting more pressure on the Stone line. They have the weapons, and they are mimicking our discipline, he thought. It is a compliment of a kind. How long that discipline will last is quite another matter.

The heavy infantry came down the slope, then broke into a run, not a headlong charge but a steady lope. At the last moment, just before their shields crashed against those of the Stone soldiers in the front rank, they let out a ferocious battle cry. The Stone line bulged inward on both sides, then steadied. The noise of clashing shields and slashing swords was thunderous. And Jasaray loved it.

Ahead the advance up the hill had started once more and Bran had been drawn into the fighting. Jasaray swung and stared back at the golden figure on the white horse. "Come," he said softly. "Pay a visit to your old friend."

Bane had ridden through the night, using two of the rebels' horses to conserve the energy of Connavar's white gelding. Leaving the spare horses behind the lines, he rode through the heavy infantry, their cheers washing over him, and then onto the slope. From there he could see Fiallach riding down from the hillside, leading ten thousand Iron Wolves. Slowly they filed across the field, just out of bowshot of the enemy rear, forming up into five well-spaced lines, ready for the charge when the signal came. As Fiallach drew rein, he grunted, the swollen boil just below his belt sending a stab of pain into his back. Should have had it lanced yesterday, he thought. It was throbbing mercilessly now. Fiallach absorbed the pain, allowing it to fuel his battle fury.

Bane galloped the gelding down the hillside and out onto the flat land beyond. The Iron Wolves drew their swords and sent up a welcoming roar as he approached. Fiallach rode to meet him. The big man came close, and Bane, despite the full-faced helm of bronze that showed only his eyes, felt nervous under his scrutiny.

"By heavens, Conn, you had me worried," said Fiallach.

"I am here now," said Bane, deepening his voice and hoping that the metallic echo of the helm would disguise it sufficiently.

Fiallach looked at him closely for a moment. "Well, Bran is in trouble. Do we charge?"

Bane was about to agree. Laying his hand on the hilt of Connavar's sword, he drew it. As his fingers touched the weapon, he felt a cold breeze whisper into his mind. "Not yet, my son."

The shock was so great that he almost dropped the sword.

"I am with you for a little time. Ride to the center and wait for the right moment."

"How will I know it?"

"You'll see the wheels of fire. Now, I think Fiallach is suspicious. Our eyes may be the same, but I am a little weightier than you."

Bane turned to the silent Fiallach. "Did you get that boil lanced?" he asked.

Fiallach laughed. "Thought I'd wait and ask some Stone soldier to do it for me. Are you all right, Conn? Your voice sounds strange."

"Never better, my friend," said Bane, touching heels to the white gelding and moving into position.

High in the sky, just below the scudding white clouds, Banouin's spirit watched the battle. The great square of the Stone army was moving inexorably up the hillside, and already some three thousand Keltoi had died.

The arrival of Connavar stunned the young druid, and he sped instantly to the Circle of Balg. There he saw the body of the king, a young, yellow-haired boy sitting beside it. Returning to the battlefield, he knew instantly that only one person could be impersonating the king: the son who despised him and who had refused to fight alongside the Rigante.

Banouin floated above the carnage, high enough so that he did not see the horror of blades cleaving flesh. From there the battle was bloodless, the giant square of Stone moving slowly northward, pushing the Rigante back toward the river.

Once more the Rigante banner was waved from side to side.

On the hillsides to the left and right of the square horsemen appeared, hauling wagons onto the crest. Flaming torches were thrown into the wagons, and oily black smoke drifted up into the sky. There were three wagons on each hill, and the horsemen pulled on the ropes, dragging the burning vehicles out onto the slopes. Slowly they gathered pace. The horsemen loosed their ropes and rode clear of the blazing wagons as they hurtled toward the Stone square.

The soldiers below, seeing the wagons bearing down upon them, tried to break lines, allowing them to pass through. Not everyone managed to escape, and several soldiers were crushed beneath the wheels. Inside the wagons the huge pottery jars of lantern oil cracked in the heat, spilling their contents to the damp straw that surrounded them. Other jars exploded, spraying burning oil over soldiers nearby, setting fire to cloaks and leggings. Two of the blazing wagons smashed into the ranks of bowmen, scattering them. Smoke and flames belched out in a roar of thunder.

Standing with his unit among the men of the reserve Panthers, young Maro tore off his red cloak as flames licked at it. Throwing it to the ground, he stamped out the fire. His eyes were stinging with heat and smoke. Around him several of the men also were trying to beat out the flames on their clothing.

The northerly breeze sent the smoke drifting toward the south. Maro saw that very few men had been injured by the attack. The wagons had come to a stop now and were burning brightly, but the line had closed once more. The archers were regrouping, and all was returning to normal.

Then he heard the thunder and glanced at the sky, expecting to see storm clouds. But there were none, and in that moment he realized the truth. There was no storm. The thunder was coming from the south, and it was not emanating from the sky. The ground was shaking beneath his feet.

From out of the smoke came the charging horsemen of Connavar's Iron Wolves, and at their head was a figure in gold with a shining shield.

It seemed to Maro at that moment that time slowed. He saw the Stone archers, still trying to regroup, string their bows and send a ragged volley toward the charging horsemen. The arrows seemed to hang in the air forever. Then they slashed home, and scores of horses fell. Not one shaft struck the golden rider, though many were aimed at him. They bounced from his shield or sailed past him, plunging into the riders close by. Smoke billowed back over the archers, causing many of them to cough and splutter, their eyes streaming.

Despite their losses the Iron Wolves continued to thunder toward the square. Maro found himself suddenly thinking of Cara and his son and the sunlit garden behind the house. He felt a great sadness upon him as he thought of all the letters he had written and had never been able to send.

He drew his sword. The Iron Wolves came out of the smoke, bright swords in their hands. From behind he heard Heltian

order the advance. The reserve Panthers began to form a
fighting line, locking shields.

Maro closed his eyes for a moment and sent a brief prayer
to the Source. "Let me live to see my son," he whispered.

Bane leaned low over the gelding's neck as it thundered
toward the Stone archers. A volley of shafts slashed through
the air. Raising his shield, Bane glanced left and right. Alongside him horses went down, their riders thrown through the
air. An arrow slashed the gelding's flanks and ricocheted from
the bronze greave on Bane's right leg. Another arrow glanced
from the rim of his shield.

Hundreds of shafts sliced into the riders, then hundreds
more, but the charge continued. Bane risked a glance forward. Some of the bowmen had begun to run, seeking the
transient security of a place behind the reserve Panthers, who
were trying to form a shield wall. Their efforts were ham-
pered by the fleeing archers.

The gelding galloped into the square, knocking several
bowmen from their feet. The Seidh sword slashed down, cutting through an iron helm and crushing the skull beneath.
Bane had never known such a weapon, light as a wand yet
able to cut through armor and bone. Beside him he saw Fiallach, an arrow jutting from his left shoulder, ride into the
mass of bowmen, striking left and right. Another arrow hit
him high in the back, but he ignored it and carried on cutting
and killing. Bane dragged on the reins, then charged the
forming shield wall, scattering the soldiers.

The gelding went down. Bane kicked his feet free of the stirrups and jumped clear. A Stone soldier ran at him. The Seidh
sword slashed out, cutting through the man's sword arm at the
wrist. Hand and sword fell to the grass. The man screamed.
Bane killed him, then swung to face another attack. Riders
forced their mounts around him, pushing back the Stone soldiers. Fiallach, grabbing the reins of a riderless horse, brought
it to Bane, who swung into the saddle. Smoke from the burning
wagons billowed about him as he charged again at the reserve
Panthers.

Higher up the slope, some eighty yards away, Jasaray
ordered a change in formation. Command trumpets were

sounded, and several ranks on the left and right faded back to reinforce the reserve. This had the effect of weakening the square, and Govannan urged his men to greater efforts. Osta and the horse archers rode in behind the Iron Wolves. Dropping their bows, they drew sabers and launched an attack against the inner left side of the square.

Bane's second horse was killed under him and collapsed headfirst. Bane was thrown from the saddle and landed awkwardly. A Stone soldier ran at him. Rising to his knees, Bane blocked the thrust. Then Fiallach rode his horse at the man, sending him spinning from his feet. An arrow slashed through the throat of Fiallach's mount, and it reared and fell. Fiallach jumped clear and ran to stand back to back with Bane. Stone soldiers hurled themselves at the two men. A blade hammered against Fiallach's mail shirt, snapping a rib. The big man's fist slammed into the soldier's face, knocking him back, then the Rigante's sword cleaved his skull.

Once again the Iron Wolves rallied around the golden figure, leaping from their mounts to form a shield wall of their own. Bane glanced at Fiallach. There was blood on the big man's face, and he was breathing heavily. "That boil troubling you?" shouted Bane.

Fiallach grinned. A sword lunged for the older man's face. Bane blocked the blow, killing the wielder with a reverse cut across the throat. On the left several hundred Iron Wolves had breached the Stone line. Breaking into a gallop, they rode behind the reserve, which struggled to form its own defensive square. Bane and the Iron Wolves around him attacked again. Bane beat aside a shield and sent his sword slashing through the bearer's leg. The man fell. Fiallach, following in, killed him.

A young dark-haired officer stepped in front of Bane. It was Cara's husband, the young Maro. Maro's sword slashed toward him. Bane swayed back, deflecting the blow with ease. Fiallach's sword smashed through the young man's skull, sending blood and brains splattering over Bane's golden armor.

On the hillside at the north of the square Jasaray drew back his front lines, ordering Heltian to reinforce the rear with another two Panthers. "Oh, and forget what I said about taking Connavar alive. I rather feel that his death would be advantageous at this point."

Jasaray stood calmly, arms clasped behind his back. The charge of the Iron Wolves had been well executed, the use of the fire wagons quite brilliant. But the charge was over now, the battle still to be decided. Jasaray's expert eyes scanned the scene. More than half the Rigante army had been killed or wounded, whereas he had lost around a third of his force. The death of Connavar would turn the tide. It was always the problem with heroic leadership. Yes, the men would be inspired by the golden figure at their head. But when that man died, so, too, did the inspiration, and in its place came despair. Connavar was the pumping heart of the Rigante. Every tribesman fighting there was performing above his abilities as a result of his presence. They would break and run when they saw him fall, Jasaray knew.

The emperor watched dispassionately as Heltian led another six thousand men into the fray. They charged into the Iron Wolves who had made it to the rear of the reserve square, killing the horses, toppling the riders, and stabbing them to death. Then, forming a fighting wedge, they began to push back at Connavar and the men with him. Connavar, as Jasaray had expected, gave no ground, and the Stone Panthers surged around the Iron Wolves. Now Connavar was fighting within his own defensive ring. The losses suffered by the Panthers were very high, for they were fighting not lightly armored tribesmen but Connavar's elite warriors, picked for their courage and strength. Even so they were cut off from the main force of Iron Wolves and outnumbered some six to one. It was, Jasaray considered, but a matter of time before the golden-garbed warrior fell beneath the stabbing iron of Stone.

On the outside of the square Govannan saw Connavar's plight. "The king! The king!" he shouted. The heavy infantry, having already lost more than half its number, tore into the shield wall ahead of it, fighting like demons now. Govannan rammed his shield at the line, which suddenly gave. Moving into the breach, he killed two startled soldiers. A third dealt him a terrible blow to his helm, which shattered. The sword smashed his skull, and Govannan half fell, righted himself, and sent a vicious cut into the man's shoulder, half severing his arm. With a cry of pain the soldier fell. Govannan's men poured through the breach after him. It was as if a dam had burst. The soldiers of Stone peeled back in disarray, and the wall broke in a dozen places. Govannan staggered forward, bright lights exploding around his eyes, blood pouring to his neck. He knew he was dying but hung on grimly, staggering toward the men surrounding his king. Several hundred infantry warriors followed him and fell upon the rear of the force surrounding Connavar. Surprised by the suddenness of the assault, the Stone soldiers had no time to regroup. Some tried to turn to face this new attack; others shuffled back in an attempt to make a shield wall.

At the center of the fighting Bane, his armor soaked in blood now, cut a path through to Govannan, Fiallach beside him. Just before they met, Bane stumbled. Two men stabbed out at him. Fiallach leapt to shield Bane. A sword plunged into his shoulder. He killed the wielder, then a second blow slashed into his side. Fiallach fell. Bane plunged his sword into the heart of the soldier, dragging it clear to hack through the skull of a second man. As he reached Govannan, he saw the general slump to the ground, blood bubbling from a split in his skull. The soldiers of Stone fell back. Bane crouched down beside the kneeling Govannan. "Getting . . . to be . . . a habit . . . saving you, Conn," whispered Govannan. "But that damned . . . bear was . . . less troublesome." He pitched forward. Bane caught him, but he was dead.

On the far side of the square Osta's horse archers, dismounted now, drove through the Stone lines, linking up with the heavy infantry beyond. Jasaray's square was in ruins.

The dawning awareness of defeat permeated the Stone lines. At first a few men started to run toward the south and the transient safety of the night fortress. Then a few score threw down their shields and took to their heels. The trickle became a stream and then a flood as the army of Stone crumbled and fled.

Heltian tried to gather a wall around Jasaray, but Bane rushed at him, slashing his sword through the officer's throat. Heltian fell at Jasaray's feet and even in death tried to raise his shield to protect his emperor.

Jasaray stood calm as ever, his hands behind him. "I take it you haven't come to surrender?" he asked the man he believed to be Connavar.

Bane pulled clear the full-faced helm and saw the shock register on the emperor's face. "Where is Connavar?" asked Jasaray.

"Murdered by his brother," Bane told him.

Jasaray suddenly laughed, the sound full of humor. "So, in the end I have been defeated by a boy with no understanding of battle strategy. How droll!"

"You are a brave man," said Bane, "and I wish I could let you live. You have any gods you would wish to pray to?"

"No," said Jasaray.

The Seidh sword flashed in the morning sun, slicing through Jasaray's thin neck. The head fell to the ground and rolled a few feet. The body sagged sideways and sprawled to the grass.

Bane walked back to where Fiallach lay on the ground. The big man was still breathing, though his face was pale.

"They . . . lanced my boil," said Fiallach, forcing a smile. "I knew . . . you were not Conn." Arrowheads had pierced the rings of the chain mail and lodged in the flesh beyond. The shoulder wound was deep, but the mortal blow had been struck against Fiallach's left side, where the chain mail had parted.

"You fought well, big man," said Bane.

Fiallach gripped his arm, drawing him in close. "Where is the king?" he whispered.

"Dead. Killed by his brother Braefar."

"I misjudged you, Bane. Always been too quick with my temper. Damn, but we beat them, eh?"

"Aye, we beat them."

"Wish . . . I could . . . be there when we march on Stone . . ."

Fiallach's head sagged back. His eyes closed. Bane rose to his feet.

All around now the Rigante were moving among the wounded Stone soldiers, hacking them to death where they lay. Bane saw Bendegit Bran making his way through the warriors. Bane took up the reins of a wandering chestnut horse. Stepping into the saddle, he rode back across the battlefield. Far to the left he could see Connavar's gelding, Windsong. It was standing now, reins trailing. Bane was glad it had survived. He touched heels to the chestnut and rode past Bran.

"Wait!" called Bran, but Bane had kicked his horse into a run.

As he moved across the battlefield, soldiers stood and cheered him, waving their swords in the air and chanting his name. He rode to the top of the hill and swung his mount to stare back at the blood-covered field of the fallen.

"Proud of you, boy," came the voice of Connavar in his mind.

Epilogue

THROUGHOUT THE LONG afternoon Brother Solstice, Banouin, and twenty other druids moved among the wounded men. They were aided by a hundred more warriors who had experience with battle injuries. Even so, many died before they could be reached and helped.

In all some seventeen thousand Rigante, Norvii, and Pannone tribesmen had given their lives to protect the land and more than twenty-five thousand soldiers of Stone had surrendered their souls to feed Jasaray's ambition.

The injured among the Rigante numbered in the thousands. Among the dead were the generals Govannan, Ostaran the Gath, and Fiallach. A little way from Fiallach lay the bodies of the former outlaws Wik and Valian and Furse, the son of Osta. Finnigal had survived despite having his left hand cut from his body. Four thousand five hundred Iron Wolves and horse archers had died after the charge, with another thousand carrying wounds.

Bendegit Bran sent out scouts who returned to say that the surviving Panthers had fled the previous night's fortress and were heading south. He had had no choice but to let them go.

With the afternoon sun dropping toward the mountains, Bran and twenty Iron Wolves rode to the east and the golden Circle of Balg. A stoop-shouldered man and a young boy were sitting with the body of the king, who was once more wearing his armor of gold. Of Bane there was no sign.

Bran dismounted and spoke to the man. He was the father of the boy and had come seeking him. Bran thanked them both for tending his brother.

"Where is the warrior who was with him?" he asked the man.

"I saw no one, sir," he said.

"What about you?" Bran asked the boy.

"Another man came, sir, just before my da found me. This man cast great magic. There was a bright light in the circle, and he walked into it and was gone."

"Gone?"

"Yes, sir."

"And that was all you saw?"

"I saw mountains, sir, beyond the circle. White mountains."

And coming in July, the hardcover event of the
year . . . *RAVENHEART* by David Gemmell.

Eight hundred years after Connavar and his bastard
son, Bane, faced the invading army of Stone, the saga
of the Rigante continues. . . .

PROLOGUE

The sun was setting, and Lanovar sat slumped against the
stone, the last of the sunlight bathing him in gold. There was
a little heat in the dying winter sun, and the brightness felt
good against his closed lids. Lanovar sighed and opened his
eyes. The huge figure of Jaim Grymauch stood close by,
gazing down at him.

"Let me carry you to the Wyrd, Lan," he said. "She'll cast
an ancient spell and heal you."

"In a while, my friend. I'll just rest here and gather my
strength."

Grymauch swore and turned away. Loosening the strap at
his shoulder, he swung the massive broadsword clear of his
back. The black hilt was almost a foot long, crowned with
an iron globe pommel. The curved quillons were beautifully
crafted to represent the flared wings of a hunting falcon.
Drawing the fifty-two-inch blade from the scabbard, Grymauch examined the sword in the fading light. There were
still bloodstains on the blade, and he wiped them away with
the hem of his black cloak. Beside him Lanovar lifted clear
the wedge of blood-soaked cloth he had been holding to the
wound in his side. The bleeding had slowed, and the pain
was almost gone. He glanced up at Grymauch.

"That monstrosity should be in the Druagh museum,"
said Lanovar. "It is an anachronism."

"I don't know what that means," muttered Grymauch.

"It means out of its time, my friend. That blade was

created to rip through plate armor. No one wears plate anymore."

Grymauch sighed. Returning the blade to its scabbard, he sat down beside his friend. "Out of its time, eh?" he said. "It is like us, then, Lan. We should have been born in the days of the *real* highland kings."

Blood was leaking slowly from the cloth plugging the exit wound in Lanovar's lower back, a dark stain spreading across the outlawed blue and green cloak of the Rigante. "I need to plug the wound again," said Grymauch.

Lanovar made no complaint as the clansman pulled him forward, and he felt nothing as Grymauch pressed a fresh wad of cloth into the wound. Lanovar's mind wandered briefly.

He saw again the standing stone and the tall black-clad man waiting there. Regrets were pointless now, but he should have trusted his instincts. He had known deep in his heart that the Moidart could not be trusted. As their gaze had met, he had seen the hatred in the man's dark eyes. But the prize had been too great, and Lanovar had allowed the dazzle of its promise to blind him to the truth.

The Moidart had promised that the turbulent years would end: no more pointless bloodshed, no more senseless feuds, no more murdered soldiers and clansmen. This night, at the ancient stone, he and the Moidart would clasp hands and put an end to the savagery. For his part the Moidart had also agreed to petition the king and have Clan Rigante reinstated to the roll of honor.

Lanovar's black warhound, Raven, had growled deeply as they walked into the clearing. "Be silent, boy," whispered Lanovar. "This is an end to battle—not the beginning of it." He approached the Moidart, extending his hand. "It is good that we can meet in this way," said Lanovar. "This feud has bled the highlands for too long."

"Aye, it ends tonight," agreed the Moidart, stepping back into the shadow of the stone.

For a fraction of a heartbeat Lanovar stood still, his hand still extended. Then he heard movement from the undergrowth to the left and right and saw armed men rise up from hiding. Six soldiers carrying muskets emerged and surrounded the Rigante leader. Several others moved into sight, sabers in their hands. Raven bunched his muscles to charge, but Lanovar stopped him with a word of command. The Rigante leader stood very still. As agreed, he had brought no weapon to the meeting.

He glanced back at the Moidart. The nobleman was smiling now, though no humor showed in his dark, hooded eyes. Instead there was hatred, deep and all-consuming.

"So your word counts for nothing," Lanovar said softly. "Safe conduct, you said."

"It will be safe conduct, you Rigante scum," said the Moidart. "Safe conduct to my castle. Safe conduct to the deepest dungeon within it. Then safe conduct up every step of the gallows."

At that moment a bellowing war cry pierced the air. A massive figure rushed into sight, a huge broadsword raised high. His lower face was masked by a black scarf, and his dark clothes bore no clan markings. Lanovar's spirits soared.

It was Grymauch!

The surprised soldiers swung toward the charging warrior. Several shots were fired, but not one ball struck him. The massive broadsword swung down, slicing a soldier from shoulder to belly before exiting in a bloody spray. In the panic that followed the clansman's charge Lanovar leapt to his left, grabbed a musket by the barrel, and dragged it from the hands of a startled soldier. As the man rushed in to retrieve the weapon, Lanovar crashed the butt into his face, knocking him from his feet. A second musketeer ran in. The warhound Raven gave a savage growl and then leapt, his great jaws closing on the man's throat. Lanovar raised the musket to his shoulder and sought out the Moidart. The nobleman had ducked back into the undergrowth. More shots rang out. Smoke from the guns drifted like mist in the clearing, and the air stank of sulfur. Grymauch, slashing the great blade left and right, hurled himself at the musketeers. A swordsman ran in behind the clansman. Raising the captured musket, Lanovar fired quickly. The shot struck the hilt of the swordsman's upraised weapon and ricocheted back through the hapless man's right eye. Across the clearing three more musketeers came into view. Raven, his jaws drenched with blood, tore into them. One went down screaming. The others shot into the snarling hound. Raven slumped to the ground.

Lanovar threw aside the musket and ran toward Grymauch. The musketeers, their weapons empty, were backing away from the ferocious clansman. The swordsmen were dead or had fled into the woods. Lanovar moved alongside the blood-spattered warrior.

"We leave! Now!" he shouted.

As they swung away, the Moidart stepped from behind a tree. Grymauch saw him—and the long-barreled pistol in his hand. Vainly he tried to move across Lanovar, shielding him. But the shot tore through Grymauch's black cloak, ripping into the outlaw leader's side and out through his back. "That is for Rayena!" shouted the Moidart.

Lanovar's legs gave way instantly. Grymauch reached down, hauled him upright, and draped the paralyzed man across his shoulder. Then he ran into the thicket beyond the trail. At first the pain had been incredible, but then Lanovar had passed out. When he awoke, he was here on the mountainside and the pain was all but gone.

"How are you feeling?" asked Grymauch.

"Not so braw," admitted Lanovar. Grymauch had plugged the wound again and had settled him back against a rock face. Lanovar began to slide sideways. He tried to move his right arm to stop himself. The limb twitched but did not respond. Grymauch caught him and held him close for a moment. "Just wedge me against the rock," whispered Lanovar. Grymauch did as he was bidden.

"Are you warm enough? You look cold, Lan. I'll light a fire."

"And bring them down upon us? I think not." Reaching down, he pressed his left hand against the flesh of his left thigh. "I cannot feel my leg."

"I told you, man. Did I not tell you?" stormed Grymauch. "The man is a serpent. There is no honor in him."

"Aye, you told me." Lanovar began to tremble. Grymauch moved in close, pulling off his own black cloak and wrapping it around the shoulders of his friend. He looked into Lanovar's curiously colored eyes, one green and one gold.

"We'll rest a little," said Grymauch. "Then I'll find the Wyrd."

Jaim Grymauch moved out along the ledge and stared down over the mountainside. There was no sign of pursuit now, but there would be. He glanced back at his wounded friend. Again and again he replayed the scene in his mind. He should have been there sooner. Instead, to avoid being seen by Lanovar, he had cut across the high trail, adding long minutes to the journey. As he had crested the rise, he had seen the soldiers crouched in hiding and watched as his greatest friend walked into the ambush. Masking his face with his scarf, Jaim had drawn his sword and rushed down to hurl himself at the enemy. He would willingly have sacrificed his own life to save Lanovar from harm.

The sun was setting, the temperature dropping fast. Jaim shivered. There was precious little fuel to be found that high. Trees did not grow there. He moved back alongside Lanovar. The Rigante leader's face looked ghostly pale, his eyes and cheeks sunken. Jaim's black cloak sat on the man's shoulders like a dark shroud. Jaim stroked Lanovar's brow. The wounded man opened his eyes.

Jaim saw that he was watching the sky turn crimson as the sun set. It was a beautiful sunset, and Lanovar smiled. "I love this land," he said, his voice stronger. "I love it with all my heart, Jaim. This is a land of heroes. Did you know the great Connavar was born not two miles from here? And the battle king, Bane. There used to be a settlement by the three streams."

Jaim shrugged. "All I know about Connavar is that he was nine feet tall and had a magic sword crafted from lightning. Could have done with that sword two hours ago. I'd have left none of the bastards alive."

They lapsed into silence. Jaim felt a growing sense of disorientation. It was as if he were dreaming. Time had no meaning, and even the breeze had faded away. The new night was still and infinitely peaceful.

Lanovar is dying.

The thought came unbidden, and anger raged through him. "Rubbish!" he said aloud. "He is young and strong. He has always been strong. I'll get him to the Wyrd. By heaven, I will!"

Jaim rolled to his knees and, lifting Lanovar into his arms, pushed himself to his feet. Lanovar's head was resting on Jaim's shoulder. Moonlight bathed them both. "We're going now, Lan."

Lanovar groaned, his face contorting with pain. "Put . . . me . . . down."

"We must find the Wyrd. She'll have magic. The Wishing Tree woods have magic."

In his mind he saw the woods, picturing the path they must take. At least four miles from there, part of it across open ground. Two hours of hard toil.

Two hours.

Jaim could feel Lanovar's lifeblood running over his hands. In that moment Jaim knew they did not have two hours. He sank to his knees and placed his friend on the ground. Tears misted his eyes. His great body began to shake. Jaim fought to control his grief, but it crashed through his defenses. Throughout his twenty years of life there had been one constant: the knowledge of Lanovar's friendship and, with it, the belief that they would change the world.

"Look after Gian and the babe," whispered Lanovar.

Jaim took a deep breath and wiped away his tears. "I'll do my best," he said, his voice breaking. His mind, reeling from the horror of the present, floated back to the past: days of childhood and adolescence, pranks and adventures. Lanovar had always been reckless and yet canny. He had a nose for trouble and the wit to escape the consequences.

Not this time, thought Grymauch. He felt the tears beginning again, but this time he shed them in silence. Then he saw Gian's face in his mind. Sweet heaven, how would he tell her?

She was heavily pregnant, the babe due in a few days. It was the thought of the child to be that had led Lanovar to trust the Moidart. He had told Jaim only the night before that he did not want the child growing up in the world of violence he had known. As they sat at supper in Lanovar's small, sod-roofed hut, the Rigante leader had spoken with passion about the prospect of peace. "I want my son to be able to wear the Rigante colors with pride and not to be hunted down as an outlaw. Not too much to ask, is it?" Gian had said nothing, but Lanovar's younger sister, the red-haired Maev, had spoken up.

"You can ask what you like," she said. "But the Moidart cannot be trusted. I know this in my soul!"

"You should listen to Maev," the raven-haired Gian urged, moving into the main room and easing herself down into an old armchair. One of the armrests was missing, and some horsehair was protruding from a split in the leather. "The Moidart hates you," she said. "He has sworn a blood oath to have your head stuck upon a spike."

" 'Tis all politics, woman. Peace with the highland Rigante will mean more tax income for the Moidart and the king. It will mean more merchants able to bring their convoys through the mountain passes. This will bring down the prices. Gold is what the king cares about. Not heads upon spikes. And as one of his barons, the Moidart will have to do what is good for the king."

"You'll take Grymauch with you," insisted Gian.

"I will not. We are to meet alone, with no weapons. I'll take Raven."

Later Maev had come to the hulking fighter as he sat in the doorway of his own hut. Normally his heart would beat faster as she approached him, his breath catching in his throat. Maev was the most beautiful woman Grymauch had ever seen. He had hoped to find the courage to tell her of this but instead had stood by as she and the handsome young warrior Calofair had begun their courtship. Calofair was now in the north, trading with the Black Rigante. When he came back, he and Maev would walk the tree.

Jaim glanced up as Maev approached. "You'll go anyway," she said.

"Aye, of course I will."

"You'll not let him see you."

Jaim laughed. "He's a bonny swordsman and a fine fighter, but he's a hopeless woodsman. He'll not see me, Maev."

Gian came walking across to them. Maev put her arms around the pregnant woman and kissed her cheek. Jaim Grymauch wondered briefly how it would feel if Maev did the same to him. He reddened at the thought. Gian stretched and pressed her palms into the small of her back. This movement caused her pregnant belly to look enormous. Jaim laughed. "Pregnancy suits some women," he said. "Their skin glows; their hair shines. They make a man think of the wonders of nature. Not you, though."

"Aye, she's ugly now, right enough," said Maev. "But when she's birthed the rascal, she'll become slim and beautiful again. Whereas you, you great lump, will always be ugly." Maev's smile faded. "Why does the Moidart hate Lanovar so?"

Jaim shrugged. The truth clung to him, burning his heart, but he could not voice it. Lanovar was a fine man, braw and brave. He had many virtues and few vices. Sadly, one of his vices was that he found women irresistible. Before wedding Gian the previous spring, Lanovar had been seen several times in Eldacre town. Few knew the woman he had met there, but Jaim Grymauch was one who did. He suspected that the Moidart was another. Rayena Tremain was beautiful, no doubt about it. She was tall and slender, and she moved with an animal grace that set men's hearts beating wildly. The first affair with Lanovar had been brief, the parting apparently acrimonious.

Rayena wed the Moidart four months later in a great ceremony in Eldacre Cathedral.

Within the year there were rumors that the marriage was foundering.

Lanovar began acting strangely, disappearing for days at a time. Jaim, concerned for his leader and his friend, had secretly followed him one morning. Lanovar traveled to the high hills, to a small, abandoned hunting lodge. After an hour a lone horsewoman rode up. Jaim was astonished to see it was Rayena.

Beside him now Lanovar groaned, the sound jerking Jaim back to the painful present. Lanovar's face was bathed in sweat now, and his breathing was shallow and labored. "I was never . . . frightened . . . of dying, Grymauch," he said.

"I know that."

"I am now. My son is about to be . . . born, and I've . . . given him no soul-name."

In the distance a wolf howled.

It's the hardcover event of the year,

■

RAVENHEART
. . .coming in July 2001

Eight hundred years have passed since King Connavar of the Rigante and his bastard son, Bane, fought the invading army of Stone. Connavar has become a legend, and the Rigante have become a conquered people who live and die under the iron rule of the Varlish. The laws are oppressive and severely enforced: No Rigante can own a sword nor wear the clan colors. Any who disobey the law will answer to the Moidart, the cruel and vengeful Lord of Eldacre Castle. They will answer with the swift punishment of death.

Only one woman follows the ancient paths. She is the Wyrd of Wishing Tree Wood—and she alone knows the nature of the evil soon to be unleashed on a doomed and unsuspecting world. In this perilous land, facing an uncertain future, the Wyrd finds her hopes pinned on two men: Jain Grymauch, the giant Rigante fighter, a man haunted by his failure to save his best friend from betrayal; and Kaelin Ring, a youth whose deadly talents earn him the rancor of all Varlish.

One will become the Ravenheart, an outlaw leader whose daring exploits will inspire the Rigante. The other will forge a legend—and light the fires of revolution.